Contents

I0635931

PIZA FOR TWO

Geneviève Montcombroux

ISBN 978-1-987946-43-7

Cover: Getcovers.com

Published by Solitude Publishing
solitudepublishing@gmail.com

To Suzanne
pour commémorer notre longue amitié

Pain hammered in Piers' head. He winced and pulled the covers over his ears to block the insistent ringing. All efforts failed to shut out the noise. With every movement, a lightning bolt seared the back of his eyes. He snaked out a hand to grab the phone, but knocked it to the floor. More pain. More hammering. More ringing. More blood thundering through his brain.

He finally identified the sounds. Someone was ringing his doorbell and pounding on the door.

"Go away!"

His yell brought on a wave of nausea. Shouts came from outside. The pounding resumed. Unaware of his naked state, Piers rolled over and got to his feet. Eyes only half-open, he lurched across the room into the hallway. His fingers fumbled with the deadbolt. The door burst open. Focused on nothing but his pain and his roiling stomach, he propped himself against the wall.

A shrill whistle drilled into his ears.

"Well, my friend, look at you!"

The words reached him through a fog. Piers opened his eyes fully. His tongue slurred. "Clayton! What the hell... you doing... here?"

Clayton Tomlisson cast a glance at the man behind him. "I told you we'd find him hungover. Let's chuck him in the shower."

Recognition seeped through to Piers' consciousness.

"Mark... I'm dying. Read my will..."

"Shut up and save your strength. It's way past noon and we've got to talk before the police arrive."

Half carried by his friends, Piers ended up in the shower. In an unkind gesture, Mark Bergson opened the cold tap. Piers yelped and cringed in the corner of the stall. After a while, the water numbed his throbbing head. He shivered, turned off the tap and staggered out. Mark held up a thick terry robe. They pushed him onto his bed and got clothes out for him. Somehow, he managed to get dressed.

Escorted by his friends, Piers made it to the living room.

He sat gingerly on the couch. Clayton handed him a mug of coffee. Without a word, Piers drank. While not hot enough to burn his mouth, the pungent liquid was warm enough to stop his shaking.

Mark pressed a couple of aspirin into his friend's hand. "Swallow them. You'll feel better in a few minutes."

Before any time had passed, Clayton exploded. "Do you realize what you have done?"

Piers' head split in two. With effort, he willed the pain away. "What did I do? I don't remember a thing."

Clayton lowered his lanky frame onto the arm of the couch.

"Ask us if we're surprised. Apparently, you were the life and soul of the party."

"The party... I left."

"You drove off with Tracy."

An instant of silence. Piers closed his eyes. The memory hit him. He wailed. "Ooh! No!"

From somewhere deep inside, a rebellious flame sparked to life. Piers shook his head and immediately regretted it. By sheer willpower, he stiffened his shoulders. "We argued. She told me she was pregnant, but she was going to have an abortion. I didn't want her to do it. I promised support. She told me there was no need. It was her body. I think I was angry. I yelled at her, too. We were fighting. Then the bang."

"How did you leave the scene of the accident?"

"I don't know. I was in the grass. I was sick. I don't know after that."

Clayton stood up. "I'll make more coffee. Muffins are thawing in the microwave."

"Mark, what happened?"

"You hit a minivan. Two people and their baby were killed. Tracy was killed. If you hadn't left the scene of the accident and called 911, they could possibly have been saved. By the time a car drove by, it was too late."

Piers closed his eyes. "NO!"

"The police traced your car to your sister,, and your father called me."

"They're coming to arrest me."

"Yes."

Clayton returned with a plate of steaming muffins and a pot of coffee. Piers ate in silence and managed to keep the nausea at bay. His head was still painful, but clear.

"I'm going to prison?"

"We'll get you a deal. Your father already stalled the police to give you time before they come for you."

Piers swallowed and drank the black coffee. Tears pooled around his eyelids. "No, I don't want any privilege... I committed a crime." He bent his head. "I'm sorry, so sorry." He lifted his head. "Clay, Mark." He held up a hand. "You're my witnesses. I vow never to touch booze again. Not to my dying day."

"That's a step in the right direction. Here, have another muffin. You'll need all your strength and it'll absorb the left over alcohol." Mark pushed the plate toward Piers.

"I'll have to tell dad. I won't be available."

"It's not as if you had an executive position."

Piers laughed bitterly. "You're right there. And what about the fitness commercial scheduled for... I can't remember when?"

"Well, maybe your brother can step in."

"T-Bo doesn't work well in front of the camera."

Mark chuckled. "You mean he doesn't like the groupies waiting for you at the store to beg for your autograph?"

Bitterness laced Piers' tone. "If they buy, who cares whether they use the equipment or not? Like the commercials say, Reddington Sporting Goods – all your fitness needs." He put his head in his hands. "Those poor people... I killed them. They lost their lives because I was a drunk... Do they have family?"

"A ten-year-old daughter who was away at camp," Mark said.

"How will she ever forgive me? How can I ever forgive myself?"

The doorbell rang. Clayton opened the door to the uniformed officers.

Chapter Two

Piers shuddered as the prison gate slammed shut behind him. He had been released. The dying sun caressed his face. Free! Older, wiser maybe, and a lot tougher. This was just like in a movie. He blinked in the pale April sun. Mark, his lawyer, took him by the elbow.

"Come on! Your father's waiting."

"I'm not going."

Mark propelled his friend to his car. "Everything is behind you now. You must get on with your life."

"Yes, my life. Tracy doesn't have her life. Mr. and Mrs. Brockton don't have theirs. Baby Carmen doesn't-"

"Enough! You made a mistake and paid your dues to society. Wallowing in bitterness won't change the tragedy, but you can make a difference with your life. Start with your father. He's holding a job in the company for you."

"Reddington Sports can do without me."

Mark sighed. "Let's go to my place for tonight and talk."

The bitter fold on Piers' lips remained while he settled himself on the plush seat of Mark's BMW.

"My father didn't forgive me. I want to go far away."

"Your mother-"

"They didn't come when I needed them most. When I was in the depth of despair. When I wanted to die. Now I want to go away to find who I can be. How can I live when a young girl is mourning her parents, her baby sister? When parents are mourning their children and their grandchild."

"You're not going to do something stupid, are you?"

Piers gave a rough laugh. "I could have done it my first day in prison. Let the inmates kill me any time after that. Somehow I didn't.

I've been granted a life. I need to find out what to do with it. But I can't do it here. I'll go west or north. Yukon. Yes. I'll go to the Yukon Territory.

Mark remained silent for a while. "Maybe you're right. When do you want to leave?"

"Tomorrow morning."

"It's Sunday, the banks are closed."

"I'm not touching my account. I've got a few bucks in my pocket from working in the jail. I'll take a few clothes."

Mark shook his head and pulled into his parking spot. "Your stuff is in the spare bedroom. I have a couple of hundred with me. I can go to an ATM for more."

Piers straightened in the seat, hand on the door handle. "That will be enough. I can work. Thanks for all your support."

"Friendship means something, Piers. Don't you forget my number."

For the first time in two years, Piers smiled.

Chapter Three

Piers stared again at the hand-written sign taped to the store window.

HELP WANTED - APPLY WITHIN

He shifted his carryall from one hand to the other. The gray street with the piles of road sand left over from winter filled him with gloom. He looked again at the sign. A job in a tacky pizza parlor was not his idea of a great career move. But they were looking for help and he was looking for work... desperately.

He had made it on the bus to Ontario. The end of winter wasn't a good time to travel. Then he had so little money left he had to get off in the middle of nowhere, near a place called Shekak, which wasn't even a hamlet, just a place like a hunting lodge somewhere in the bush. He walked. And walked. A road repair crew gave him two days of work holding the stop-and-slow flag while their signalman was sick. A worker gave him a ride to Longlac. He had enough money to buy a meal and continue on the bus up to Thunder Bay. The Yukon was still a long way away. Finding work was taking longer than he had expected. His stomach growled again. If it hadn't been for the independent trucker who gave him a ride, he'd still be huddled at the outdoor table of a roadside café. He had noticed the loose tie-downs on the truck's load and had run up to stop the driver.

He shut his eyes and tried to recall how long it had been since his last real meal. It must be at least two days. Even a couple of nights at the Salvation army hostel had drained his meager funds. At least he'd been able to clean up. At the soup kitchen, he was turned away because he wasn't registered. As he walked out, a small hand had pushed a wrapped bun in his. The petite Asian woman smiled and hurried away. He chewed on the piece of sausage and white bun slowly to make it feel like a meal.

Last night, he had found a park and considered spending the night on a bench. Then thought again. The Prairies in late April were not the place for sleeping rough, not when it still dipped way below freezing at night. Back in the Annapolis Valley, flowers would be in bloom. His sailing boat would be bobbing at her mooring. Here, crews hadn't gotten around to cleaning up the mess left by the snowplows. The Saskatchewan River was still encased in ice. His last dollar paid for a bed at a homeless shelter.

No one would have known his job prospects would narrow down to employment at Flavio's Pizzeria. If they wanted him. After so many job rejections since he had arrived, a tremor of apprehension clawed at the back of his neck. It was only a small prairie town. Job possibilities were limited. This time, they had to want him. It was his last chance. He glanced again at the building. Flavio's Pizzeria and the empty store next to it stood in the middle of a large vacant lot, a sort of overflow parking lot for nearby offices, and a couple of small factories.

He squared his shoulders and pushed open the door. He had hardly crossed the worn threshold when a soft feminine voice greeted him.

"Good morning, sir. And what can I serve you with?"

Piers' eyes focused on the slim brunette behind the counter. A shockwave darted through his body. The sight of a woman had never done that to him before. His throat tightened. He forced out a few words. "Good morning. I... I see from the sign you're wanting help."

The woman smiled. Piers reckoned she was in her mid-twenties.

"That's why it's there."

"I'm looking for a job." The words still sounded alien on his tongue, even after having said them perhaps a thousand times. At this point, he was reduced to begging.

He watched the brunette's smile widen. It lit up the otherwise dingy interior.

"You've come to the right place," she said. "You drive, don't you?"

"I drive."

"We need a delivery person. You might also have to help out in the kitchen. How do you feel about that?"

Piers shrugged. "I'll do whatever is needed. I've no experience in the pizza business, mind you, but I'm willing to learn." He couldn't wrench his gaze off her face. The exquisite oval was illuminated by almond-shaped, green eyes, a green so deep it mesmerized him. Her absence of makeup and lack of sophisticated manners were a refreshing change from... He decided it was time to stop thinking about his former life.

The young woman pulled open a drawer and took out a sheet of paper. "Fill this in, please. It's a standard application form."

Piers took the offered pen. He swiveled the paper toward him and began filling in his personal details, with the careful omission of the last two years and a slight spin on his former employment. His hand shook. Lying didn't come easy. A faint sheen of perspiration dampened his brow. He wrote his first name and printed his second name in bold, but left out his last name. If she asked for his driver's license... He added Reddington in small scratchy letters, spilling all of it into the adjacent printed space.

The woman's voice startled him. "Tell me, why is a guy like you applying for a job here?"

A surge of panic coursed through his chest. He looked up to find those green eyes drilling into him.

"I beg your pardon?"

"I can tell you're not a working man. Your hands are too smooth. Your nails are neat and trim. Neither do you strike me as a student looking for part-time work. Why are you here?"

The forcefulness of her tone paralyzed him. He marveled at the way she seemed able to pin him down. A specimen on a display panel. It scared him. He scrambled to come up with a convincing answer. "Er, I used to have an office job."

"So what happened?"

"Got downsized." He sliced the air with his hand. "My position was eliminated. Cut." He wondered if she would ask for references.

She nodded. "It's happening more and more."

He bowed his head and resumed the task of filling in the form. This job search was a tougher assignment than he had imagined. After being rejected from countless retail and construction jobs in cities along the way, he was down to working in a pizzeria in Otter Lake. His stomach gurgled, the hunger a constant reminder that things weren't running smoothly.

"You're a young guy. There must be tons of jobs in a city like Saskatoon, Winnipeg or Alberta, if that's where you're heading."

"Yeah, and two hundred applicants for each one."

He caught the look of curiosity in her eyes. Curiosity mingled with a suspicion that compressed her lips. He promptly returned his attention to the form. Again, her voice, now with a harder edge, intruded on him.

"You're wearing too expensive clothes to be an ordinary office worker. And if I'm not mistaken, that's a Gucci bag you have there."

Piers summoned all his inner resources to remain calm. This woman was too darned observant for his liking. He regretted his lack of attention to details before embarking on this madcap journey. "I just happen to like neat clothes. I spent all my spare cash trying to look... trying to impress potential employers." The lies now rolled off his lips so easily, it scared him.

She leaned over to examine the form. Piers got a close up view of her tight chignon. Not one shiny hair out of place under the invisible net.

She straightened. Again, the third-degree gaze. "From Halifax? Why Otter Lake?"

Piers took a deep breath. He hadn't come from Halifax. Montreal was home. But he had a cottage in the Annapolis Valley. So it was only half a lie. What rotten luck, finding a woman with a mind like a steel trap in a joint like this.

"You know the old saying, go west, young man, seek your fortune."

He wasn't going to tell her Otter Lake was only a stop on his way to the Yukon, a place where they didn't ask many questions. Yukon Territory, Dawson City, the end of the road.

"Fat chance of making your fortune here. Ever since Flavio's heart attack, we've been struggling to stay afloat."

"Flavio's the boss, right?"

The woman nodded. Piers detected a new softness in her eyes.

"How many employees do you have?"

"Only me. I'm the manager and chief cook rolled into one. I also do deliveries when Mrs. B. comes in."

A silence fell between them. She looked away, giving Piers a chance to admire the graceful profile of her face and the tantalizing sweep of her neck. Her Flavio's Pizzeria apron molded her shapely figure.

He mentally shook himself.

When she spoke again, her voice carried a hint of vulnerability behind the tough exterior. "I just hope I can get the business going again now that you'll take over deliveries. Flavio has helped with some of the food prep, but he's busy with his therapy."

"How bad are things?"

"Only a handful of loyal customers remain. Yet our pizzas are the best in town. Handmade from scratch. No premixes."

At the mention of food, his stomach complained audibly.

Her face melted into a grin. "Hungry?"

"It's been a long time since breakfast." He omitted to tell her he meant breakfast the previous day. Or was that the day before yesterday? He had lost track.

"Come over to this side and we'll have a slice."

"You mean I'm hired?"

"Sure."

Relieved, Piers smiled. "What's your name?"

"Nicole Desmond. And you're..." She picked up the form. "Piers Sonder." She looked at him, half smiling, half frowning, as if made nervous by his closeness. "Piers. That's a nice name. Unusual."

He sidled around to her side of the counter. "Not to me. I've carried it around for three decades." His fear and fatigue dropped away. She obviously didn't recognize him from the fitness commercials. She obviously didn't associate him with the sorry case the media had made of his fatal drunk driving accident. Though perhaps people's memory was short and what was national news three years past was now archived at the back of the brain.

Nicole's lips formed a smile. Piers guessed she hadn't been doing a lot of smiling lately. No wonder if the pizza business was heading south.

"This is the kitchen. Needless to say, we keep it spotless. That's ensuring the health of our customers as well as satisfying the health inspector."

Piers dropped his bag by the door. Nicole took a pizza out of a warming oven and cut it in four.

"I must keep a slice for old Mr. Knopf. He never fails to come in at noon."

She slid the generous slice onto a plate and handed it to Piers. The two of them ate in silence, standing up. Piers made a huge effort not to wolf down his portion.

The door chimes jangled.

Nicole glanced at the wall clock. "That must be him now."

She packed a slice of the remaining pizza in a carton and brushed past Piers. He eyed the last slice but gauged it was impolite to snag it. She was probably saving it for her boss.

His boss too, now.

She returned and must have read his mind.

"Yes, that one is for Flavio. He should be back soon. I should teach you the basics of preparing the dough."

In another time, Piers would have been tempted to crack a joke about knowing how to make dough. His sense of humor had vanished on that Sunday early morning when his good friends Mark and Clayton had shaken him out of his post-alcoholic stupor to tell him he had killed four people.

Though relieved at having finally landed a job, he knew his situation was still precarious. Besides, from the look of it, there wasn't much about Flavio's Pizzeria to provoke mirth.

Over the next half hour, Piers was initiated into the secret of making pizza dough of just the right consistency. From there, he graduated to mastering the various toppings.

The back door opened and a tall, corpulent man came in.

"Hey, *mia* Nicole, guess what? My weight went down and the doc is satisfied."

Piers reckoned that in the past, Flavio had been a walking ad for his pizza shop.

Nicole clapped her flour-white hands. "Congratulations! And how were the exercises today?"

Flavio shook his head. "It's hard on a guy who's never exercised since high school. But I do it. Got me a membership at the gym."

"Good for you."

"Mrs. B. been in?" His inquiry had an embarrassed ring to it.

"Not yet." Nicole's eyes sparkled with glee. "But she'll be here soon."

A look of anticipation flickered over Flavio's face. Piers moved from the corner of the kitchen.

Flavio acknowledged the newcomer. "And who have we here?"

"Flavio, this is Piers Sonder, our new jack-of-all-trades. Piers, meet Flavio Bellini, our boss."

Flavio extended his hand. "Hi there, young fella."

Piers shook the hand, aware of the man's eyes boring into him. Once more, he felt like a bug under a microscope. He schooled himself to remain calm. Flavio struck him as the kind of man no one could fool.

"So, you come and learn to make pizzas? Good! And you can drive. You're a godsend." His eyes receded into his head as he gave Piers the once-over.

Piers clamped his jaws. He mustn't falter now or the man would see right through him and trick him into revealing why he should want to work in a pizza parlor.

Yet he figured he owed his new boss some kind of explanation. "I fell on a streak of bad luck a while back. Gotta thank you for giving me a break." In that, he wasn't lying. His inability to get a job in his area of expertise, an euphemism if there was one, or any job at all, was rotten luck.

Flavio's look under his taught eyebrows sent a shiver of fear down Piers back.

"You'll do."

An intense relief washed over Piers. He had no doubt that the man knew he was a criminal, just out of jail. Gratitude swept through him.

The phone rang. Flavio picked up the receiver. "Sure, ma'am. We'll have them to you at four o'clock on the dot." He jotted down an address. "Thank you. Goodbye."

He turned to Nicole and Piers, a grin on his face. "Okay, we have two extra large bacon pizzas for a birthday party."

"Great," Piers said. "Where do I deliver them to? I've got to learn the town."

Flavio extracted a dog-eared map from under a heap of papers and spread it on the counter. "We are here." A stubby finger traced a line on the map. "The delivery is over here, Baker Bay, in the New Town." He folded the map and handed it to Piers. "Now, let's make those pizzas."

Chapter Four

Nicole removed the *Help Wanted* sign from the window. She lingered behind the cash register. A worry line creased her forehead as she eyed the kitchen. The sight of her new employee wearing expensive but rumpled clothes troubled her. Yet there was something appealing about him. She couldn't place the feelings he aroused in her. Probably relief that he was willing to work for basic wages. All the same, he was just too good looking, too refined to be mixing pizza dough and making deliveries.

There was something hard about him, something tragic.

She should have asked for references, which she ought to follow, but she didn't even want to read his application past his name in case she had to reject it. She desperately needed someone to help. If no one, the business would have to close. Flavio would assess him. Her boss had an infallible knack for detecting bad guys. Nobody knew that he had sometimes hired a released convict to give him a chance and a reference. Was Piers one of those? That haunted look in his eyes when he didn't know she was watching wasn't the look of the everyday man. Why else would he have emphasized a second name, making his real surname almost illegible? It didn't ring a bell of known wanted men. But then, those wanted men were not likely to come and ask for a job with their stomach growling with hunger. And she couldn't explain why she somehow trusted he wasn't a criminal.

The chimes sounded. A middle-aged woman in a faux-suede jacket and gray pleated skirt entered. "Hello, Nicole. How's it going today?"

"Great Mrs. B. I hired a new helper this morning. He's in the kitchen with Flavio."

"What's he like?"

Nicole paused. "I don't really know."

"What do you mean, you don't know? You hired him, didn't you?"

"What I mean is I can't make heads or tails of him."

"Ha!" Her eyes twinkled. "A young man."

Nicole nodded.

"But not a teenager?"

"No, I'm not hiring kids these days. Most of them work hard when they're here but then they disappear on us just when we need them most."

"It doesn't mean they're all like that."

Nicole sighed. "I know, but at a time when we are stretched so thin we have to have someone reliable."

"What else about this young man?" An amused look lit up her face.

"Why don't you go and check him out for yourself. Then let me know what you think. Flavio's initiating him into the finer points of pizza making."

Warmth colored Mrs. B.'s voice. "Flavio's back from therapy?"

Nicole nodded. Lynne Bancroft walked into the kitchen. Nicole followed close behind.

"I hear we have a new employee." Lynne dropped her purse on a chair.

Flavio straightened his back. "Lynne, I'd like you to meet Piers Sonder. Piers, this is our award-winning volunteer, Mrs. Lynne Bancroft."

Piers held his hand out. Lynne put hers behind her back.

He glanced down at his floury hand and laughed. "Pleased to make your acquaintance, Mrs. Bancroft."

"I'm delighted, Piers. Don't believe a word of what Flavio is going to say. But somebody's got to look after him."

"Uh-oh, I know what's coming," Flavio said.

"Right. Have you taken your walk for today?" Her voice carried an intimate edge.

"Not yet. Must show our new worker the way around the kitchen. We've got a birthday party order for this afternoon. The dough needs to be tossed just right."

"Then I'll wait for you." She turned to Nicole. "Are classes nearly finished? How's it going?"

"Very well. I got top marks on my last assignment."

Piers lifted his head. His eyes met Nicole's. Then he returned to his task.

Flavio pointed to the mixing bowl. "Now, take that dough in your hand. But you've gotta concentrate."

Piers scooped up the dough. It stretched and he caught it with his other hand.

"Gently, boy, gently. It's like caressing a woman's breast, soft yet firm. Now, a little twist of the wrist and up it goes in the air. Catch it lovingly."

Nicole flushed and busied herself with cleaning one of the ovens. Heat rose in her cheeks. It was not the first time she had heard Flavio explain handling the dough in words of lovemaking. Previously, it went past her with no more effect than if he had said "Use steel wool on the oven." Her reaction disturbed her.

Piers applied himself to his task and won the gruff approval of his boss. Flavio hung around until Nicole had shown Piers the correct method of adding the required toppings.

Flavio ripped off his apron and tossed it aside. "Okay, enough. See I'm sitting down and resting. It's been a busy day."

Nicole took up a mop and set about cleaning the pizzeria. Lynne pointedly stood by the door. Flavio heaved himself up and paused. "Don't stay too long, Nicole, okay?"

Nicole bristled. "Flavio, we can't afford to close up shop early. We do our best business with the movie theater crowd. At least at the end of the week."

"I still worry about you walking home alone in the dark."

Lynne interrupted. "Now, now, don't you fret. Nicole's been doing that trip for how many years?"

Nicole laughed. It had become their little ritual but deep down she appreciated Flavio's fatherly concern. "Closer to ten than I care to admit. You know I'm careful even though this neighborhood is safe. Off you go, you two. I'll keep an eye on our apprentice."

Flavio was about to add another recommendation but Lynne dragged him out with her.

After the door closed behind them, Nicole grinned at Piers. "He's supposed to work only half a day and take a nap in the afternoon besides the therapy. If it wasn't for Mrs. B., he'd never do it and he'd be heading for another heart attack."

"He's lucky to have two caring ladies looking out for him."

Memories crowded Nicole's mind, but she shook them off. "He was good to me at a time when I was young and inexperienced."

"Did I hear you are studying?"

"I'm in my final year of an accounting degree at the university online campus. The school has organized it so that students who have to work, like me, can meet and take courses here. My accounting classes are on Mondays. Studying part time takes longer." Her voice quavered with a hint of self-consciousness. He was going to think she was a slow learner or none too bright. She couldn't explain that taking only one class at a time left her with a little cash with which to continue the search for her baby, a little boy now. But that was none of his concern.

"Don't apologize. Lots of students do their degrees part time."

She sighed. "It's been a long haul." Her attention came back to his hand. "Cut the green peppers thinner." She deftly caught the offending piece and sliced it neatly in two. Electricity zinged up her arm as her fingers brushed his.

"You're a whiz with a knife."

"Practice, that's all."

She eyed him up, not trusting his sexy voice or his persuasive charm. The sound of his voice, soft yet rich, but not deep like Flavio's, sent tiny shivers up and down her spine. She could begin to like this man too much.

The timer pinged on one of the ovens. Nicole donned a pair of mitts and dragged out a fragrant, golden-crust pizza. Before she could place it in the warming oven, the front door chimes sounded. She dropped the mitts and went out to greet the customers.

"Hi Jack, hi Betty. What'll it be?"

"Two slices of your best," Jack said.

"You're in luck, I just this minute took one out of the oven."

Betty patted the back of Nicole's hand. "Congrats! Jack told me you got top marks again on an assignment."

"Thanks."

At that moment, Piers appeared with two slices on a plate and handed them to Nicole. She wrapped them and pushed them across the counter.

Jack paid, and the pair went out.

Piers bent toward the window to look at the retreating customers. "Who are they?"

"The guy is Jack Wilshire. He's in my class. Betty too but I don't know her as well."

"I stuck the two birthday pizzas in the oven. When they're done, what do I carry them in?"

"Here, I'll show you." She led the way to the kitchen. "These are the insulated containers. Bring up the map on your phone."

Red invaded Piers' cheeks. He bit his lip.

"I…I no longer have a phone."

A moment of silence stretched uncomfortably.

"No problem, we have a good old-fashioned paper map. Here, I'll show you."

They spend a minute bent over the map while she explained the route.

"Make sure you take the map."

With Nicole's help, Piers studied it, then refolded it and stuffed it into his back pocket. The timer went off. Nicole deftly slid the pizzas onto a disposable platter and placed it inside a carton.

"Do you know how to use the mobile terminal?"

"Er… I learn quickly, if you show me."

She did. It wasn't all that complicated.

"Just remember we cannot take credit cards, only debit cards. Unzip the container, please." She put the carton into the holder. "Thanks. In the van you put the insulated holder on the middle rack of the metal cabinet. It's normally heated, but something's broken."

"An electrical problem?"

"I wouldn't know."

"I'll take a look at it tomorrow morning. Not that I'm any good at that sort of thing, but I like to tinker. You never know, I might get lucky."

Nicole smiled with an unexpected warmth. Despite her deep feeling that something was out of place with her new employee, she had to recognize he had a winning way about him. Maybe it wasn't going to be so bad, after all, having him around. She liked the way he pitched in willingly. "You're on. Getting a pro is expensive."

Piers opened the back door. A bark stopped him. He looked down at a black pup, standing squarely on his legs.

"Good dog, Snowflake. Sit and shake a paw," Nicole said.

"Snowflake?"

Nicole bent and patted the dog head. "He turned up starving in the middle of a snowstorm last February. Just a little pup."

"How old is he now?"

"Probably six months according to the vet."

Piers shifted the container to one hand and offered the other to the dog to sniff. Snowflake made a thorough inspection of Piers' hand. He then diverted his attention to Piers' shoes and pants. His wagging tail stirred the air.

"I made him a shelter in the corner made by our shop and the shop next door."

Piers stepped forward to view the dog enclosure. "The store next door is bigger than yours?"

"It is by a good ten feet. Lynne got the chain link pen. We close the gate at night. He's never moved from here and he stays out of the way of customers parking in the back. The vet thinks he might be a pure Labrador."

"A jet black dog called Snowflake!" Piers chuckled. "I guess he doesn't mind."

Nicole laughed. "It took him all of five minutes to learn his name."

"See you later." Piers stowed the pizzas in the van.

Chapter Five

For a long while after Piers had driven off, Nicole stared at the empty parking lot. Snowflake nudged her hand, and she absently stroked his head. Unanswered questions hummed through her brain. Mostly, questions about Piers Sonder. She had the distinct impression he was being driven by something more than the need to earn a few dollars at minimum wage. In her mind's eye she could see him getting a role in a Hollywood blockbuster without even trying. That voice of his... Surely they didn't all speak like that down East. There was something special about him, a compelling mix of intimacy and authority. Yet there was a bleak look in his eyes. She shook herself out of her trance and went in. Still troubled, she wiped down the already gleaming oven door.

A flush came to her cheeks. She imagined the scores of women that he must have enthralled with his sexy smile. His stylish clothes troubled her too. Close up, her eye had detected that he hadn't changed his shirt in a couple of days, but that did nothing to diminish the obvious quality of his clothes. Didn't he have a place to sleep?

And the man was educated. Anyone could tell that from his speech and manners. He was the first employee to hold open a door for her. Not that she expected it from anyone, but she liked it. The old-fashioned gesture spoke of good breeding. Piers was an enigma, one she didn't have time to wrestle with at that moment, and to be honest didn't want to.

She had one more phone call to make to yet another agency.

Her heart tightened whenever she thought about the baby they'd taken away from her. With the new awareness of adoptees to discover their biological parents, she prayed that the same applied to mothers seeking their surrendered children. The internet had proved a rich source of information. She spent as much time as she could surfing the net. There was little chance that a nine-year-old would be looking for his birth mother. All the same, she had to try.

Her savings had been used up paying the private investigator she had hired to trace the nurse who had handed the baby over to the agency representative. If only at the time she had thought of demanding the name of the agency. Only a teenager, and emotionally distraught, she'd been unable to think straight. They sedated her to calm her down. When she had come round, they accused her of being ungrateful. The baby, they said, would be much better taken care of by adoptive parents. In the depth of despair, she had fled the hospice for single mothers. Soon be eighteen, she could find a job and collect her sister. At the time, she had no plan on how to achieve this.

With Piers helping in the business, she'd have more time for her search. She sighed. Her thoughts drifted back to Piers. There was something about the way his light brown wavy hair framed a perfect face. His face was new to her, yet she had the impression of having met him before. She couldn't pinpoint it though. If he had confessed he was really an out-of-work movie star, she wouldn't have doubted it for one second. She tried to brush off the image of those brown eyes. No, not just any brown, more like a warm chestnut. The long lashes, lean cheeks and stubborn chin below a well-defined mouth sent her heart leaping every time he came close. His high forehead contributed to that killer appeal of his. He'd make a great TV hero.

Whatever he was, she sensed only too well the blatant sensuality he exuded when their eyes met. She was used to men ogling her with lust on their faces. Piers was different. Respect and kindness shone in his eyes when he looked at her.

Her last relationship had scared her. The moment she told the guy about her search for Christopher his interest cooled off. He wasn't prepared for commitment. In retrospect, nor had she been. At least not with him. She placed her faith in finding Mr. Right. Until he came along, she wasn't about to bestow the gift of her person on anyone else.

Once when she was an innocent girl of fifteen, she had fallen under the charm of a too-good-looking man. Little Christopher was the result. Not again, never again.

She wondered if the child's adoptive parents still called him Christopher. It was on his hospital bracelet. The nurse who took him knew she had named him Christopher. For two months before the birth she had known in her heart that it was a boy. Full of wonder at the life growing inside her, she had talked and sung to him.

A tear pooled in the corner of her eye. She grabbed the phone and dialed.

Chapter Six

Piers navigated his way through what passed as the downtown rush hour traffic. Otter Lake wasn't an industrial hub. At the red light he consulted the map. He turned onto a wider roadway.

Finally, he entered the New Town and located the Baker Bay address. He parked and glanced at the bare trees. Back home, green leaves were emerging to give the landscape a sheen of tender spring color. Here, the buds were barely forming.

Shrieks of laughter greeted him as he strode up the walk to where a somewhat harassed young woman stood in the open doorway.

"Pizzas for a birthday party."

"You're a savior! Thanks for coming on time."

"Nothing like a few mouthfuls of pizza to keep the youngsters happy."

The woman laughed. "At least for a short while." She handed Piers a couple of bills.

Piers jaw sagged. "Sorry, ma'am, I don't have enough change." He reddened in confusion holding the terminal.

"That's fine. Just keep the change."

He recovered from the momentary surprise. "Thank you very much."

Piers turned back to the van, and the woman disappeared into the house. The heat of embarrassment didn't fade immediately. This was new for him. He drove the van down the block and parked. While the big tip made him happy, he was struck by the strangeness of it all. This was the first time in his life that someone had actually tipped *him*. Normally, he was on the giving end.

Well, you got yourself in this situation. So get used to it. Maybe the humility will help atone for your crime.

Taking himself to task helped restore his self-control. *I'm successful in a job! A real job.* A brief second, he wished his father could have seen the scene on the doorstep of that house. No. He didn't want to think about his father.

He put the van in gear and drove to the plaza. The aroma of baking bread from the Crescent Moon Café made his nose twitch. His stomach tightened painfully. Later. Later he would have a piece of pizza to satisfy his endless hunger.

There must be only one bank in this place and it was still open. He walked up to a smiling teller and asked for change for one of the bill. A warm glow of satisfaction accompanied him all the way back to Flavio's Pizzeria. Maybe this job wasn't going be that bad after all.

He patted Snowflake's head and whistled a few bars. The dog cocked his ears. The back door squeaked as he opened it. Nicole stood by the center table. He flashed her a warm smile as he handed her the money.

"So, how did your delivery go?"

"No problem. I even got a tip. How do we share?"

Nicole laughed. "No, it's all yours. That'll be the first time someone offered to share a tip with me."

He let air out from his chest. "A tip is a welcome bonus."

"Indeed."

"Do you have something to oil the door hinges?"

"How about WD-40? We seem to use it on everything here." She bent to look inside a cupboard and brought out a spray can. "Will this do?"

"Perfect."

Piers set to work on the door. "I was wondering if you knew where I could find some cheap accommodation."

"Actually, I was thinking you might need an apartment. There's a basement suite in the block I live in. It's been empty for ages. I'm sure the landlady could let you have it right away."

Piers didn't know whether he had to marvel at her insight for guessing he needed lodgings immediately or fear she might guess too much.

"Is it... expensive?"

Nicole chuckled. "Why do you think I rent there? It's only a grand old house that has been converted into suites. Two floors and a basement, five apartments in all. Nothing fancy, just two rooms, kitchenette and bathroom, but it's clean. Only one room in the basement. There are few takers."

"I don't mind."

"Mrs. Harlow, she's the landlady, lives in a suite on the top floor. We can go and see her now, if you like. I'll phone Mrs. B and ask her to come and take care of the shop. I've prepared enough pizzas for the evening."

Piers' eyes followed Nicole's graceful movements as she reached for the cabinet where she stowed her bag and got her phone. He shook his head. He had enough on his plate without becoming attracted to his beautiful supervisor.

Try as he may, he couldn't throw off the urge to unclasp the copper-hued hair so severely pinned at the back of her head. He imagined burying his face in its fragrant mass. He longed to forget his troubles in the warmth of those sea-green eyes. He wanted to find out what lay beneath her strict outer shell. That cynicism he detected had to be a front. Then again, he'd be courting disaster if he followed his impulses.

Lynne Bancroft's entrance put an end to his musings. "So, you'll be staying?"

Piers nodded. "Yes, ma'am."

"We're off to look at an apartment for him," Nicole said.

"There, take my car." She handed Piers the keys.

Nicole grabbed them. "I'll drive. He doesn't know the way, and we need to get to the thrift store before it closes."

"Thrift store?" Piers gave her a bemused look.

She didn't reply until they were seated in the car. "I seem to remember there is an army-type cot in that apartment. And a small table plus a couple of chairs."

"What about the thrift store?"

The glance she threw him showed her amazement. "Because you'll need some basic household equipment. At the Helping Hand store you can pick up second hand items for a song."

A second hand store would be a novel experience for him. He was going to need time to adjust.

He looked at her profile against the car's side window. "One teeny problem. I don't have money to buy anything." The admission hurt. He wondered how people managed for whom poverty was an everyday reality. There must be hundreds who never had enough money to buy the necessities in life... let alone Gucci bags.

"I guessed you didn't have much money. I'll advance you what you need."

"Why should you do that?"

Nicole lifted her eyebrows and shrugged. "Because I must be crazy at times. I reckon I just have to put my trust in you. As long as you work hard, you'll be okay by me."

"Thanks!" He settled in his seat and decided to take her remark as a back-handed compliment. There was no time for deeper analysis.

Nicole stopped the car in front of a weathered sandstone ornate house that had to date from the nineteenth century. Stone pillars supported a covered entrance and half a dozen steps. Molded carvings framed tall windows.

The negotiations didn't take long. Piers penned his signature to the rental agreement on Mrs. Harlow's kitchen table.

With a regal bearing, the old lady eyed him over her gold-rimmed glasses. "You're working at Flavio's. See that you do well by him. Do you want me to leave the bed and the table in the apartment?"

"Yes please, unless it's extra."

"I wouldn't charge you for them. They're not worth much."

"Except to someone who has nothing." The words sounded strange on his lips. He had had so much in his other life. Yet here he didn't. Here he was obliged to shed his privileged skin to become one who had nothing. Prison had given him an education in the lowlife of society. Here, he was getting an education in how the rest of the world lived.

Mrs. Harlow smiled and shook her head. "You're a good man, Mr. Sonder. Nicole, would you show the gentleman where the laundry room is, please? And how to work the machines."

"I will, Mrs. Harlow. Is there anything you need? I'm going shopping after I show Piers his apartment."

The woman pursed her lips. "I should really get a car and drive again. If it's not too much trouble, I could do with a carton of milk and a bag of potatoes." She reached for her purse and handed Nicole some money.

Piers opened the door for Nicole.

"Thanks." On the landing she pointed to the door opposite. "That's my apartment."

Piers followed her downstairs.

"There are two young couples on the main floor, and now you in the basement. Here's the laundry room. Washing machine and dryer. This is your apartment door."

Piers opened the door and eyed the drab room.

Nicole looked over his shoulder. "The lime green paint must date from the nineteen fifties. Decorators in those days didn't have a lot of imagination."

"You're not kidding." He breathed in the musty odor common to closed-up rooms. "It'll do fine." A strange sensation gripped his stomach as he took in the prison-like windows set high on the wall and the metal cot in a recess off the main room. At least it was a shelter.

"I've some spare drapes. I'll get them for you when we come back."

Without further examination, Piers put down his bag and locked up. He let Nicole drive him to the thrift store. She parked by the entrance. The stucco of the low building showed cracks below the eaves. The glass doors were in need of washing.

They walked in. Piers halted in his tracks. Another alien smell assaulted his nostrils. It wasn't quite mustiness, nor dampness. It wasn't anything he was accustomed to. Not even like the prison smell. It was, he reckoned, the sharp, pervasive smell of second-hand clothes and furnishings.

A glance at Nicole heading down an aisle lined with women's dresses told him she wasn't aware of anything unusual. She and other shoppers milling in the aisles probably detected nothing out of the ordinary.

He followed his female mentor, all the while trying to remember where he had once smelled that odor. A kid dashed from behind a row of suits and brushed past him. A memory flashed through his mind. Back in the elementary school in his district, where his father insisted he attend, he remembered a boy who carried that smell on his clothes. No private school for the Reddington heir and a couple of his privileged friends. His father wanted to prevent any sense of entitlement in his sons, as did his best friends. Clayton had commented that it was the odor of poverty.

He repressed a sigh. Now that he was poor, maybe in time he too would begin to smell like that kid.

Nicole seized a pair of sheets. "Still in their factory wrapper. Sometimes you're lucky and get new items like these that stores unload from their inventory. The Helping Hand committee is always on the look out for bargains."

"Good." He was at a loss to know what else to say. Her smile made him feel that this low-keyed shopping spree might be worthwhile. If not for the sheets then just to hear her triumphant cry after rummaging through shelves and bins.

"It'd be best to start with a comforter. You can get a blanket later."

"Whatever you say, ma'am."

"Didn't you have an apartment before? Didn't you ever shop?"

Shop he did, for clothes and sundries at the most exclusive stores in Montreal, Toronto and New York.

"I shared the apartment with... er... a girl. She took care of all the household stuff."

Nicole pulled a face. From a stack she picked up a forest green comforter with a fall leaf motif. "Feel this." She thrust the corner into his hands.

"Seems nice enough to me."

She spread the comforter out and examined it closely. "Good, no bugs. What happened to the girl?"

"She told me to move out after I lost my job." Lying was still not easy. He visualized his bungalow on the grounds of his parents' mansion in Montreal's Westmount. Testing comforters was the last thing he needed to worry about. Every two years his mother had the place gutted and sent in her interior designers.

"That was pretty mean! You're better off without her."

Piers, still thinking about his mom, had to do a quick mental gear change to realize Nicole referred to his fictional ex-roommate. He shrugged. "Life sucks."

"Doesn't it just. This comforter is defect free. I think the dark green won't clash with your walls."

"You're right." What did his mother say? *Men don't like shopping. That's why I never take you or your father along.* Mom made all those kinds of decisions. Just like Nicole was doing.

"Let's go and look at the china."

Piers followed, his arms cradling the comforter and the sheets.

"You probably think I'm pushy, but the store is about to close and you need some dishes."

"You must think me dumb. I wouldn't know where to start. I appreciate your help."

One of her rare smiles rewarded him. Nicole shook her head. It struck him she likely shared his mother's view on men and shopping. Not only did men not like it, they mostly hadn't a clue what to buy or how to buy it. And Nicole and his mother were spot on as far as he was concerned, at least when it came to household furnishings.

A young female store clerk pushed a cart toward Piers. "Would you like a cart, sir?"

"Ah, yes, thanks." He flashed her his movie star smile.

The clerk watched spellbound as he dropped his load into the cart.

Nicole dragged him over to a shelf of utensils. "Saucepan, frying pan. They're good. Now for some dishes."

His extended arms received the items. He placed them in the cart. "Where does the store get all this stuff from?"

"People donate things they no longer need. Estates, store closings, returns or factory unsold or seconds. You name it. The store is operated by local people. It's money well spent."

His eyes followed her swift hands. "I like the plate with the roses you just put aside."

"It's too old-fashioned. Don't you want something more abstract?"

"I have a soft spot for roses."

He saw her try to hide a smile. But she selected two rose-patterned dinner plates, two dessert plates and two cereal bowls. A kettle joined them. She inspected a set of forks, spoons and knives.

"There are a few items missing but that should be enough for a start."

A disembodied voice over the intercom announced the store was about to close.

"Just in time," Nicole said.

They moved to the checkout. While Nicole paid, Piers eyed the door to the outside and realized that in the excitement of watching Nicole select his household needs, he'd forgotten about the smell. Nonetheless, he took a deep breath once they cleared the exit.

"And now for some groceries. No rush, it closes at eleven."

Piers laughed. "What a relief. I feel a whole lot more confident buying food than I do bed sheets."

Minutes later they were in the grocery store. He reached out to bag some mangoes. Nicole stopped him with her hand on his arm. "Apples are far cheaper and have the same food value as mangoes."

Chastened, he dropped the mango he was holding. "Spartan apples are the cheapest. I guess they're as good as any of the more pricey varieties. What do you think?" He saw the look of approval on Nicole's face. The effect of her smile and the fleeting touch on his arm spread a growing warmth through him.

"You only need to buy food for breakfasts. You can eat pizza for lunch and dinner."

"That's a great advantage for the time being." Weird. He found it weird that he should feel happy about getting free food on the job.

"A small perk. It does help with the food bill, at least until you've got yourself organized."

It didn't take long to carry Piers' purchases into his apartment. He stowed the food in the fridge while Nicole went upstairs to fetch the promised drapes.

When she returned, Piers noted with approval that the loaner drapes were russet brown. Had they too been green, he might have been tempted to bang his head against the wall. They spent fifteen minutes fixing the drapes to the existing hangers.

Nicole placed her hands on her hips to survey the transformed apartment. "There, you're all set."

"Thanks for your help. Let's take the car back to Mrs. B."

"And have a pizza dinner."

Piers' mouth watered at the thought. The hunger pangs that had plagued him all day returned in strength. All this was a new experience. He wondered if he might have two slices. Probably after he had been around pizzas for a while he'd grow to hate the very sight of them. For the moment, they were manna from heaven.

Lynne greeted them with a cheery wave. She took off her apron. "It's been busy while you were out. But there's a couple of pizzas left in the warming oven."

Nicole gave Lynne a hug. "Thanks so much."

"Thanks for the use of the car," Piers said.

"Did you get what you needed?"

"Nicole did it all. I'd have been lost without her."

"Then make sure you take care of her." With that Lynne put on her coat.

Piers watched bug-eyed as the woman picked up her purse and keys and disappeared out of the door.

"Don't pay much attention to her. She's a real mother hen." Nicole opened the door to the warming oven.

Piers grinned. "I guess she means I must watch my p's and q's as far as you're concerned."

Nicole burst out laughing. "Well, wouldn't you, anyway?"

Piers' smile widened. His Nicole had soft edges. *His* Nicole? He startled himself at having thought of her in a possessive way. Perhaps there was something happening in his subconscious that he ought to know about.

It puzzled him too how his brain could have led him in that direction. A direction he'd never again take. A ghost rose in front of him. Four lives, no five really, snuffed out by his fault. No, never again.

A rumbling in his stomach interrupted his somber thoughts. Nicole was already at the kitchen counter expertly running the cutter through the perfect disk of a pizza.

A late customer threw Piers into a minor panic when it appeared the man wanted to take the whole sixteen-inch pizza. Piers breathed easier when he saw Nicole package two slices and flip the CLOSED sign on the front door.

"I'm sure you must be hungry. Go ahead and lick the platter clean. We don't keep pizzas overnight."

"I hate to say this but that's the most welcome news I've heard all day. That and you giving me the job." He wondered if hunger could have warped his brain.

Piers helped Nicole tidy up the kitchen and store. He carried out the garbage and played fetch with Snowflake for a while.

When he came back inside, Nicole was sitting on a stool at the front counter.

She glanced up from the piled up money and debit receipts from the till. "You can head off home. I've got to deal with the cash and feed Snowflake. See you tomorrow. Oh, can you find the way?"

Piers reassured her he could and tapped the map in his pocket. A last goodnight and he ambled to the place he'd better start calling home.

***

Nicole hurried upstairs to deliver Mrs. Harlow's groceries. As she prepared for bed, her thoughts drifted to Piers. His confessed ignorance of even the existence of thrift stores puzzled her. They had to have such stores where he came from. But obviously, he didn't buy hand-me-downs.

She liked the eagerness he put into learning the pizza trade, even asking if he should share his tip. A smile coursed on her lips. Previous employees not only didn't offer to share tips, they sometimes tried to hide the sale money when customers paid cash.

Piers was a puzzle. Something was amiss. He hid something. He didn't look, speak or act like someone who had done time behind bars. Or did he? Was that the haunted look in his eyes? Not that she had much experience with ex-cons apart from those Flavio agreed to hire. Like Walt, a hard worker determined to put his past behind him. He had succeeded too. She could never forget the look in his eyes, the look of a misled youth who had finally reached maturity in prison. From time to time Walt came back with his wife and baby girl for a pizza treat.

But Piers was no Walt. Obviously, Flavio liked him and had approved him. She had no alternative but to trust Piers. As far as business matters went that is. On a personal level, she resolved to keep her guard up. The way women flirted with him was not lost on her. Like the adoring smile of the young thrift store clerk when she offered him the cart. And the way the girl seemed close to fainting when he dazzled her with his words of thanks. Everyone he had met succumbed to his charm, from Flavio to old Mrs. Harlow and the customer who gave him such a big tip.

It wasn't going to work on her. She had no intention of being fooled again. Her thoughts drifted back ten years to the mature man who persuaded a naïve fifteen-year-old that he loved her.

Her heart tore anew. At the home for teenage mothers, they had coaxed her to sign forms the very day she arrived, alone and very pregnant after living several months on the streets. "This one's for hospital insurance," they said. These are for admission to the home, for the baby, for so many other things, she had lost track.

Since she had been young and uneducated, the due date had been a matter of guesswork. So vague that Christopher was born only a few days later. Just before driving her to the hospital, they had made her sign yet another paper. *For the new parents.*

Racked by pains, she had faintly asked what parents. Words like "better off", "good life," numbed her brain.

For three glorious days, she held, bathed and fed her baby.

Then they came and took him away.

Chapter Seven

Piers flicked a spot of sticky dough off his sleeve. "Nicole, what was business like before Flavio had his heart attack?"

"Really good. We were open from ten in the morning to two the next morning. The shop was packed all day, and the phone rang all night. When Flavio took sick, I had problems with the staff. I had to spend all my time cooking. Although the pizzas were just as good, business dropped off. I had to cut back on the hours."

"What kind of staff problems did you have?"

"Some wouldn't accept my authority and left. Others talked back. So I fired them. Then others stole, pocketed money from deliveries, pilfered supplies. Mostly small stuff. It all added up though. By then we were understaffed. Orders were not met on time. And the result was..."

"Loss of business." Piers finished her sentence for her.

Her shoulders slumped. "We almost had to close."

"We have to win back the old customers and attract new ones."

At the conviction in his voice Nicole looked up. "Sure, but how? I've phoned some of the regulars. We keep all the info for deliveries on the computer. A few came back. That's all."

"Posters are the answer. We need to make posters and flyers. Get the flyers into people's mail boxes. Staple posters to service poles and get them inserted in newspapers."

"We only have one newspaper. The Otterian Gazette." A grimace tugged at Nicole's lips. "All that costs money."

"We can do it on the cheap and distribute them ourselves." He tossed the dough he was kneading in the air.

His enthusiasm drew her to him despite herself. "On the cheap? Cheap doesn't look good. How anyway?"

"On the computer. You've got a printer?"

"A decent color laser, but its expensive to run."

"Then we're all set. Let's try something." He pointed to the computer desk.

"What looks homemade doesn't attract people." Her tone was dry, expressive of an inner weariness.

"Don't be defeated before we try."

"It's a waste of time."

His voice took on a beguiling tone. "Time is never wasted if you give it your best. If only two more customers come back, they can tell others."

Nicole struggled with herself. If he kept talking in that persuasive manner, she'd agree to anything – even to go to bed with him. She quickly dismissed that dangerous idea and gave herself a mental shake. "I suppose there's no harm in giving it a try."

Piers raised his hand to give her a high five.

Nicole took a step back. "Easy! Your hands are plastered with dough."

She tapped the side of the big mixing bowl. "First, we finish the prep of these pizzas."

They worked in silence. When the dough was ready and safely stowed in the refrigerator, she hung up her apron, washed her hands and sat at the computer.

It didn't take her much time to set up a frame and pull up some pictures. "I have these photos of pizzas, but if I print a photo on each flyer, we'll soon run out of ink."

"Then let's transform the picture into a line drawing."

"I don't know how to do that."

"Let me."

With her body language screaming *futile, futile!* she stood up and waved him into her chair. "I still reckon it's a waste of time and money. When people find flyers they toss them into the trash."

He swiveled on the chair to look at her. "Not everybody. Some people read them. We only need to get through to a few to make it work."

"Ordinary white office paper it isn't going appeal to the eye. It's too amateurish."

"It's all in the message. Now, look at your pizza picture."

Nicole bent to examine the image on the screen, her face next to his. She quickly resumed her standing position. The unexpected closeness, and the heat from his body were too intimate for comfort. "I will admit it looks better than the photo. It looks done by an artist."

"I'm no artist. Your photo program is."

"So, what's next?"

"The all important message. Customers who came into the shop liked Flavio, right?"

"Of course. He's really chatty, always has a kind word for everyone. He remembers customers."

"And they know he's been sick? How about starting with something like *Greetings from Flavio!*? Then we'll write something like *Flavio has recovered and welcomes you to a big Pizza Celebration Special. Order from Flavio's Pizzeria on Thursday and get a two-for-one pizza deal!*?"

"Hey, wait a minute. Two pizzas for the price of one is going to cost us a ton of money."

"When the customers come in or phone, they'll discover things are back to what they were. Flavio will be there to greet them. Plus they'll get a deal they can't say no to. You watch. They'll be back again for more."

"We won't make any profit."

"Perhaps not at first, but they'll know Flavio is back in business and will return in droves. Tell their friends too."

She remained thoughtful. "I'd have to clear this with Flavio first."

"...And what is it you want to clear with me?"

Piers and Nicole spun round to find Flavio framed in the doorway. They had been so absorbed over the computer that they hadn't heard the back door open. After Piers' work with the spray can it no longer squeaked.

Piers held up the sheet the printer had just ejected. "A promotional flyer."

"He wants to do a two-for-one deal for one day. I say it's too expensive."

"*Mia* Nicole, we got to spend money to make money. Lemme see." Flavio put on his glasses and took the sheet from Piers. "Mmm, I kinda like the look of it."

Nicole frowned. "You've got three 'Flavio' in there. It's repetition."

"On purpose," Piers said. "You must get the name out in every sentence to sell the product."

She raised her eyebrows at Piers. "You sound like a business textbook." She saw him bite his lip. Surprising really, she hadn't seen him nervous before. Then again, she hadn't known him long.

Flavio beamed. "What a smart guy you are."

"Then we go with that?"

"Start printing."

Nicole rolled her eyes. The door jingled, and a customer came in. Shortly afterward, Lynne arrived and immediately offered to mind the shop while Nicole and Piers distributed the newly printed flyers.

"Nicole, do you have a cell phone I can borrow?" Piers asked.

"No." Nicole's answer was curt, a clear message that he was taking charge and she didn't like it.

Lynne rummaged in her shoulder bag. "I'll lend you mine." She handed him a shiny pink phone. "You're smart. Like that if there is a delivery needed, I can call you."

Nicole busied herself stacking the flyers as they dropped from the printer. "We'll take the van, so we can go as far as we have flyers."

"I'll carry the flyers." Piers followed Nicole out to the parking lot. Snowflake ran for a pat, then ambled back into his enclosure.

They started at the end of the nearest residential block. Each took one side of the street. The spring sun, still not very high, warmed the pavement. Residual heat wafted upward every time they got back on the street after running up driveways bordered by brownish lawns where tiny green shoots were struggling.

When they came to the last of an armful of flyers, Piers would sprint back to advance the van. Nicole watched him over her shoulder, long legs unfurled in a fluid motion. An office worker, he'd said. No office worker in her experience possessed that kind of athletic body. Piers struck her as someone who put in long hours in the gym or in some sport. Whether she was right or not, she couldn't take her eyes off the agile way he jumped behind the wheel of the old van. A strange tightening in her chest surprised her. She watched him drop the final flyer through a mail slot.

He held up his hands, palms out. "That's it. Let's go back. That printer will have coughed out another batch by now. We can tack some to service poles."

"Why you're doing all this?" A sharp rasp to her voice threatened to disturb the friendship that was developing between them.

He motioned her into the van. "This is my job. I'd like to make sure I bring in more business. It would be nice to get paid at the end of the week. Every week." He glanced at her and turned his attention back to driving.

At a loss to know what to say, she stared idly out of the window. The breeze blew an old plastic bag off the sidewalk. His argument for marketing pizzas was strong. Then why did it set her nerves abuzz? She shot him a quick look. "When we come back, I'd better drive. I know the best spots to put up posters. And where the community board is."

"I noticed there was a bulletin board in the entrance of the thrift store the other night."

"We'll go there too."

"Maybe I could pick up a pair of jeans."

Her suspicions came back in force. "For a guy who says he likes clothes, you don't seem to have many."

Piers swung the van into the parking behind the pizzeria. "I left most of my stuff at my brother's."

Another lie. It wasn't his brother but his lawyer and best friend.

"You have a brother?"

"A handful of years younger than me. I'll send for my things when I've got the cash."

Piers parked the van and cut the motor. The sudden silence discouraged further conversation. A quiver ran down Nicole's spine. She watched him jump down, his toned muscles apparent under the white T-shirt. He had discarded his jacket.

Piers Sonder was so tempting.

He was also an outright liar.

That T-shirt, her critical eye had noticed, was not your discount store generic brand. She could tell from the cut and the fine weave of the material. The shirt fitted beautifully. A pizza delivery boy dressed in a hundred-dollar T-? It made no sense.

Nor did anything else about him.

With the dog at his side, he held open the backdoor for her. She walked past him, head high, not daring to look at him. Belatedly, she murmured her thanks. What poise he had. He acted with that casual assurance all people had who were born rich.

She had seen that same assurance in Howard Witherington. Howard, her baby's father and number one jerk. Pangs of regret assailed her. If only she could be fifteen all over again. She'd do everything differently. No one would browbeat the new and assertive Nicole into giving up her baby. No one would walk in and take her child from her. Nor would she repeat anything as stupid as kidnaping her own little sister from their foster parents, the same foster parents who'd kicked her out because she had gotten pregnant.

Right now there was no time to dwell on the past. Customers were coming in. Piers had left on a delivery.

When the modest rush was over, Lynne brushed a few crumbs off the counter. "Time to take Flavio home. He's got to put his feet up. I'll be back. Like that you and Piers can distribute the rest of the flyers."

"Thanks. It feels good to be busy."

"Maybe the flyers are already having an effect."

"Let's hope so."

Lynne shook her head. "You're pretty pessimistic for someone so young."

Nicole shrugged. "I'm getting older by the minute." The bitterness in her heart wasn't something she wanted to share. Not even with someone as understanding as Lynne.

Her two favorite people left. Good-natured Flavio bickered about having to rest and exercise, but followed Lynne.

Alone in the kitchen, Nicole snatched up a cloth and set about cleaning the cupboards. Anything to help blot out the memories. She had prided herself on keeping the hurt bottled up. Somehow, Piers' arrival had brought her sorrows gushing to the surface.

The best that could happen would be he'd soon lose interest in pizzas and move on. Because, if he didn't, if he hung around, she'd have to come up with a few clever strategies to survive. Working alongside him was too distracting for words.

It had been her mistake to hire him. She couldn't understand what had prompted her to give him the job. Worse still, she had found him an apartment in *her* building. The more she thought about it the more he reminded her of Howard, though in a very different way.

Piers sported Howard's killer good looks. His accent carried the same refinement. He must have gone to the same prep school as Howard. And like Howard, everything about him screamed money. The only difference, and that remained the big mystery, was that Piers had shown up with empty pockets. The haggard look that hunger gives was something she had experienced herself and recognized right away. She had been in the same penniless situation when Flavio without asking awkward questions gave her a job.

Yes, Piers was a mystery, one she was nowhere near solving. Maybe she'd discover that like Howard, Piers too was married. That thought pitched her mind into free fall. More than anything else, the longing to know where her baby was engulfed her with a searing pain.

She wallowed in gloom until the backdoor burst open and Piers came in. He waved a fistful of bills and printouts grinning from ear to ear.

His arrival ended her temptation to brood. Shortly afterward, Lynne returned to take charge of the shop.

Piers picked up the heap of flyers. "Ready, Nicole? Time to hit the bulletin boards."

Half an hour later, the stapler clicked empty.

"How is it you always run out of staples right before the very end?" Piers glared at the staple gun in his hand.

Nicole reached down to the lower edge of the bulletin board. "Here, use a thumbtack."

Piers pinned up the flyer. He shook Nicole's hand and held it longer than necessary.

"Well done, ma'am. People who shop get hungry, and the pizzeria isn't far away."

A sudden wave of heat streaked from her hand all the way to her cheeks. She freed herself from his grasp. "Okay, you've convinced me it was the right thing to do."

"But deep down you still think it's a waste of time and money."

"I don't go in for psychoanalysis, especially while standing in a supermarket entrance. What I do know is that thanks to all those flyers the printer now needs a new color cartridge, and a black one too. Do you know how expensive they are?"

Piers held his arms out at his sides. "I guess when money is tight everything is expensive. Do you think we can get to the thrift store before it closes?"

"We can if we hurry."

They arrived just as the woman manager was about to lock the front doors. Piers smiled at her through the glass. The woman waved them in. Nicole had the impression that if it had been anyone else, the woman would have turned them away. Piers' looks and winning smile, Nicole had discovered, opened lots of doors, real and otherwise.

She helped him pick out some jeans in near-new condition, waited outside the booth while he tried them on, and found him a three-pack of tees in white, gray and black still in their unopened plastic packaging.

At the cash register, Nicole pulled her credit card from her purse. Piers placed his hand on hers. The simple contact was enough to set the familiar quivers spiraling up her arm.

"I have tip money. With the next tips, I'll reimburse you for the rent and house stuff."

"There's no rush."

A grin rewarded her. "Of course, that all depends on how much I get in tips."

They left the store after thanking the Piers-dazzled manager.

Lynne was boxing up a whole pizza when they got back to the pizzeria. "Not too many customers while you were out. But the gentleman who just left said he came because he saw the flyer. You had an excellent idea, Piers."

"One order isn't going to make a fat lot of difference." Nicole's tone wiped the smiles off her co-workers' faces.

"Nicole," Piers said. His voice both gentle and firm. "We just put them out. Give people a chance to see them. Former customers will remember and want to come and see for themselves. You've got to have faith."

"You're right. Sorry. It's just that this last while hasn't been easy."

Lynne retrieved her jacket from the hook. "Things will get better. You know the saying, what goes down comes up again."

"Isn't it what goes up comes down again?" Nicole didn't hide the sarcasm in her voice.

Piers held Lynne's jacket for her. "Depends on your outlook. If your glass is half-empty or half-full."

Nicole tilted her chin. "What if your glass has tipped over, spilled and smashed on the floor? No, don't bother to reply. I know, I'm being a pain."

Lynne opened the door. A repressed smile on her lips. "Goodnight, you two." The balmy spring night air wafted in with the smell of damp earth after rain. "Tomorrow, I'll plant some spring flowers in the tubs out front. It's that time of year." Lynne closed the door behind her.

The sound of the chimes faded. Piers scrutinized the shop walls, ceiling and counter. "It would improve customer relations if we repainted the old place."

Nicole looked up from cleaning the floor. She leaned her weight on the mop handle. "Another one of your genius ideas? Repaint?" The textbook again. The feeling of unease came over her once more. "Out of the question. Imagine the cost."

"I don't know. I only see that an attractive shop has more appeal for customers. Here, let me do that." He took the mop from her hands.

Nicole bit her lip. Ever since he had arrived on the scene, she had the feeling she was doing everything wrong. Flavio's Pizzeria didn't seem big enough for the two of them. Her opinions seemed destined to clash with his, even though she was supposed to be in charge.

A customer came in.

Piers said, "Good evening, sir. How are you?"

"Just fine, thank you."

"Lovely night out there."

"Yes, summer can't be far away."

From behind the counter, Nicole pasted a smile on her face. There, Piers was doing it again. Mr. Smoothie with the velvet voice. She straightened. "What can I get you?"

"Excuse me interrupting, sir," Piers said, "but if you haven't tried it before the new bacon and pineapple topping is simply mouth watering." His confidential tone implied one gourmet talking to another.

The man smiled. "Hey, that sounds inviting." He turned back to Nicole. "I'll take a nine-inch, please, miss, with the bacon and pineapple."

"You'll forgive me butting in yet again, but if you order the twelve-inch pizza, you get double the topping at no extra charge."

"Is that so? Then, miss, you'd better make that a twelve-inch."

Nicole glowered at Piers. "It will just be a few minutes."

She disappeared into the kitchen. While she prepared the order she could hear Piers and the customer chatting in the front.

The oven timer sounded. She slid out the pizza and carried it to the counter.

The man eyed the piping hot pizza. "Mmm, that smells delicious. I'm glad your new manager put me onto it." He paid. On his way out he gave Piers a thumb up sign.

Nicole waited until she saw the man climb into his car. "New manager, indeed! Did you tell him you were the manager?"

"Nope. All the time he waited we talked hockey. He's a PrairieEagle fan."

"And I suppose you are too."

"Me? I know next to nothing about hockey. But he was happy to talk to me about it."

Nicole pouted. "I guess he assumed that because I was out back baking the pizza, you must be the manager."

Piers lifted a shoulder, an innocent look on his face. "I don't know why he would. I was mopping the floor when he came in."

"And what do you think you're doing offering extra topping at no extra charge?"

Piers grinned. "I did a quick mental calculation. If I talked him into buying the larger pizza, we could offer the extra topping and still come out ahead."

"Where do you get all this?"

"You must have covered that concept in your business studies. It's called creative promotion."

Nicole's lips tightened. "We mustn't have gotten to that page in the textbook yet. I'm worried you're going to run Flavio's business into the ground with your harebrained schemes." If she thought her tough talk would deflate him she was mistaken.

With a sweep of his arm he encompassed the empty space in front of the counter.

"You know what we need here?"

Nicole rolled her eyes. "Not again. Tell me."

"A couple of tables and chairs so customers can eat-in."

"This isn't a restaurant."

"Not everyone wants to carry a pizza home with them. Maybe they just want a snack. You know a drink and a slice of pizza. And they'd appreciate being able to sit down while they wait."

"We've never had problems in the past with people waiting."

"Well, it's just a thought." He put away the bucket and mop. "It's time to close up."

"I'll take a slice home. You can have all the leftovers you want." Nicole surprised herself with the unexpected softness in her voice. "We make fresh tomorrow."

"That's quite a lot. Are you sure you don't want more than one slice?"

"One's enough for me. Besides, I've done some baking at home."

"I don't mind admitting I'm hungry enough to wolf the lot. I'll carry them... home, too. Like that you don't have to wait for me to close the shop."

They walked together to their apartment building. Nicole made sure the conversation remained firmly focused on neutral subjects like the weather.

A glance at the clock in her apartment and Nicole took a quick decision. She'd go to the thrift store and get that dress she'd seen at the end of the rack. Good clothes didn't stay long. The dark blue satiny dress with its abstract white and mauve circles would be perfect. Perfect for what she didn't know, or rather didn't want to acknowledge the reason. Normally, she wasn't one to buy many clothes, not unless they were practical clothes, and definitely not on a whim.

Her inner voice urged her to be honest with herself. She didn't want Piers always to see her in her work clothes.

In the store, she made a beeline to the dress rack. The dress was gone. Disappointment killed her joyful expectation. Maybe the clerk had hung it in a different place. She rifled through the hangers and almost let out a whoop of jubilation. Here it was. The dress! She checked the label. Medium as she'd expected. A quick look at the seams and the fabric. Almost new. No spots.

The dress on her arm, she strode to the fitting room. The sleeveless blue dress with its décolleté and its tiny white lace trim emphasized her feminine allure. She liked the image the mirror sent back to her. It restored her confidence.

Happy with her find, she walked out of the fitting room to go to the checkout.

Chapter Eight

After another long day, Piers shut his apartment door and leaned his back against it. He couldn't believe the hours he worked at the pizzeria. Was this the way to atone for his utter stupidity? There has hardly been a moment in the last two years when he hadn't thought about the people he killed. The hard work prevented him from dwelling as much on the fatal accident, but the memory didn't fade.

A new life was his goal. A life that could make him proud. Or so he told himself. Pride and now a dark-haired girl living two floors above his head.

Swearing off drink had been the easy part. Two years abstinence in jail had seen to that. The two hundred dollars Mark had given him, hadn't taken him far. Not that the lack of cash made him really miserable he discovered. Maybe he needed to prove he was made of sterner stuff than his father gave him credit for. His father hadn't visited him in prison, but had sent a message that on his release he could come back to the company and sweep floors. Reddington Senior hadn't accepted that his son had rejected the use of his influence to get his sentence commuted. What hurt most was that his mother hadn't gone against her husband to come to see him. She had sent clothes and delicacies with Mark, all of which he refused to take. Poor Mark had a trunk full of clothes in his spare bedroom.

His business degree was soon put to good use when he was asked to teach a class to the inmates. They weren't hardened criminals but most of them had no skills and were likely to re-offend simply because they could only get menial jobs, or no job at all. There had been a deep satisfaction to see those men improve their reading and writing skills, and learn simple budgeting.

Working alongside Nicole might threaten to derail his plans to go on to the Yukon. Under that austere chef's uniform and flour-dusted apron lay an intriguing woman. Only, now that he had learned how hard it was to get a job he had no intention of losing the one he had got. Why did he want to go North? For a while he had forgotten the reason. The Yukon Territory was a long way from home, the end of the road, a place where he could pit himself against nature, and become someone else. A place where he could shed the idle, carefree Piers.

He shook his head. As much as he'd love to see what it would take to get Nicole to unpin her chignon for him, he reminded himself that it was perhaps just as well she was so prim and proper.

Survival was priority number one. And that included keeping body and soul together. He opened his box of pizzas on the kitchen counter. Fifteen minutes into taste-testing the different toppings, he decided that the bacon-pineapple was his favorite. He rounded off his solitary dinner with an apple. At least, he was no longer hungry.

His dinner over, he stretched out on his paper-thin mattress. With hands locked behind his head, he let his eyes wander over the lime-green decor. A laugh rose in his chest and nearly choked him. His prison cell hadn't been much different from this room.

But this prison isn't because of a criminal act. It's the result of my newfound poverty. Poverty is a prison. It may not have bars on windows but it did prevent people from escaping to a better life. Until I saw homeless men brought into the prison, I had believed they were on the streets because they were too lazy to work. But no, they had tried and failed. Prison was almost a welcoming change. Food, heat and showers. I hadn't been sentenced to a maximum security prison, nor were those homeless men. They were safe there, too, which probably wasn't always the case on the street.

For the first time in his life he realized that poverty forced some people to live their entire lives in similar dingy surroundings. He understood how despair could overcome the best person. How it could lead them to do things they wouldn't otherwise do and sometimes land them in prison.

His lengthy job search had taught him that poverty is a vicious circle. Look poor and employment doors shut in your face. That was true for the lowest level jobs just as much as high- paying positions. Mix poverty with a lack of experience and even a Harvard MBA was not worth the parchment it was printed on. And his coveted world championship in Tae Kwon Do had no monetary value whatsoever.

Worse still, if you can't provide references you may as well go and live like a hermit in the desert. No prospective employer was ever rude to his face. But Piers soon recognized the particular smile and handshake that meant "Thanks, but we won't be needing your services."

Going hungry for a forty-eight-hour stretch was an experience he had no desire to repeat. Once, in a year-round Farmers' Market, he'd almost stolen an apple off a stand. Just as humiliating was the gray-bearded man behind the neighboring stall who, without a word, handed him a piece of honeycomb on a paper plate.

Piers wondered if the man guessed he was about to filch the apple. Maybe he thought that by offering the free sample he wouldn't get ripped off too. At the time, his clothes were not really wrinkled. Nor did he have the air of a drifter. Maybe the man with the honey recognized a certain look about the homeless and unemployed.

He remembered how Nicole had commented on the quality of his clothes. Then again, she had an eye for detail. The honeycomb guy never said anything except, "I'm a beekeeper." As if that gave him the power to see through the people who walked by his stall.

Piers grinned up at the stained ceiling tiles of his room. On the other hand the man might have heard his guts rumbling.

He had experienced humiliation again when he had bought a movie ticket and they wanted to check his bag. He had gone in not to watch the movie but to catch up on some sleep out of the pouring spring rain. He was curious to know how many homeless people did the same thing.

Poverty sucked! Poverty led to depression. Waves of darkness had hit him as he walked from place to place. This he had recognized as deep despondency. Too much of it and it'd become clinical depression. He fought against it.

He had chosen to turn his back on his family's wealth. Yet at times he did wonder if it wouldn't be better to sweep the floors in his father's sports empire. Then the sharp pain of regret and sorrow would wash over him and he'd lift his chin up. There was no respite for two grieving families. There would be none for him either until he had become a better man, done something useful with his life.

On the second trip to the thrift store, Piers realized that the smell hadn't bothered him the way it did on his first visit. He could see now how someone could slide so low as to end up on the street. He himself had almost been there. Once on the street, a person is launched on a downward spiral. Piers had never thought about it before. Now he knew otherwise.

He preferred not to think about where he'd be if Nicole hadn't offered him the job. He liked to think he had the strength of mind to persevere. There was no way he'd have called Mark to have him wire some cash. No matter what. Yet at the same time he wondered.

Nicole. She was something else. A woman so easy to love. Piers jerked his head off the pillow. *Hey no, I don't mean it in that way. People like her and so do I. But I can't afford to let a female get to me.*

Sleep overcame him. He awoke in the middle of the night, in the chilled room. He undressed and wrapped himself in the comforter. Manual work, he determined, tired the body a lot more than hiking in the mountains or spending the whole day in his sail boat.

In another minute, he was fast asleep again.

Chapter Nine

The day brought in many returning customers who had seen the poster. Lynn helped in the kitchen while Piers ran deliveries non-stop. Finally it was closing time. Over the week Nicole had the chance to observe Piers in action behind the counter. During the day Flavio's Pizzeria had more walk-in customers than phone orders. He'd greet male customers in a businesslike fashion. His charmer smile he reserved for the women. Nicole's ear picked up the sexy edge to his voice. She had to admit that customers left happy and came back again and again.

"How do you do that?"

"Do what?" Piers beamed a smile on her.

"Get them to return for more. That's the third time those two women have been back in less than two days."

Piers shrugged. "Maybe they're hooked on pizza."

She pursed her lips. "You know that's not the reason."

"When serving the public, you have to smile and engage the customer. Make them want to come back for more whether they need it or not."

"Which charm school did you go to?"

His rich laugh echoed around the kitchen. "It's common sense, really. Make the customer feel he wants to come back. I still think tables and chairs and a coat of paint would-"

"I told you, no money." Her tone was more snappy than she intended.

The phone jangled. She stood and listened while Piers smooth-talked the caller into ordering the twelve-inch with extra topping that had now become a fixture on the menu. Piers made up the order and set off to deliver it.

She went to the window and watched him climb into the van. He stuck his head out of the window and flashed her his killer smile. Her hand made a fist in her jeans pocket. Unlike the pizza-addicted women, she wasn't about to succumb to his spell. That was a no-no.

At that moment Flavio returned from his therapy. "Lost in thought, *mia*?

"I was thinking about an idea Piers has."

"He does well that boy. Do you like him?"

Lynne's arrival saved Nicole from answering. After Nicole finished serving some customers, Flavio came and leaned on the counter. "You were saying Piers had another idea?"

"He said we should paint the interior and put out tables and chairs so that customers can eat-in. Says it would boost sales."

"Hmm. Maybe not a bad idea. Can we afford the paint?"

"A definite no."

"Maybe not the paint," Lynne said. "But the tables and chairs are a good idea. I've got a round café table at home and some tablecloths I never use. The tablecloths are plastic but quite pretty. We could find at least one other table. I have a couple of chairs in the basement I can spare."

Piers burst into the kitchen breathless. "I took two big orders from the house next door to my delivery. Promised them for five o'clock."

His news was received by a round of applause, which Piers acknowledged with a theatrical bow. Nicole rolled her eyes. She could just picture the scenario. The woman out in her yard. Piers leaning over the fence and charming her into ordering pizzas instead of having to cook dinner.

"We need to have an account to take credit cards on the terminal and we need to get one of the buy-online software to take orders on the computer or phone."

"You're out of your mind! Think of the cost!" Anger put red spots in Nicole's cheeks.

"Well, Nicoletta, the lad is right. We'll have to look into it."

Nicole's voice rose a notch. "Then with tables we'll need a restaurant license."

"No, we won't," Piers said. "People are buying a takeout, where they chose to eat it doesn't matter. There're some hamburger joints that have picnic tables out front, and a table indoors. No different from what I'm proposing."

"The boy is right," Flavio said.

"Okay, let's get going." Nicole went to the kitchen to start on the dough.

Lynne went to serve a customer.

"I like the idea of offering eat-in," Flavio said.

Piers' face lit up. "I'm glad. Do you think we could rustle up a couple of tables and chairs?"

"Mrs. B. has already offered us a table and some chairs." Nicole surprised herself with her abruptness. Piers' enthusiasm irritated, no, not irritated, *antagonized* her. Somehow, she always seemed to react sharply to him. Normally, she liked to think of herself as easy going, someone with a ready smile and a nice word for everyone. She let no one suspect the pain locked away in her heart. Her tone softened. "She also has some tablecloths. That should make the place more homey."

"I can fetch the stuff with the van," Piers said.

Lynne pushed her head through the door. "When you get back from the five o'clock delivery, we'll go over to my house."

While waiting for the pizzas, Piers went out to the rear parking lot. He came back a few minutes later. "Do we have a screwdriver?"

"Why? Is Snowflake's gate loose again?" Nicole asked.

"I need it for the van."

"For the warming cabinet?"

Hands deep in flour, Flavio pointed with his chin. "Second drawer from the right. You'll find all the tools you need in there. What's broken?"

"The van's heating cabinet. I believe I've solved the mystery why it isn't working. A couple of wires are short-circuiting."

Nicole watched from the other side of the worktable. For no apparent reason, her heart beat faster. Perhaps it was the lock of hair sweeping his forehead or the long eyelashes casting a shadow over his cheekbones. Or perhaps, like the cheese on the pizza topping, she too was melting. It wouldn't work to fall for him.

She hadn't spent these years avoiding entanglements with men for nothing. Yet she was slowly accepting the truth that his ideas and enthusiasm had injected a positive note into the flagging business. She no longer resented it when she saw female customers swoon over him. If it meant they ordered more pizza, that was fine by her.

Two men with name tags on their shirt front came in. "Monytiz. We're here to install the terminal."

"What?" Nicole's voice rose to a high pitch.

"Mr. Flavio Bellini ordered the terminal. The bank sent us."

Lynne bustled in. "It's all right, Nicole. Flavio opened an account. We can take credit cards now and on the mobile for the van."

"I'm going to faint. How are we going to pay for it?"

Lynn laughed. "By doing more business."

"Piers has really got you wrapped around his little finger," Nicole said. Bitterness edged her voice.

"Cheer up, girl. I think that man knows a lot about running a shop. You'll see, it's going to be really good," Flavio said.

After Flavio and Mrs. B. departed the evening got busy. Yet Piers managed to pick up the chairs and tables. It was late when he came back from making the last delivery. Nicole waited.

"Let's close up," he said. "How about if I drive you home in the van?"

Again, he was taking charge. But he was right... as usual. "Thanks. We'll have to be here early tomorrow. It's your Special Thursday, remember? We have to make double the quantity of pizzas."

Piers paused and pointed to the formerly empty space to the left of the counter. "Don't you agree those two tables look attractive?"

"I'll grant you that. It gives a different look to the shop. I didn't believe there'd be enough room."

Piers played with Snowflake then locked the dog gate and opened the van door for Nicole. As Nicole placed her foot on the step, Piers put his hand to the small of her back. A jolt shook her, but already he was closing the door. She breathed deeply. The drive home was short. Mercifully short.

Her answering machine blinked at her the moment she stepped into her apartment. Under a wave of anxiety she sucked in her lips. A sigh escaped her while she pressed PLAY and went about peeling off her work clothes.

Jack's voice came on. "Sorry I missed you, but I had to rush. I finally persuaded the clerk at the Toronto General to check the records when I went to see my parents over the weekend. She told me a nurse by the name of Bea Riemer was on duty the evening they took your baby away. But Nurse Riemer doesn't work there anymore."

A thrill of happiness filled Nicole's heart. At last a name, a concrete clue she could follow up on. This Nurse Riemer could be traced and would be able to tell her which adoption agency had taken her baby. Nicole went about the task of cleaning her apartment, playing reunion scenarios in her head.

She wished she had the time and money to go and find the nurse right away. A rush of anxiety swamped her moment of joy. The question nagged her whether she even had the right to look for her child. He might be perfectly happy in a loving home. Her sudden appearance in his life might unsettle him. Yet she couldn't shake off her intuitive feeling that something had gone wrong. Her little boy needed her. It isn't like she hadn't wanted him. She had.

From the day he had moved in her belly, since the day he was born, she had grieved for him. And every day over the past nine years.

Last night, her dream came back. In it Christopher was calling to her, his arms outstretched But in the dream he had no face. Something had happened. More urgently than ever, she had to find him. And if it was all wrong, if he was happy and loved, she would just watch from afar and leave. Then she would wait until the time he might want to know his biological mother.

***

Piers let the kitchen tap run cold. He filled a glass and sat at his rickety table to eat the last of his pizza for breakfast. Even cold it tasted good. He turned his mind to figuring out how he could get the pizzeria to make more money. The product was excellent. The decor was the pits. Sure, the tables were an improvement. But it was going to be a long haul before the business could be called a success. His belief that the pizzeria needed to invest in a shop-online cart couldn't be shaken. People turned to their phone to search and order. They would order a pizza and it would be ready by the time they collected it. No waiting, though there would always be people who preferred to walk in, wait, have a chat and take in the ambiance, the new ambiance he was planning that is.

And the paint? He wished he was a little more in touch and knew how much a gallon of latex cost. Never in his life had he set foot in a paint store. He had bought plenty of varnish for his boat. He simply charged it to his account at the ship chandler and settled the total bill at month end, giving scant heed to the individual items. He wondered what Nicole would say if she knew that little fact about him. He chased the thought away. That was his past life, a time he'd never go back to.

In business school they teach that in order to sell your product you have to promote it. You have to package it right. Then you have to know your market. Once you've got a toehold, you must expand that market. *Okay, today's big two-for-one is promotion. That's a start in the right direction.*

And tomorrow, I'll buy a can of paint out of my tips. Something cool yet conservative. Eggshell white, perhaps. Conservative considering the clientele I've seen so far. That'll deal with the packaging angle.

He tried to picture Nicole's face when he'd come into the shop with his gallon of eggshell. Too bad there was no way he could get it on the walls without her knowing. She might be so excited that she'd kiss him. Unlikely. And he'd best put such ideas out of his head.

Piers hit the shower. It bothered him that his thoughts returned more and more often to Nicole. The woman had a persistent effect on him. Droplets of water flew everywhere as he shook his head.

Maybe he'd have time to go the thrift store before taking her to the pizzeria.

Chapter Ten

The alarm on his watch sounded its annoying buzz. Piers grabbed the watch and fumbled with the off button, then remembered he had to get up early to call in at a paint shop. He didn't think there were any thrift stores for paint. Maybe he should find out. It suddenly occurred to him that in so few days he had already adopted the mentality of people who, without being totally destitute, didn't earn enough to buy brand new items for their homes.

He backed the van out of the parking spot. Amazing how well he had already learned his way around Otter Lake. It wasn't a big town by eastern standards, more like an overgrown village, but he found it interesting with its nineteen century buildings, some with intricate ornamentation. No office towers rose above smaller buildings and houses to mar the skyline.

The thrift store wasn't yet open. Stymied, Piers paced the sidewalk in front trying to decide what to do. The air hadn't yet warmed up. He shivered despite his woolly sweater. Across the street, on the edge of the parking lot, buds were beginning to sprout tiny leaves on a row of young trees. The store opened at ten. That wouldn't do, he and Nicole were to be at the pizzeria by nine. A girl passed him, stopped and retraced her steps.

"Hi, you need something from the store? It's not open."

She stated obvious but Piers refrained from saying so. "I was wondering if they sold paint."

"No, we don't."

"*We*? You work in the store?"

The girl smiled and nodded. He recognized her as the checkout clerk when he had bought his jeans and sweater. She had made eyes at him, like she did right now.

"If you want paint," she said, "Try Habitat. They sell a lot of recycled stuff. They have brand new cans of paint too, leftovers from commercial projects."

"Great. But what time do they open? I have to be at work at nine."

"They open early. We open late and close late. I'm coming in earlier today to sort a shipment of inventory ends from a factory." She stepped closer, her smile inviting. "D'you want me to save you some clothes? Shirts and pants maybe? There'll be some winter things too."

In his own social circle, he'd have no trouble brushing off such a blatant come on without causing offense. But in this world of working folk he was unsure how. He didn't want to upset the eager young woman. She was sweet and sincere. Telling her that by next winter Otter Lake might be a distant memory just didn't seem right.

"My only problem is I can't buy anything right now. You know, a cash crunch."

"That's okay. I can put stuff in a box with a reserved label on it." She eyed him up and down. "I think I know what size you are."

Her pretty face was so earnest he didn't have the heart to refuse. "I guess I do need another pair of jeans, a couple of shirts and a sweater."

The girl laughed. "I can save you a good jacket or a parka. You'll need more than a sweater for our winters. And we get the best stuff like now, at the end of winter."

He gave her a dazzling smile. "You guessed I'm not from around here."

"Your accent. I can tell you're from down East."

"You're right. And I'm Piers."

With a smile, the sales girl laid her hand on his arm. "I'm Jenny. Get going or you'll be late. The HFP store is three blocks down, on the left. I'll mark a box for you."

Piers beat his way through the light morning traffic and pulled into the recycling store's parking lot on the edge of town. On all sides the yard was surrounded by piles of lumber, metal posts, frames, heaps of stones, bricks, concrete blocks and a whole collection of items he couldn't put a name to. His frivolous ex-friends would have called it junk. He'd never doubted the value of recycling, but never thought it would hit so close to home. For a minute he wondered why he even thought about his former gilded life and the friends he had rejected when they refused to understand why he wouldn't accept a deal to avoid prison. He parked and headed for the entrance just as the open sign lit up.

Inside, he was met by a scene that resembled no other store he had been into. Arranged on the floor in neat family clusters was an assortment of toilet bowls, sinks, plumbing fixtures and kitchen cabinets. Stacked on metal shelving were boxes of door knobs, light fittings and sundry hardware. And more shelves extended the length of the cavernous building.

"Hi, may I help you?"

And they even had courteous employees.

He smiled at a youth with 'Ed' embroidered on his blue shirt. "I'm looking for paint."

"Indoor or outdoor?"

"I'll start with indoor."

"Right here. We've got a good selection, but not all from the same lot. How much do you need?"

"I don't know. I want to paint a room about thirty feet by twenty."

"You'll need a couple of gallons. Right now I don't have that much all in one color. Do you have a preference?"

"Not really, I'm looking for something bright and happy." Bright and happy. Not conservative eggshell. For a moment his thoughts strayed to Nicole, her friendly manners to customers, her caring for Flavio, her affection for Lynne. She was certainly bright, but he sensed she wasn't totally happy.

"A gallon should do just under six hundred square feet. That's if the walls are primed. I have a gallon of sunflower yellow. That would cover the two larger walls. You could do the other two with this royal blue. It goes well with the rich yellow. You'd have some left over.

I've also got about a half gallon of light blue but you might just be short a few feet."

"Better take enough. You're sure that the royal blue and the yellow will go together?"

"Absolutely. You have brushes?"

"What do I need?"

"Those two. The smaller one for the edges around windows and doors and the larger one for the walls. A roller would be better. You could have this roller and tray set real cheap."

"I'll take the lot."

The clerk rang up the total. The low price came as a surprise to Piers. He had tip money left over. There was no time to waste to get back to the apartment block if he wanted to pick up Nicole before she suspected he had been out paint shopping.

Piers whistled a few bars of a new song he picked up from the van radio. His footsteps echoed up the stairwell. He knocked on Nicole's door. A tantalizing odor rushed at him when she opened the door. His stomach complained that his meager breakfast had been a long time ago.

"Piers! You're up extra early. Had breakfast?"

"Good morning, sweet lady. Breakfast was the last of the pizza. Cold."

"Come in. I've made extra waffles."

"Do we have time?"

"Of course."

Piers entered her apartment. His eyed drifted to the photos of Snowflake adorning the cream-colored wall. He stood in front of a silkscreen wall-hanging of a ballerina. The polished furniture, simple but stylish, made him aware of the contrast with his own grungy quarters down below. She waved him to the kitchen table and pushed a plate toward him.

"Help yourself. I'm done. Here's the maple syrup."

He licked his lips. "Hey, these are great. You make them from scratch?"

"With corn and chickpea flour." Nicole slid the last waffle onto his plate and deposited the empty platter in the sink.

Piers devoured the corn waffle as slowly as he could. Nicole burst out laughing.

"You must have a hole in your stomach. Here, have an oatmeal cookie. I baked them yesterday."

Her laughter did something inside him, something he preferred not to analyze at this point. At the pizzeria, he unloaded his two cans of paint and stacked them at the far end of the shop.

Nicole's eyes blazed. "You bought paint!"

He hesitated. "A bargain I couldn't refuse."

"For heavens' sake! We can't afford paint even at a bargain." The earlier warmth in her voice vanished.

"The business can't but I can."

"You can't pay for it if you're going to repaint the shop."

"Why not? I'm investing in my job."

She softened. "You sound like my management textbook. When I saw the paint in the van, I thought you'd bought it for your apartment."

"The apartment can wait."

"What color did you get?"

"There wasn't a lot of choice. So I got sunflower yellow, enough for two walls, and royal blue for the other two."

Nicole tilted her head, her hand coming to her chin. Piers closed his eyes. Her apron covering her simple T-shirt and jeans with her hair tightly pinned at the back of her head sent longings through him. That was not what he wanted to dwell upon if he was going to keep his sanity.

"Since you've got the paint, we should paint part of the wall with a big diagonal or a wave in one color and the rest in the other color. Make a sort of motif. Perhaps a big star-burst behind the tables."

He inclined his head and opened his hands. "That sounds pretty artistic. Okay, direct me and I'll do the grunt work."

Their carefree laughter united them for a moment.

Nicole pointed to the kitchen. "Before we splash paint around, there's dough to mix."

Not long afterward Flavio arrived, then Lynne. The four of them concentrated on the work with only a word or two to break the silence, a fast and efficient team. When everything was ready, Lynne went to open the shop. Piers found himself in the way.

"Go and prepare the sunburst," Nicole said.

"I don't draw that well. What about you?"

"So, so. I'll come in a minute."

Piers made a mock bow and moved to the store front to wash the walls and prepare the paint.

Flavio looked up. "What's going on?"

"Piers is going to paint the shop."

Flavio cocked his head to one side. "Is he now? Well, well. The man's a real eager beaver. I thought you said there was no money for paint."

"He bought it with his tip money."

Flavio caught his dough and held it suspended for several seconds. A smile broke out on his jovial face. "He's got guts that guy."

She looked up to the ceiling. "He thinks it will bring in more customers."

"Smile, Nicole, smile. It will. That young man is good for business."

Nicole didn't want to listen to Flavio extolling Piers' virtues. Instinct told her that Piers was more than the usual pizza delivery boy. A lot more. Flavio and Lynne didn't see him the way she did. Added to that was the effect Piers had on her. The way she responded to his closeness troubled her. His presence reminded her she was still a young woman. A woman with needs and wants.

She didn't welcome those disturbing quivers she experienced whenever he brushed past her. Not welcome. Yet she wondered what it would be like if she kissed him. The way he looked at her with eyes that turned dark chestnut brown in their intensity awoke sensations she'd prefer to leave dormant.

No fantasy. No private dreams. Not until she found what happened to Christopher. A ray of hope lightened her features. Nurse

Riemer. Perhaps she'd remember something.

Next week, she'd take her day off to contact her and try possibly to meet her. And if she had to go to Toronto, she'd take a couple of days off. A customer left and for a while the store was empty. Everyone sat down.

Lynne produced a carton of milk. "Sorry, no coffee today."

Nicole and Piers groaned. Flavio muttered something too low to be heard.

"You're not allowed coffee yet," Lynne said to Flavio. "It'll be quiet for another couple of hours before the evening rush. Why don't you and Piers start on that drawing?"

Piers shook his head. "Delivery in a few minutes."

Nicole handed him the insulated container. "Here you go."

"Flavio, we've got enough dough prepared. You have to go home now and rest." Lynne backed up her words with a fierce frown.

"I'm okay."

"No, you're not. I can see fatigue written all over your face. You've been working too hard. Do you want another heart attack?"

"Don't be dramatic, woman. I know what I feel. We're busy. Look, the shop's still full."

"Two customers are finishing their slices. If you won't do it for yourself, do it for me, please." Lynne's abrupt change of tone caught his attention.

"You're bullying me." Flavio took her chin in his hand. "And you take good care of me. Why Mrs. B.?"

"Because I care for you. You loveable old fool."

"That's what I like about you. You say it like it is."

He let out a long breath. "I guess I'd better listen to you. What healthy dinner have you prepared for me today?"

"You'll find it in the fridge. And no cheating."

"How could I possibly cheat in your house? Everything in the kitchen is health food. Maybe I should go to my own abode."

"Don't you dare. And don't forget fifteen minutes on the stationary bicycle. Slow speed. Get your blood circulating after standing two hours at this work table."

"Yes, ma'am." He bent his head as if he was about to kiss her. Instead, he feathered a lingering caress on her cheek.

Lynne watched him go. "What a guy!"

"He actually listens to you." Nicole had come in to fill an order. "But does he carry through with it?"

"He could do better."

"Then marry him."

"Nicole!"

"I know what I see."

"All right, I've got to admit I'm in love with the impossible man. Have been for some time. He doesn't seem to get the message."

"Maybe he's shy."

"That heart attack scared him more than he cares to admit. It could take him a while to accept that he still has a future ahead of him."

The timer pinged. Nicole snatched up a pair of oven gloves and slid out the pizza. "You might have to spell that out to him. We actually need more dough."

Nicole disappeared to the front. Lynne put more pizzas in the ovens.

Piers bounded in. "Hi Lynne! Any more deliveries?"

"Not at the moment. We need to make more dough though. Scrub your hands. I'll go and relieve Nicole up front. She's faster at making toppings than I am."

"Just as you say, Mrs. B." He grabbed his apron and waltzed with it to the sink.

At that moment Nicole came to the kitchen doorway. She saw Piers, his back bent over the sink, and paused. If she herself hadn't reminded Lynne more dough was needed, she'd swear Lynne had set her up.

Piers wiped his hands and went to the work table. So intent was he on the task in hand that Nicole realized he was unaware of her watching from the doorway. A warm thrill coursed through her as she watched the long, supple fingers turn the sticky paste into elastic dough. With an effort she squelched her wayward thoughts. He looked up and smiled, as though he'd known all along that she'd been observing him.

"I see it's almost ready," she said. "I'll cut the pepperoni."

"You know, I've been thinking."

"Uh-oh, I see danger ahead."

"Seriously, I think we should open up the wall and have a hatch. Like that the pizzas can be passed to the serving girls... I mean serving personnel, instead of having to carry the orders out front through the door. It'd save a whole lot of labor."

"I admit you have some good ideas—"

"Hey, thanks!"

"But you don't seem to understand the lack of money around here." She gave an exaggerated sigh.

"But I do. You just have no idea how much I do."

Nicole sucked in her lips. His seemingly innocent words confirmed what she'd suspected all along. Piers wasn't exactly who he said he was. His attitude toward money wasn't that of a working man. He had only recently learn the value of money. It unsettled her, but she stared him down. "I don't mean that on a personal level," she said. "I mean if you run a business you can't lay out money you know isn't going to come in."

"You say that because you're in a defensive mode. In business the best approach is to attack. That means spending money to earn money. It's called investment. You invest in promotion and the sales go up. You cover the debt and make a profit."

"You do speak like a textbook." Though she tried to keep her tone neutral, her voice shook with suspicion. "You said you worked in the office of a computer firm. You didn't say you were in sales."

"The company sold computer systems to schools and organizations. That's no different from selling pizzas." Piers swallowed hard. Lying still didn't come easy, but he was getting good at it as long as he didn't have to do it too often. He only had to substitute the word *computer* for sport equipment. A wave of shame submerged him. Yet, what could he do?

Thankfully, a call came in for more pizzas. The flurry of

deliveries put an end to further discussion. It was closing time before the last customer left the shop.

Lynne flopped into a chair. "Piers, you're a genius. The two-for-one promotion really worked. I reckon we took in more today than we normally do in a week. And we had many new customers who came from Silver River. We'll have to extend deliveries to other towns."

Piers looked up from the oven he was cleaning and grinned. "Thanks for the vote of confidence."

He returned to scrubbing. Nicole looked round from the sink. "Don't forget we also spent more. Not to mention the gas for the extra deliveries."

"I don't know why you're always down on poor Piers," Lynne said. "He's come up with another genius idea. He divided the map in sections, took extra pizzas with him when he went out on deliveries. Before leaving one area, he phoned in to find out if there were other deliveries needed in that part of town. I call that brilliant."

"And if we had an online cart, it'd be even more efficient."

With a furious shake of the head, Nicole wiped her hands on a towel, then tossed it into the dirty laundry hamper. "He thinks money grows on trees, but I have to agree, very clever to try to group the deliveries by areas. Though how would you know what size or toppings the other customers requested?"

"If the pizzas in the van didn't match the orders, I just talked the customer into accepting a substitution so they could have a pizza right away instead of having to wait."

"I bet you did." She thought it uncharitable to add that because usually women answered the door. They'd fall all over him and let themselves be sweet-talked into whatever pizzas he had on hand.

He winced. "Actually, it only happened twice, and the ladies were satisfied with the product. I got a good tip from both."

"That's precisely what I was talking about."

Lynne gave Nicole a playful jab in the ribs. "The tables and chairs were a definite advantage. People also asked about the intriguing design sketched on the wall."

"I hope you told them it was Nicole's idea."

"I just said our young people were behind it and they'd have to wait till it's painted." She smiled at Piers. "What are you proposing after the mural?"

"I'd like to make a serving hatch and paint the outside of the shop. Then maybe do a mural on the other walls."

"See what I mean?" Nicole said. "He wants to spend all the money he helped earn today."

Lynne repressed a smile. "People like to see a clean and fresh interior. It boosts their confidence in the product. Especially a food product."

"Mrs. B., you're talking just like Piers."

"It's common sense, really. Now, step aside so that I can tally the till before I fall asleep."

Nicole was immediately contrite. "I'm sorry, Lynne. You've had a long day. And you still don't want to be paid."

"Money isn't why I do this. I enjoy it." She pulled the cash drawer from the register and set about sorting the credit card receipts and putting the bills into their separate denominations.

Piers and Nicole finished cleaning the kitchen and the storefront. They sat at one of the tables, not speaking so as not to distract Lynne.

"Was it a good day?" Piers finally asked in a soft voice.

Nicole detected a waver of anxiety in his voice. She looked at him. Wrong move. Her pulse raced. A million butterfly wings fluttered in her stomach.

Lynne put down her pencil and consulted the notepad.

"After all expenses are paid, today's profit is more than three times what we've been making in a regular week. Since Piers arrived, there's has been a steady increase in sales."

Elbows on the table, his chin on his hands, Piers nodded. "That's good news."

Nicole wrenched her eyes off him. If all the female customers reacted to him the way she did, it was no surprise that sales had gone up.

"The fact we can now take credit cards is just wonderful," said

Lynne. "Now, let's put that money in the safe."

They closed up and said goodnight to Lynne. Piers insisted on driving the van to the apartment.

"We can walk, you know," Nicole said.

"You're thinking about the expense of the gas. I'm thinking about your safety."

"I've always walked."

"Maybe not the smartest thing to do late at night. Okay, this is a safe neighborhood. But it's not the local residents you've got to worry about."

"You have a point. Anyway, my feet will be glad of the rest. I'll just feed Snowflake and I'll be ready."

When he smiled at her all her fatigue vanished as if by magic. As he helped her into the van, the warmth of his touch permeated deep under her skin. She reminded herself that it meant nothing, that he meant nothing to her. For the hundredth time, she told herself not to let him get close to her heart. She couldn't afford to let him affect her in this way.

Snowflake barked. She glanced in the wing mirror. A shadow, fist raised, receded at the far end of the parking lot. She frowned, then dismissed the idea there had been someone. Then Snowflake went straight to his house to sleep. When customers parked at the back, he always stood by the gate, tail wagging a mile a minute. It never failed to get him a pat and a few kind words. Fatigue made her see things that weren't there. The dog had only barked once as if to mean *see you in the morning.*

Chapter Eleven

The next day, between deliveries, Piers started on the sunburst design. The pizzeria wasn't as busy as on the previous day, though the flyers and posters had attracted attention. Word of mouth was spreading. He made a point to remove the Thursday Special posters while he was out.

"If you left them, people would know about us," Flavio said.

"Our publicity would lose its impact. The eye is attracted to something new. Leave a poster up too long and people will cease to pay it attention."

Lynne folded her arms. "Piers is right, Flavio. If we left the old posters up, no one would take notice when we do the next two-for-one offer."

Flavio let out a wolf howl. "You're right."

"We've got to move with the times," Lynne said. "These days, if a store doesn't have an end-of-the-month or some other kind of sale going on, customers stay away."

Nicole sighed. "I guess that's true. So when is the next event, Mr. Marketing Manager? I'm off on Monday. I have classes in the morning."

"We should wait two weeks before doing any further promotion."

Flavio nodded. "I agree."

Nicole smiled at Piers. "Your day off will be Tuesday. It's always quiet on Mondays and Tuesdays."

A grin stretched his lips. "Then we ought to find a way to liven them up."

Nicole groaned. Lynne chuckled and went to serve a customer.

"The community social media. Every other week, we post a picture and a few words."

"I suppose this could work. Opening an account is free."

"Good. I'll set it up when we close."

For most of the day, when they weren't needed elsewhere, Piers and Nicole worked on the mural. Customers paused to admire the artwork and make appreciative comments. Piers declared the mural finished that evening.

A couple of mornings later, Piers and Nicole walked to work. Nicole still found the easy companionship that had developed between them addictive. Since he didn't come on to her, she saw no harm in lowering her guard a fraction. Piers was fun. She enjoyed his company. Though the sweet sensations that inundated her at the slightest touch alarmed her.

They had scarcely opened up the shop when the phone orders started to pour in. The trickle of customers became a steady stream.

"If this continues," Nicole said, "we won't have enough ingredients to make pizzas for the day!" She hauled a batch of dough out of the fridge, took two pizzas out of the oven and rushed to the front counter.

Flavio mopped his forehead. "This is getting just like the old days. Is Mrs. B. in yet?"

Piers straightened from his search in the smaller fridge. "Not yet. I hope she arrives soon. We're out of bacon and mushrooms."

"*Mama mia*! I'll get on the phone."

Piers pointed to the receiver. "We should have a second phone line. This one rings non-stop."

At that instant, the kitchen door swung open. Nicole burst in. "A second line! Do you know what that would cost?"

His face calm, Piers smiled at her. "Remember the old business maxim we discussed? You've got to spend money to make money."

"That's easy enough when it's not your money."

"The boy's right, you know, *bellissima*. Without a second line we're missing orders."

Nicole shrugged. "Maybe you're right. After having been so close to disaster, I get cold feet. I can see this bubble burst one of these days and we'll be left worse off than we were before."

Piers answered her with a grin. "Bye. I'm off to Zone A. Six deliveries."

"Zone A? What's that all about?"

"That's the north-west part of the town and include Silver River. Didn't Lynne tell you? We've divided it up into segments to better coordinate deliveries. We really need more than one vehicle out there. I bet we're losing business to the chains."

Nicole rolled her eyes and distributed pineapple chunks onto a row of unbaked pizzas. "No chains here! This is the country. We're the only pizza shop for miles around. But going to Silver River cost a lot in gas. It's too far. We can't do it."

Piers shook his head. "Customers had no problem paying for the delivery. They said otherwise they would have to drive and pay gas, so they pay our gas. We all win."

Nicole repressed a sigh. He always had the last word. "Do you have any extras with you?"

"Just two."

"Hang on a few minutes and take a couple of these. I'll whip up some more for the walk-ins."

Now that she had bought into Piers promotional plans, she was determined to help him sell as much as he could. If his women customers could be suckered into ordering more because of his boyish charm, that was fine by her. She went out with him to the van and helped him stow the insulated containers.

His vitality made her insides churn with unfulfilled longing. As he drove away, giving her his customary wave from the window, she shook her head. He was not for her.

Snowflake stood guard, and she played with him for a short while. A sense of peace came over her. Dogs did that to people. She kissed the tip of his nose. "I love you, puppy." In response he beat his tail against her leg.

Chapter Twelve

The First City Bank stood austere amid the low stone and brick buildings nearby. Piers glanced up and went in.

He approached a wicket where a middle-aged teller thumbed some papers. "Good morning. Would you be kind enough to give me change for these twenties, please?"

The clerk set aside the heap of papers and checks she was tabulating, her lack of smile probably due to her desire not to create any more wrinkles. "Do you have an account with us?"

Piers was taken aback by the frosty reception. He chose his words with care. "I'm not asking you to cash a check or anything. I'd just like some change for these honest plastic twenties."

"Bank regulations require you to have an account with us first."

The woman's sharp tone attracted the attention of the neighboring teller, a slim blonde about the same age as Piers.

The young woman exchanged glances with Piers. "Sheila, I've got lots of change in my drawer that I wouldn't mind getting rid of."

The unsmiling Sheila tilted her chin a fraction. "No need, I can do it."

The smile of thanks Piers flashed the young woman brought a pretty blush to her cheeks. Piers' teller counted out the required amount in smaller bills, dimes and quarters with deliberate precision. She then pushed the money toward him.

He pocketed the money. "Thank you, ma'am." Piers turned his smile on her. "Tell your manager I'll think real hard about opening an account here."

The teller's jaw sagged. Piers sauntered to the exit. *It was not as if could go to another bank since it was the only one and served a large rural area. Still, it was an eye opener. Do bank tellers always behave like this when people turn up in second-hand work clothes?*

Is that why those casually employed go to money lenders instead of the bank? Then they get caught in a vicious circle. Their small checks docked by the sharks keep them poorer and poorer. What this place needs is a money co-op, like a credit union, I guess. A sort of community credit union. I wonder who could start one.

In the van, he sorted out his tips and put that money in his right pocket, the pizza money in his left. Piers drove to the Habitat store. Before looking for lumber, he punched the pizzeria's number into the cell phone. Lynne answered. No, there were no delivery orders right now. Just as well, there was only one small pizza left.

In the HFP store the same helpful Ed took Piers under his wing and walked him through the whole process of cutting a hole in a wall for a serving hatch. The store carried plenty of recycled materials with which to construct the hatch.

"Okay, Ed, tell me what I need to get started. Right now I only have fifty bucks."

"Since it's just a hatch you're framing, it won't cost you very much. Let's see..."

By the time they loaded two-by-fours, planks and trim, there was enough money left over for paint.

"This can of mauve is almost full. It'll go nicely for a trim with the blue and the yellow. Here's a free how-to leaflet. Toss in an extra quarter and you'll get one of our neat carpenter's pencils. You'll need one."

In his other life, Piers would have tipped the young man. On this occasion, he thanked him with a handshake.

Back at the shop, he unloaded his purchases under Nicole's watchful eye. After her initial protests, she received his new scheme, if not with loud enthusiasm, at least with resigned acceptance.

She couldn't help hope sweeping over her as she watched Piers stack the wood by the kitchen door. His toned body exuded health and self-confidence. She envied him the latter. "You should buy furniture for your apartment not spend your tips on the business." With a wave of her hand she encompassed the pile of materials. "All this was presumably bought with your tip money."

"I've got all the furniture I need for my apartment. The bed is comfortable enough for me. Besides, I spend more time here than I do in the apartment."

In the face of Piers' nonchalant charm, Nicole's resistance crumbled. "Okay, but don't complain if your apartment gets you down. We wouldn't want you to get discouraged and quit your job."

The words were spoken in jest but contained an underlying anxiety. Another worry sprung in her mind. One day, without warning, he might just walk away. She chastised herself. It was against her principles to become too attached to anyone. Flavio and Lynne were exceptions. They were the family she no longer had.

A flurry of activity around noon created such a frenzy that Nicole had no time to think about anything but filling orders. Although the kitchen was hot, the work helped smother her super-heated emotions. There was no way, an insistent inner voice told her, she'd allow herself to fall for this smooth-talking man. He was hiding something behind that handsome exterior of his.

When she had started her accounting course, the university had appointed an aging assistant professor in charge of the campus. He came three times a week and had hit on her. The experience left her with a definite wariness. Aging and balding, he had given her extra help. Then he proposed a weekend of private tuition at his cabin by the lake. She quit school rather than follow the online counselor's advice to lodge a complaint. There was no way she would have complained with the fear that the authorities would pry into her life and discover she had kidnaped her young sister from the foster home. Until Paula turned eighteen, that was a secret only Flavio shared. Later, she had gotten a note from the counselor. The prof had resigned. That incident had cost her a year of her already part-time studies.

Although she hadn't told a soul about her experience, it had somehow filtered into the Otter Lake community. The town took matter in their hands raising money to buy a house for the next director so he would have to live right there, where they could keep an eye on him or her. She assumed that Andrea, the motherly coordinator of the campus, had been behind the new arrangement. A graduate who had realized he had no hope of becoming a professor any time soon in the city had jumped at the chance to move his young family to Otter Lake. The satellite campus expanded enabling high school graduates to take their first year university in their town.

The early afternoon lull lent itself to reflection. She speculated on the Piers Sonder's mystery. Or, more specifically, on the past that he so masterfully avoided discussing.

Woman trouble was the most likely answer. Yet somehow she couldn't imagine Piers angering a woman so much as to have to flee his native province. Then again, maybe he didn't really come from Nova Scotia. She hadn't run a check on him. Taking chances, that's what desperation did to a person. She didn't want to have a reason to reject his application. All right, maybe, not running from a woman's anger. A woman's *husband's* anger, perhaps. No, that was too melodramatic. It didn't fit the image. She couldn't picture sexy Piers needing to pursue a married woman, not with any number of unattached women making themselves available. Even if he did, she could see him talking his way out of any predicament he found himself in.

The end product of her conjectures was a throbbing headache.

Piers and Flavio sat on stools at the counter.

In front of them was Piers' sketch of the proposed hatch. She had watched him draw up the plan with the aid of the how-to leaflet.

Lynne glanced across from the table, where she relaxed with a cup of coffee. "Flavio, don't even think about wielding a hammer, okay?"

She responded to his deep-throated chuckle with an inelegant snort. "May I remind you it's time for your afternoon exercise and rest?"

Flavio sighed. "I've gotta go, Piers. Start it. Just make sure the whole caboodle doesn't come crashing down on your head."

Nicole fetched a long drink of ice-cold water from the kitchen and joined Lynne at the table. The two women watched Piers measure where the hatch should go. Careful taps with the hammer revealed the location of the existing studs. He picked up his carpenter's pencil and drew the lines for the saw cuts.

Nicole massaged her temples. "I must agree having a hatch will be more practical."

Piers glanced their way. "We might have to shift the counter and move the cash register the other way."

"Can't move the register far because of the phone connection."

"Let me see."

A customer came in while Piers was measuring. Lynne dragged Flavio away. After that the phone rang three times in quick succession. The rest of his afternoon occupied Piers with deliveries. When Flavio and Lynne returned, they found Piers standing on tiptoe on a chair in an effort to reach the ceiling.

Lynne's mocking laughter echoed round the room. "You're tall but not tall enough. Ever heard of a stepladder?"

Piers laughed. The rich tone sent a delightful shiver down Nicole's spine. Her headache receded.

Lynne disappeared and came back thirty minutes later with a stepladder, a power saw and a power screwdriver. Piers was given no time to use any of it. Business became brisk right until late evening, when Nicole announced they were closing.

"I want to saw one side of the wall while we're shut."

"Do you realize how late it is?"

"Why does that matter? We have no neighbors."

"Eleven p.m. seems an odd time to be hacking a hole in a wall."

"I don't know. Lots of interesting things happen in the middle of the night."

His provocative reply, coupled with the gleam in his eye, set Nicole's imagination running wild, but she quickly squashed it.

"At least stop for a bite to eat." Flustered, she went to the kitchen. She reappeared carrying a laden tray. "Put down that power saw and come and eat." She set the tray down with more force than necessary. "Now!"

"My pleasure. I'm starving." He took a seat opposite her at the table. "Wow, a twelve-incher! What's the celebration?"

"The destruction of one perfectly good wall. Eat up." Her gaze focused on his white teeth sinking into a juicy pizza slice. Not trusting herself, she lowered her eyes to her own plate.

Perplexed, she struggled to make sense of why she reacted so strongly. She hadn't dated much over the years. After being ditched a couple of times, Nicole wised up to the fact that she was not destined for romance. Too much pain crowded her heart. More than that, she had come to believe that romance was a starry-eyed delusion that existed only in the minds of the naïve. Yet, she still couldn't help hoping for some kind of loving relationship... eventually. Sometimes, she found it hard to cope with her contradictory feelings.

Since it might take her another decade to track down Christopher, she'd better put the prospect of love on the back burner. At nine years old, Christopher may not even know he was adopted. Later, though, he'd learn. He'd ask questions and would want to know about his biological mother. That's what adopted children did, if she believed the articles and books she had read on the subject.

The only young man she knew, Piers aside, was Jack. But Jack was a friend, a good friend and a fellow student. He didn't count. The fact he was so attentive to her, much more than toward his other friend Betty, sometimes made her wonder if he meant more than friendship.

Much to her dismay, Piers had already chipped away, consciously or unconsciously, at the defensive barrier she had erected around her heart. Liking him was easy. Loving him would be dangerous. He could easily deflect her from her self-imposed course of action. Curbing the physical attraction she felt for him was difficult but not impossible. Doing the same for those imperceptible emotional threads that threatened to ensnare her was a whole new reality. For one thing, she wasn't even sure of the rules of the game.

Piers wiped his mouth on a paper napkin. "Let's shift the counter. I checked. It's only held down with a few screws."

Tempted to nix his suggestion, Nicole bit her tongue. After all, she had seen him measure it.

The power driver easily removed the screws. She steadied the counter while he shoved it to its new location where he secured it with an additional length of wood.

"Like that, it won't wobble anymore." He grinned then turned his attention to reinstalling the cash register and credit cards terminal.

They stood back to assess the new arrangement.

"Now that it's in place, I agree. It does seem to fit better there. When the hatch is made, the counter won't be in the way. Lynne was right. You are a genius... an infuriating one."

He smiled wryly. "Thanks."

She helped him spread the plastic sheeting to protect the kitchen area from the dust. For the next forty minutes, talk was impossible. The sound of the power saw ripping through drywall and the supporting studs rent the air. Nicole fetched a pan and broom to sweep up the dust and debris as Piers enlarged the opening.

Streaked with plasterboard powder, Piers stood back to examine his handiwork. "Ladies and gentlemen, I declare the serving hatch officially open."

"You're crazy. You know that? Only a lunatic would be up at this hour cutting a big hole in a wall."

"You must admit, we make a fabulous team, you and I. Let me secure the top." He leaned a two-by-four on each side of the opening and jam another horizontally between them. "Tomorrow, I'll cut the wood and frame up the hatch. Let's go home."

"We'll take the van."

When they arrived at the apartment building, they lingered in the common entrance hall.

Piers grinned at her. "You've got plaster on your nose." He used his fingers to brush away the speck of white dust.

A shock as strong as an electric current darted through her. "I'll... I'll grab a shower. Thanks."

Piers bent his head and touched his lips to her nose. "Even coated with drywall dust, you still look pretty."

Her breath came in labored gasps while a zillion stars danced in her eyes. "Please don't."

"Don't worry. I know my limits."

"I'm glad to hear that. Goodnight." Blindly, she took the stairs. Once behind her own door her shoulders sagged. To rid her mind of images of Piers, she forced herself to think about Christopher.

The dream had come back again.

Chapter Thirteen

Before his pizza delivery career, Piers used to spend his ample leisure time sailing between the Caribbean Islands or, if the season was appropriate, jetting to some trendy ski resort. Except when intensively training for the next Tae Kwon Do tournament, or filming a new commercial, Sundays found him lounging in bed, cappuccino in hand, tablet in the other and surrounded by magazines or papers.

All this had changed. Now, as an honest working man, he rose at six. If anyone had told him in those days that he'd be feasting on cold pizza leftovers, and enjoying it, he'd have told them they were crazy.

The contentment he was finding in his new life didn't prevent the haunting memories of his mistake. Nothing ever would. In counseling, he had learned that he needed to forgive himself. He hadn't been able to. Especially after the families had expressed their forgiveness. Their generosity had torn him apart even more. He owed his life to the prison chaplain. Without the goodness of this man of God, he would have ended his wretched life. *Make your life count*, he had told him. Would that be here? In the pizzeria that he helped stave off bankruptcy?

Piers pocketed the last apple and headed out to start the van. The imperious need to take a good long run to get his body back in shape increased. He doubled back inside to scribble a note.

To make sure Nicole would see it, he slipped the folded paper into the edge of her mailbox at the main entrance. He ate his apple while jogging to work.

June had rolled in. The sun had crowned the elms on either side of the street with gold when he arrived at Flavio's. The cool morning heralded a hot day. Piers sighed. It would be a great day for sailing. When the walls of the prison threatened to crush him with despair, he'd close his eyes to remember the freedom of the wind, the slapping of the water against the hull, the salty tang in the air, the cry of a gull. It calmed his inner turmoil. When he thought about the end of his incarceration, he planned to live on his boat, feel the peace of the sea and perhaps feel peace himself. This idea didn't last long. Living idle on his boat wouldn't bring the redemption he sought.

The noise of his hammer prevented him from hearing the van pull into the rear parking lot. But he heard the door slam with more force than necessary.

An angry voice sounded behind him. "Why didn't you come and wake me?"

He looked up at Nicole. "I thought you might appreciate a little sleep. We worked late last night. I didn't need my teammate right away."

Disarmed by his grin, Nicole made a face and went into the kitchen. "Call if you need me."

Piers had thought of waking her. He had imagined creeping up the stairs in the predawn gray and letting himself into her apartment. Without waking her he would have nestled beside her on the bed. Only after the first rays of sun filtered through the drapes, would he have kissed her. That would have awoken her for sure. Whether they would have been able to get off the bed was another question altogether.

That was a fantasy destined never to take place. The guilt burden he carried weighed on him. There was no room for beautiful things like love. He shook himself. That life he had promised to make count didn't include a romance. He could fantasize about a beautiful woman, but he couldn't forget. Always at one point in the fantasy, it shattered and a wave of regret and despair assailed him. He was free from the jail walls, yet imprisoned by the memories.

At the start, the little town on the prairies hadn't featured in his future plans. It was just a stop on the way north. His brief stay had begun to change his views about the previously unknown plains town. It certainly represented the opposite of everything he used to cherish back home. He used to live for sailing. Otter Lake lay land-locked, though a couple of lakes weren't far away. He loved old-world towns and gracious houses. The New Town, which he had been told was already more than twenty years old, had struck him as the epitome of brash newness, but he had developed a fondness for the remaining hundred-year-old houses, the few ornate buildings and the green canopy of big elms bordering residential streets. He had heard some inhabitants talk proudly of how they had saved the elms where other cities all over the North American continent had lost theirs to the Dutch elm disease.

By now he knew the town as well as any Otterian. He had seen the old neighborhood and recreational spaces. Many green spaces attracted resident and migratory birds and the air always resonated with harmonious trills and chirping. It was the country at his best. Although he didn't have the money to do anything other than work and sleep, the newspaper carried announcements of ballet performances by the local school and its company. Music had put the town on the map and many concerts toured here making it a vibrant a vibrant center of culture.

His growing attraction for Nicole would complicate his life too much. He imagined taking her to the dance and holding her in his arms. He swept the fantasy out of his mind and returned to his task. A few choice words and one sore thumb later, the hatch was framed. Only the painting remained to be done.

"Here's breakfast."

Nicole's voice was as welcome as the mingled aroma of baking and coffee that preceded it.

Piers gave an appreciative sniff. "This is heaven."

"No pizza today. Biscuits with melted cheese."

"Hey! Why not make it a standard menu item?"

"We're a pizza parlor."

His mind worked overtime. He paused, a feather-soft biscuit in his fingers. "That doesn't mean we can't offer other things besides pizza. What about offering an assortment of biscuits for kids? That would be less messy than gooey pizza at those birthday parties."

She pulled a face. "Grocery stores sell pizza pops for that reason."

He put on a scandalized face. "You can't compare our stuff to factory-made pizza pops."

"*Our* stuff! You've really made yourself part of us. You don't consider yourself just an employee on an hourly wage, do you?"

"You're dead right. If I'm going to work here, I want to be part of it. I'll give it my best. Why should I behave differently?"

Nicole smiled. That was all the reward he needed.

"One thing you hadn't thought of," she said. "With the hatch, we'll get kitchen smells out here in the shop."

"Only a faint smell. The kitchen exhaust fan does a good job. Besides, so what if customers smell the pizzas cooking? This is a pizza parlor, not a hospital. Just think. That wonderful aroma will make their mouths water. They'll be tempted to order two instead of one, even on days we don't run the two-for-one special."

Nicole chuckled. "Maybe. But let's get working. I'll open at ten today. Over the last few days, I noticed a couple of people arriving before eleven and waiting."

Her laughter cascaded through him like a caress. He wanted to ask her why she didn't laugh more than she did. She nurtured in him the desire to take her in his arms and squeeze her till she laughed. With effort he turned his mind back to his task. Not for him.

Chapter Fourteen

After the noon rush hour subsided Nicole borrowed Lynne's car to drive Mrs. Harlow to a medical appointment. When Nicole arrived back at the pizzeria, Piers had just finished washing the floor. Lynne and Flavio came in late, faces drawn and shoulders squared. Work grounded to a halt. Nicole didn't need to be told the pair had been fighting. She watched them assume a false air of normalcy.

With a body language that spoke volumes, Lynne ensconced herself behind the counter. Flavio, in his rich baritone, hummed a tune from *The Marriage of Figaro*.

Piers nudged Nicole and whispered. "Do all Italians sing bel canto?"

"Flavio only sings when he's upset."

"Looks like they've been arguing, wouldn't you say?"

During a lull between orders, Nicole sidled up to Lynne. "Did you draw guns on him?"

"It's such a beautiful day. I had something I wanted to tell him. He didn't go for it. So I told him to forget about coming into work. I told him to do his exercise then lounge all day on a lawn chair."

"But he came anyway."

Lynne lifted her shoulders with a sigh. "Why do I bother with the pigheaded man?"

"That's what love does to a person."

Lynne snorted. "Look who's talking! What does little Ms. Nicole who rebuff all males know about love?"

Nicole stiffened. The telephone rang. She didn't have to reply.

Whether it was the warm spring weather or the return of Flavio's Pizzeria's fame, Nicole didn't care. What mattered was that customers flocked to their door. The phone jangled off the hook nonstop. The new local-only website channeled more orders. It continued that way, leaving no time to rest, for most of the day.

When the last delivery was made, and Flavio and Lynne had gone home separately, she finished up in the kitchen and went to see what Piers was doing. She found him applying the final coat to the wood trim of the new hatch.

She stood and watched silently so she wouldn't break his concentration. Her heart wanted to sing with the pleasure of being near this vibrant man. Yet the sight of him disturbed her in ways she couldn't comprehend. If it were a case of simple physical attraction, she could have dismissed her feelings with the reminder he was just an employee. And like all the employees she had hired for Flavio's he'd soon get bored and start looking for other work.

Deep inside she knew that Piers was unlike any employee she had hired. More than that. He was the most exceptional man to step into her life. That knowledge lay at the root of her emotional turmoil. Now and then she'd catch that haunted look in his eyes.

Unanswered questions filled her brain and clamored for answers. Like why he did all this work. Even dressed in his thrift store clothes he looked like he belonged elsewhere. She could see him sitting on some patio, sipping an iced drink, while a bevy of carpenters worked on his house. Maybe she should run that check on him. But she knew she wouldn't. Just in case she found cause to dismiss him.

The door chimes tinkled. A man wearing a windbreaker stepped in.

"Hello, Jack. You're up late."

"Hi, Nicole. I just dropped round to see if you'd like to grab a coffee at the Crescent Moon. We can chat."

"Thanks. That'd be nice." She turned to Piers, now cleaning his brushes. "You'll close up for me?"

His eyes narrowed. His easy grin disappeared.

"Sure. I'll finish up here," he said. "Like that we'll be able to use the hatch tomorrow."

Jack waved his hand to encompass the storefront changes. "Did you guys do all this?"

"Nicole planned it all." Piers' tone was dry.

"Don't believe him. I only helped some."

Jack nodded and turned his attention to Nicole. "Shall we go?"

"Just let me get my purse."

While he waited, Jack leaned on the counter. With his back turned to Piers he studied the menu board on the wall.

Piers watched them go. His features creased into an uncharacteristic frown. He had taken an instant dislike to Jack. The moron had his eyes glued on Nicole. This raised Piers' blood pressure. Paint brush in hand, he attacked the wood so vigorously that he splattered the new paintwork and had to spend ten more minutes undoing the mess.

Later, when he went to the washroom to clean a brush, he laughed at his reflection in the mirror. "You're the moron, you idiot!" It amazed him that he should have reacted as he did just because a guy asked Nicole out for coffee. Jack would be around long after he had made his way to the Yukon. Unless he'd go back to Montreal, not Nova Scotia as he had led her to believe. Not that this was likely, unless he really made something of himself. No, after due consideration, he would never go back to Montreal. Maybe he hadn't completely lied when he said Nova Scotia, that's where his boat was moored. He, Piers, had no claims on her. Neither did he need to feel protective of her. Attentive to his task once more, he tried to put Nicole out of his mind.

Chapter Fifteen

At the Crescent Moon, Jack took a seat opposite Nicole. A silence fell. She sipped her latte. Jack's cappuccino remained untouched.

"How come you're always hanging out with that fellow in the shop?"

The hint of aggressiveness in his tone surprised her. "I'm not hanging out. We work together. We're bound to spend time in each other's company."

"I had the impression you'd rather be with him than with me."

This didn't sound like the Jack she knew. "Of course not. We've been incredibly busy and working much later in the evenings."

"You haven't come to our weekend get together for a long time."

"I know. But we've started as early as eight in the morning and not finished till after midnight some days."

"Okay. First, I have some news." The corner of his mouth gave a nervous twitch. "I've got me a good job lined up right after graduation."

Happy for her friend, Nicole's eyes shone. "Congratulations! Is that what makes you so jittery?"

He reached for her hand over the table. "No. You are."

Surprise and disbelief froze her expression. "But Jack-"

"I know, I'm not very good at this. What I want is you to marry me. I mean Will you marry me?"

She closed her eyes for a few seconds. "I'm in total shock."

His nervousness increased. "I told you I was no good at that."

She pulled her hand from his. "I'm touched. I can't possibly answer immediately. We need to know each other better."

"I realize I'm a klutz. I've never asked a woman to marry me before."

"If it's any comfort, I've never been asked before. We should get used to the idea first."

He twisted his fingers, his features drawing into a point as if overcoming pain. "You're right."

"I feel honored." Panic simmered just beneath the surface.

He fidgeted. "I know. Maybe you can get used to it? Think about us."

"I'll have to think about what you just said." Nicole repressed the urge to flee at the hard edge in his tone.

"Promise you will think of me... us every night."

An unyielding glimmer came into his eyes. A ripple fear stirred in the pit of her stomach.

"Well... You're my friend. I can't think about you other than a friend."

"Please, think of me. Think of marrying me."

Begging didn't suit him and it made Nicole even more uncomfortable. She stretched her lips but no smile came. "You're different, Jack. Let's go now."

"All right. I told you. I'm really no good at this."

Nicole wrestled with her confused feelings. Images passed before her eyes. The images were not of Jack but Piers. No matter how she tried, Piers' face refused to go away.

Jack walked Nicole back to her building but didn't go in. He took her in his arms and placed a light kiss on her mouth. His lips were cool and dry, the kiss not unpleasant. Yet she couldn't wait to get to her apartment and take a shower.

As she went upstairs, the memory of Piers' touch made her shiver. This was all too crazy. Piers was like an alien who had landed at the pizzeria and one day would return to his own world just as swiftly as he had arrived. Of course, he could just as easily be an angel sent to help good old Flavio restore prosperity to the pizzeria.

Whoever Piers was, she'd better think of him as temporary help.

Besides, she didn't believe in angels.

Chapter Sixteen

Piers went home, carrying a whole twelve-inch bacon pizza in one of the new wax-coated paper box they were now using. Before entering the lobby, he glanced up and saw a light on in her apartment window. He almost climbed the stairs under the pretext of borrowing something, a cup of sugar, anything. A glance at his watch reminded him that one didn't make calls so late at night.

The last thing he needed feel was jealousy. Nicole was a woman a man married, not played around with. And marriage couldn't be further from his mind. At the same time, the thought barely formulated outraged him. The man upstairs better not take advantage of her.

I'm going crazy! He's probably an ordinary guy, ready to put a ring on her finger. Good luck to him.

After a restless night, Piers was eager to get back to the pizza parlor to examine his carpentry. Okay, a pro might have made those joints a little tighter. And the top trim could have been a closer fit. But the hatch was neat and functional. The cost minimal.

He checked the paint he had stacked in a cupboard to see what coverage he could get out of it. Lynne came up behind him.

"Planning more artistic endeavors?"

"Hi, Lynne. I've got enough to do another sunburst behind the counter but in reverse colors."

"Sounds good. Let's prepare the dough. Then I'll give you a hand."

"When I finish inside, I'll start work on the outside."

Her smile showed her interest. "What colors?"

"Your guess is as good as mine. I'll see what Habitat's got."

"Good luck!" She tipped the flour into a bowl.

Luck was with him when he finally got to the recycling store. A truck was unloading building materials. Ed was busy running back and forth. After a moment's hesitation, Piers joined him and helped unload. He didn't want to go into the store and have somebody else wait on him.

Ed straightened his back. "Don't think customers are obliged to pitch in."

"Yeah, but I think I saw some paint I could use in all this lot."

"That's one way to make sure you get what you came for. Thanks anyway."

Between the two of them and the driver, it took no time to unload the truck.

Ed wiped his sleeve over his forehead. "I've got to price this lot before I put it on the floor. You said you needed paint?"

"Exterior this time. Something to go with the interior yellow and blue."

"Let's find it for you."

In spite of Ed's claim that he had to price the new consignment, he took a full fifteen minutes to examine the cans of paint.

"It's often impossible to read the labels but I reckon your best bet is go with this gallon of green and these two half gallons of red."

"Do those colors clash?" Piers considered Ed had an eye for color but couldn't help asking.

"Let's find out." Ed took a church key out of his hip pocket and pried off the lids. "This is a lovely green, like new grass. The red is a good warm color. I think they'd go well together. Red and green are complementary colors. Are you going to use this for the window trim and doors?"

"I'd like to paint a mural of green fields with flowers and maybe a sunset sky behind, but I don't have that kind of skill. Maybe I'll stick to something abstract. I've seen many beautiful murals in town. Otter Lake seems to be the capital of murals."

"I agree. Many great ones. Get someone to draw the mural for you, then fill in the spaces."

Piers laughed. "Paint by numbers. Even that'd be too skilled for me."

"Could do worse, you know. If you'd like, I could drop by after work."

"Hey, that's swell. You like to draw?"

"I take art night classes at the school. When I've enough money saved up, I'm going to college to study fine art."

"It's a deal. Let me pay for the green and the red, plus whatever you'll need, which you can bring."

Weighed down by his purchases Piers returned in triumph to the pizzeria. Lynne stood by the door contemplating the hatch.

"I think it's finished or do you see something I missed?" His voice betrayed his anxiety.

"It's perfect."

"Tonight we're getting help from a professional artist for the outside."

"An artist?"

"My new buddy Ed from the Habitat store has artistic abilities. He's coming round this evening to sketch in the design for the front of the pizzeria. It's amazing the hidden talent out there."

A satisfied look settled on Lynne's face. "That's super! I better make a start scraping the old paint off."

"There isn't much left."

"The grime needs to be scrubbed off, otherwise the new paint won't hold."

The phone interrupted them. Customers came in and expressed their appreciation of the new look. Piers kept a low profile. Inwardly, he felt he'd accomplished something worthwhile. For once it was something that required more than simply the expenditure of money. Renovating and growing Flavio's Pizzeria had become the combined effort of many hands and minds under his leadership. That was where the satisfaction lay.

When he returned from an early evening delivery, he found Ed perched on the stepladder in front of the shop. Black lines crisscrossed the wall. Wire brush in hand, Lynne was busy with the preparation on the lower part of the wall.

Ed came down and moved the stepladder to one side.

"It looks great!" Piers said.

"We need to stand farther back to get the big picture."

The two men stood in the middle of the street to admire the sketched in mural of rolling fields, woods and flowers.

Piers clapped Ed on the back. "It's just what I was dreaming of."

Lynne came out and pushed the two young men back to the sidewalk. "Are you two out of your minds? You're going to get yourselves run down by a truck. Come in and have supper on the house. You like pizza, Ed?"

"Love it."

They ate in the kitchen at the center worktable.

"I'm really impressed with the drawing," Piers said. "But I'm not sure I can follow the mix of colors."

"It's easy, really. There's enough light for another hour tonight, so I can start and I'll come back tomorrow."

That was another thing Piers had become aware of. Here in the West, the sun seemed to rise earlier and set later.

"Good. I think I can paint the bottom foot of wall since it's uniform green."

Ed nodded. "That's where the dust gathers, so no point on doing too much there."

"And there are Mrs. B.'s planters which will have real flowers in them. They'll fit in with the picture. Neat."

Piers and Ed worked until the lack of light rendered it impossible to continue. Ed left for home. Lynne changed her shoes and put on her coat.

"Mrs. B. Don't tell Flavio about the outside mural. We want it to be a surprise."

"I won't be seeing the stubborn old mule tonight. Or tomorrow if I have any say in the matter."

A chuckle escaped Piers. "He's lucky to have you."

"I've fed Snowflake, taken him for a short walk and closed his pen."

"Thanks. Goodnight, Lynne."

Left alone, Piers tidied up the store and the kitchen. It was past closing time but going home didn't appeal to him. He realized he missed Nicole. Her classes didn't run all day. Jack must have taken her out on a date.

Why should I care? I'll be out of here sometimes, when the place is looking good and doing good business. I have a little money saved now, and then I can save the tips too.

He slung his jacket over his shoulder and strolled to the apartment. Perhaps she was home and he could beg a cup of coffee.

He went straight up and knocked on her door, half expecting her to be out, or asleep in bed. To his surprise, she opened the door. An even nicer surprise was that she was wearing a sleeveless blue dress with an interesting pattern of white and mauve circles and lace around the collar. It gave her an altogether different appearance from the work clothes she normally wore.

He pulled himself out his contemplation. "Hey, you look great. What's the occasion?"

"I went to class today." A blush came to her cheeks.

"Oh, yes, I'd forgotten. How is it going?" Of course he hadn't forgotten, but he wasn't about to tell her how much he missed her.

"Fine. Our term's almost over. I should graduate in a few weeks."

"Congratulations!"

"Why am I keeping you standing here? Come in."

Piers stepped into the apartment and kicked off his street shoes. Her floors, unlike his own, gleamed with polish. "You've really made your place cozy."

"Thanks. It's surprising what paint and a few nice pieces of furniture will do. I don't need to tell you that, after what you've done to Flavio's. Do you want coffee? I made a strawberry flan before I went to school."

"How could a guy resist?" He took a seat on the living room couch while Nicole busied herself in the kitchen alcove. A surge of quiet contentment swept over him. Here he was in a tastefully appointed apartment, about to be served coffee and flan by a beautifully dressed woman. What more could he want from life?

Maybe he felt good because she hadn't, as he had imagined, spent the day with Jack-the-Jerk.

Nicole pushed the low table closer, went back to the kitchen and returned with two mugs of coffee. Then she brought out two plates of strawberry flan topped with whipped cream. "First strawberries of the year."

"Luscious! I can't remember the last time I had dessert. And whatever it was it didn't compare to this."

He made short work of the strawberry flan, then stood to help with the dishes. He hung the dish towel. "Let's relax a moment before I head back to my quarters."

She sat in the armchair opposite. Not for the first time, Piers' gaze lingered on her slender legs. Twenty times more graceful than any of his sophisticated casual dates back home.

The two of them talked, mostly about their work at the pizzeria and the changes that were being made.

Nicole chuckled. "I took Snowflake to the park for some training."

"What kind of training?"

"Sit, come, stay, that sort of thing. He's really good."

"When was that? I didn't see you."

"You were out on deliveries. I wish I could bring him home, but Mrs. Harlow, for as nice as she is, has a phobia about pets in her building."

"Lots of landlords are like her."

"It used to be her whole house. Even had a maid. But after her husband death she had to do something to survive."

"Very unfortunate and it often happens. But, it's getting late. I can see you're yawning. I must go."

Despite her pleasant appearance, Piers was struck by a fugitive look of sadness in her eyes. She saw him to the door, waited till he'd put on his shoes. He was seized by an irresistible urge to kiss her. His reason overcame his desire. Instead, he let his eyes caress her face and squeezed her hand softly.

"See you tomorrow."

"Take care on the stairs."

***

He hadn't kissed her. Nicole chastised herself. That was due to the boundary she had set, and he appeared to respect her enough not to trespass. She pushed the door but left it open a few inches so she could follow his footsteps. When she finally heard his door close with a solid click, she shut her own door and turned the deadbolt. As soon as she had invited him in, she had regretted it. This was not the way to keep him at arm's length. A big sigh escaped her chest. She was full of contradictions.

Yet, all afternoon she had been wishing he would come. The flan, she had baked it just for him. The dress had been for him too. She had willed him to come so hard he must have sensed it. Despite the lateness of the hour, he had appeared at her door. She mentally scoffed at herself for being foolish. Any other person would have changed into some shapeless housecoat to relax. Nothing was going to occur between them. Which was exactly what she wanted. She had received a proposal from a steady, reliable man who was going to be an accountant. Businesses always need accountants. The future was ensured. All the while she was excited about someone else. A questionable man at that. On one hand she wanted him to kiss her, on the other she wanted him to keep away. It was all very disturbing.

Damping down her emotions, though, proved a difficult task. Her mind went back to the major disappointment of the day. Jack told her that the Bea Riemer he had found through the internet was an eighty-year-old woman living in a Phoenix retirement village. And she had never been a nurse in Toronto.

The phone rang. Maybe Piers. Her heart beat faster. She picked up the receiver. It was her sister not Piers.

"Paula! What's up?"

"I got a summer job as a park ranger in Canmore!"

The pitch of excitement in her sister's voice made Nicole smile. "Wow! Better than waitressing, I guess."

"For a student in biology and environmental sciences, definitely. But it also means more money, so you won't have to help me pay the rent. You can put that into your search fund."

"You know I've always been happy to help you."

"Yes, but I can't wait for the time when it my turn to help you. One more year and I graduate."

"In your field you need no less than a Master's degree to make waves. You should continue on to grad school."

"I'll be able to get a good job. Don't worry, there'll be time for grad studies. After all you did for me, I want you to be proud of your kid sister."

"I am already."

"Unfortunately, I won't be able to spend the summer vacation with you and Flavio."

"Maybe a long weekend?"

"That's when the park is busiest. But I'll be able to get a few days for a short visit sometimes in between. I must go and pack now. Love you."

"I love you too."

Nicole hung up with a feeling almost of maternal pride. At least for the last three years she had stopped fearing she'd be charged with kidnaping or something. It had been worth it, the running away, the hiding and meeting Flavio. The man with a heart of gold. A heart that nearly stopped beating.

But she'd miss not having her sister around for the summer.

The phone rang again. Indulgence made her smile. Paula frequently phoned two or three time with a tidbit she had forgotten.

Nicole picked up the receiver. There was only silence at the other end. She shrugged. It must be a wrong number.

Chapter Seventeen

Shortly after six, Piers eyed the slice of cold pizza that was breakfast. *It's good food and it's free.* Should he zap it in the microwave? No, it was oozing wholesomeness even cold. And it tasted good. He licked his lip and made himself a promise never to throw food away. Not when so many people went hungry every day. Now he understood what real hunger meant. A tap on the door cut short his thoughts. With a smile on his lips, he opened the door.

Nicole smiled back at him. Her low rider jeans and crop top gave him an exquisite glimpse of skin. Too much to take this early in the morning. His blood rushed in his veins. In his former life he had never been as moved even by the most blatant advances from his female acquaintances. But then his former life dated more than two years ago. It was the life he never wanted to go back to. Pain stabbed at his heart. He didn't deserve those feelings of happiness.

A sudden shyness made her hesitate. "It's your day off, but would you like to have breakfast with me?"

"With pleasure!"

The aroma of fresh coffee greeted him at the doorway of the upstairs apartment. The herb omelet and toast were a welcome change from his leftover pizza and he certainly had enough room for it. After knowing the desperation of hunger, his body clamored for food. Maybe it would calm down, eventually.

He watched her pour coffee and pictured her with Jack. The image made him clench his jaws. Last night, she hadn't told him whether she had spent the day with Jack or not. He had just assumed she hadn't. Not knowing twisted his insides. *I don't need to care,* he reminded himself. Then, why could he not stop?

***

After breakfast they set off to the pizzeria. They were half way to there when Nicole stopped.

"Hey, what are you doing? You're not working today. There's no need to walk me to work."

"I've got painting to do."

"You can take a day off. It'll wait."

"There's nothing I want to do and nowhere I want to go."

"I know the feeling."

As they arrived, Nicole halted in her tracks. "Look at that! Did you do it? You said you couldn't draw."

"Nothing to do with me. This is the work of an artist. You'll meet Ed this evening."

It took a while for Nicole to regain her composure and hold back the mild rebuke on her tongue. Nothing she could say would change his mind. It was his right to spend his money the way he chose. Which made her even more suspicious of him.

A truly struggling worker would save every penny he earned. Piers acted as if didn't need the money. She knew his wages would cover his rent but leave very little left over. The tips? Anybody else would hoard them to buy clothes and furniture. He didn't. It was as if he had no worries about the future. Yet he didn't have the air of a drifter about him.

The fear that he could soon leave insinuated itself into her thoughts. The void he'd leave in her heart would be huge. At the same time, she didn't want to be concerned. What he did with his life was none of her business. She had no wish to feel anything for him. She bit her lip and went to answer the phone.

All business again, Nicole smiled at Piers at work outside the shop. "I've got a problem."

"Tell me."

"We have six pizzas to deliver for an office party. Lynne won't be here for a while. I can't leave the shop."

"I'll be most happy to do the deliveries for you."

"You're not supposed to work today." She scrunched her lips in that gesture of thanks no-I won't-cry-but-I-almost-did. "I'll make an extra three. By the time you get there, they could want more."

"I'll come in and help with the dough."

He scrubbed his hands and donned an apron. They worked in silence until Lynne arrived.

"It's your day off, Piers, so what are you doing here?"

He grinned. "Making dough, Mrs. B."

"Joker! Nice to have your sunny personality around."

He chuckled. "That'll be the first time someone pays me that sort of compliment."

"Don't let it go to your head, though," Nicole said. "Here's our grocery truck pulling in. Can you get our cartons while I put those pizzas in the ovens? Please!"

Piers hid a smile. She said *please*. He wiped his hands and went out. When all the cartons were in the kitchen, he signed the delivery sheet. "Is this the standing order?"

"I ordered double." Lynne said. "We ran short last week."

"Good planning." Piers whistled a tune while they stored the supplies in the two fridges and freezers.

The oven buzzer sounded. Piers loaded the pizzas into the van and took off. With Snowflake nudging her hand, Nicole continued staring at the empty back lane.

"He'll come back."

Lynne's voice shook her out of her reverie. "It's not that. I'm still amazed how he has turned our lives upside down."

"I wouldn't say upside down but he sure changed things around here."

Nicole's features relaxed. "Although we've had to work harder, Flavio seems to be thriving."

"It's done him good to see the business prosper again."

"I guess we'd better be grateful to Piers." Nicole hid her face from Lynn and furiously cleaned the table.

"Is something troubling you about Piers?"

Lynne was too perceptive. It made Nicole uncomfortable.

"He's good at his job. He's educated. Why is he working in a pizza parlor?"

"Nothing wrong with a good honest job."

Cloth in hand, Nicole leaned against the table. "He's a phony. He spends money like he didn't need it."

Lynne fell thoughtful for a moment, her eyes scrutinizing Nicole's face. "Money isn't everything. He strikes me as a man who, faced with a challenge, forges ahead to conquer it. He fell on some bad luck. You gave him a chance by hiring him. He saw the state of the business and took on the challenge of making it successful. Even if that meant using his own funds."

Nicole gave a feeble laugh. "You're quite the psychologist, Mrs. B."

"I've lived a long time. Chalk it up to experience."

"Are you going to check on Flavio?"

"He's at the gym today. I hope that all those endomorphins will put him in a better mood."

"Is he still sulking?"

"Sort of. I have a little money that came to me a month ago. I said I wanted to invest it in the pizzeria. He took the offer badly. Wants to make it or break with his own funds, he said."

"Just too proud."

"Misplaced pride. I'll get around that somehow. Let's have lunch. I made some biscuits from quinoa flour."

Nicole smiled. Another health food product, but it certainly appeared to do a lot of good for Flavio. They had barely eaten when a flurry of customers kept them busy. Only after the last one had gone did Nicole wonder aloud about Piers' whereabouts. She didn't want to think about him, yet she kept looking at the clock. "He's taking a long time."

Before Lynne could answer, a satisfied whistling preceded a jubilant Piers.

Nicole faced him. "Did you get lost?" Then immediately regretted her words. It was his day off.

"No danger of that. You know the three extra pizzas? Well, I sold them."

"You do that all the time. So if you want compliments, make this a standing order."

Piers took a bow. "Thank you, gracious lady."

"Sorry. I'm a little prickly."

Lynne laughed. "Okay, tell us, Piers."

"There's a small factory and an equally office block across from the birthday party. Workers were out on the street enjoying the balmy weather, some with their sandwich bags. I opened the van's door and stood there with a pizza in my hands and sure enough someone approached. I sold her a slice. Then a dozen people came to buy a slice. The three pizzas are gone."

The door opened to let Flavio in. "What's gone?"

Piers recounted his story. "I think we have potential there. I could take some pre-cut pizzas, park outside factories and offices at lunch time, and sell pizza by the slice."

Flavio nodded. "We'd need a vendor's license."

A grin spread across Piers' face. "So, it's a good idea?"

"I think it's a super idea."

A frown marred Nicole's brow. "How long would you be in any one place?"

"I thought I'd go at the noon hour, one day a week. People would know that's the day they can treat themselves to our delicious pizzas."

There he was doing it again. *Our* pizzas. "But what if you have a noon delivery on the other side of town?"

There was silence until Lynne broke in. "In that case I could do the delivery in my car."

Everyone then spoke at once. Finally they agreed twelve-inch pizzas would make the best slices. Not too big, not too small.

"We should have some wedge-shaped boxes in case someone wanted to take a couple of slices back to the office," Lynne said.

"That's a great idea," Flavio said.

Lynne phoned their carton supplier and ordered the necessary boxes. Paper plates would do for those who wanted to eat on the spot.

"We should consider making a very crispy crust that could be held in the fingers without bending," Nicole said.

The fear of bankruptcy always kept Nicole silent about her own many ideas for the pizzeria. She could see the benefits of Piers' salesmanship. Yet all her being was reluctant to agree to his new ventures. On this issue, however, she'd be out-voted if she protested much more. If she gave it serious thought, she'd have to admit it was a good way to make extra money, as long as the rest of the business didn't suffer.

A hand landed on her shoulder. She looked up at Flavio. He was all smiles.

"I had a call."

By now Nicole accepted that sometimes her sister would phone Flavio and not her. Paula refused to call collect. It was three minutes for her and three minutes for Flavio. "What did she say?"

"La Bambina's got a job. I told her she could come and work here."

Nicole had to laugh. "I know, but she said she'll only come when she can afford to work here for free. So we won't see her any time soon."

"It's good she has a job in her field of study."

The telephone and customers put an end to the chatting.
***

Piers went back to painting the outside. When Jack walked into the shop, he followed and nearly told him Nicole was out, but the hatch gave a good view of the kitchen. He couldn't do that. No matter how he chastised himself for bristling every time he saw Jack, he didn't like him. Nicole talked to her friend while arranging a bunch of flowers Lynne had brought. After a while, Jack squeezed her shoulder in a way that spoke of familiarity, and said goodbye. Piers noticed Nicole looked upset.

"Bad news? Something I can help with?" Genuine concern ran in Piers' voice.

"Huh...Thanks, no." She smiled but her eyes didn't.

Ed arrived. He and Piers worked on the facade until the light faded. On the way home that evening, Piers joked in an attempt to draw Nicole out of her silent mood. He was rewarded by her laughter. At the foot of the stairs, she thanked him.

"I can go up on my own."

"Never! What if a vampire was hiding on the landing?"

She chuckled. "Vampires don't know the security code."

"What about bats? They could come in through the vents."

"You're getting batty yourself. Goodnight."

He flashed her his best smile. "How about a cup of coffee at my place?"

"Piers! You don't even have any coffee."

He sighed theatrically. "True."

"I see. You're fishing for an invitation. Let's make it tomorrow. I have letters to write tonight."

"Okay, tomorrow." His hand came up to her face and he brushed a tendril of hair back. A finger slowly descended along her cheek. "Goodnight." His voice was soft and seductive.

He watched her climb the stairs two at a time. When he heard the clunk of the door closing, he took the stairs down to his own apartment.

Piers, you're an idiot!

But she's the nicest woman I've met in long time. And so damn attractive.

That's where the danger lies.

He heaved a quiet sigh. He hadn't had a problem living like a monk the last two years. But right now, sweet, perceptive Nicole made it mighty difficult.

In the shower he did his best to put her out of his mind.

***

Her purse landed on the sofa and she dropped next to it. Nicole didn't want a man in her life. Not until she knew about Christopher. The thought that it might be years before she found him crossed her mind. By that time she'd be too old for romance. She pictured herself telling a man "Oh, by the way I have a child somewhere and I want to find him. One day he'll want to know about me. Or, I may have to go to court to get visiting rights." She had experienced it twice already and wasn't about to try a third time.

What Piers' reaction might be, she didn't want to even think about it. He probably would encourage her. Offer to help. Only Piers Sonder wasn't a man to commit himself. There wasn't that air of permanence about him. Like there was with Jack.

A sigh escaped her. Jack, the man who wanted to marry her. Jack who was so nice. Jack, so predictable.

Jack, so boring.

Chapter Eighteen

Piers returned elated from the Noon Hour Pizza Run, as they had dubbed this new venture. "It's absolutely great! I sold the lot. And there was competition from the hot dog stand."

"That's no competition for our pizzas." Flavio spoke deadpan.

His excitement softened Nicole's features. "Congrats!"

"I felt I should have had drinks to sell."

All the joy drained from Nicole's face. "You'd need a cooler for the van. Another expense!"

Flavio tossed the dough with an expert flick of his wrist. "The boy's right. Folks want to eat *and* drink."

The last customer went out and Lynne joined the conversation. "I agree. We should even offer drinks here. Since we put in the tables, lots of customers have sat down to eat a slice and asked for a glass of water. Water!"

"True." Nicole was prompt to recognize the strength of other people's argument even if she refused to agree. "I hope you're not talking about one of those big ugly drink machines."

"There isn't enough room for it. We'd keep the drinks in the fridge," Lynne said.

"We can't have too many choices. It's not practical," Nicole said.

"What goes best with our pizzas?" Piers asked.

Between serving customers, making more dough, cleaning ovens and counters, the debate continued about the best drink.

"Nicole's right," Piers said. "Plain water is best. It doesn't take the pizza taste away like sodas do."

Nicole shrugged. "We call them soft drinks in these parts. But I'm not sure we can make a profit selling bottled water."

"The accountant has spoken." Piers had a teasing gleam in his eye. "Perhaps it isn't necessary to make a profit on the water. Plain water is free from the tap, and plain bottled-water a few cents at cost. The customer enjoys the full taste of the pizza and wants more. That's where the profit lies."

Nicole looked heavenward. "Why do I feel accountants are killjoys? We've just got out of the red, but only just."

There was a moment of silence. Then Piers waved the knife he was cutting peppers with. "You haven't tabulated the Noon Hour Pizza Run sales yet. How about saving that money to buy a cooler?"

It was agreed. The shop became busy again and Piers went out on more deliveries.

A few days later, the van was equipped with a large picnic cooler which could work on the vehicle's battery or ice.

Flavio heaved a sigh and lowered himself on a chair. "Isn't it about time we stop for lunch?"

A burst of laughter greeted his complaint.

Lynne pulled a bag out of the fridge. "The noon hour rush has ended. I made sandwiches last night. Then you'll go and rest."

"We've got too much to do."

The back door opened and Piers came in. "Time to get another helper."

They all look at each other. Nicole broke the silence. "The business is really picking up, but another employee would strain the budget and put us back in the red."

"If we could sell to restaurants, it could double," Piers said.

"Strange you should have gotten that idea. I thought about it too before Flavio had his heart problem," Nicole said. "But then I couldn't see how to manage the shop, the deliveries and supply restaurants all at the same time."

"It's simple. We go and visit the restaurants. They put pizza on the menu, phone in the order and I deliver same as to any regular customers."

"Don't you reckon the restaurant customers would get impatient waiting for their pizzas?"

"We're now preparing quite a bit of dough in advance. The toppings don't take any time to make. We know the orders would come around noon and in the evenings."

"Anyway, people always wait for food in a good restaurant," Lynne said.

Nicole hesitated. "It would double the number of deliveries."

"Isn't it time to hire someone?" Piers' eyebrows arched. His mouth curved. The picture of perfect logic.

A shiver raced down her spine. Why did he look so attractive even when he made faces?

"I thought you realized money doesn't grow on trees!"

Flavio had been watching, a hint of a smile on his lips. He turned to Lynne and breathed deeply, like a man gathering up his courage. "Why don't we let those youngsters organize the business and go for a stroll, Mrs. B.?"

"A great idea. It's a beautiful day."

Lynne winked at Nicole who nodded in return.

Flavio grinned. "I've recognized the value of rest, you'll be happy to hear. Friends again?"

Lynne took his hand in hers.

After Flavio and Lynne left, Piers stood up. "How about looking at the accounts together?"

Nicole pulled out a ledger and a calculator. "I do all this on the computer, but I like to write it down too. It makes the picture clearer in a different way. I can printed the spreadsheet out if you want."

"No need. Let's look at the spreadsheet."

"Grab a chair."

Shoulders touching, they peered into the monitor screen and its tiny figures. A tremor coursed along her arm and poured into the rest of her body. She took a deep breath to steady herself.

For the next half hour they threw figures around. A pleasant warmth had invaded Nicole. She wished they didn't have to answer the phone which rang for the second time. She'd better shake herself out of this kind of exquisite torpor.

Piers answered. His warm voice caressed her ears. She imagined it caressing the customer's too. Piers was repeating, "Make that two?" His tone became intimate. "Of course, ma'am, the Fifteen DeLuxe is the best. Yes, ma'am. I'll be right there as soon as they're baked."

Nicole wondered if any woman could resist him. She cocked her head to hear the end of the call while preparing the topping.

"We bake each order fresh. None of our pizzas sit waiting for customers. That's why they're the best."

His deep and sexy laugh rang in the room. He hung up.

"Okay, I'll deliver that order. On my way back, I'll look into phone prices. Two sets that can handle split lines, hold function and leave your order in a mailbox."

"Piers, I just said we can't afford it. We're almost in the red."

"All businesses are in the red to start with."

"Before Flavio's heart attack we were never in the red." Nicole shook her head, troubled with contradictory feelings. "This business must provide for Flavio, your wages and my wages. Whenever we're in the black, something for Mrs. B. Although she refuses to be paid, she now works here all day. She uses gas. She needs clothes too."

"Not to mention operating expenses, but the only way to get this business on a profit making basis is to expand it. We have to get the name recognized beyond a two-block radius. To do so, we must spend money."

A frown creased her forehead. "Why do I feel that you'll do it, anyway?"

"Because you know I'm right. The risk is small compared to the benefits."

She took her head in her hands. "I'll phone the company to get another line put in. But we're headed for ruin, I'm telling you."

The door chimes rang. She went to greet the customer. It wasn't a customer but Jack.

Jack spent no time on pleasantries. "Have you been avoiding me? You haven't phoned in days."

"Sorry, we've been very busy. I've been putting in overtime."

"I hope you're getting paid for it."

"Jack, we're trying to get the business back on its feet. Sit down. We can talk until customers come in."

Piers appeared, his face bland. "And what will it be for you, sir?"

A scowl marred his face.

Jack turned to her. "Are you turning this two-bit place into a restaurant? Tablecloths and now a waiter?"

"Do you have any objections?" The sharp edge to Piers' voice brought a red blotch to Jack's cheeks.

"You shouldn't make Nicole work overtime."

Her eyes flashed. "I work because I want to. We're a team and each one of us pulls his or her weight."

Piers remained stoned-faced. "Would you care to try our cheese biscuits? They're still in the experimental stage but I can vouch for them being good."

Jack flushed. Piers went to the kitchen.

A smile floated on Nicole's lips. "He's a good salesman. I made the biscuits."

"Then if you made them, they must be good. Have you given any thought to what I asked you?"

She started. She had just about forgotten about his proposal. "We're friends and I'm not comfortable with the idea... not yet."

His lips drew into a thin line. "You will marry me."

Stunned at the commanding tone, she had no chance to reply. Piers returned with a steaming cheese biscuit on a paper plate and a bottle of water. A customer came in at that moment. Nicole got up from the table. She noticed the satisfied smirk on Piers' face. It annoyed her but at the same time she couldn't help an inner chuckle. Jack was notoriously tight with his money, avoiding to buy anything except the basic groceries. Piers had sold him a biscuit and bottled water.

Though she understood well enough that as a full-time student, Jack had to budget carefully, he was what she termed a comfort animal. Life with him would be regulated. Intimity Monday to Friday. Shopping on Saturday. Church on Sunday. Two weeks vacation in summer. A house with a white picket fence or whatever it was these days. She wasn't sure she liked him enough to marry him, not to mention love him. There was no question that she'd have to love the man she eventually chose as her life partner. The more she thought about it, the less certain the path ahead appeared.

That night, she and Piers walked home exhausted. Piers took her hand. On impulse, she wanted to snatch it away, but she didn't. A gentle breeze soothed the prickling over her skin and cooled the flush that colored her cheeks.

They went up to her apartment. The final cup of coffee of the day had become a ritual. Those brief evenings of easy talk led to discoveries of common interests. All her being screamed to lay her head on his broad chest and give in to her innermost feelings.

She resisted.

At her door, Piers pressed a butterfly kiss on top of her head. A battle raged within her. She wanted him to take her into his arms. She needed to feel his strength around her. But she made no move to encourage him. The imprint of his lips remained with her until the following day.

By now she had contacted every adoption agencies on her list. A few refused to talk to her. A couple were downright nasty. These she earmarked for contact by a private investigator, when she'd have saved enough money again. The familiar feeling of despair enveloped her. She had to find her little boy. Deep in her heart she knew he was unhappy. Something had happened.

Yet, she may never find him.

That probably meant she'd become an old maid. If she were to make a life for herself, make a happy home with a man she could love, it wouldn't take anything away from her search. She shook her head free of the impossible daydream.

Piers wasn't that man. The thought startled her, but she had to admit she liked him.

The more she analyzed him, the more the word *phony* rang in her ears. Granted, his charisma was genuine enough. It attracted customers on the Noon Hour Pizza Run. She'd bet her last dollar they were mostly females. To be fair, she recognized that male customers also enjoy talking to him. He could talk about any sport and every sports star just as easily as he could talk ballet with Vera Louden, the instructor at the nearby dance studio.

There were too many puzzling inconsistencies about him. She was certain he had never work in a store before. Yet he fitted in as if he had been born to the trade. His business ideas seemed to come out of a textbook. Yet he had no books and no time to go to the library.

No, Piers was not a man she could trust. If he were lying, as she was sure he was, that was his problem. She would have nothing to do with him. Even if his contact had awakened her body. For a long time, she had suppressed her feelings, both emotional and physical. She could do the same for a while longer. At the end of the month, she'd graduate as a qualified accountant. Then she could find a job with fewer hours and more money so she could continue her search.

Leaving Flavio's would be hard, but the pizzeria was rebounding. She sighed, rebounding thanks to Piers. Flavio could hire a manager. She'd do the books for free of course. That way, she wouldn't have to meet Piers at all, and she could still help Flavio. Maybe she'd find a new apartment too.

Maybe she should marry Jack.

The phone rang. She put the receiver to her ear. There was silence at the other end. Slightly troubled, she checked her locks and went to bed.

Chapter Nineteen

Another two-for-one day came and went with the now habitual resounding success.

Flavio leaned against the counter. "That's it, Nicole, hire someone. I've been on my feet all day. If I sit now, I won't be able to stand again."

Lynne turned on him. "You stubborn mule. I told you to go home to do your exercises and rest up. You skipped therapy today."

"You know I couldn't leave you short-handed."

"Well, I'm taking you home now. Piers and Nicole can close."

"Your obedient servant, Mrs. B."

After Lynne and Flavio left still squabbling, Piers looked at Nicole. "How do you hire someone? I mean where do you advertise the job?"

"Why? Do you have a friend in mind?" She didn't mean to be sarcastic. Sometimes Piers had that effect on her.

"Just figured that a notice in the window doesn't reach enough people. Wouldn't an employment bureau recommend someone?"

"Got to pay a fee."

"They have to make money too. There'd be more applications to choose from, I'm sure."

"I just hate to spend money."

He laughed. "Don't I know."

Nicole switched off the store lights. "I should really wash the floor tonight. I'm beat. I'll do it in the morning."

"I'll come in early and do it. How about getting a high school kid to come in and wash the floor every day? That wouldn't cost much."

"You're out of your mind. Did you have servants in your previous life?"

A shadow flitted on Piers' face. He chuckled. "I'll check the family records. Do you know if the thrift store is still open?"

"We might just make it."

"Let's take the van."

They did and arrived just minutes before closing time.

"What do you need?"

"I have a small table and two chairs in mind."

"This way."

There was a good assortment of tables and chairs. Piers stood in front of a round table of solid maple.

"This is too big, but perhaps I could cut a slice off it. Then it'd fit against the wall."

Nicole looked puzzled, but her sense of humor took over. "Cut off a slice? You've been around pizzas too long! What is it for?"

He grinned. "I could also cut it flush on the other side. It'll then be perfect."

"You don't want to cut up a good table like this!"

"I do. I'll take the two matching chairs."

The loudspeaker crackled. "Closing time."

Piers seized the table and carried it, while Nicole followed him to the check out with the two chairs. They loaded them into the van and drove to their building.

"I'll give you a hand to carry the chairs."

Piers locked the van. "It's for the shop. We'll take them in the morning."

"For the shop? But we've got two already."

"I studied the traffic in the shop. There's one dead corner next to the door by the yellow wall. It needs a table for two, but a small one. That's why I want to cut it down."

She opened her door. "Piers! You have no furniture and you bought the table for the shop. It doesn't make sense."

"I'm spending more time at the pizzeria than in the apartment. It makes plenty of sense to me."

"It's your money you're spending!" Her face reddened.

Piers sat in the armchair. "I'll get it back when you give me a raise. This coffee smells heavenly."

She poured a cup. "You're changing the subject."

"It's a boring one. Thanks. You make the best coffee in the West."

"Can you sleep after it?"

He trailed a finger along her arm. "Does it keep you awake?"

She quivered. "Not as long as I put lots of milk in it." What kept her awake were the longings that he aroused in her. But she wouldn't tell him that.

They stood up at the same time. Piers never stayed long. A shadow passed over her. Nor would he stay long in her life.

At the door he leaned over to place a light kiss on her forehead. Startled, she raised her face. He didn't move. Their breath mingled.

His hands inched over her shoulders, down her back until she was completely enfolded in the power of his arms. His lips lowered to hers.

Shockwaves hit her in quick succession. Her body trembled. Her arms snaked around his neck. As if he'd been waiting for her signal, his lips took hers. The electrifying contact wiped out any remnants of resistance. She let herself go against his solid chest with a sigh.

For one precious moment, nothing existed but the incredible thrill of floating on air. Then he released her and reality came crashing down.

Gently, she pulled back. "Goodnight."

His eyes had become dark and sultry. A different type of hunger shone in them. He too was obviously fighting for control. A last fleeting touch of his lips on her nose, and he was gone.

Her forehead rested on her hand braced against the door. She waited until her blood cooled. If only Jack's kisses were as stirring, she'd marry him in a shot. But, there was more to a man than the power to make her body crazy. Qualities that weren't physical. An urge to scream seized her. She was so confused. Since the day Piers appeared at the door of the pizzeria she had been living on an emotional roller coaster. For a moment she longed for the quiet life she knew before he came into it.

***

Piers plodded down to his apartment, berating himself non-stop. He had lost control. His strong determination vanish into thin air when she had lifted her face to him.

I'm a heel to deceive her like this.

I don't know what she'd do if I told her who I really am. What have I done?

Probably tell me to beat the heck out of here. Then what? How would I get another job? She might even confide in Mrs. Harlow and get me thrown out.

A wave of muddled feelings rolled over him. He didn't want to move away. He liked it here. He liked her. He cupped his chin and stared at the wall. Sometimes he could really shake her for acting like a prim and proper old maid when she really seethed with passion. He wondered why she acted the way she did. It wasn't her true self. Always on her guard, as if she, too, was keeping a secret.

He sat on the bed, his head in his hands. The specter of the tragedy still hung over him. Before prison, he had kept his emotional distance from women. Marietta was never a serious affair. Neither was Tracy. None of his girlfriends ever were. They knew the score in the fast lane. But Nicole was different. She didn't belong to the crowd where material possessions took the place of honest happiness.

For a second he was startled. *Honest happiness*! A smile stretched across his face. That was what he had been experiencing these last few weeks. The awareness sent his heart beating faster. He ended up here on his way to oblivion, to some place where he wouldn't be known, where he'd know nobody. Yet landing here, had transformed his life beyond simple existence. He surprised himself laughing and joking. Only in the quiet of the evening did the pain of his foolishness haunt him. In the weeks before his trial, funerals for the family and Tracy had been held. Hidden at the back, he had cried with the families.

After his sentencing, Tracy's parents, Elgar and Ruth Dewilt, had come and forgiven him. That Christian gesture had deepened his pain even more. The worst pain bludgeoned him when the Brockton family had turned to him. Ten-year-old Clara, tears brimming at the edge of her eyelids, took his hands in hers. She couldn't speak but her uncle John Brockton did. "Thank you for the trust fund you made for Clara. We only want one thing: turn your life round. We'll pray for you."

When he had set out West, it was to escape the memories, escape a life he had come to hate. It was to find who he could be without the trappings of his family's wealth. The rundown state of the pizzeria became his challenge, and he actually enjoyed seeing the business grow. He couldn't tell Nicole he had an MBA, and that he may as well use the expensive education he had received. In addition, he could apply the theories and the knowledge he had reluctantly gained with Reddington Sporting Goods under his father's tutelage.

He couldn't even tell her his real name. If she had deciphered his scribbling, it had meant nothing to her. It seems incredible that she had never heard of Reddington Sporting Goods. He might tell his father one day that the commercials didn't reach everybody.

He was lying by omission, and that still didn't sit well with him.

Chapter Twenty

Spice bottle in hand, Piers sprinkled the tomato paste he had spread on the dough.

"What are you doing?" Nicole asked.

"Do you like the new blue table?"

"Yes, you had a good idea. It looks attractive against the yellow wall. I want to know what you're doing with this dough and the bottle of spices. It's not even ours."

"The other day I did some shopping for Mrs. Harlow. She told me about tarragon, a herb Nicole, not a spice, so I'm trying it."

"You can't put tarragon *herb* in a pizza!"

He kept on working. "Sure you can."

"Well, you can eat that one." She turned impatiently and went back to the computer to tabulate wages.

"We'll all try it."

Customers and calls came in. Soon Piers was out on deliveries. It was afternoon before Flavio, Lynne and Nicole sat down to taste Piers' pizza experiment. He anxiously watched them bite into their slices.

They seem to take forever to chew. Then exclamations of delight resounded in the room.

"Delicious! Mostly cheese. You didn't use pepperoni. What is it?" Lynne chewed some more and inhaled the flavor.

"I thought pepperoni would overpower the subtle taste of tarragon, so I bought a sort of garlic sausage at the Farmers' Market. It's homemade and the taste blends well."

"What d'you think, Nicole?" Flavio asked.

She raised her head. "I think we have a winner here. A mild pizza, it could do for children too."

Piers glowed with pride. A compliment from Nicole meant the new pizza was a success.

"What do we call it?" Lynne asked.

Flavio frowned. "Why does it have a name?"

"To promote it," Piers replied.

Nicole grasped her head in a theatrical gesture. "You can't spend any more money."

Flavio chuckled. "Trust Piers to do it cheap."

For the next half hour they debated names. At the sound of the door chimes Piers glanced at the door. Like a bullet, he shot from his chair.

"What the hell are you guys doing here?" He kept his voice low, his back to the hatch.

Charlotte, Clayton and Mark's faces took on an air of feigned surprise. "We're just checking out this great pizza joint."

"I don't want you here. How did you find me?" Piers turned toward the kitchen, almost shouting. "Three Fifteen DeLuxe."

He knew there were three fifteen-inch pizzas in the oven. He wanted his friends gone.

Nicole, her face reflecting curiosity, passed the boxed pizzas through the hatch.

Piers had taken his friends' money and pushed the boxes in their hands. "Get out!"

"We need to talk."

Piers sighed. "Call at my place after eight. You obviously have the address."

Bemused, they ambled out and climbed into the BMW parked in front of the door.

Piers struggled to recover his cool.

A suspicious look in her eyes, Nicole's voice was dry. "What was that all about?"

"Customers from the Noon Hour Pizza Run." His devil-may-care tone of voice didn't ring true even to his own ears.

"In which office can they afford Jaguars?"

"BMW. It was a BMW."

Flavio cleared his throat. "Hmm... we haven't decided on a name yet."

"How about *Picnic*?" Lynne asked.

They all looked at her. She leaned against the counter a shrewd expression on her face.

"It's a nice name," Nicole said.

"Good, we'll adopt it," said Flavio. "How about you, Piers?"

"Sounds good to me."

A family came into the shop and sat down. Nicole and Piers went out front.

Flavio raised Lynne's chin with a finger. "So, Picnic it is. Tell me Mrs. B. what made you think of a picnic? People taking the pizza on their weekend outing? You have that look on your face which makes me think you have other reasons."

"*Pi* for Piers, and *nic* for Nicole."

He chortled. "You maybe right, Mrs. B. But they have a long way to go."

She nodded. "Time for your exercise, I'll drive you to the gym."

"But it's too busy here."

"Good. That'll keep Nicole from asking questions Piers doesn't want to answer."

"You're talking in riddles."

"I know, but can't say more. It's just my observation."

"And us men don't see things like that, I suppose. All right, let's go."

Chapter Twenty-One

Piers fidgeted for a good part of the evening. He hoped there would be some late deliveries and he could slip by the apartment before closing time. Unfortunately, it was a Sunday and they closed at eight. Although there were many customers in the shop, no late deliveries were required. With dread in his heart that he and Nicole would walk home and find the BMW parked in front of the building, he started closing up, until inspiration struck. If he drove the van, they could come in by the back door.

"Ready Nicole? I'll drive you in the van, I think you're tired."

Surprised, she turned to him. "I'm a bit. But I can walk. I used to run every day, but that was before Flavio's heart problem. I haven't had time since then. Walking is good too."

"We should think about running to work, but it's been a long day. We'll get here earlier tomorrow."

"Okay. I admit my feet are beginning to complain. I'll feed Snowflake first."

Relieved, Piers played a while with the pup. Nicole put the dog through his paces before locking his gate.

Piers drove carefully and took an indirect route for the last couple of blocks before their building.

"Is this a tour of back alleys?"

"I find them interesting. Some houses are so posh in front and their backs are just awful. And the junk some people keep in their backyards is something else."

She turned her head as she looked at the cans against a fence. "I suppose they also put out good stuff which anyone can pick up if they need it."

"That's right. We never know what useful things we can find."

Pleased he successfully diffused Nicole's suspicions for his reason for driving home through the back lanes, he escorted her to her apartment.

"You didn't take a pizza for supper."

Piers shrugged. He'd go hungry tonight unless his friends and his sister had the good idea to bring the pizzas with them. "I've got some leftovers. I'll skip coffee tonight. I'm beat too. Goodnight."

He held the back door for her. Surprised and mildly suspicious, she watched him take the stairs two at the time.

Adrenaline flowed in his veins. A sigh of relief escaped his chest when he heard Nicole's door click shut. He rushed out and checked the street. The BMW was parked a block away. His sister and his friends stood waiting on the curb. Relief flooded him. At least they had some sense. They spotted him.

"Come in!"

"My, my, Piers, working life doesn't make you very polite," Charlotte said. She hugged her brother.

"Sorry, guys. I didn't tell my boss who I am. I don't want to lose my job. It was hard, very hard to get work."

Clayton crossed his arms over his chest. "Why did you sell us three pizzas and push us out of the shop?"

"I wasn't going to introduce you to my boss."

"You didn't tell him?"

"Her."

Charlotte shook her head and pointed to the room. "How can you live in a dump like this?"

"It's a bit empty, but it's clean. What did you do with the pizzas?"

"They're in the car," Clayton said.

"Then go and fetch them."

"Sure, boss. What's the code?" The sarcasm fell flat.

"Did you drive all the way from Montreal?"

Mark scoffed. "Nope. I rented the car at the airport in the city."

Charlotte put her hand on Piers arm. "I'm dismayed to find you living in a one-room slum."

"It isn't a slum. How did you find me?"

Clayton let himself in with the pizzas and proceeded to unwrap one.

Mark pulled a chair for Charlotte and took the other one. Piers and Clayton sat on the cot.

They bit in the crisp crust and for a short moment no one talk. Finally Mark wiped his mouth. "You filed a late Income Tax Return. Simple enough."

"Mom is very upset, Piers. She and Father have been arguing a bit too much. She isn't feeling well. Mentally that is."

"They turned their backs on me."

"Mom didn't. Father prevented her from contacting you."

"She could have paid me a visit if she had really wanted to. You had no problem coming to see me."

A silence fell.

"Maybe they weren't right," Clayton said. "They suffered too. They didn't know how to cope, and they were hurt because you refused a deal and wanted to do the whole prison term."

"Expiation," Piers said.

Charlotte exploded. "Why didn't you come or phone or something when you were let out?"

"I explained it to Mark. I guess he told you."

His friend shrugged. "I did."

"I still don't understand. And why the Yukon? And why are you stuck in this hole of all places?" Rancor underlay Charlotte's tone.

Piers took a shuddering breath. "I was making my way north. I got a job here. I'll stay until they throw me out."

"Why would they?" Clayton picked at the crumbs in the pizza box.

"If and when they learn about who I am."

Mark shrugged. "Decent people will understand. You paid your dues to society."

"It doesn't feel like it for me. The pain I caused innocent people is weighing heavy on my heart. I live, I work, I laugh, but I don't forget. I can't forget."

"You haven't forgiven yourself," Mark said. "It's time you do."

"I promised Mom I'd find you and bring you home. I know her depression would lift instantly."

A frown appeared on Piers forehead. "Tell her I'm alright but I can't go home just yet."

His friends and kin heaved a collective sigh.

"At least phone her."

"I don't have a phone. I'd have to use the Pizzeria's. Can't do that."

"No phone? How come?"

"My dear sister, there is something that's called money. It costs more money to have a mobile than I earn."

Her mouth formed an O. She shook her head. "Could you at least write to Mom? A stamp should be in your budget." She put on a dramatic air. "And it'll keep your secret when you post it *discreetly*."

Piers thought for a moment. "Then they will trace it back here. I'll think of something. Do you enjoy the Porsche?"

She smiled. "Thanks for signing it over to me."

"The best I could do since I totaled your Explorer."

"Let's not talk about that," Clayton said. "Among other things, the Canadian Tae Kwon Do Association has contacted you, i.e. Mark, to represent Canada at the international tournament in Tokyo. He replied you were at a religious retreat."

Piers rolled his eyes. "Gee, thanks. They'll think I'm a monk or a nut case. I thought they'd taken me off the roster."

"They know about you, but still want you."

"Tell them no thank you. That's another part of my life I don't want to go back to."

Charlotte hugged him. "I think I understand you. There's more here than just getting a job, isn't there?"

With a few words, Piers told them about his work.

"And that's why you live in this simple basement suite," Charlotte said.

Piers grinned. "Not a dump?"

They all stood. His friends clapped him on the back. He promised again to write a good old-fashioned letter and include one for his mother. He showed them out and opened the front door.

Charlotte put her arms around him. "You simply amaze me. Oh, by the way Marietta is desperate to get in touch with you. If I'm to believe her, she is the love of your life."

"Don't give her my address. She never counted."

Charlotte laughed. "I'll tell her."

A last hug and they left. He turned to go down to his apartment. A door slammed on the upper floor.

It had to be Nicole's. Worried that she should have come down and seen him hugged his sister, he climbed upstairs, taking the steps two at a time. He knocked on her door. No answer. He knocked again. After a long wait, Nicole opened the door a few inches. Enough for him to see that her table was set for two.

"Nicole, I think we need to talk."

"Do we? There's no need... I... I'm expecting a friend."

"No, you're not."

She reddened. "You're a liar. I'll see you at work. Get out of here."

"I know you're upset because my friends came to visit."

"Who are you, Piers Sonder? A down-on-his luck guy whose friends drive BMWs and dress in Armani suits?"

His shoulders sagged.

Suppressed anger darkened her face. "I don't count, either. Please don't waste my time."

Her stormy outburst tugged at his heart. She had heard some of the conversation. "Let me explain-" He stepped back to avoid the slammed door.

I guess deserved that. I should tell her the truth, but I'll lose her if I do. But maybe I've lost her, anyway.

He dragged his feet down to his apartment. The two remaining pizzas sat staring at him on the table. He wouldn't be able to eat all of them and throwing them out was not an option. He grabbed the van keys and headed out with the boxes.

On one of his recent deliveries he'd noticed an institutional-looking set of interconnected houses in the middle of a residential area in New Town. Curious, he'd asked his customer about them. A seniors home was the reply. The occupants lived independently and some with assistance. A nurse and a night-watch were always on duty.

Surely, they wouldn't mind receiving some free pizzas? He found the place again and rang the bell. A woman answered.

"Delivery for the Home."

"We didn't order anything. You must have the wrong address."

"No, ma'am. Someone is sending you these. It's all paid for. Enjoy."

Her eyebrows lifted in surprise. "Well thank you." She reached for a can on a shelf by the door. "Here, take this."

Piers pocketed the small tip with a smile. A warm feeling washed over him. Some people were going to be happy and excited wondering who the mysterious donor was.

His contentment evaporated on the drive back. Nicole didn't want to see him in any capacity other than an employee. His spirits fell further. Tomorrow was her day off. He wouldn't meet her again until Tuesday. He had to tell her.

Chapter Twenty-Two

Nicole curled up on the sofa and looked at the crisp tablecloth and the shiny glasses. The shrimp appetizer in the center was wilting. No matter. Her constricted throat would prevent any food from going down. All this had been for Piers. She knew he hadn't eaten since lunch. She had taken care that there was nothing remotely pizza-ish about the meal. He had kissed her. Yet all the while he had a woman. He had rich friends. How stupid she'd been to think maybe he meant something with that kiss.

She had and now it hurt.

Well nine o'clock wasn't too late. With effort, she dialed Jack's number. Bitterness flowed over her. She had been right. Piers was a liar and a cheat. For whatever reason she didn't even begin to guess. From now on she'd make sure she treated him just like the employee he was. She'd love to give him his marching papers, but she knew she couldn't. She needed him to keep the pizzeria going as he had done since he had arrived.

A pent-up sigh escaped her throat. It was going to be difficult working next to him, but she had years of practice giving the cold shoulder to male employees. And this week, she'd be interviewing some applicants. Maybe she could hire two and fire Piers. That wouldn't do. Flavio wouldn't allow it. He liked and admired Piers. Another sigh pushed in her chest. Like it or not, Piers was good for the business.

The knock on the door startled her. Jack entered and handed her a small bouquet of drooping forget-me-nots. "My landlady trimmed her flower bed this afternoon, so I picked those."

"Thank you."

"Very nice of you to invite me over. Did you have a cancellation?"

"Don't be sarcastic. I just had a lot of food on hand and thought I'd like to share it with someone."

"Then it's my pleasure to be that someone despite the late hour."

"You know I work odd hours."

They ate in silence. Jack sat back while she cleared the table. "I haven't made any other discoveries on the internet. I didn't have that much time with the last exams to prepare for."

"I appreciate everything you've done already."

"You should also give some thought to your personal life, Nicole. I'd like to take you out and show you a good time. Maybe we could have a date? You wanted us to get to know each other better."

"I know I'm obsessed with finding what happened to Christopher. I can't help it."

"We can do both."

She forced smile. "You're right, I'm sure. I'll give it a try after my grad."

A knock on the door interrupted them.

"You're expecting another visitor?"

She shook her head. "It must be Mrs. Harlow."

Piers stood at the door. "Sorry to disturb you. I wonder if you'd lend me some coffee. I forgot to buy some."

Nicole opened the door wide enough to allow him to see Jack. Now he'd believe that she had been expecting a friend. She ought to slam the door in his face. She didn't know why she spoke. "I'll get you a packet." She took her time in the kitchen to compose herself before coming back to the door.

"Here's the coffee. There's leftover pea soup in this container. You're welcome to it if you want."

"Thank you."

Nicole closed the door slowly and breathed deeply. She turned a smiling face toward Jack.

Chapter Twenty-Three

Piers ground his teeth and made his way downstairs. He was sure she had prepared dinner for him. Maybe he was wrong. Maybe she had something going with that man. The guy looked at home.

No way, the jerk's all wrong for her. I felt like punching his face.

He was puzzled why she should give him the soup after she had slammed the door on him. On the other hand, she always had endearing touches, always seemed to sense someone's needs.

If she was mad at me because she overheard my friends, she wouldn't give me soup, would she? How do I know what she really feels? How he'd like to break down her reserve, find out what she kept hidden behind her cold mask. When that mask fell at unguarded times, she was a bubbly, easy-going person.

He warmed the soup in the microwave. The pea soup and an old apple washed down with strong coffee did little to assuage his real hunger. The day had been a mess. He fell asleep trying to make sense of it all.

The next morning came too fast. After a cup of warmed up coffee, he hurried upstairs to offer to drive Nicole to class. Fear rippled in his guts as he speculated whether Jack spent the night there.

He'd never know. She had already left the apartment.

Dejected, Piers hurried to the pizzeria. He took out his frustration on cleaning the shop and the kitchen. When Lynne arrived, she looked at Piers and at the sparkling place.

"My oh my, I need dark glasses. You've done a great job. The kitchen's never been so shiny, not even right before the health inspector's visit."

He used his best charmer smile. "There was nothing else to do. Only one order. So I kept busy."

A thoughtful look on her face, Lynne nodded. "I see."

Late in the afternoon, the chimes tinkled and a beaming Nicole breezed in. "My GPA is 4."

"So *mia*, what's the mark?"

"It's an A."

The two waiting customers clapped. The universal congratulations brought a rosy flush to her cheeks, but she kept her back turned to Piers. "I thought I'd drop in to let you know."

"That's nice of you." Lynne's eyes followed Piers to the door. "Delivering your order?"

"That's right."

The door closed behind him. Lynne motioned Nicole to the small table for two. They sat down.

"What's going on between the two of you?"

"Nothing."

"Ah...! Nothing. That's why. What do you want him to do?"

Nicole thought for a second. "I don't know. I thought he cared for me."

"I think he cares a great deal."

"He's a liar. He's got a woman back wherever he comes from. Those people who came in yesterday are his friends. I heard them say the woman's name. She's called Charlotte."

"And you love him."

Nicole's eyes dampened. She turned her head to look out of the window. "I don't really know. I like him. I don't want to fall in love with him."

"But you have. Perhaps there's a logical explanation about his friends? Why don't you ask him?"

Nicole shook her head in denial. "Perhaps. He had the opportunity to tell me, but he didn't. Anyway, I'm not interested. I'll get over it. I'd better go now. I'll take Snowflake to the park for the rest of the day."

Lynne watched her leave, back stiff and straight. When Piers returned, he wore a casual air on his face. His eyes promptly scanned the shop and the kitchen. A cloud passed before his business smile returned.

"It's her day off," Lynne said.

"I know, Mrs. B."

"Did you two have a tiff?" Lynne straightened.

He sighed. "Let's call it a gross misunderstanding."

"What have you done to rectify it?"

"She threw me out before I could speak."

A threatening mask came over Lynne's features. "Just a warning. Don't hurt her, because you'll have to answer to me. That goes for Flavio, too."

"I wouldn't do anything to hurt either of them. I love them both." He was startled by his own words. "I mean, I respect and like..." He was bogged down again.

"I think I know what you mean. Though, about Nicole?"

"She's got herself a boyfriend."

Lynne guffawed. "Jack? That'll be the day!"

"He was at her place last night."

"Which means nothing. So what got between you and her?"

"I kinda didn't tell her all the truth."

"And what is the truth Mr. Piers Sonder Reddington, ex-con and heir to the Reddington Sporting Goods empire?"

Horrified, he stared at Lynne. "How—"

She waved her hand. "It's not important how I found out. The internet is such a marvelous medium to find out about so many facts, including facts about people. Why did you withhold the information?"

"I had to prove myself."

"So you left your daddy's boardroom to see how the other half lives, is that it?"

For a long silent moment, Piers remained slumped on the chair. "I have no desire or inclination to succeed my father."

"But why the pizzeria?"

"Serendipity. I was looking for a job." Pain marred his features. "After jail, I couldn't go back and pretend nothing had happened. There was the possibility of my return creating another media circus. People are still grieving back home."

"You've taken on all the responsibility for the accident, but, according to the court report, Tracy Dewilt was found equally responsible. Her phone was on and it recorded the event."

"I don't remember. I know we were fighting, but I was... I was behind the wheel."

"Why do you need to take all the blame?"

"Lynne, I was in charge of the vehicle, so drunk I couldn't control her or the car. It *is* my fault."

"And Nicole? You're not going to stay here forever."

"She was an unexpected part of the bargain."

"So what now?"

"I don't know. But please, don't tell her who I am."

The telephone crew arrived at that moment to install the second line.

"Do you have a really good reason not to tell her?"

"I don't know. Fear? But it must be me to tell her."

"Come clean with her as soon as you can. Now let's deal with these guys."

Chapter Twenty-Four

When Nicole arrived at the pizzeria, five applicants for the post were already there waiting. While she interviewed the four young men and one middle-aged woman, Piers kept glancing at her trough the hatch.

Flavio elbowed him. "What do you think of those?"

He kept his voice muted and Piers did the same.

"They're too good looking for the job."

Silent mirth shook Flavio's large frame. "Look who's talking!"

"Okay, I think the dark fellow has a more intelligent and determined air about him than the others."

"And the woman?"

"She looks like a whiner who's already got tired feet."

"I wonder who our Nicole'll pick." He grinned. "She's got good judgement."

The hint was obvious. Except Piers wasn't so sure anymore.

The last applicant left. Nicole came into the kitchen, clutching the forms in her hand just as an insistent honking sounded outside in the yard. Piers opened the back door. A van was parked in front of it, with a radiant Lynne at the wheel. She jumped out.

"There, have a look."

"It's got Flavio's Pizzeria on the sides," Flavio exclaimed.

"Of course it has. It's our new delivery van."

Nicole grabbed her head with both hands. "Lynne! You didn't go and lease it. We can't afford a van *and* a helper."

"I know, that's why I leased it in my name."

A tired smile came to Flavio's lips. "Mrs. B. you are doing too much. You come here to work like a slave and you don't even get paid. I told you to keep your money for your old age."

"Am I a partner in this joint or not? Besides, I have a good pension."

"Do you really want to be my partner?"

Piers pulled Nicole back into the front. "That conversation isn't for our ears."

"You're right."

"About Sunday night,"

"We don't have to talk about it. You've got your life and your friends. I've got mine."

She walked to the desk. He followed.

"I have to tell you what happened."

On hearing the serious tone in his voice, Nicole whirled around. "How come you were so poor and looking for a job, yet you have friends who drive a BMW?"

"At one time, I thought I could belong to their crowd. It looks so good being rich." Piers tried to keep the tenseness out of his voice.

"Being rich sure brings more happiness than being poor. Poverty sucks."

"Happiness doesn't depend on money. There are many things money can't buy."

Gloom came over her face but she made no reply.

"I know you heard Charlotte talking."

"It's none of my business."

"What I want to tell you is that I do care about you-"

She spun away from him. "It doesn't matter. My only concern is that you do a good job here."

Piers bridged the distance between them and took her shoulders to turn her to him. His arms encircled her. "I mean it." He lowered his head and took her lips. She stiffened. He kissed her nose, her eyelids and came back to her mouth. "Charlotte is my sister."

Nicole pulled back in shock. He smiled and drew her close. She softened then stiffened again. His sister!

"Hmm...springtime, I guess."

At the sound of Flavio's voice they leaped apart. Flavio searched for something in the cupboard under the cash register.

Lynne came in. "Something happening?"

No one replied. Lynne frowned but said nothing more.

"I really don't see how we can afford another employee but we have to." Nicole sounded her normal calm self even if her voice wavered.

"Who's your choice?" Lynne asked.

"The dark fellow by the name of Roger Thomas. He's taking acting lessons as well as theater management every morning. If he can start at one p.m. he's willing to do anything."

Flavio and Piers exchanged an amused look.

"How much does he want?" Piers said.

"Whatever we can afford, which is only minimum wage. Not that we can really afford that."

"But his being here will help us do more business. I'll be able to develop the Noon Hour Pizza Run to reach other communities. Already we had some office parties as a result of it. I'll do some promotion. Then I'll work on the restaurants."

"And then?" The words were out of Nicole's lips before she'd time to think.

"Then we'll hire another crew to keep the shop open till two in the morning. I figured that's when it makes big money."

Nicole wailed. Lynne burst out laughing.

Flavio chuckled. "He's right. We always take good money late at night."

Business picked up and they were too busy to continue the conversation.

As soon as Nicole closed the shop, she started walking home without another look at Piers. He caught up with her and took her hand. She pulled it away.

"Nicole, I meant it when I said I care for you like I have never cared for anyone before."

"Sometimes I believe you. I don't know why, but I do. However, I don't want any involvement."

"I'm not asking for anything."

A bitter note crept into her voice. "Give an inch take a mile. A simple kiss can lead where I don't want to go."

"I can respect that."

"Good. See you tomorrow."

They reached their apartment house. She bounced up the stairs leaving a dejected Piers to stare after her. Her brain was about to explode with thousands of contradictory thoughts trying to think back to what she had said. She had told him that she believed him. Yet she didn't. Perhaps she believed that he cared for her. It was just like a man to say that in order to foster intimacy. Or like a friend.

Jack and Betty were very good friends. Betty, with her privileged background, studied accounting so she could keep an eye on her personal fortune and the charitable foundation she had just established. In her own words, having nothing to do was boring. Betty wasn't in the least uppity, but she had that ease of manners and the poise that go with a wealthy upbringing.

Just like Piers. Poise and confidence came naturally.

An orphan like her, Jack had been shuffled round foster homes and had left the system at sixteen. He had worked and saved so he could continue his studies. Yet he and Betty were the best of friends.

It was hard to believe Piers really cared for her as in dating seriously. The memory of his kiss still tingled on her lips. No matter how much she tried, she had been unable to remain passive. Her whole body came alive in a way it never had before. Of course, she hadn't let anyone that close for a long time.

She couldn't determine what her reaction to Piers were. Her emotions kept shifting. She listed his good points. There were many. Reliable, polite, cheerful, and a sense of humor. The man wasn't afraid of working hard for long hours. He was adept at charming the customers. They came back and often ask for Piers. He was generous.

Trying to list his bad points proved more difficult. He never talked about his family or his past. And now he had a sister and two rich friends. Of course, he had arrived with a Gucci bag and expensive clothes. Though, it didn't mean that much. She too had a designer dress, one she had picked up at the thrift store. Although she badly wanted to, she avoided questioning him since she didn't want to be questioned in return.

There was no adequate way to tell a man that she had fled the foster home at sixteen, five months pregnant in the wake of her foster father's wrath. Actually, she needn't worry about that because men never stayed after she murmured the words, "I had a child."

While she prepared a salad, her mind went back to what Jack had said about having a personal life. Since Christopher was born, she had been denying herself the fun of youth. Sometimes she wondered whether it was punishment for the teenager she had been. The naive girl who had fallen for a handsome face and a smooth talker. When she stopped to think about it she had to answer yes. A mountain of regrets assailed her. Only, regrets led nowhere. Nor did they help solve problems.

And somewhere out there was a little boy of hers.

No matter how much she tried to convince herself that he had been adopted by parents who must love him, she couldn't just put him out of her mind. A day didn't go by when she didn't think about him. In her recurring dream he called to her. She had to find out where he was. Then her dilemma would grow even more. One part of her said she mustn't take him away from a loving family. A family who had raised him all these years, not knowing he had been stolen from her. They might accept the fact he was stolen from her... she could never prove it. Her signature was on the papers. Trying to explain she didn't know what she signed sounded lame.

Pain clutched at her heart. Sorrow weighed her down. She had to know where he was. After that, decisions, if there were any to be made, would be taken. When she found him and told the story to the parents, she'd go away and perhaps when he was older, he would ask to meet her. Perhaps they'd let her into their lives.

Since she was used to discouraging any man who showed a bit of interest, she'd carry on as always. Unless the man was loving enough to accept and support her search.

Piers could be that man, but he didn't intend to stay around. He denied it, but she sensed it. There was too much she didn't know about him. Too much she had to take at face value. Too much she had to guess about what was hidden behind his smiling exterior. Of course, she could do a search on him, like any employer would have done. That scared her more than not knowing.

On the one hand, the heartache that was sure to follow if she gave in to him wasn't worth the temporary happiness she'd gain. On the other, she'd never know if she didn't give Piers a chance. There was Jack too. A man she could trust. A man who wanted to marry her.

And this summer she wouldn't even have the comfort of Paula's carefree chatter.

When she arrived at the pizzeria, she found Piers perched on the ladder that Lynne was holding. He struggled to fit the flag pole into the holder above the door.

"Push it straight against the wall then pull toward you," she shouted.

The holder clicked and the flag unfurled. They contemplated it as it fluttered in the light breeze.

"We'll go watch the Canada Day parade in turn," Lynne said. "You two can go first, then Flavio and I will go afterwards."

Nicole nodded. "Sounds good. Then we'll all go to watch the fireworks after we close."

Toward the end of the morning, Ed came in with a young woman. He introduced her as Helma and ordered a slice for each of them. "I brought Helma to show her the art work."

"Everybody asks who the artist is. We should hand out your business card," Nicole said.

"We could have a small box of them by the cash register. Who knows, you might get commissions," Piers said.

They chatted until Ed asked, "Why don't all four of us go for coffee one evening?"

"Great! It'll be Sunday on our early closing night. Nicole?"

She hesitated. "Okay, I'll come."

Piers flashed her a smile that sent a tremulous response throughout her body. And that didn't stop while they watched the parade, jostled by the crowd, nor did it abate during the fireworks display. It took all her strength to close her door on him that evening.

Chapter Twenty-Five

In between customers, Piers sat at the computer.

Nicole looked over his shoulder. "What are you cooking up now?"

"Posters which I'll put around my noon hour haunts to tell customers when and where I'll be."

"But they already know."

"Nearby streets don't, though. If I put up posters, they're sure to walk a block or two for a pizza treat."

"I suppose you're right."

When they strolled home, Nicole wondered if he would take her hand.

He didn't.

During the next few days, Piers was pleasant, attentive to her but kept his distance. Nicole rebuked herself. She wanted him to break the rules she had made. But he wouldn't. Yet in his eyes she often saw what she could only describe as tenderness. Lust too, maybe, especially when he saw her to her door. Whatever his feelings, he controlled them.

Deep inside her admiration began to take root. When he had said he respected her, he meant it. It gave her a warm rush she didn't want to analyze.

Lynne along with Roger ran the Pizzeria on Sunday night so that Nicole and Piers could go out early with their new friends.

After a lively conversation at the Crescent Moon Café they took a walk in a nearby park. Laughter alternated with more serious topics. They finally parted with promises to get together again soon.

The banter and easy camaraderie painfully underlined for Nicole what she had missed all these years. At her door, she said goodnight. Piers nodded. Silent, his intense gaze fell on her face.

A shot of adrenaline ran through her. Her lucidity vanished. She raised her face to him. In a second she was enveloped in his strength and she abandoned herself to the excitement of his burning lips.

Dizziness overwhelmed her as wave after wave of emotion submerged the last of her reason. Her body molded itself against his, vibrant with contained desire. She swayed inside the room.

Cool air wafted over her face. Piers had broken the kiss. Although her body screamed for fulfillment, she was thankful he had stopped. Because she sure couldn't.

Chapter Twenty-Six

At four-thirty in the morning, Piers jogged to the pizzeria, with a detour through the park for good measure. It had been a long time since he'd had a good workout. It hadn't been too bad in the slammer since he was able to use the gym room. His body, used to regular exercise, had been protesting for weeks. Cool air filled his lungs. Exhilaration washed through him, soon tempered by the memory of last night kiss. He had almost carried her off to bed. That wasn't going to happen.

The revelation that she liked him for himself, not his social or financial status gave him a rush of happiness. Her anger hadn't completely abated, but she hadn't shut him out. His steps bounced higher until he remembered he still hadn't told her about serving time. Sobered, he put on speed and reached the shop.

For the next five hours, he worked at making a stack of nine-inch pizzas. Lynne and Flavio came in. Immediately behind them, Nicole appeared.

"Hi Nicole. You're not in class?"

"Classes are over."

Their eyes locked. Nicole turned away. Lynne smiled.

"It's still your day off."

"I know but I may as well come and help after I take Snowflake for a walk. What's this stack? Not orders so early?"

Piers took his apron off. "Samples for restaurants. I've contacted them by phone already."

"Samples? You mean free samples?"

"Of course."

"We can't afford it!"

"They'll put our specialties on their menu and that will pay hundred times the cost of these samples."

Nicole shook her head. "It won't work."

"Of course it will. We could prepare a stack every day and they just would have to warm them up. We could even freeze them."

Flavio howled together with Nicole. "Frozen? No way!"

"It's terrible bad." Flavio was shocked enough to mangle the language.

"Okay, okay. I'll discuss the technical details with the managers. Mrs. B. you got the list?"

"I've got your schedule. I'll do your Noon Hour Pizza Run."

"Thanks again. See you later."

As soon as Piers had gone, the telephone started ringing. Customers came in. Nicole was kept running non-stop. Brows were damp, but all the orders were filled in good time.

When Piers returned, he pitched in immediately. No one talked much. Finally, closing time chimed in with the last customer. Nicole locked the front door and dimmed the lights.

"Let's have a staff meeting," Flavio said. He looked pinched and tired.

"I've made a Picnic and a DeLuxe," Nicole said. "We should eat first."

A collective sigh of relief welcomed her announcement. They pulled up chairs around the kitchen worktable. For the next several minutes they enjoyed the food and began to relax. Lynne produced a bag of oranges.

Flavio teased her. "Here comes the health food."

"It completes the meal," Nicole said. "Our pizzas are a full homemade meal."

Flavio leaned back his chair. "We need more staff. We can't continue at this pace."

"Agreed." Concern sounded in Lynne's voice. "Nicole, could we have a few figures?"

Nicole was already sitting at the computer. She printed a couple of copies of a summary account. A whistle of admiration made her look up. "It *has* been good."

Lynne nodded. "So you don't see any problem hiring two more helpers?"

Nicole suppressed a sigh. "I guess not."

They smiled at her reluctant tone.

"Good. I like to hear that," Flavio said. "Now Piers, tell me about the restaurants."

"I approached independent family restaurants in Otter Lake, Silver River and Porcupine Creek. They have agreed to carry our pizzas daily. Two of them offer Italian cuisine and said the pizzas would fit right in. The others will put it on the menu and I said we'd deliver if customers order."

"How will they carry the pizzas? And what about the traveling time?" Nicole asked.

"*La Trattoria* was the first one I went to. Mr. Leoti was really impressed. He suggested that we deliver three pizzas a day, uncooked, and his chef will cook them as per our instructions."

Flavio frowned. "I don't know if my pizzas should be sent out uncooked."

"They'd have to be refrigerated," Roger said. He had been listening intently.

"We can fit a fridge in one of the vans, though the pizzas can be carried cold in the insulated containers," Lynne said.

"The chef should come here and be trained," Flavio said.

"That's a good idea," Piers said.

"How about the others, what do they want?" Nicole asked.

"Here is the list of orders."

Whistles greeted Piers' list.

"So, basically, we have to make over ten extra pizzas a day, or more," Flavio said.

"The managers, the chefs and staff were all impressed. They wolfed down the samples. It was an easy sale. They're eager to promote it on their menus as it'd make them stand apart from other places by offering artisan pizzas."

Flavio's eyes strayed around the kitchen. "Standing room only. We'll remove the table."

"Actually I thought we should lease the store next door," Piers said.

A stunned silence greeted his proposition. Nicole reacted first, almost leaping from her chair.

"You're out of your mind. We can't afford rent and stay in the black."

A chuckle came from Flavio. "Piers read my mind."

"That place has been empty for years," Nicole said.

"Precisely, I... Flavio could bargain for a lease."

"There's a man after my own heart. He could do it better than me. Piers, you're the one to go and negotiate a lease." Flavio leaned against the back of the chair.

Nicole's eyes flashed with anger. "No way, we cannot afford it. We have to manage with what we've got here."

Lynne cleared her throat. "In fact, the store was for sale but I think the owner gave up."

Roger followed the exchange with an interested look on his face. "The owner will probably be happy to carry a mortgage. He still has to pay tax and insurance on that empty building."

Nicole pushed back her chair. "Where's the money going to come from? We'd have to renovate the place. Already we have to add ovens here."

In deep thought, Flavio rubbed his chin. "Ovens, mixers and fridges."

"We'd better get a loan." Piers' quiet statement brought dead silence to the room.

"How do you propose to repay it?" A flush crossed Nicole's face.

Lynne beat a tattoo with her pencil on the table. "We're selling more and that will continue, and continue even more as soon as we perfect that veggie pizza. We are also getting the workers from the new minerals mining site. They drive two hours to buy pizzas."

"We could drive up with the prepared ingredients and finish the pizzas on site from time to time," Piers said.

Lynn stood. "That is a great idea. Let's adjourn. We need to start early tomorrow."

"I have a week before summer session starts," Roger said. "I can come in the mornings. And my friend Helma said she can come every day, either at eight to clean the shop before you open or before closing time."

Cheers exploded. They stood and replaced the chairs.

"She doesn't mind? For just an hour?" Nicole asked.

"Better one hour than none. She hasn't any other summer job."

An animated discussion of the potential expansion continued as they gathered up their belongings and went their separate ways.

Nicole and Piers walked home together. At her door, Piers held her loosely in his arms. She gave up her inner struggle and responded to his gentle kiss. He strengthened his hold and took her lips with a renewed hunger. Warmth invaded her body. Every nerve ending tingled. Luminous points darted in the darkness under her closed eyelids. She floated into a surreal world until butterfly kisses teased her lips. There was nothing better in the world than this shared sublime moment. He tightened his arms with tenderness. She opened her eyes. Reality intruded.

"Do you really not have a girlfriend?"

"No, I don't. I want to stay with you."

She didn't reply.

He contained a sigh. "I know it's late."

Reason took over. Nicole let the breath out of her lungs. "It isn't that. I'm worried. You are pushing Flavio. You shouldn't make him take on a loan."

"You want him to retire soon, with health and money. The only way to do that is by getting the pizzeria going full tilt. Expansion is the way to go."

"I admit you have a good business sense but what if it fails? What if it can only grow so much? This is a small town."

"We won't fail."

"You did it again. You use *we* all the time as if you were part of..."

"But I am, aren't I?"

"What I mean is that you're not going to stay here forever."

"You don't know. Maybe I want to stay."

"I'd like to believe you."

"Try. Good night, sweetheart." Piers turned and ran downstairs.

Nicole leaned her weight against the door and shook her head. Finally she dragged herself to the bathroom. The shower washed away some of the exhaustion but not the imprint of Piers' lips on hers.

If only she could resolve her dilemma. Finding Christopher was her top priority. It didn't have to exclude love and being loved in return. Such a revolutionary idea startled her. She couldn't possibly be in love with Piers. No one could fall in love with someone who lied the way he did, someone who was just passing through. Women fell in love with men like Jack, who were correct and dependable.

Shortly after she hired him she noticed Piers never again wore the good clothes he had on that first day. Not that was any proof. Maybe he saved them for a future occasion, just like she saved her better clothes to attend school. He hadn't known about thrift stores. In these uncertain times it was only the very rich who knew nothing of second-hand clothes from thrift stores.

"*Maybe I want to stay*," he had said. Maybe he was hoping that a couple of kisses meant she'd relent and jump into bed with him. No, he must have realized she wouldn't consider it without a total commitment. *Maybe I want to stay*. Maybe he really meant it the way she wanted to understand it. That he would stay if she agreed to a relationship. He had thrown himself wholeheartedly into the pizza business. He was capable of commitment of some kind, like developing a business, though, that wasn't the same as committing oneself to another person for life. Also it wasn't his money. If it failed, he'd walk away unscathed.

He was probably like any other men. More lust than love. She had no yardstick to measure the tenderness he surrounded her with. It could just be his inbred politeness. She was aware he wanted her... as much as she wanted him. But he controlled himself. Unless he didn't find her attractive. She ruled that out. She wasn't vain, but she knew her figure was attractive enough to turn men's heads. Even without makeup, her sea-green eyes in the oval of her face drew attention.

The question now was to decide whether she'd tell him about Christopher before or after. *After* what? Her head spun as she reviewed the options. She could let the relationship develop to the point his *"Maybe I want to stay"* became the reality of wanting to stay for her. Then and only then would she tell him about her son. Or, she could tell him now before he made a move. Then she'd know the depth of his feelings.

A wave of cold despair hit her. Piers hadn't talked about love. And there was no reason why he should. A passionate kiss and hand holding didn't mean he had fallen in love. There was a whole side of him she couldn't grasp. And this frightened her even more than her burgeoning feelings. She turned down the bed and dropped into it, with the promise to herself she'd keep Piers at arms length, and well out of her personal life before she got hurt.

The phone rang. As she put it to her ear, she heard the word 'bitch' spoken by a gravely voice. Then silence. Fear invaded her soul.

Chapter Twenty-Seven

Against her own best judgment, Nicole hired two experienced short-order cooks to work shifts, and a part-time delivery girl recommended by Roger.

The rush hour over, everyone collapsed with relief onto chairs. Nicole took out the pizzas she had cooked for their lunch. Lynne brought out a salad.

Nicole was licking her fingers when the door chimes tinkled. It was Piers.

"So did the owners agree to sell us the store next door?" Nicole asked.

Piers nodded. "Yup."

The owners, an older couple, were delighted with the offer Piers made them. The vacant premises had been a drain on their limited resources.

In the afternoon Piers and Flavio put the last touches to their proposal and drove to the bank.

After several minutes reading the business plan, the loan officer raised his steely gaze. "Mr. Bellini, I fully understand your need for expansion. However, your liabilities far exceed your assets. I don't see how we could grant a loan or credit line for such an amount."

"Business goes good since I have Piers Sonder as the manager. He gets better when we have more space."

The man shook his head.

Piers' eyes narrowed. When Flavio was upset, his English slipped.

"I'm sorry, Mr. Bellini. The regulations are-"

"Dang the rules..."

Piers cleared his throat. "Mr. Renfrew, can we start over from the beginning? I will co-sign the loan."

"*You?*" The manager's dismissive glance would have made anyone but Piers feel small.

"First of all, I'd prefer to speak to the director himself, Mr. Leonard, I believe."

"There is no need, I'm the one-"

"No you are not. Anything above ten grand you have to get approval from above. So let's not waste our time."

The authority in Piers' voice clearly unnerved Renfrew. He fidgeted with his pen. Piers stood up. "If you're not going to make the call, I'll ask at the front desk."

"No, no. No need to. You *are* wasting your time. However, I'll put a call through to Mr. Leonard."

A withering glance was all the answer the bank official received. He picked up the phone. A moment later, he escorted Piers and Flavio to the director's spacious office.

Surprised, Eugene Leonard, shook hands and pulled two chairs forward. "Mr. Bellini, Mr. Sonder, please take a seat."

Mr. Renfrew was about to pull an extra chair to sit by the desk when Piers' curt voice stopped him.

"You may go, Mr. Renfrew."

The man opened his mouth at the quiet authority in the tone and threw a glance at an impassive Mr. Leonard. The door closed behind the retreating red-faced Renfrew.

Eugene Leonard speed read the sheet of paper on top of Flavio's file. "You're requesting a rather large amount, Mr. Bellini. What collateral do you have?"

"I'm co-signing the loan," Piers said. He pulled out his wallet. "I don't have any documentation with me, but you can check my account and my credit rating." He plucked up a gold pen from the holder and wrote a few words and a series of numbers on the director's notepad. He then pushed his driver's license and the pad toward Eugene Leonard.

Flavio looked at Piers, curiosity etched on his face. He didn't speak.

Leonard picked up the license, then looked at Piers. His face assumed a puzzled expression. "If you don't mind waiting a minute, I have to verify this." He left the office.

Flavio scratched his ear. "Tell me, how come you have such pull?"

"I have good credit."

"Is that all?"

"Maybe not but I'd rather not go into the details."

"I guessed so. What about you and Nicole? She's like a daughter to me."

"I must win her over, Flavio. I have feelings for her. I respect her..."

"But you're keeping something from her. From us all."

Piers sighed. "I hadn't planned on meeting a woman like her when I applied for the job."

"But why, Piers? Why? You don't need a job."

Pain drew lines on the young man's face. "Why do you say that?"

"I don't know. Instinct, I guess. When you came to us, my guts told me to trust you, though you don't seem to be who you say you are."

A smile came to Piers' lips. "Can you believe there are two persons inside a man, Flavio?"

The older man nodded.

"The other guy in me took off when I started work at the pizzeria."

Flavio chuckled. "Nicely put, Piers. Nicely put. One day you'll tell me everything. Just one thing, don't hurt Nicole." The threatening tone in his voice was unmistakable.

Leonard returned, his features relaxed with a hint of a smile. He bowed slightly as he handed Piers his driver's license. "Thank you, Mr.-"

"Sonder." Piers prompted.

Leonard started but recovered promptly. "Mr. Sonder, yes. Let's proceed with the paperwork. Perhaps you'd like to enter your own details." He passed the wireless keyboard across the desk and turned the monitor half-way, enough for Piers to see it.

"Thank you." Piers typed away thankful the man who now knew his true identity had been discreet enough to keep his mouth shut. It was even smarter of him to get him to fill in the form on the computer himself rather than have him verbally answer the questions.

But this loan wasn't for his benefit. He had to tell Flavio the truth. Lynne already knew. Maybe all this secrecy wasn't needed. Yet Flavio and Nicole might become upset enough and tell him to get back to his idle life and his trust fund.

Leonard printed off the agreement. Flavio and Piers signed.

"Good, you're all set. When is the work starting, Mr. Bellini?"

"The contractor is a friend of mine. He promised me he'd start the moment I give him the go ahead."

Piers grinned. "Like tomorrow."

More handshakes and thanks. Piers and Flavio left the bank and climbed into the van.

"You noticed I upped the loan amount, Flavio."

"I did. Why? Or is this another secret?"

Piers laughed. "No secret. I suddenly thought we need another van. Not a lease because you can't alter a leased vehicle. So we'll buy one we can fit out with fridge, shelf and warming cabinet for the Noon Hour Pizza Run and deliveries."

"Something with a serving hatch in the side you can open up and you have a shop inside?"

"Exactly."

"Good. Really good. So we'll have three vans. The old beater, stubborn Mrs. B.'s and your shop on wheels. We can drive it to the mining site, right?"

"And I have applied for a street vending license."

"And the clerk rushed to give it to you." The lines around Flavio's eyes crinkled.

Piers grinned. "I can't help it."

"So what happened to the silver spoon?"

"You mean the one I was born with in my mouth?"

The two men laughed heartily.

"I knew right from day one that you weren't who you said you are, Piers. You did time, I thought. I won't ask why, where, how, because I saw there was a real man behind all that."

Throat constricted, Piers just managed to thank his boss.

They arrived back at the shop and immediately plunged into the work.

Chapter Twenty-Eight

When the evening drew to a close, Nicole dropped into a chair and turned to Piers.

"By the happy look on your face, I assume the bank approved the loan."

"They did."

"In my opinion it's a dangerous thing to take on a debt. We've just got out of the red, and now..."

"We'll increase our sales and revenues. Will you plan the layout for the renovations?"

She sighed. He always won. "I'd love to. Lynne and Flavio will have to be in on it too."

"Of course they will be. I think you have the best ideas so you should make the rough plan and then they can input their ideas."

"What about yours? After all, it's been your ideas that turned this place into a much better pizza parlor."

"If you'll have me, we could do it together."

She nodded. "Let's take a pizza home. I'll make a salad and coffee." All the while she berated herself for failing to stick by her decision. This was important for business she told herself, aware it was a pitiful excuse for her desire to be close to him.

Piers grinned at Roger, who was cleaning the kitchen. "Will you close up for us?"

"Will do as soon as Helma's finished the floor."

A Pizza under his arm, Piers took Nicole's hand. She pulled it away. Since she hadn't been able to stop herself to invite him, she'd do her best to treat this as a business meeting. He made no comment.

On the way they talked about all the possibilities the expansion would open. Once in her apartment, Nicole slid the pizza into the oven while she prepared the salad. She put yogurt and apples on the table.

After dinner they both pored over sheets of paper, using rulers and pencils to sketch out their ideas. Thrills stampeded through Nicole's body. She was seized by a longing she had never experienced before. At one point she thought Piers was going to throw the papers aside to take her and kiss her senseless. But he didn't.

She admired his self-control and tried bravely to tell herself a strictly business relationship was exactly what she wanted. Many times her determination to keep him at arm's length was in danger of being undermined. His velvet smooth voice interrupted her wayward thoughts.

"You could have been an interior decorator with your tasteful ideas. Why accounting?"

"The security of a nine-to-five job is important to me."

"Is there no security in working for an interior decorating firm?"

"Not as much. It depends on getting new clients all the time. But every business needs an accountant. All the time."

"So you'll leave Flavio now that you graduated?"

She toyed with her pencil for a moment. "I'll stay as long as he needs me, then I'll continue doing his books and taxes for free."

"You're very devoted to him."

It was a statement, but she sensed the question behind it. "Flavio is a good man with a truly great heart. He's been more like a father to me." She paused. "I want to make sure he can retire comfortably." Her features softened.

"He will. The business is flourishing."

Her lips compressed and her voice hardened. "But now you've made him take on a big loan, he's got to keep on working."

Piers smiled gently at her. "Of course not. The loan stays with the business. He can retire at any time without the loan affecting him."

"Why not? He's the sole proprietor, so he's responsible for any outstanding loan."

Piers shook his head. "Not the way we've set it up."

"Is this another of your distorted truths, Mr. Sonder?"

"It's a fact."

"Good because I don't want Flavio to suffer by your fault, or anybody else's. I owe him that."

Piers waited for her to continue. Their gaze locked. "Flavio gave me a job when I was a mixed-up teenager." A crease of pain marred her forehead. "I... I had left home." As the memories came flooding back, she couldn't go on.

"What did your father work at?"

She appreciated Piers' tact. Anybody else would have asked 'why?' "My parents were killed in a plane crash when my sister Paula was only six. I was twelve. We were put in a foster home. My foster father was an autoworker. My foster mother was a seamstress. We lived in Windsor," she added, *Ontario*. "When I came to Otter Lake, Flavio didn't ask any embarrassing questions. He just offered me a job."

"He's a good man."

"He set me up with Susan. She's his friend Aldo's daughter. Susan was looking for a roommate. I'm grateful to him. I worked, saved. When Susan got married, I found my own apartment. It was closer to work."

Nicole braced herself. Now was the time to tell him. Tell him about Christopher and about her abducting nine-year-old Paula. Tell him how they lived in fear for the following ten years. She opened her mouth to speak, but he was already speaking.

"You did well for yourself. Do you mind if I make a last cup of coffee? Then I'll have to go and let you sleep."

"I'll make it."

They both stood and went into the kitchen.

"You said you have a sister. Any other siblings?" This was a good opening to ask about him.

"Just T-Bo. We get along fine."

"And your parents?"

"Happily married."

Nicole sensed he was reluctant to talk about his family. "What do they do for a living?"

"My father works... in a sports store. We don't get along too well. Mom's busy with different jobs."

More questions burned on Nicole's tongue but she instinctively knew Piers wouldn't answer them. At this point, she didn't want to upset the delicate balance they had reached. They still had to work together. To be totally honest with herself, she didn't want to do or say anything that might send him packing his bag and leaving. Not just because he was now the driving force behind the pizzeria's new success but because she wanted badly to see him, talk to him. Now was the opportunity to tell him about Christopher.

"Piers..."

"I know, it's late. Goodnight, sweetie."

A sigh escaped her. He had misunderstood. Maybe it was just as well. She wasn't yet sure where she wanted to go with him. Her resolution kept wavering. If only she could thrust her unwelcome feelings aside and concentrate on the work at hand. Perhaps he'd go away and she wouldn't have to deal with the added anxiety of what his reaction would be.

Of course, he had once said *Maybe I want to stay.*

When he was away from her, whether in his apartment or on a delivery, she had no doubts about wanting to keep him out of her life. But all her arguments collapsed the moment he breezed in through the door.

Dejection wasn't productive. Nicole stretched just as the phone rang. She picked it up. There was silence at the other end. About to put it down again she heard the word *bitch*. Fear froze her. She double checked the lock.

Chapter Twenty-Nine

Piers headed straight for the shower. He and Nicole couldn't spend time together without talking about themselves, their families. The last thing he wanted to do. Living a lie was far too uncomfortable. Pride and the need to prove something to himself meant he'd carry on. But he couldn't confide in her. Not yet. To relinquish his previous privileged life had been made easy by his stay in jail. It was a minimum security facility but there he had seen how despair and greed drove men to cheat, steal and drink. The cursed alcohol which made men believe they could drive better but took lives and left destruction in its wake. Like he had done. Not because of despair and greed but the insouciance of those who don't have a care in the world.

While he toweled himself dry, the resolution to stay at the pizzeria struck him as newfound freedom. For the first time the word redemption came to his mind. He still carried the grief of the tragedy but could now look toward the future. Was it true that fate directed the path people had to take during their lives? He combed his wet hair. Was it a twist of fate that put him on the road at that particular time? Without it he'd never have met Nicole. He'd never have faced the challenge of building up a business. The realization that he had talents and was using them came as a great satisfaction to him, but didn't erase the sorrow he still carried.

A look around his sparse apartment made him laugh. He hadn't even missed the comforts of home. This was home because Nicole was close by. His stomach tightened as her image flitted in front of his eyes.

The next time they had a quiet evening together, he'd talk to her. If she accepted him for who he was now, it would be easier to tell her the whole truth. Then he'd tell his father about his new line of work.

What his father's reaction would be was anyone's guess. Piers had to prove to him he wasn't just an idle waster.

In the meantime, he had to earn Nicole's trust. He didn't see where that would lead him, though. Something had hurt her and she had never got over it. He knew all the signs. The past still haunted him were ghosts that he could never put to rest. He had sworn never to fall in love, but he just had.

Friendship could be a good substitute for love. After all, he loved Flavio and Lynne like family. That wasn't what he felt for Nicole though. Of course, he could be a friend to Nicole without experiencing this wild desire to kiss her. Amend that to go all the way to bed with her. Every day and every night. That was just normal healthy lust speaking. He couldn't shut the voice in his head, *I love Nicole, I love Nicole...*

No, that wasn't love. It had to stop. They were working together and he wanted to preserve their friendly and cooperative relationship. It was necessary. Making the pizzeria successful had become not only a personal challenge but a selfless goal to help someone who had been compassionate and generous.

Piers bobbed his head. Flavio had known on the first day he'd done time and wasn't who he said he was, but he had given him a chance. The same way that beekeeper in the market had seen right through him.

Hey, I should go and buy some honey.

What was the sign? Ames something? Ames Lake Farm. That's right. Could put in on pizza. That's it! A veggie pizza with honey!

I must run that by Nicole.

Sleep canceled reality till morning.

Chapter Thirty

In the early morning, Piers knocked on Nicole's door. "I'm jogging around the park. Want to come?"

"I haven't run in ages. I'm so out of shape."

"Me too. We'll take it easy."

"Just a minute I throw my work clothes in my backpack."

The morning was shaking off the coolness of the night. The sun barely pierced the green foliage. Anemones displayed their delicate white corollas and tiger lilies made a vivid orange splash here and there amid the tall grass.

Piers and Nicole alternated between running and walking. They were still the first to arrive at the pizzeria. Preparation of the pizzas for the restaurants started in earnest.

"Let's work on one thing at the time. We put the ingredients in all the mixing bowls we have. I knead the dough and you roll it out. How does that sound?" Piers asked.

"Like factory work, but it's economical on time. Are you sure they will return the pans?"

"Of course. They're professionals. I've got an idea for a vegetarian pizza."

"So tell me." She let out a sigh.

He told her about the delicious honey from Ames Lake Farm which he thought could be coated on a non-meat pizza. When she didn't jump with enthusiasm, his mood plummeted. They worked on in silence.

"We'll try your veggie pizza when this is done. It sounds good."

Relief flooded Piers. He'll have to remember she took her time to consider new ideas. Unless they cost money, in which case she shot them down fast. He wanted to smile and kiss her but refrained.

The rest of the team came in and each of them took on one part of the job. By mid-morning, Roger went off to deliver to the restaurants. Flavio turned his attention to training the two new cooks until his friend Aldo Egidio pushed the door open in his usual jovial manner.

"Hey Flavio, what do you want me to build?"

"My young people have drawn up plans. Take a look."

"First let me see the building."

Piers took him next door. Then for the next hour, they studied the plans.

Aldo straightened. "So you need more kitchen space. I can make an arch in this wall. No problem."

"What about the sunburst?" Lynne said.

"Oh, it's beautiful." Aldo laughed. "We'll take the wall board down and put it on the wall in the next room. Exactly as it is. When you're looking straight at it, you won't see there is an opening. Okay?"

"Thanks, the sunburst is very important to us."

"I'll put a wall in the middle there, so you have a long room with tables, and the rest is kitchen, no?"

"Yes, that what we drew up. Is it workable?" Nicole asked.

"Of course it's workable. We just put a beam in the kitchen part so the roof doesn't fall on your head. You want to keep the window?"

A chorus of yeses answered his question.

"Good, but we'll make the door an emergency exit. That's code."

Aldo went around with his tape measure and his clipboard. Finally, he sat in front of a steaming slice of pizza and wrote up his estimate. "We'll do the real one in the office, but here are some figures. Friend's price."

They crowded around him. "This is very reasonable. Are you sure that's enough?" Piers asked.

Aldo smiled before switching to rapid Italian with Flavio. The two men laughed and clapped each other on the shoulder. Aldo stood up to go. "I'll get the building permit. We start the day after tomorrow. *Ciao*."

Flavio didn't tell anyone what their conversation had been about, but a half smile remained on his lips for the longest time. For the rest of the day, the topic was the construction and the changes it would make.

On the way home, Piers took Nicole's hand.

A moment of hesitation, then she removed it. "Did I hear Lynne order a new van or was I mistaken?"

"Didn't Flavio tell you? We are buying a van to fit it out with a drop side for the Noon Hour Pizza Run. It will have a fridge and can be used for evening restaurant deliveries."

She threw up her hands. "I just can't believe this. This is just plain crazy. A customized van costs the earth."

"It'll pay for itself within the year."

"I need to enter the details of the expenses in the books. Why do I have this feeling of doom all the time?"

"Everything will all work out." He took her hand again.

Although she heaved a sigh, she didn't withdraw it. "I admit I'm amazed on how well it's been going. Ed phoned to invite us for coffee tomorrow evening."

"We can discuss with Ed about painting the front of the extension."

She unlocked her mail box. Her exclamation attracted his attention.

"Something wrong?"

She thrust her mail into her purse. "No, just a letter I've been waiting for." She didn't elaborate. "If you don't mind, I'll go straight up."

Resigned, he trailed a finger along her cheek and leaned in just enough to plant a light kiss on her lips. "If you need me, just call." He watched her go upstairs.

He didn't start down to his own apartment until he heard her door close. There was some coffee left in the canister she'd given him. He made a pot and sat at the table to eat the pizza he had brought home. A knock on the door made him jump and sent his heart on an erratic beat. She needed him. He opened the door with a flourish.

Chapter Thirty-One

Rob, his upstairs neighbor, stood on the threshold.

"Hi Rob."

"Hi old buddy. Haven't seen you around in a long time."

"We've been incredibly busy."

"I know. Tina and I came to the Pizzeria the other day and found the place buzzing. That's good. It had really gone down the drain."

"We've got a good product."

"That's for sure. By the way, Tina and I just bought a house. We're moving next month. I thought I'd let you know so you could ask Mrs. Harlow to let you have our apartment."

"That's really nice of you. I'll see what my budget can afford. Thanks."

Piers returned to his cold pizza and warmed up coffee. Moving upstairs would bring him that much closer to Nicole. Yet maybe that wasn't a smart move. His gaze trailed around his shoe box apartment. He didn't mind the bare walls, the lack of furniture. Now that he made better wages, he could look into refurbishing the place.

***

Nicole put the letter on the table and forced herself to change before opening it. Preparing her supper took more time than it needed. Her hands fumbled with the utensils. Although she wanted to tear the letter apart, another part of her found excuses to delay its opening. There had been so many disappointments from other adoption agencies, she held little hope that this one, the last on her list, would be any different.

Finally, she slit open the envelope. She only saw one word, *sorry,* and knew the rest would be they couldn't help her.

The letter fell to the floor. Tears she wouldn't shed hurt her eyelids. It seemed she had become emotional ever since Paula had left to go to college. She missed her.

Chapter Thirty-Two

The phone rang. Nicole picked it up. "Flavio's Pizzeria. May I help you?" Her face registered surprise. "Us? You're sure?" She grew agitated. "Alright. Yes, this afternoon, then."

She hung up the phone and sat on the nearest chair. A chorus of voices rose. "What's that?"

"AMKC-TV is coming to video the pizzeria for the Homebred Enterprises program this afternoon."

"Excellent!" Piers looked pleased.

"Did you have anything to do with it?"

"Not the tv. They must have picked it up somehow. I only put in a plug with the *Otterian Gazette*."

"Thanks for telling us."

"I was about to when the phone rang. They must have tipped off MKC."

"The construction isn't even finished," Nicole said.

He shrugged. "Does it matter?"

"It'll be good exposure for Aldo's business too," Lynne said. "I've got to go and fix my hair."

Good humored laughter greeted her words.

"You're beautiful just as you are," Flavio said.

An intense look passed between them. Nicole broke the spell.

"You're the only one who looks good in the hair nets we have to wear."

Flavio chuckled. "They're invisible!"

Piers joined in. "The best part are those butterfly hair pins that hold them."

A wave of protest arose just as Roger came in. He asked what was going on. The prospect of appearing on TV excited him.

"That's great. I hope I'm not on delivery. They usually interview all the employees and I'd like to be in on it."

"Of course you'll be seen. Anything that can help your career. Give a good show. I'll do deliveries if there are some at that time," Piers said.

They returned their attention to the work. Nicole reflected on Piers' last words. What he meant was he didn't want to be seen on TV. She was now more certain than ever he was hiding something. A glance at him as he discussed some technical points with Aldo and his workers made her heart spin. Yet when Jack came in, she didn't even notice him until he tapped her on the arm for attention.

She served him without a smile.

He grabbed her arm. "You're deliberately avoiding me. You go home with *him* instead of calling me."

"We live in the same building."

"You're engaged to me but you hold his hand."

She was taken aback. How did he know? "I'm not engaged to you."

"We're going to marry."

"I haven't said yes. Not yet. I told you we need more time."

"I gave you time to think. We know each other. It's been enough time."

A prickle of fear descended Nicole's spine. There was an aggressiveness in Jack she had never suspected before. "Are you the one phoning me at midnight?"

His eyes went hard. She turned to see Piers standing behind her.

"Sorry to interrupt. You're needed in the back, Nicole."

"Bye, Jack. See you later."

Relieved to have an excuse for getting away, she still worried. Jack hadn't answered her question. In the kitchen, she prepared a topping. Piers came close and took a knife to cut peppers.

"You've been receiving late-night phone calls, but no one talked?"

"Yes."

"Why didn't you tell me?"

"I thought they were wrong numbers, except..."

"Except?"

"The last two ones, someone said *bitch* to me and hung up."

He frowned. "That's no wrong number."

"It wasn't Jack's voice. Slice this pepperoni, please."

"But you thought maybe he did make the other calls?"

"Pass me the tomatoes, please. He can be persistent when he's got a bee in his bonnet."

"What's his bee?"

"He wants me to go out with him but I really don't have the time."

"Do you want to go out with him?" A hint of challenge insinuated itself into Piers' words.

"I don't even give it a thought. Between here and finding time to play with Snowflake, I really don't have time."

Piers gave one of his dazzling smile. "Then that's fine. He needs to understand. But I'll walk you home every night from now on."

"Surely..."

"No buts. Excuse me a moment. Aldo's signaling."

Nicole watched him stride away. Even dressed in fading jeans and second hand T-, Piers commanded authority, the sort that came with breeding and higher education. She had seen it on campus among graduate students. Whether clothes were expensive or cheap made no difference, it was the person that mattered. Piers' charisma had everybody bending over backward for him. Herself included. The image brought a flush to her cheeks.

For a brief instant she wondered what it'd be like to make love to him. Horrified by the way her thoughts were running, she went to the washroom and splashed cold water on her face. When she came out, Piers had left for the Noon Hour Pizza Run. It brought little relief to her tortured mind.

The lunch hour rush wasn't over when a cameraman appeared on the doorstep. From her post behind the cash register, Nicole beckoned him in.

"Hi, I'm Dwight from MKC-TV."

"I'm sorry that we seem to be rather busy at the moment. If you'd care to take a seat."

"If you don't mind, I'll just take a few background shots with customers while you're going about your biz. The real thing as it happens. I'll stay out of the way. The rest of the crew'll be here shortly."

"That's just fine. I'm Nicole."

Dwight smiled and hoisted his camera on his shoulder. He went around the room filming the bustle of activity, even the walls and the outside mural. Still filming he entered the kitchen and began filming the pizzas making. Roger burst in, a big smile on his face. Dwight went out the back door and filmed the van, with Roger re-enacting his arrival. Snowflake ran into his enclosure and hid in his house.

Dwight went next door to film Aldo's construction workers renovating the new addition. By the time he had finished all the background shots, the crush was over, and the rest of the TV crew arrived.

They spent half an hour setting up. Nicole kept glancing at the door. The Noon Hour Pizza Run must be over. Piers should back. What was taking him so long?

He finally arrived and left immediately.

An hour later, the TV people were still filming and still asking questions. Orders came over the phone and Roger went on deliveries along with the cameraman and Ms. Tremblay, the reporter.

"Good, I think we can wrap up here," Dwight said.

Debbie, the producer, nodded. "It was great talking to you all. We have a nice human angle story on the decline and revival of Flavio's Pizzeria. We have shots of the area before your renovations in our archives."

Flavio frowned. "But you haven't tasted the pizzas yet. Please take some back to the studio."

The crew cheered and accepted the pizzas. Curious customers looked on.

"They're hoping to be on TV. Should have come earlier," Roger murmured.

Piers opened the kitchen door and looked in before stepping in.

"The crew was here for two hours, all that for a half-hour or less program," Nicole said. "How did you get the TV interested?"

"They'd seen the van, bought a slice and decided to look up the business. They told me that's how they noticed the pizzeria."

Nicole shook her head. "That was really lucky. And a coincidence. You sure you didn't leave some clues about your whereabouts?"

"Just a word to the newspaper. I didn't know who they were. People come up to the van all the time. I can't see much around me."

At that moment, Aldo called out and Piers went to talk to him. It struck Nicole that Piers was in charge. The construction workers deferred to him, not to Flavio. The worst was that Flavio didn't mind. But when it came to the TV reporters, Piers was conspicuously absent.

Flavio had spoken eloquently about the business he had created. His dignity was impressive. Yet she knew that the real boss at the back of all this was Piers.

Nicole wasn't sure she liked it. In fact, she didn't like it at all. Yet what else could she do when the business was prospering.

Now that there was more staff, Piers and Nicole didn't have to wait until closing time to go home.

"Darn, it's raining!"

Piers' outburst made her laugh. "It does rain from time to time on the prairies. Actually, this is soft rain. You wait until it pours buckets during a thunderstorm."

"I guess I was getting used to the dry weather. We're going to get soaked."

"Here, I've got an umbrella."

"Allow me." He took it from her and opened it, sheltering her more than himself. She looked up into his face. He grinned back and wrapped his free arm around her waist. "Close up like this is much more efficient."

She chuckled. "I'm not so sure."

The rain cooled the air but didn't do anything to quench the fire that burned where his arm rested on her waist. The heat nurtured such a deep yearning that her body began to tremble. She vainly tried to control it.

"You're shivering?"

She was about to reply that it was just the chill in the air. Before she could, he tightened his hold and brought his face close to hers. His warm breath fanned her ear and died gently on her cheek. It took all her self-control not to turn her lips to his.

At her door she lifted her troubled eyes with a longing so deep it was hopeless to try to hide it. He released his hold on her while he put the umbrella in the bathtub to dry. This allowed her to regain some of her composure.

"I'll get us some supper." Her voice sounded strangely detached. Piers joined her in the kitchen.

She turned and brushed against him. "Your shirt's all wet!"

"No big deal. It'll dry."

"Better if it dries on the chair than on your back."

He grinned and shrugged out of his shirt. Nicole hurriedly open the microwave and put in the casserole she'd prepared earlier. A flush darkened her cheeks. She forced herself to look directly at him. There was no way was she going to let the sight of a bare chest rise her inner temperature. Even if that same chest was powerful, with rippling muscles She took a deep, slow breath and pressed the microwave's start button.

In summer she often saw good-looking guys jog bare-chested in the park. So why was a bare-chested Piers troubling her so? The answer was obvious. This handsome male stood beside her in her small kitchen. Much more personal than sighting the joggers in the park.

Not only was it the sight of so much attractive flesh but also a tangy masculine scent that made her blood run faster in her veins.

His voice spoke in her ear. "Something wrong?"

She turned to find him so close that she felt the heat from his body invade her own. When he closed his arms around her, she knew he was going to kiss her. In a brief moment of panic she bent her head toward his shoulder. Fatal mistake. A musky scent rose in her nostrils. The damp skin tingled her lips.

He gently rubbed his chin over her hair. Her barrette, already loose, came undone, releasing a cloud of dark tresses. Fighting her body, she lifted her head to push him back. His lips descended to take hers.

Hot waves threatened to drown her as her arms rose to clutch him. She abandoned herself against his rock-like body. His kiss deepened and she responded with a desperate need. Her hands roamed over his naked back.

He lifted his head. A sense of loss overcame her as she raised herself on her toes to reach his lips again. He swung her in his arms and turned toward the bedroom. She opened her eyes and saw the raw hunger in his.

He sat on the edge of the bed and, cradling her, leaned back. His hand roved the length of her denim-covered thigh.

His voice was low and hoarse. "I want to make love to you."

For a moment longer she clung to his strength, then shook her head. Dizzy with want, she shook her head again. "No. I can't."

With a tremendous effort, he lowered her back onto her feet and held her a while longer against him, then freed himself from her embrace.

Years ago it had started in the same way, with her unable to control her passionate body. Reason began to scream inside her. *Not again!*

Piers kissed the top of her head. "I'd better go."

"You haven't had supper."

"Not hungry." With those words he grabbed his shirt on his way out and was gone before she could protest. She wanted to tell him about her past. Tears sprung to her eyes. He was so considerate. He could have persuaded her easily. She knew she wouldn't have resisted much longer.

But he didn't.

He was true to his word to respect her. A growing feeling of confusion welled up inside her. This was a measure of proof that she could trust him. Yet another part of her refused to. Maybe she should go down to him and explain that Jack had asked her to marry him. If she did that Piers would surely give up on her. In truth she wasn't sure she wanted him to. But she couldn't use that lame excuse. She had to make it clear to Jack that she wasn't going to marry him. Although it scared her, she found it exciting to be near Piers. He occupied her thoughts. His dynamism and his gentleness were infectious. Energy flowed through her when he was near.

On the other hand, maybe she should say yes to safe old Jack. In plain contradiction to her feelings, she straightened her clothes and headed down the stairs to the basement apartment.

***

Behind his closed door Piers ran his hand through his hair. He exhaled a deep and frustrated breath. He then pushed himself off, wasted no time to change into his running gear, and launched himself out of the door. The rain was tapering off to a steady drizzle. He ran in direction of the park. Taking his habitual route he ran fast for half an hour before his body kicked into its normal athletic stride.

He asked himself why Nicole had suddenly backed away. Not through shyness. Of that he was certain. She cringed as if some unnamed fear had surfaced. He was sure she was holding something back. But then so was he. He exhaled a long breath. Tomorrow wasn't going to be easy. They had almost made love.

One thing was certain. She had wanted it as much as he did.

A pang of hunger reminded him he had left the slices of pizza they'd brought home in her apartment. Too bad. A glance at his watch and he directed his steps toward the pizzeria.

Roger was cleaning the kitchen when Piers walked in. "Hey, look at the drowned rat!"

They shared a good-natured laugh.

"The rain's stopped now that I've finished my run."

"Don't you go to the gym?"

"Are you kidding? With what they pay us in this joint, I can't afford it."

Cloth in hand, Roger propped himself against a table. "The business is doing better, though."

"It is. Since I'm here, I wouldn't mind a slice if you got any left."

"Help yourself. I made one DeLuxe to take home."

They closed shop and sat in the kitchen to eat.

"So how is it going with Nicole?"

Startled, Piers dropped his slice. "What do you mean *going with Nicole*?"

"I see the way you devour her with your eyes and how she tries hard not to look at you."

Piers sighed. "I didn't know it was so obvious."

"So?"

"Stalemate. She needs space and time."

"That's why you're jogging in the rain."

Piers laughed. "You could make a song out of that."

"Yeah, in my next life."

"I'll jog back home."

"I'll walk. So long."

They parted. When Piers arrived at the apartment, he glanced up at Nicole's windows. All dark.

Chapter Thirty-Three

After a listless night, Nicole packed her work clothes in a backpack. A long run before getting to the Pizzeria would calm her rattled nerves. Maybe Piers too would run this morning. Until now she had enjoyed their morning jog together. Today, though, she wasn't sure she could face him. No, this was not a good time. Then again, she might meet him 'by accident' in the park.

She took the stairs one at a time, slowly. His windows were on the parking lot side so he wouldn't see her. This was about the time he normally left for his run.

Running on her own didn't bring her the peace of mind she looked for. When she arrived at the shop, Aldo and his crew were already at work. They greeted her enthusiastically.

"That's how you keep beautiful? Want me to install a shower in the corner of the staff washroom?"

Piers appeared behind her. "Not a bad idea. Then we could get the staff onto a fitness program. Hi, Nicole."

The banter continued, but she remained tongue-tied. She could see Piers had run this morning. His hair was still in disarray. Her hand almost went up to smooth it. The heat that suffused her cheeks had nothing to do with the run.

This couldn't work. They'd been on the point of making love last night. Now, he greeted her as if nothing had happened. To her, this was a sign that he, like all men, had only sex on his mind. They could take a woman to bed and next day, for them, nothing had changed.

Fortunately, she got so busy the moment the shop opened she had no time to dwell on her disastrous evening. Though she had first refused to make love, she had then changed her mind and gone down to him. To her dismay, she had discovered he was not in his apartment.

The amazement that Piers could be so casual about what had happened between them stayed with her. The more she thought about it, the more it proved her right. He was a typical man driven by lust. It was so much a man's thing to whisper *I want to make love to you.* Admittedly, her resolution to keep him at arm's length crumbled last night, but never again.

She'd seize the first opportunity to tell him about Christopher. If nothing else, that would cool his ardor. Her thoughts strayed to Jack. He was so restrained about his needs. She could never imagine him saying "I want to make love to you."

The Otterian Gazette reporter and photographer arrived mid-morning. The article would appear before the TV program. It was all good for the business, They insisted on a staff picture. Everyone, including a couple of customers, crowded together. Although Nicole did her best to be at the opposite end from Piers, they ended up being pushed side by side until the phone rang and he slipped out to answer it.

All day she watched Piers come and go, and answer questions from the building crew. His acting as the boss still irritated her. Yet she had to admit he filled the role superbly. Up to now, she had been the one in charge. She wasn't sure she liked being sidelined.

She picked up her bag and said her goodbyes all round. She took the time to feed her dog and play with him. Piers wasn't around and she was glad to walk home on her own. Her relief didn't last two minutes. He caught up with her and fell into step at her side.

"Thought you could give me the slip, did you?"

"I didn't see you." Her cheeks turned red. She chided herself for showing her emotions so easily. Maybe he'd think she had tried to sneak away without him noticing. He couldn't possibly know that his voice had a soft intimate caress when he spoke to her and that it made her lose her head, well almost. He exuded a sexiness that went right down her spine.

Piers looked at her and reached for her hand. Evasive, she switched her shoulder bag to his side.

He dropped his hand.

"We agreed that I'd walk you home every day. Had any more phone calls?"

"No. It obviously wasn't anything."

"Don't be so sure. By the way, the newspaper article will appear on Tuesday."

"And the TV on Wednesday. That's close. Wouldn't it be better if it could be a week later?"

"That's called a publicity blitz."

"Do you realize that Thursday is a two-for-one day?"

"It did cross my mind. We'll start early. Aldo promised enough of the kitchen would be finished by then."

"That'll help."

They'd arrived and Nicole promptly took her leave.

"Nicole..."

She waved without looking his way. "See you tomorrow." She was already half way up the stairs. Her heart beat too fast. Her body prickled from a heat that had nothing to do with the air temperature.

Though she promised herself to tell him, she was too unsettled to let him into her apartment. Her feelings were no longer so confused. Being honest with herself wasn't difficult. Despite her misgivings and resolutions, she was aware she had entered a new phase in her life.

She was in love with him.

Her dilemma grew more intense. She had to stop herself from loving. Not something she realized was possible, but perhaps she could hide it. As long as Piers didn't know she loved him, he wouldn't press her.

Unless, of course, she played safe and married Jack.

The dice were loaded in Jack's favor. He knew about Christopher, accepted her search, and actively helped her. He wanted to marry her. Like every other men, he didn't say he loved her. Perhaps men took it for granted that if they asked for a woman's hand she'd assume he was in love with her.

Nobody else at the pizzeria seem to notice the ease with which Piers commanded everyone, an efficient CEO. Nobody was surprised that he had taken to overseeing the renovations right from day one. She had entered the loan into the books, and she knew that no bank would have lent that amount of money against Flavio's assets. Flavio and Piers remained closemouthed about what had happened that day. A dazzling smile and an overload of Italian charm was not enough to sway a bank manager.

Unless that manager was a woman.

A sigh that sounded more like a sob raked her chest. She'd end up an old maid after all. Before that, though, she'd find out what had happened to Christopher.

The phone rang. She looked at it with apprehension. Too late to wish she had an answering machine. Too late to wish for a cell and voice mail. With a hesitant hand, she picked up the receiver. No one was on the line. She thrust back the phone onto its cradle and bit her lip. There was a knock at the door.

Perhaps it was Piers? Her hand on the knob, she was about to turn it, when instinct took over. She looked through the peep hole. There was nobody on the other side. Uneasy, she chewed her lip then turned the deadbolt.

Chapter Thirty-Four

Piers grimaced all the way down to his apartment. This was a ridiculous situation. He had to tell her who he really was and why he was there. She'd be angry, of course at not being told the truth from the start. Eventually she'd calm down. Though he didn't think that would make any difference. If she didn't trust him in his present persona, she wouldn't trust him any better if she knew his story, not after he lied for so long. The passion she had demonstrated the night before still made him dizzy. How could they go on from there? Only if he told her the truth.

The memory of Tracy's death floated up from his subconscious. The old pain gripped his heart again. Although not in love, he'd been thrilled and ready to marry her when she announced her pregnancy. She wanted a passionate adventure, not a family. Until tragedy struck.

Nicole was different from other women he had known. But she couldn't possibly love him. It must have been hormones speaking. In fact, the more he thought about it, the more sense it made. He had seen how quickly she regularly dismissed male advances. The only reason things had progressed that far between them was because of their closeness at work and living in the same building.

Although he swore to himself he wouldn't get involved with her, he couldn't help but love her. How he would like to start all over, meet her without falsehoods, and see where it led to. Then she'd trust him. Now, he was at a loss to know how to win her trust.

The simplest way would be to confess everything. Eyes closed, he let himself dream of her.
***

The morning was young when Nicole awoke. Breakfast of milk and a banana didn't take long. She didn't like to run on a full stomach. She'd eat when she'd arrive at the pizzeria. After much hesitation, she went out. Not five minutes into a jog in the direction of the park she heard footsteps behind her. A momentary fear gripped her. Although the morning light was already putting gold touches to the tops of the trees, there weren't many people around.

A quick glance over her shoulder erased her worries. Piers was gaining on her. Except for a brief greeting, they ran in silence. They arrived at the Pizzeria where Aldo hammered away and sang at the top of his powerful lungs.

Moments later he stopped. "I'll hang the door in just a moment and your shower will be ready."

Nicole's jaw dropped. "You were serious... but—"

Aldo jerked his thumb in Piers' direction. "The boss said to finish the shower first."

"The boss, huh?" Her eyebrows knitted together.

Piers laughed. "Go on. Be the first. Christen it."

She threw him a dark look. The boss! But she couldn't resist the attraction of a shower after a run.

Saturdays were always busy and many children came into the shop. Nicole's eyes always scrutinized every little boy who looked about nine years old. Although she knew Christopher would never be among them because he had been adopted in distant Toronto, her eyes avidly picked up small details. Like that she could imagine him. She had been doing that for years, observing the regular customers' children. It was a while before she noticed Jack standing in the corner by the window.

"Jack, have you been waiting long?"

"Not long. I forget time when I watch you."

She chuckled. "Good job we don't work in the same place. Did you want to order something?"

"Betty's having a small party tonight. I wanted to take along a pizza. I was also wondering whether you'd be free to come. You know? On a date."

Nicole smiled. She almost told him not to be so pompous. Maybe he was shy and tried to hide it. That would explained the aggressiveness he had displayed the other day. Piers appeared at that moment with a cloth to wipe down the tables. He looked at her and she reddened. Annoyance swept over her. The tables had already been cleaned. He did that because he didn't like Jack. It was so obvious. About to refuse Jack's invitation, she changed her mind.

"Thanks, Jack. What time should I come?"

"Whenever you're free. We're getting together at about seven."

"Then I'll be there shortly afterwards."

"Would you like me to come and pick you up? I don't have a car yet. We can walk."

"No need to. I'll meet you at Betty's."

A murderous look filled Piers' face. Nicole saw it and reddened again. She handed Jack his pizza and saw him out the door.

It was close to seven when Piers returned.

Nicole shouldered her pack and said goodbye. Piers held up his hand.

"I'm walking you home. I guess you want to change." His tone was flat.

"It's alright. I can manage."

"Of course. So I walk you home. Then I'll call you the cab. And you'll take it to come home after the party."

Her frown would have cooled anybody else. "Bossy, aren't we? I've lived a long time in this town. I'll walk."

He opened the door for her. "Practical is the key word. Walking takes too long, and you want to get there early enough."

She had no rebuttal for his argument. A shiver of fear ran down her back. After the previous night phone call and phantom knock on the door, she didn't want to argue. Once in her apartment, she changed her mind about going to the party and almost phoned Betty. The little blue dress hung in her closet like an invitation. The memory of wearing it for Piers tugged at her heart. She moved the dress aside and reached for a pink tank top with its matching short sleeve cardigan. That and her best jeans would do. Her hair fell to her shoulders. At the last minute, she grabbed a hair slide and gathered the shiny mass more formally.

Piers waited for her by the taxi. He handed a bill to the driver and leaned in to say a few words.

"Piers, I can pay."

"I know. Have a good time." He closed the door and watched the cab drive away. He saw her turn her head. He waved.

Now that she was gone he could vent his wrath. How he would have like to punch that idiot who stood for half an hour in the shop undressing her with his eyes. *The jerk could have come to pick her up with a rental or the cab. The only taxi in Otter Lake was not that busy. In my world, if you invite a girl, you pay. But he probably didn't even think about it.*

Then he scolded himself. The man was a better prospect for her than he was. The guy would probably end up by marrying her.

Piers went back to the Pizzeria. He didn't have to but he couldn't face his dingy lodgings while thinking about Nicole and Jack. Besides, he had no real food in his fridge.

Aldo was on his own putting the finishing touches to the renovations and welcomed Piers' help.

"So, you need to expend some energy?"

"I find it very relaxing."

The big man chuckled. "Maybe I could hire you full time, hey?"

Piers pointed to the hatch. "I did it all."

"I know. Flavio told me. And it's even square. What I like best are the fancy half-moon decorations. Takes a good hammer to miss the nails."

They laughed heartily and got down to work.

Chapter Thirty-Five

When Piers arrived home, Nicole's windows were dark. Despite his fatigue, he couldn't fall asleep. His ears strained toward the stairs. It took a supreme effort for him not to go and wait for her by the main entrance. Unless she was already home.

In the morning, Piers lingered in the lobby, idly studying the mail boxes. He waited a long time for her door to open.

She came downstairs and halted on the bottom step. "Waiting for me?"

Her bright and chirpy tone brought a smile to his lips. "Caught in the act. How was the party?" What he really wanted to say was: *Did the jerk bring you back in the cab? Did you kiss him?*

"Nice and quiet."

"And did you take the cab after?"

"Are you my angel guardian?"

"I care for you. Does that make me your guardian? Though, I wouldn't mind if you'd let me."

"Well, I'm a big girl. As a matter of fact, I did take the cab home. It was idling by the curb." She stopped talking and looked at him frowning. "Did you tell the driver to wait for me?"

"I gather he doesn't have that many clients."

"Taking over again. Anyway, thank you."

A jolt of happiness caused Piers to miss a step at the news that Jack hadn't bothered to see her home. It could be she hadn't wanted him to. That didn't tell him though whether he kissed her goodnight. The idea gnawed at his stomach.

They talked in a friendly manner, though Piers noticed that she made sure to leave a space between them.

Customers came in non-stop. During a pause, Piers wiped his forehead. "Wow, that new Picnic pizza is a hot favorite."

"I wonder if it's because people associate the word picnic with an outing to the lake," Nicole said.

"It sure looks like it. We sell more of those over the weekend. Mrs. B. you're a genius for naming it."

Lynne smiled. "No flattery, please. I came up with the name but you invented it." She turned to Nicole. "To change the subject, my neighbor has finished some more baby clothes for your charity."

"Oh, thanks! The Safe Home shelter has just welcome a young woman and her newborn baby. I was intended to go shopping for her," Nicole said.

Piers took two steps back. "I guess I'd better find something to do some place if the talk is about babies and shopping."

They laughed as Piers made his way to the back of the shop. They couldn't know that even after more than three years, talk of babies brought a deep sadness to him, no matter how much he suppressed it.

Customers came in and kept everyone busy.

In the afternoon when the two shifts met Flavio called a special staff meeting. A tray of dainties appeared on the table for all to share.

"The good news first." He looked at Nicole who nodded. "Everybody gets an immediate two percent raise."

Cheers and laughter rocked the kitchen.

"As you noticed I don't work so many hours now. Have you any suggestions that would make your work easier and more profitable?"

The babble of voices rose until Piers called for order. "Perhaps we could improve on how we work around here. At the moment, everybody does everything. It'd be more efficient to specialize the jobs. Division of labor, that is unless a crush happens in which case we all pitch in, regardless."

Quiet returned and all heads turned to him.

"What are your preferences? It's important to do the job you like best."

Nicole leaned back in her chair. There he was doing it again, taking over. The door chimes tinkled. She jumped up to deal with the customer. She rejoined the discussion as they were brainstorming about a more efficient way to pass orders from the front counter to the kitchen.

"Unless we put a wire and a pulley between cash register and kitchen with clothes pins to hold the paper, we'd better go with a computer and a printer."

Nicole scowled at Piers. "Spend, spend and spend again."

"Have we not made what we spent on outfitting the vans?"

"Okay, we did. It's just I'm always fearful of yet more outlays. We have no reserve." The admission cost her. She couldn't help it. For years she'd managed so carefully both her personal finances and those of the pizzeria that it was hard for her to think about risking any funds at all. Even if she knew the returns were bound to be healthy. Not for one moment did she forget the burden of the large loan.

"Trust me. It'll work."

She sighed. Again, *trust me*. From the business point of view, she did trust him. "Alright, explain."

"We'll change the cash register to an automated computer register. You enter the order, take the payment all in one, press the print button and the printer in the kitchen spits out the order."

"You mean one with a button for each pizza?"

"No, that's just too limiting. We'll code the topping ingredients and you enter the code on the pad. There are always customers who have a special request. In that case, you type it in. The computer will keep track of pizzas, cheese biscuits and any other products we might offer. It'll give us statistics."

"What about customers who need a receipt?"

"How many do you get a day?"

"None really, but I had one several weeks ago."

"All you need is a pad with our letterhead, and we can write it by hand," Lynne said.

"Actually, we can print two receipts from the terminal since it is likely the payment will be made by debit or credit card."

Laughter punctuated the lively discussion about what job each of them liked best. Piers glanced around the table. "So you're happy with your positions?"

They nodded. Nicole raised her eyebrows in his direction. "Why was I squeezed out of the pizza making? What am I supposed to do now?"

Piers smiled. "You have your own office in the extension, and you'll spend the rest of your time supervising the new shop."

A stunned silence greeted his words. Then Flavio burst out laughing. "So, you do want to open another pizzeria?"

"Two actually, so that Flavio's Pizzeria covers the countryside in a triangle."

Nicole took her head in her hands. "He's crazy!"

A few seconds later, she straightened up. "But he's right."

"There's a former steakhouse for lease, in Silver River," Roger said.

"Is that the Olde House of Steak building?" Lynne asked. "I know it. The owners retired."

Helma, always a bit shy, pushed the folded newspaper across the table. "There are units available in the new strip mall in Porcupine Creek."

"Perfect."

Between phone calls and walk-in customers, plans were sketched for opening the first of the two new outlets.

A well-dressed man and woman came in. Piers stood up. "My turn to serve."

The couple ordered slices to eat-in. With his usual flair Piers entertained them, offered them bottled water and left them to their food. Four different flavors which they shared while talking.

The moment customers came in, the staff hushed their voices.

"We have lots of ideas now thanks to you all," Piers said. "Anything else you think of, we can discuss next time there is a lull."

Nicole took her dog for a walk while she waited for Piers to finish up.

Finally, he came into the rear yard.

Nicole gave him a critical stare. "Tell me, why were you so eager to serve that couple this afternoon? You were so intent I thought maybe they were more of your so-called *friends*." The caustic emphasis on the last word was deliberate.

"I don't know. Something about their uppity look made me think they were inspectors of some kind. Either that or reviewers. I should've let you go and deal with them. You're very good with customers. For some reason I felt I needed to explain the pizza business to them."

She sighed. "Your instincts have been successful so far."

"We'll see."

They entered the apartment house.

Piers paused at the foot of the stairs. He scratched the back of his neck. "I've run out of coffee again."

"You're just fishing for an invitation."

"I promise I'll be a good boy."

A smile came to her lips while a battle raged inside her. "Do you always get your way? No don't answer that." She opened the door.

The evening passed rapidly until the phone rang. Nicole jumped up, a worried look on her face.

"Aren't you going to answer it?" Piers asked.

She nodded and picked up the receiver, but didn't speak. Her faced paled. At Piers' questioning look, she shook her head. He stood and grabbed the phone from her.

"Hello, buddy, how are you tonight?"

A distinct click was heard, and the line went dead.

"Did someone say something?"

He raised his eyebrows. "No, but now the creep will think that I live here and shouldn't bother you again."

"I hope that does the trick."

"You had more of those?"

She nodded. "And a knock on the door."

"But nobody there, right?"

"Correct, but I thought afterwards I was a long time going to the door. Mrs. Harlow could have knocked and thought I wasn't at home.

By the time I looked through the peephole, she'd have gone home. It's only a few steps to her suite."

"I don't like that. We should call the police."

"We've got nothing to go on. Don't worry. I won't open unless it's you wanting coffee."

They chuckled. True to his words Piers merely squeezed her hand when he took his leave. She raised herself on tiptoes and looked into his eyes. Her lips reached his as powerful and as brief as a shaft of lightning. She closed the door after him.

Her mind spun out of control. What was she doing? She hadn't been thinking. Definitely not thinking. There was a way to remedy that. For the next few evenings, she'd try social media groups in her search for Christopher. It took forever to comb the groups' archives. It'd distract her from thinking about Piers.

With this resolution in mind, she prepared for bed. Sleep didn't come. The empty phone calls bothered her more than she wanted to admit to herself. Unless it was Jack. He was shy. Maybe he wanted to speak, but hung up. That must be it, unless his male lust was finally overcoming his reserve.

Chapter Thirty-Six

As the door closed behind him, Piers stared at the paneling and the brass number plate. Finally, his brain clicked into drive and he made his way down to his own apartment.

Maybe that's what it would take. Be a real friend to her and let her take the initiative. At least until he could see they were getting somewhere. His moves would have to be subtle. Nicole was prickly. Yet there was a different person underneath that defensive exterior. The mystery of what lay beneath the mask intrigued him. He mentally chastised himself as he remembered his vow to respect her.

How unlike this was from the dating game with his crowd back home. Even so, it wasn't much different. Lust drove him then as it did now or was it just lust? Nicole was vulnerable and that prevented him from taking advantage of her. Though he had never taken advantage of any defenseless woman. Of course, he seized every opportunity that offered itself, except there weren't really many, to be candid. Young women had ideas of their own. After he eliminated those who were after a wedding ring and his trust fund, the pool of available women was drastically reduced. Anyway this was a long time ago. In his former life. But Nicole... she was different and he loved her. He didn't know what love was until Nicole. Now he knew it wasn't just jumping into bed.

Because of the thoughts cascading through his brain, sleep eluded him. He switched on the light, snatched up the pad he had brought from the shop, and studied his notes. For the following two hours, he wrote and planned the setting up of the second pizzeria in time for Labor Day. A smile floated on his lips as he imagined a third Flavio's Pizzeria. Then one more in another town, and more again in the neighboring province. There was no limit to dreams.
***

If someone had asked Nicole whether she believed in miracles she'd have replied in the negative but would have qualified her answer with "But Piers can make them happen." The negotiations for the second pizzeria went quickly and smoothly. He worked from early in the morning to late at night. She began to resent it until he assigned her the decorating of shop number two.

"Why do you think you can order everybody around?"

His arms fell to his side. He pulled a face. "I did say please."

"Don't twist what I said."

He took a deep breath. "Alright, I do it because Flavio can't. Even though his recovery is going well, this is beyond his strength."

"We didn't need another outlet in Silver River. People love to drive out and come here. Then the restaurant will order from them so we lose that custom."

"We have to admit that it is driving us crazy to prepare the pizzas for the restaurant. And Flavio still isn't happy about having the chef finish and bake them."

"True. So the new manager will be trained by Flavio, is that the idea?"

"Exactly. As I explained before, there's a huge potential for the type of business we run. Artisan pizzas. That's unique. When it comes to food, people are more critical than we usually give them credit for. They might grab a burger on the road, but when they want real food, they come to us."

A sigh escaped her lips. "And our pizzas are better. I know that."

"Therefore, we have to exploit our strength."

"People drive here from Silver River. Now they'll go to the new pizzeria. Loss of business here."

He shook his head. "We're overwhelmed even with the extension. Since we appear on TV and the social media ran with it, we don't have enough hours in the day. And, now the tourist bureau has included Otter Lake as THE place to visit for pizza, biscuits and music, we'll be working twenty-four hours in the summer with the music festivals."

A note of apprehension seeped into her voice. "How are we going to pay the new staff?"

"Same as here, with the proceeds."

Nicole was about to retort something just as Flavio and Lynne came in. They glanced at Piers, then at Nicole. Piers shrugged. Tight-lipped, Nicole went out front to serve a customer.

Piers caught Lynne's eye. "Mrs. B., do you think I could borrow your car? I want to drive over to Silver River."

Lynne handed him her keys. After he left, she went and stood next to Nicole.

"Okay, what's bugging you?"

Nicole looked at her hands. "Nothing. Why?"

"You've not been your usual smiling self lately."

"I think Piers is going too far with this expansion nonsense." The words blurted out in an accusatory tone.

"Ah, Piers!" Lynne waited for Nicole to continue.

"I just don't know what to do. He's a liar, but then I am, too."

A silence stretched between them, interrupted only by the door chimes.

"We've got to get rid of those annoying bells now that we always have someone at the front counter," Lynne said. "Come and have dinner with me after work."

Nicole nodded and work resumed until Piers came in with a handsome young man. He introduced him as Vinny Devoz.

"Nicole, would you do the formalities? I hired Vinny to do the Noon Hour Pizza Run."

"I thought we were supposed to discuss all new applications."

Piers made a gesture of looking contrite. Instead of apologizing he grinned. "I met Vinny outside the community arts center where he'd just been singing. I had to offer him the job before someone else grabbed him."

"Are you crazy? We're not in the music business."

Although Nicole let her anger show, she couldn't help but recognize that Vinny seemed like a good choice. Magnetic charm radiated from his whole person. His good looks would appeal to customers. His amused air showed he could take flak without bending.

Vinny grinned at her. "Ms. Desmond, look at it this way. If the customers are slow in coming, I can string them a tune on the guitar. That should attract some attention."

His smile defeated Nicole. She had already recognized they needed someone. It was the way Piers had gone about it that irked her. "Okay, fill in this form, please."

Chapter Thirty-Seven

"Girls night out? Go my beautiful ladies. I'll stay and do your two jobs." Flavio dismissed Lynne and Nicole with his usual good humored banter. He reached for Lynne as she went past and enveloped her in a quick bear hug.

A short drive took them to Lynne's home. Nicole got out of the car and looked at the white two-storey house, surrounded by a profusion of flowers and berry bushes.

"It's so nice to have dinner in a real house rather than an apartment."

"You never go out?"

"I've been concentrating on my studies."

"I've noticed you decline invitations."

"If you mean invitations from male, yes. I haven't met one who was interested in a serious relationship. Anyway, I'm not ready for one."

"Even with Piers?"

"Especially with Piers."

The two women entered the house. In the kitchen, while they prepared the dinner, Lynne gave Nicole a searching look. "Has he made a move? Not that it's any of my business. Though if you need a sympathetic ear, I'll lend you one."

"I like him a lot. Maybe, I even...." She cut short her words. Her eyes became misty.

Lynne finished for her. "...even love him?"

"I'm stupid."

"You're not at all stupid. You're a woman in love. For the first time maybe?"

Nicole sighed. "Can you believe you're in love and yet later you find out it's not really love after all?"

"Many people experience that. Some more than once."

"I was in love when I was fifteen. Really believed I was." She told Lynne about Christopher and the dream that haunted most of her nights.

"Does Piers know?"

"I haven't told him."

"Is this why you have been giving him the cold shoulder?"

A half smile spread over Nicole's lips. "We manage to work together. We used to run to work most mornings. We don't anymore. He goes much earlier than me. I make no attempt at getting up before dawn. We're polite to each other. Occasionally we've had dinner or coffee together, but since..." She stopped and blushed.

"Since he kissed you?"

Nicole shook her head. "Since *I* kissed him."

Lynne laughed. "Way to go."

"I don't want to enter a relationship, not while I'm looking for my little boy."

"Nicole, why do you do such a thing? What make you sure Piers wouldn't support you in your search?"

"What if I found my son and his adoptive parents don't want him anymore? What if my rights were recognized and he could be returned to me? Or if at least they agree to visiting rights? I'll have a child. No man wants a woman with a child."

"It depends on the man. Some can be very responsible."

"I know it's not a valid argument. That's why I'm in such a quandary. But I don't trust Piers. That's not entirely true. I do and I don't. He's good for the business. I'll admit that."

"Why don't you trust him?"

"I know deep down that he's living a lie. I can never forget the way Howard lied to me."

"The only thing you can do is talk to Piers."

"I've tried to get my courage up. Right now, he's fully occupied with the business. Unless he's avoiding me."

"Or giving you the space you tried to put between the two of you. You both need to talk seriously."

Nicole brushed her hand across her forehead to repress her weary sigh. "It seems that every time I open my mouth something happens and he isn't available."

"You went out with Jack, that's why."

"Jack is a study friend. I'm good with numbers and he is super in management, my weak point. He taught me how to search the internet too."

"That's what you do together?"

Nicole blushed and nodded. "I help him with the accounting proper and in return I have made progress on management."

Lynne chuckled. "Are you trying to make Piers jealous?"

Nicole stared at Lynne. Her voice shook. "Not in the least. I must admit that sometimes I think I could do worse than accept Jack."

"Has he declared himself?"

"He asked me to marry him. But... something about him..."

Lynne frowned. "Have you reached the kissing stage with Jack? Not that I should ask, mind you."

Nicole's cheeks flushed bright red. She couldn't speak.

"I thought so," Lynne said. "You have to make the first move... before Piers commits murder."

Lynne burst out laughing at Nicole's startled expression. "You obviously haven't noticed the daggers in Piers' eyes whenever he sees Jack. If you've told Piers to back off, he's going to give you enough slack for a while."

"Or, forever. That would suit me fine. In fact, I really think I should ignore the attraction. That's just what it is, an attraction, an infatuation."

A shake of the head was Lynne's only response. Nothing more was said about Piers or Jack. The two women cleared the table and loaded the dishwasher.

"I'm in a real mess," Nicole said.

"I wish I could say more to help you."

"It was good talking with you. I'm going to sit down with myself and give a lot of thought to everything that's happened recently. Even though Piers and I don't talk much anymore, he appointed himself my bodyguard and does his best not to miss an evening."

"Really? That's a new twist."

"I get crank phone calls where nobody's on the other end."

"You must report that to the police and your phone company. They'll trace the calls and block them."

"It's going to be okay. Piers picked up the last call. The caller will think he lives with me and won't call again. Anyway, I'm going home earlier and in daylight now at least for another month or so."

Lynne blew a breath. "I'll drive you home."

The drive didn't take long. Nicole climbed the stairs. For once, her cozy apartment didn't feel as welcoming as before. Sleep didn't come for a long while. By morning she'd taken only one resolution.

She was going to tell both Jack and Piers that she didn't want either of them in her life.

Chapter Thirty-Eight

The morning run in the park held no appeal for her. A fatigue that wasn't entirely physical plagued her. As she went downstairs, she heard a door close which she identified as Piers'. A moment of hesitation then she continued. They met in the lobby. He greeted her with a smile that could charm tigers.

His eyes raked her from head to foot. "No running gear?"

"I'm not sure I feel up to it."

"C'mon, you'll feel better afterwards. I'll wait for you."

"Bully!"

"I've missed you."

"You shouldn't have opened that second shop."

"We're on our third now. I've got a lease in a great location in Porcupine Creek. A small strip mall newly built. The management is doing the alterations to suit the clients. That'll save time."

Her brows knitted. "I thought number three was only a joke."

"Not at all."

"Who's directing all this?"

"If you go and fetch your sneakers, I'll tell you while we jog. We can take it slowly."

"You mean if I don't, you won't tell me?"

He winked. "You'd just have to wait until the staff meeting this afternoon."

"Hang on, I'll be down in a minute." This was the first dent in her resolution to ignore him. And it wasn't just because she wanted to know about the other outlet. His smile had already brightened her morning. A warm wave rippled through her. It reminded her of being a child on Christmas Eve with her beloved parents and her baby sister.

They arrived still arguing at the pizzeria.

"You don't need to hire two managers. I can take one shift."

"You're the personnel department as well as the accounting office. It's a full-time-plus job."

Without seeing the enquiring faces turned her way, Nicole stormed into the shower. Hands raised Piers shrugged.

"I can pour a bucket of water over your head if you need cooling down," Flavio said. He narrowed his eyes to a gesture that would sent cold shivers into any employee, except Piers.

"Thanks no. I'll wait for the comfort of the shower."

Her damp hair loose over her shoulders, Nicole strode straight past him to her office in the extension.

Flavio glanced at Lynne. "Should we tell them now?"

"I don't know. I've never seen Nicole so touchy."

"It'll smooth her ruffles. It's just a lovers' tiff."

Lynne shrugged. "I don't know about that. Let's wait until the change of shifts so we have everybody here."

"I'm an impatient man."

"Really? I'd never have guessed."

With work in full swing, talk became difficult. The noon hour rush over, Roger pushed open the door waving a copy of the Otterian Gazette in his hand. "We've done it again!"

"Done what?" said Piers.

"We got a review on the *Food Around Town* page. Must have been that stuffy couple you served, the other day."

Flavio growled. "Get your vocabulary right, boy. We stuff customers. They are stuffed, but are never stuffy."

Repressed chuckles greeted his words.

Roger shot Flavio a rueful glance. "Sorry, boss."

When all the staff were assembled, Flavio asked Roger to read the review. When he finished applause erupted. Roger bowed with a flourish. Everybody talked at once. Flavio raised his hand to get their attention. Nicole squirmed and tried to move away from Piers who came and stood directly behind her.

"That review stole my thunder," Flavio said. "I have some personal news to tell you."

A hush fell over the staff.

"Mrs. B., here, proposed to me yesterday."

A loud cheer bounced off the ceiling.

"And I have decided to accept."

More cheers and good natured banter followed the announcement.

The smile on Nicole's lips was genuine. "Absolutely fantastic. When's the wedding?"

"Friday," Lynne replied.

"But that's just four days away!"

Flavio chuckled. "I was told I'd wasted enough time, and I agreed. We'll go away for a few days. But now, for the big moment."

The murmur of voices ceased. Flavio pulled a black velvet box from his pocket, opened it and showed it to Lynne.

"You sly old fox! It's such a beautiful diamond!" Emotion smothered her voice. "How long did you have it in your pocket?"

"Much too long. Allow me." Flavio took her hand and slipped the ring on her finger.

Several customers came in at that moment and the phone rang.

"Now you two lovebirds go and celebrate," Nicole said.

Flavio winked at Piers. "You're my best man in business. Would you like to be my best man at my wedding?"

"I'd be most honored."

"Nicole? You'll be my maid of honor?" Lynne asked.

"Nothing would give me greater pleasure. Thank you."

Vinny stepped forward. "Will you have music at the wedding? I'd be real happy to provide it."

Nicole jumped up. There was a way to make amends for her unpleasant reaction the day Vinny had been hired. The young man's engaging personality had won her over a thousand times as well as a thousand new customers. "That would be great. Thanks, Vinny. I've heard you and you're superb."

Vinny smiled. She could have sworn it was relief she read on his face. It made her feel guilty.

The newly engaged couple were moved by the offer. Although they wanted to keep the ceremony simple, they agreed to hold it in the park where the hiking or skiing trails cross each other in a large clearing.

Flavio pulled Nicole aside. "Will you tell *La Bambina*? She can make it, no? I pay for her plane ticket."

"I'll phone her right now. I can pay for her."

"It's my wedding gift to me. So I pay."

Nicole laughed as she watched Flavio squeeze Lynne's shoulder. Everyone returned to work. For a moment, neither Nicole nor Piers moved.

"Finally, they're happy," Nicole said.

"Happiness is there to be grabbed." A look of tenderness softened his face.

A glance at him unsettled her.

"I'll walk you home tonight?"

"I... I'm not going straight home."

His expression darkened. "Another Jack's evening?"

"No. Actually I want to do some shopping. I want to buy a laptop. My computer is outdated and slow."

"Then allow me to carry it home for you."

The velvety tone of his voice send tremors up and down her spine. She had to laugh. "You've got to win all the time, don't you?"

He clamped his jaws shut, then took a deep breath. "Only when it's important."

She looked at him out of the corner of her eye. "You know lots about computers. I wouldn't mind your advice."

He blinked. His smile was as smooth as his voice. "I'll do my best. I need to go over Flavio Porcupine again. I'll be back in time."

Nicole's eyes followed him until Vinny attracted her attention.

"If you have a minute, we could go over what music would be appropriate for the happy couple."

She shook her head to clear her brain from the question that had just popped into her brain. *Why did he look taken aback when I asked for his advice on a laptop? That's what his previous job was.* "Sorry,

Vinny, I wasn't listening."

For the next half hour she and Vinny planned Flavio and Lynne's wedding music.

***

Piers borrowed the cook's car and drove off. But he didn't go to the new outlet. Construction was going well and they didn't need him. Instead he drove to the computer store in the Silver River, where he was less known. It wouldn't do if Nicole found out he had only a limited knowledge of computers. He could use one and was adept with it, but nothing technical. He'd told her that his fictional previous employer had sold PC systems. She would expect him to know a lot more than he did.

After Piers confessed his lack of knowledge, the store owner called his technician. An hour later, Piers' head buzzed with new knowledge. He folded the credit application form the manager handed him. This was a novelty for him - a guy who had always paid cash.

"I'm a one-man business," the manager said. "I can't carry credit for my customers. But the finance company always approves the credit as long as you've got a job."

"Thanks so much. I'll send this in." He hadn't planned on getting a laptop himself. However, with the developing business, he'd need one. That purchase could wait a few days.

He breathed easier on the way back to the pizzeria. As he negotiated the slow traffic backed up by the crossing train, he decided that since credit was so easy to obtain, he should buy a car. Borrowing Lynne's or the cook's didn't reflect well on his status. Not that he minded in the least, but driving a loaner car just wasn't practical.

Perhaps he should take Nicole with him. No doubt she'd direct him to a reputable used car dealer the way she'd directed him to the thrift store. At this moment he couldn't go and buy a new car without raising her suspicions. Besides, he had wowed not to touch his bank account back home in Montreal. In his new persona, that account didn't exist.

Nicole was ready and waiting when he sauntered in. They walked to the computer store. Without overwhelming her with his newly acquired technical knowledge, he helped her make a good choice.

"We'll set it up for you with all the software and apps you need for your business. We'll deliver tomorrow at eleven, ma'am."

"I'm at work-"

Piers lifted his hand to stop her. "You'll be home. You work such long hours. You're due for a break."

"But-"

"No buts." Piers turned to the clerk. "Tomorrow eleven." He gave the address.

After they left the store, she turned on him. "It's okay to manage the business, not my life!"

"Sorry, Nicole. I didn't mean to overpower you. You do spend too many hours at work, and that's fine. Don't go overboard though. One little morning off to take delivery of your new laptop isn't the same as shirking work."

"Damn you! You're not the boss, you know."

"I know. I only want to see you relax and happy. Am I forgiven?"

She shook her head. "Were you a lion tamer in a previous life?"

A rumble of quiet laughter came from Piers' throat. Unable to keep a grudge, she joined in. They stopped in at the Cresent Moon Café.

"I should buy a laptop for myself. There's lots of research I want to do for the business."

"You can always use mine."

"We'll both want to use it at the same time. Probably late at night in your apartment. Too dangerous."

The idea carried intimate overtones. No, not a good idea at all.

"To change the subject, Vinny and I organized a party the day after tomorrow for the staff to celebrate the wedding of our boss and his bride-to-be," Nicole said.

"Very thoughtful. Will you be free tomorrow afternoon?"

"Free for what?"

"Two things. One, I think we need to get a gift for the happy couple. Two, I need to buy a car and I'd like you to come with me to pick it."

Her eyes widened. "You want to buy a car? You don't even have furniture!"

"I'll get furniture some other time. I'm constantly going between our three shops and I can't keep on borrowing other people's car."

"I agree."

"Of course I could get a racing bike from the cycle shop down the street. Matt has got some nifty ones."

She punched him lightly in the arm. "Sure, and cause the biggest traffic jam ever when all the women drivers stop to gape at you."

"In which case, I guess I'd better have a car."

"You shouldn't have any trouble getting credit now that you're getting a decent salary."

"So you'll help me?"

She nodded. At that moment, Ed and Claire walked in.

"You won't believe it. I've got a commission to paint a mural!" The excitement in Ed's voice was infectious.

They spent some time discussing the path Ed's career might take. For the first time in a long while, Nicole relaxed. She enjoyed their easy friendship.

Chapter Thirty-Nine

"The Honda would do you just as well and it's cheaper," Nicole said.

"But the Kia Sedona is bigger."

"It uses more gas. Minivans are for people with kids and dogs."

"That's an idea. We should have one. A dog that is." Piers winked.

"We've got Snowflake. What about a hatchback?"

"Actually the Taurus or the Subaru wagon would be best. They're smaller but it still has room to carry stuff in the back."

"The Subaru and the Taurus are the most expensive. Your tastes really run to expensive things."

"The sales guy said the Taurus is in the best condition and has lowest mileage."

"He says that about every car." Nicole's tone was becoming exasperated. She strove to keep her temper in check.

"We should test drive the Subaru."

They did. They were not impressed. The car salesman handed Piers the keys of the Taurus. The smooth ride and the comfort were a winner. Piers spent the next fifteen minutes convincing Nicole of the quality and the status of such a car. She gave up her objections. After the paperwork was done, they drove the Taurus home. Happiness shone on Piers' face and rubbed Nicole's soft spot for him. For a while on the used car lot, she'd felt as though they were a couple. She chided herself, that was only because the salesman kept addressing the two of them together.

It proved one thing. Piers needed someone to look after him where money was concerned. He really didn't know how to economize. No wonder he'd turned up that day hungry and with empty pockets. If he bought a laptop, she'd better go with him. A glance at his joyful face as the auto purred sent pleasant shivers down her back. His expressive hands gripped the steering wheel. The memory of those hands on her brought a blush to her face.

"Too hot? I'll crank up the AC."

"Thanks." She had to be careful not to let her emotions show. "I was thinking about the laptop you say you need. Will you be able to afford it now you bought a car?"

"I still have a little room on my credit line."

"Can we go and get a gift for Mrs. B. and Flavio? The staff insisted in collecting some money for a staff gift. Flavio Silver also contributed. Then I'd like to call in on the Safe Home shelter."

"At your service, ma'am."

"The staff at Flavio Silver will take turns coming to the party."

This was how the new pizzeria were to be known, Flavio Silver and when the third location opened, Flavio Porcupine. It had been Nicole's idea and had been enthusiastically approved.

"That's wonderful. A good way to bring everybody into the fold."

Shopping didn't take long. They bought a wok set on behalf of the staff, theater tickets from both of them, and a small painting from an itinerant artist at the Farmers' Market.

He carried the parcels upstairs. The red light was blinking on Nicole's new answering machine. Hoping it was Paula, Nicole pressed the button. Her sister's clear voice rang in the room.

"I'm arriving by the eight-thirty plane tomorrow morning. See you at the airstrip."

Piers looked at her questioningly.

"My sister Paula. She must have got leave even though she's only a summer employee. The airstrip is a couple of miles out of town."

"See how indispensable a car is?"

She shook her head and turned her attention to the dinner. No need to ask if he wanted to stay. Piers was already setting the table for two.

Chapter Forty

Ten minutes before Paula's plane touched down, Nicole was pacing the arrival lounge.

"There she is," Piers said.

Nicole was stunned. How did he recognize her sister? She wasn't the only tall, slim and dark-haired young woman to descend the steps of the Cessna.

Paula reached them. For a second or two, she just stared at Piers and he seemed to be mesmerized by her. An elevator dropping down at high speed wouldn't have made Nicole's stomach fall any lower. She took a deep breath and introduced them.

The whole day dragged for Nicole. Paula was in the limelight, bright, witty and bubbling with laughter. Nicole decided dowdy and unintelligent was her lot. A band seemed to be tightening itself over her rib cage. It was obvious that Piers and Paula complemented each other.

What a fool she had been to think Piers might have had tender feelings for her. Her icy reserve put men off. Piers was no exception. The friendliness of their interactions was only due to the fact they worked together. She had understood earlier that she wasn't in his league. How true that was when she looked at him and Paula talking with abandon about books and plays.

When Piers had kissed her, Nicole had believed it was because he liked her and found her so attractive he couldn't help himself. The horrible truth was, at the time, no other woman was at hand. And she had kissed him back! He must have thought her a fool.

Today had been a revelation. Instead of running off to the other outlets, he'd found things to do at Flavio's Pizzeria.

While she put the finishing touches to the dinner, she could hear him in her living room, entertaining Paula. Honest with herself, she admitted that they both had helped prepare the meal. Piers had been the chauffeur and had picked-up two bottles of sparkling pear juice at the grocery store along with a basket full of vegetables and fruit.

He poured as they took their places around the table.

"Hmm, this is delicious. As good as any wine," Paula said.

"Nothing wrong with wine during a meal," Nicole said.

Piers looked at her over the rim of his glass. "I don't drink. It's a personal choice. I don't pass judgement on other people or dictate to them."

Paula cocked her head. "Did you used to drink?"

Piers shuddered. "I've done enough of it and got drunk enough. Then I sobered up."

Nicole caught that haunted look again in his eyes. What had happened to him?

"Good for you. I brought a gift for Flavio. Should I give it to him at the party tomorrow?"

"That's when we'll give them their gifts," Nicole replied.

"Great. I have to catch a flight Friday night. It gets busy at the weekend. Dak is covering for me. Today's my day off, so it worked out well."

Nicole smiled. "A short visit's better than not coming at all. Flavio would have been really sad otherwise." She was aware of the flat tone of her voice.

When dinner was over, Piers got to his feet. "I better let you ladies get some sleep."

After he'd departed, Paula chatted about her work. The knock on the door interrupted her. Expecting Piers had found some excuse to return, Nicole flung the door open.

There was no one on the landing. A cold fear ran down her back. She slammed the door in a hurry.

"What was that?"

"I don't know."

"You look scared. Has it happened before?"

Nicole couldn't help shaking. "Twice."

"What's the police doing about it?"

"I didn't call them. What do you expect their reaction would be when I tell them there's a knock on my door but there's no one there?"

"Knocks on doors don't happen by themselves."

"I'll talk to Piers about it. Since the phone calls, he appointed himself my guardian."

Paula looked horrified. "What phone calls?"

"Same sort. No one on the line. But Piers answered once. So the jerk who phones now thinks I'm not alone. He didn't phone again."

"Any idea of who could have it in for you?"

"None. I don't have any ex-boyfriend."

"What about Jack?"

"He's a good friend. He's asked me to marry him."

Paula's face lit up. "Really?"

"Frankly, I don't want to."

Paula sighed. "Too bad." She yawned. "Okay, let's turn in."

Chapter Forty-One

The party lasted all afternoon, with customers joining in. Excitement ran high. Paula's musical laughter put smiles on every face.

Nicole had never seen Piers so witty or entertaining. Although tempted to laugh, she kept a serene face and stayed behind the counter to serve customers. So that's what it meant to be the life and soul of the party. There was no way she could compete with Paula. Studying accounting and business part-time hadn't equipped her with quick repartee and humorous anecdotes. Her mind worked better with figures and spreadsheets. No wonder Piers preferred to devote his attention to her vivacious sister.

From time to time Nicole caught him looking at her. She'd turn her head. She didn't want to see his expression as he obviously made the comparison between her and her sister.

Toward the end of the afternoon, Nicole escaped to go and buy herself a suitable dress. A new one. She hadn't gone ten yards before a car pulled to a stop next to her, Piers in the driver seat.

"Get in. I'll give you a ride."

"Do you keep watch on my movements?"

Piers smiled. "Just saw you go out. Since you weren't going home, I thought you might want to go shopping.

"I do."

"In the name of efficiency..."

"Okay, okay." She wasn't going to argue. His tender smile awoke the butterflies in her stomach. Did this really mean he cared for her? No, he had good manners and it came naturally to him to offer to drive her, but he had to like Paula a lot more.

Nothing was far in town, and it didn't take long to arrive at the store. Nicole found a knee length sun dress in an aqua tencel, a kind of bamboo material, that draped like a silk gown. She was pleased with her purchase. A refreshing change from her thrift store acquisitions. For a moment, she didn't want to be the dowdy accountant. Her hand reached toward a forest green short dress trimmed in dark red with a matching jacket. Her reflection in the fitting room full-length mirror pleased her.

"What about you, mister best man?"

"I dropped by the thrift store yesterday and would you believe I found a brand new suit and formal shirt?"

"Did you charm a young lady into looking in the back room by any chance?"

"As a matter of fact it was in the back, waiting to be put out on the racks. How did you guess?"

She missed the teasing gleam in his eyes. "Just a hunch."

About to ask him how he could have torn himself away from the party and Paula, Nicole bit her tongue. It'd be bitchy to goad him. If Piers liked her sister so much, he might move to Canmore to be near her. Which would suit her, Nicole, just fine. In her continued search for Christopher, she'd quickly forget about Piers Sonder. Her life could go on without the upheavals caused by having him around.

The evening was a repetition of the previous night except that Piers had called in at a Chinese takeout. Nicole had to admit that chopsticks were fun. Piers was adept with them, proving to her that he was accustomed to dining in exotic restaurants.

Chapter Forty-Two

The ceremony unfolded under a bright sun in the Otter Lake Park large clearing. Nicole threw glances in Piers direction. Another of his killer smiles must have won the park event manager to go extra lengths to help the wedding couple, even providing a white arch decorated with silk roses and additional picnic tables despite the crowd staying for the Beethoven festival. A woman of course.

A pleasant breeze kept the bugs away. Swamped with contradicting emotions, Nicole acquitted herself of her maid-of-honor task. Vinny's repertoire of music varied from the classical to pop befitting every phase of the ceremony.

As the newly joined couple was about to walk down the grassy aisle to the picnic tables, Nicole expected to hear Mendelssohn's *Wedding March*. Instead Vinny sang a touching song with lyrics that captured everyone's attention. A spontaneous round of applause burst from the assembled guests.

Flavio brushed his eyes. "Boy, that was just wonderful. Where did you learn that?"

"I wrote it especially for you and Mrs. B."

"Thank you. It's just beautiful. You've got a good voice too."

To diffuse the emotion, Piers threw his arms up in the air, his voice dramatic. "Blessed be the gifted!" He turned toward Lynne. "And did you realize, Mrs. Lynne Bellini, we can continue to call you Mrs. B.?"

Laughter erupted and the procession resumed toward the tables that had been set under a flower-decked pergola. The Women Institute catered to most events for the benefit of their charities.

Her hand in the crook of Piers' arm, Nicole followed Flavio and Lynne. She didn't dare look at her escort. Electrified jolts shot up her army.

The two people in front of her had decided that real happiness was to be found in being together. She had denied herself that sort of happiness for a long time. Though she hadn't found anyone she wanted to spend the rest of her life with. Unless Piers... There were too many *ifs*.

Jack knew about her child and helped her in her search. He probably wanted to take her to bed too. At least she thought so. There were no sparks between them. She wasn't attracted to him. Then there was his anger when she said she wanted time to think. He never really kissed her, not like Piers did. Heat suffused her face.

Piers awoke long buried sensations. He lusted after her. She'd found it nearly impossible to resist the surge of longing that assailed her at his mere glance. Except now. Ever since Paula's arrival, he had eyes only for her. Nicole's anger directed itself inward. There she was, falling for another smooth talker despite having sworn not to repeat her youthful mistake.

A flute of champagne in one hand and a *canape* in the other, she listened to Piers toasting the newly married couple, but didn't touch his champagne. His wit and Paula's repartees kept the party humming.

A feeling that wasn't physical swelled within her chest. It grew and filled her and threatened to overflow. As much as she wanted to deny it, she had to admit it was love. Sometimes in the previous months, the feeling had snuck up on her, grown and taken over her soul. No matter how much she tried to shake it off.

Denial set in. She didn't want it to be love.

Piers didn't talk commitment and love. There was that elusive side of him which bothered her. He didn't open up about himself, and she couldn't ask questions. Just watching him flirt with Paula revealed his true nature. To think about Jack's proposal was safer. She amended that. Forget about Jack.

No, she couldn't possibly be in love. Even if a while ago she had admitted as much to Lynne. Her physical state was just a normal healthy reaction. Piers wasn't husband material. No matter how much she was attracted to him, she had to take herself in hand and ignore it. Ignore him. There was a lot more to marriage than physical attraction.

Distracted, she was still pondering her problem when the bouquet landed on her shoulder. Instinctively, she grabbed it. Paula kissed her. The guests laughed and cheered and patted Nicole on the back.

Among the amused titter, Lynne had taken careful aim before she'd turned her back to throw the bridal bouquet. Nicole was the only one who hadn't seen it happen.

Flavio and Lynne were driven off in a white limousine amidst the cheering of their friends.

Piers turned to Nicole. "Did you want to stay at the party? I'd like to go and buy my laptop."

"It's late night opening. I'll go with you. We can drop Paula off at the airstrip."

Paula came between them. "Actually, I'd like to stay a little longer. I phoned Dak and he told me to enjoy the weekend. As you know, I have to wait until a Flying Otter Air plane is available. So it doesn't matter when I leave. I'll get a message when the pilot is free."

"Sure," Piers said. "Do you want to come and help buy my laptop?"

"I'm going to party a bit longer. Someone can drop me off at my sister's place."

They waved and walked to the Taurus. For the first time in her life, Nicole was sorry that her sister chose to stay. She berated herself for the uncharitable feeling, especially since she didn't want a relationship with Piers. Yet watching Piers banter with Paula twisted her insides. It came home to her once again how well the pair was matched.

The Comp Tech store owner handed the laptop to Piers. "I'll get the desk kit for you. You're sure you can assemble it?"

"What do I need? A hammer and a screwdriver?" Piers picked up the printer.

"It comes with its own tool, an Allen key. It's not that difficult to put together."

Nicole laughed. "He's a very resourceful guy."

Piers winked at the man. "I guess that's my seal of approval."

Pride sketched over his face, Piers parked in front of the apartment house.

"You feel good about your purchase, don't you?" Nicole said.

"Oh I do. And it's all thanks to you."

"Me? I didn't do a thing."

He paused a second. "You gave me a job when I needed it most."

"And you transformed the bankrupt business into a highly successful enterprise."

He scrunched up his face before smiling. "I take that as a compliment."

"It is. I know I often sound negative, always wanting to put the brakes on."

He laid his hand on hers. "It's understandable. You've shouldered so much responsibility on your own. You did so well keeping the pizzeria going."

Her hand began to burn under his touch. The heat spread to her cheeks. "Let's take these in."

They ferried their purchases into his apartment.

"Yesterday I got a cell. Now you can call me anytime you get the urge." He grinned and pressed a card into her hand. "Here's my number."

The buzzer sounded. Paula was back. She came in carrying a bottle of Perrier and a box of goodies. "The reception wrapped up and we shared the leftovers."

"Great. Any cheesecake?"

"Sorry, Piers. All gone. Only butter tarts and fruit flans."

"Hmm, they're good too."

"First, let us go and get out of these dresses in something more practical," Paula said. "Then, Piers, you'll have to tell me how you came to work for the pizzeria."

"One boring story. How about if we took in a movie?"

"Great!"

Nicole frowned. The clamor *Three's a crowd, three's a crowd* echoed around inside her head. "It's all reruns. I'll pass." Her tone was dry.

"Of course not. You're coming," Piers said. His smile lit up the drab room with its hideous lime-green walls.

She chose to ignore his comment. The two young women ran upstairs to get changed. Nicole wore her new dark green dress.

Paula whistled. "You look beautiful!"

"Well thank you. I'm still no match for you though."

"Oh you are! Piers sure noticed."

"He does that with every woman in his line of sight."

Paula laughed wistfully. Nicole gave herself a mental shake. She had never been jealous before, and she had no exclusive rights to Piers. Didn't want any.

Back in Piers' apartment, Nicole's heart somersaulted if that was possible. He had changed into jeans but kept the white dress shirt albeit without tie. A triangle of skin showed where he had left two buttons undone. He was too good looking for her fragile nerves. Paula pursed her lips and nodded.

Nicole broke the awkward silence. "Let's set up your desk,"

Piers opened the package and took out the instructions while Nicole laid all the pieces according to their numbered labels. Paula leaned against the kitchen counter to watch. When Nicole finished, she glanced at the drawings, and pushed some small pegs into the largest piece.

"This piece goes on top of these pegs."

Piers looked at her and at the wide board. "If you say so, but I haven't finished reading the instructions."

"You don't need to. Just look at the drawing. It's obvious."

Paula burst out laughing. "Men are supposed to conceptualize problems at a glance. My sister could always visualize things faster."

Piers studied the leaflet, shook his head and screwed the piece. "I'm a dimwit. I couldn't do this without reading the instructions. Next?"

Nicole handed him the parts in sequence, and in no time the desk was assembled.

A quiver she vainly tried to suppress passed through her as he efficiently installed everything.

"Let's go to the movies," Paula said.

Outside once more, Piers opened the passenger doors and stood back. Taller than her sister, Paula moved to the front seat as if it were her given right. Nicole sucked in her lips. Then she repeated to herself that Paula and Piers were so well suited they could have each other. She didn't want Piers. Not at all.

In the small theater, Piers sat between the two girls. Nicole bit her lip. The smell of the bag of popcorn in Piers' hands made her nauseous. Whatever was on the screen didn't reach her consciousness. She kept glancing sideways at Piers' head turned toward Paula. He was murmuring words she couldn't hear. Half way through the film she had enough and stood up.

Piers looked up, surprised. "Where are you going?"

His whispering carried an intimate tone about it and sent a shiver through her body. She clenched her teeth. "Washroom."

The red exit light guided her. In the lobby, she took a deep breath and headed toward the ladies' room. Since she wanted nothing to do with Piers, it galled her she should be so het up that he was paying attention to Paula. As far as she was concerned they could kiss themselves stupid in the dark now that she was not around to poop their party.

She took her time, pulled out her little-used makeup kit and re-applied a coat of mascara, eye shadow and gloss. The mirror threw back the image of an attractive face enhanced by the green dress which flattered her trim body and enhanced her dark green eyes.

For a long moment she contemplated herself wondering what was missing. Like her, Paula had long black hair and green eyes, though her own were speckled with gold. The same regular features adorned both of them. Though when Paula entered a room, everyone took notice of her. Nicole expelled a sigh of resignation. She had brought up Paula to be a self-confident outgoing person. Until now, she had been proud of her surrogate parent role. Then she chastised herself. She was still proud. It pained her that the only man that awoke her senses had turned in a flash to her beautiful sister. A warning to Paula about the man might be in order.

The door opened and a tall woman walked in, followed by Paula.

"Hey, so this is where you're hiding."

"Sorry, I couldn't stand the smell of the popcorn."

Concern showed on Paula's face. "You okay?"

Nicole nodded.

"You missed the best part of the movie."

"Trying to read subtitles and watch the picture at the same time gives me a headache."

"Wouldn't it be nice if we could speak half a dozen foreign languages at birth? There would be no need for translations. You read one line on the bottom of the screen, but can tell the people are saying so many more words. Frustrating, really."

While talking, Paula brushed her hair and checked her impeccable makeup. "Piers is a really nice guy. I like him."

"He obviously likes you too." Nicole marveled how she managed to keep the bitterness out of her voice.

"He's so interesting. I wouldn't mind getting to know him better."

The tall woman came out of a cubicle and washed her hands.

"Appearances can be deceiving," Nicole whispered.

Paula turned her head to look at her sister and screwed up her eyebrows. "Do you have a claim on him?"

"Not at all. Remember he's an employee and I'm the boss." She spoke too loud to sound convincing.

Paula didn't notice. "I suppose it's always a problem in the workplace."

"Let's go," Nicole said.

In the car, Piers and Paula discussed the movie. They hadn't needed the subtitles. Their lively comments threatened to give Nicole a genuine headache. Yet at the bottom of the apartment stairs, she couldn't help herself.

"You can come up for a light supper if you like."

A flush of pleasure lit up his face. "That's an invitation I cannot refuse. I'll just go and put the packing materials out for tomorrow's recycling. Then, I'll be right up with the leftover goodies."

Paula pitched in and made coffee.

"Do you invite him to dinner often?"

"Sometimes. Though he'll also stay without invitation."

A thoughtful air came over Paula's face, then the hint of a smile. "I see."

Nicole sucked in her lips to gain time and turned to get plates from the cupboard. It wouldn't do to make catty comments. "There's nothing to see. We do have to work together closely."

"I must have got the wrong impression."

"Like what?"

Paula threw her hands up. "Like if he was staked territory."

"He and I are not in the same league."

"But he is an interesting man."

Before Nicole could tell her sister she was welcome to him, the object of their discussion knocked on the door and let himself in.

Nicole sat seething throughout the last of the evening. She didn't attempt to take part in the animated conversation that was going on around her.

Sunday morning rolled round and Nicole was ready to tell her sister to pack her bags. All the males at the pizzeria wore silly grins on their face and managed to get in front of Paula whenever she turned round. Customers too succumbed to her charm.

After dinner, dinner that Piers had shared at Paula's invitation, Nicole exploded.

"Why don't you go and join him downstairs? It'd make my life easier."

"Oh dear. Touchy aren't we?"

Nicole calmed down. She didn't miss her sister's mischievous look. "I see what I see. He's got the hots for you and you're drooling."

"You don't see very well. We're just enjoying each other's company. That's all."

"You could fool me." Nicole turned away and stored the dishes in the cupboard.

"Okay, I'd like a date with him. So what's wrong with that?"

Nicole wanted to scream. Instead she shrugged. "You don't know the man. He's a liar and a cheat."

"Wow! How come?"

"It'll too long to recount and I need my sleep."

"You had a bad personal experience with him?"

Nicole grabbed her nightdress and strode to the bathroom. "No, not me." She slammed the door.

"I see," Paula said. She stared at the closed door. "At least, I think I do."

Over breakfast with Paula, and Piers, Nicole made a great effort to appear her normal self. She berated herself for her jealousy. That was what it was. Jealousy. No matter how much she tried, she couldn't shake it off. In spite of her resolution to forget about Piers, that they had no future together, her inner voice kept murmuring *but you love him, you love him!*.

When Piers took Paula to visit Flavio Silver and Porcupine, Nicole closed the door to her office and gave herself a stern lecture. A knock made her sit straight.

"C'mon in."

A grin on his face, Vinny entered. "I left my guitar in your office. Would you like a tune?"

"No."

Her curt tone brought dismay on the placid features of the young man. But he didn't move away.

"You look stressed out. I'd like to help you relax."

Ashamed of her harsh response, she forced a smile. "You're right. I'm stressed. I'd like nothing better than to hear one of your songs." She leaned back in her chair.

Vinny picked up his guitar and began tuning it. For the next ten minutes, Nicole let herself carried away by the tunes Vinny sang. She smiled when he played a whimsical tune and her laugher bounced off the wall of the small room when he made up some silly song. At that moment, Piers and Paula came back and walked into the office.

Paula stuck her head round the door.

"Time to go to the Flying Otter airstrip. Plane and pilot are waiting."

Nicole froze. "You can stay longer if you want to, you know."

"I really enjoyed my visit, but I do have a job to go to. I don't want to lose it by taking more time off."

Nicole stood. "Thanks for my private concert, Vinny. You're such a talented guy. I hope you make it big one day."

"Thanks. All in a day's work." He bowed and went out.

The frown Piers gave when he saw Vinny leave her office intrigued her. He hadn't looked pleased at all. After ensuring that everything was in order, she joined him and her sister in the car.

At the side of the Cessna on the airstrip, Paula kissed Piers on the mouth. "Take good care of my big sister, okay?"

The mechanic, who was holding the door open, chuckled. Tomorrow, it would be all over town. Nicole sighed. So be it.

On the way back, Nicole couldn't remember how she had said goodbye. "I'm going back to the pizzeria."

"You don't need to. Roger's in charge and he's very competent."

"I've some paperwork to finish."

Piers grimaced at her sharp tone.

"No problem. I'll pick you up in an hour."

"You don't have to."

"I want to."

His thousand-volt smile melted her resistance.

"All right." She turned before she could blurt out all her anguish at his defection. In the quiet of her office, she'd have time to compose herself and adopt a strategy to deal with him that would be both safe and professional.

An hour later, she was still staring off into space. It didn't matter which way she looked at it, she was in love. Miserably in love.

As for him, any interest he had shown in her quickly evaporated the moment Paula arrived. Logic told her that Piers' earlier demonstrations of affection had been superficial. Bright, smart Paula was the right match for him. Nicole berated herself once more. She'd better get over loving him.

The cause of her anguish pushed open the door and stuck his head in. "Ready?"

She nodded. The ride home passed in awkward silence. At the bottom of the stairs, Piers caught her hand.

"Are you mad at me?"

Nicole made a show of shrugging her shoulders. "Mad at you? What for? I've been preoccupied. That's all."

"I wondered. It's not like you to be so quiet."

"I can't compete with my sister!" She blurted out the words full of suppressed aggression.

For a few seconds, he stared at her flushed face. "No you can't. You are so much more in everything. I suspect some past suffering has made you wise beyond your years. Yet, you've got a heart."

Surprise snuffed any retort she was about to make. After a deep breath she asked, "There are some leftovers. Want to share?"

"I thought you'd never ask." His teasing smile brought out hers. "I bought a bottle of mango juice. I'll get it."

"See you when you come up." She must be crazy to invite him but she couldn't help it.

Chapter Forty-Three

Piers watched Nicole climb the stairs. His heart twisted in a knot. An urge to rush after her to take her in his arms and kiss her senseless overcame him. This couldn't go on. He had to tell her the whole truth and then face what may come. She had been down these past few days. He was sure she had been suspecting him for a long time, but she never pried. Everything he had accomplished since that morning when she hired him pivoted on a lie. People didn't take kindly to being lied to. It made them feel like fools, too naïve to detect the falsehoods.

On the other hand, she was an intelligent woman. If he told her she'd understand that for him it had been a matter of honor. He backtracked. Honor had little to do with it. Anger at himself. possibly, but a desperate want to atone his crime more than anything.

After he had started work at Flavio's Pizzeria, the desire to prove he had the guts to succeed, enjoy it even, became his goal. This whole new life had opened doors he didn't know existed.

To be honest, he admitted to himself that every time the sun shone and a light wind ruffled the lake in the park, he missed being out on his sail boat. Those moments soon passed when his mind returned to the work he was accomplishing. His heart beat faster just thinking about Nicole.

She'd probably get angry with him. She'd forgive too. At least he hoped she would.

He made his way upstairs. For several weeks, he had been consumed with the need to tell her how much he wanted her. No, make that loved her. He paused on a step. His feelings needed sorting out. There was no way to tell her how he really loved her.

Piers you got yourself in a jam. You might want to make love to her, but she doesn't want you. If two people are in love, they know it.

If one person is in love but not the other, that person must hide her or his feelings. At least he believed so. What he was feeling for Nicole was totally different to what he had felt for Tracy, his last girlfriend. He winced with a lingering pain. He had to convince himself he didn't love Nicole. Though he had feelings for her. He wanted to wake up with her head on his shoulder. Every day. Every year. He wanted to hear her laugh, to see her with his children. No, not just feelings. That was love. Real love. He was in love, totally, irrevocably.

He resumed his upward progression.

Nicole had left the door open. He walked in.

Shop talk presided over the meal. Finally, Piers folded his napkin. "That turkey salad was delicious. And as much as I'd like to stay and talk some more, it's late. We've got to work double shift while the lovebirds are away."

"That's what happens to those at the top."

"I'll give you a ride in the morning."

She suppressed a smile. "Tut, tut, what about our fitness routine? Especially now that most of the staff is running to work. We've got to keep up with them. Set a good example."

For a second or two, Piers didn't speak. "How about running before work, then coming back here?"

"I guess that's good enough."

A fleeting kiss on her lips was all Piers allowed himself. His trembling communicated his urgency to her. She grasped his shirt front and buried her face into his shoulder.

"Do you want it too?" he whispered.

It took her a moment to recover her breath. She shook her head. "Yes...no..."

For a long while he held her without moving. He then smiled and gave her a gentle kiss. "You're not ready. I can see. Goodnight, sweetheart."

His hold loosened, his hands descending along her arms to catch her hands. He pressed them together and brought them to his lips.

His eyes smoldered with a strange emotion. He turned on his heel and ran down the stairs.

***

Nicole watched his retreating figure. She clung to the door frame for support. When he disappeared, she closed the door slowly. As her body calmed down, she heaved a sob-filled sigh. "Piers, Piers, why are you so good? Why is life so complicated? I don't want to love you. I don't even want to like you." She gave herself a mental slap in the face. Instinct clamored for her to stay away from him, to hide her growing feelings. Deep down, she knew he was only passing. Sooner or later, he'd move on. Despite his denial, he must surely have a woman in his life. The woman called Marietta. No matter what his sister Charlotte had said, and his reply. Like men everywhere, he was ready for a fling.

The knock on her door came after she had changed into silky pajamas. Her mind full of Piers she opened the door without checking the peephole. The empty landing filled her with dread. She stepped back to slam the door when a figure emerged from the side and grabbed her arm.

"Oh Jack! You scared me."

"Where is he?"

Her heart sunk. "I don't know what you mean."

"Piers, of course."

"Downstairs. He left ages ago." Panic rose in her throat at the hard look on her friend's face. "You're hurting my arm. It's rather late to be visiting."

Jack seem to shake himself. "You're right. I just wanted... wanted to know if you were thinking about us and our future."

At this point, Nicole wanted to placate him so he'd go away. "I have. But it's too late to be talking tonight."

He didn't move.

"Go! Now!" Still holding the door, she tried to reach the wall phone with her other hand.

Jack looked at her gesture and promptly turned, running downstairs.

She watched him. An uneasy feeling came over her, which grew to outright fear. He was the one who had phoned and knocked on the door without showing himself. Friends didn't act like this. His new possessiveness scared her. Her forehead prickled with cold sweat.

Chapter Forty-Four

It was Wednesday. Staff meeting day. When Lynne and Flavio walked in, an enthusiastic applause greeted them.

Piers and Roger leaped up and pulled out two folding chairs for the married couple.

"I'm glad you're here. We're about to start," Nicole said.

Routine matters were soon dealt with. They then all turned toward Colby, the manager of Flavio Silver. He rose and handed a sheet of paper to Flavio, Piers and Nicole.

"This is the first statement of our profits and expenses. You'll see that after the advertising has been paid, we're ahead. It doesn't include the lease, but that's not due till the end of the month. By then we'll be comfortably in the black."

Flavio nodded his approval. "You're all doing an excellent job."

Colby threw a look of acknowledgment at Piers. "Only following Piers' directives."

"Don't be modest. You have a good sense for the business." Piers then addressed everybody. "We're now using the services of a young entrepreneur to put up posters. He's taken charge of the design, printing and distribution."

Flavio nodded again. "I already heard he employs a small army of youths. Is he an associate of Flavio's emporium?"

Chuckles came from the group.

Piers spoke up. "I thought it'd work better if his company was associated with ours."

"Not to mention all the good business advice you're dispensing," Roger said.

Lynn looked at Darren, the other manager they'd hired. "Isn't tomorrow the grand opening of Flavio Porcupine?"

"Yes it is. We're still setting up but we've been open since

Monday. Traffic has been much higher than our predictions and I had to order double the quantity of supplies."

"That's great!"

In the lull that followed the announcement, Nicole straightened on her chair. "It certainly looks like our product is appreciated and that Piers is a great organizer. We could probably expand to other towns."

A stunned reaction greeted her words.

"We're not having a chain. We are not a factory." Flavio pronouncement fell in the dead silence.

"No, not a chain. Individual Flavio's pizzerias could be opened and staff trained right here by Flavio. That we could expand to other towns is a feasible possibility," Piers said in a calm voice.

Then the group came alive as a lively discussion broke out. Staff members gave the thumbs up to the idea and went back to their tasks.

"Where can we find the money to set up new outlets?" Flavio asked.

"I can't help thinking it'd be really good if we could pull it off somehow."

Nicole pursed her lips. "But I guess we don't have the capital to do that."

"But there's hope. Maybe later," Lynne said.

A frown marred Piers' forehead as he appeared lost in thought. He remained like that until Nicole tapped him on the arm.

"Time to go."

"Are you really okay with more expansion?"

"But where do we get capital to do that?"

"I know we can raise it. There are a number of possibilities."

"Like to share?"

"Let me put a few other things in order first, then we'll discuss the business."

He seemed so confident that on their way upstairs to her apartment the old suspicions again drifted into her mind.

"You're always so sure of yourself. You talk as if money was no object."

He was taken aback for an instant. "There are ways to acquire capital for a business venture."

"We've already got a big loan."

"Business venture is different from a loan to acquire property and renovations."

"It's beyond me. Property is an asset. Leasing a shop carries no risk if the business tank. I suppose I should trust you."

He took a deep breath. "Please do."

Since they had had a pizza dinner, she set dessert plates for the lemon mousse she had made earlier.

"You saw that the two new pizzerias are already profitable. It'll be the same everywhere," Piers said.

"You're so confident."

He pulled her to him and in his arms. "I'm not at all confident about kissing you, yet I want to so badly it just about killing me."

Shock waves zinged through her. A desperate yearning softened her being. She raised her face to him. His warm lips touched hers as lightly as the brush of a butterfly wing. So light, yet she felt it all the way to her toes. He pressed his mouth closer to hers. Her breathing stopped as the contact reverberated through her. His hands roamed, sending millions of electrical points dancing over her skin. Time ceased to exist. Reason ceased to exist.

Chapter Forty-Five

The morning sun slanting through the partly closed drapes awoke Nicole still entangled in Piers' arms. Cold fear washed over her. She had broken her vow to herself. All this to persuade herself that Piers hadn't really looked at her sister. Perhaps making love to Piers was a way to boost her self-esteem. To convince him she was as good as any woman he knew back home.

Remorse settled heavily in her stomach. Last night couldn't mean they would consider a relationship. Although she told herself Piers was different from other men, she wasn't ready for that. Since they had to work together, it would make things even more complicated. She had to tell him about Christopher. She rubbed the heel of her hands across her eyes. First she had to put some order in her chaotic feelings.

Truthfully, she admitted to herself that she loved him. She wasn't sure about wanting a relationship, as in live together. Though the big question was whether Piers loved her. There was no answer she could give. She had no way of measuring whether he had made *love* to her or had been merely overcome by passion like any healthy man would be. She lacked experience in that domain.

The tenderness he displayed could be love, though he hadn't said as much. This was going to change the way they worked together. People in love exchanged looks that spoke volumes. Their hands briefly touched at every opportunity, that's if Lynne and Flavio were anything to go by.

Her new intimacy with Piers filled her with warmth. A blush invaded her cheeks. She'd revel in it and see what the future would bring. As long as she repeated to herself that it was only temporary, she wouldn't get hurt when he left.

Slowly, so as not to wake him up, she slipped out of his arms.

***

Through the slit of his half-closed eyes, Piers followed the motions of her slender body as she extricated herself. His natural reaction was to seize her and drag her back into the warm bed. Nonetheless, he savored the innocent show of her tiptoeing to the bathroom.

Moments later, wrapped in a silk robe, she paused by the side of the bed and looked down at him. The sight send a thousand volts through his body.

"Come here my beautiful angel."

A smile floated on her lips. "Not a good idea. I'll make breakfast."

An exaggerated sigh answered her. Perhaps it was just as well. He should get dressed and tell her about himself. It was a serious matter. He could go no further until all the truth was out. A smell of waffles tantalized his nostrils. His stomach gurgled. He rolled out of bed.

For a while they ate in silence. Piers took Nicole's hand.

"I've a confession to make."

She looked up but remained silent.

"I haven't told you everything about myself."

Words weren't required. Her body language was clear. She knew he had been lying. The new look of happiness about her evaporated. She pulled back her hand.

"When I filled in the application form, I only put the first part of my name. I couldn't give my whole name because you'd have recognized who I was."

The corners of her mouth tightened. "Go on."

"I'm finding this very difficult. Almost three years ago, I attended a party-"

"Never mind the party. Your name? What *is* your real name? Who are you, exactly?"

"Piers Sonder Reddington."

Nicole's face registered a blank expression. "So? Am I supposed to know the name?"

Piers' jaw sagged. "I assumed everyone knew about the Reddington Sporting Goods company. You must have seen the TV commercials."

"I don't have time to watch TV. Wait a minute. Now I remember. Is that the chain that boasts *All your fitness and camping needs*? Matt from the gym carries equipment by that name."

"Right. My great-grandfather founded it. My father is the current owner and CEO." Piers had hoped for a more lively reaction to his admission. When she made none, he was left hanging, like he did when he was a little boy and his mother discovered some misdemeanor.

Nicole folded her arms over her bosom. "I'm waiting for this confession of yours."

"My father and I don't get along too well. He wants me to learn the business from the ground up. Unlike my younger brother, T-Bo, I'm not that interested. I did get a Harvard MBA. So I know the ropes, and I'm all for fitness. Dad wants to groom me for an executive position in the company. To be honest, I don't want anything to do with it. Until I came here, I really hadn't done much with my life. My biggest achievement to date is winning a Tae Kwon Do championship."

"You mean you didn't work? What do you do for money? No don't tell me. It's none of my business."

"I live off the interest of my trust fund. That and commercial endorsements. I only did token work for the firm, like being the featured star of the company's publicity promotions. I spent most of my time goofing off with a small circle of friends."

"The ones who came here?"

"Clayton, my most serious and best friend, Mark my lawyer and my other best friend. Charlotte who you know is my sister. I started telling you that I attended a party, just one of many..." In a flash, the memory returned, vivid and painful while he recounted it. "We all got ...er, inebriated. No, let me be truthful. I was drunk, but I decided to drive my girlfriend home. She was drunker than me and telling me about a baby. It finally registered she was pregnant with my child and she was planning to abort it. We fought in the car. I lost control and crashed into an oncoming minivan. The driver, his wife and their three-month-old baby were killed. Their ten-year-old Clara was at camp. She was left an orphan. I went to jail."

His eyes brimmed with moisture.

"You could have told me!" Anger simmered in her words.

"I know and I wish now I had." Misery oozed out of his voice. "I didn't want anything more with my former life when I came out of the pen. I was on my way to the Yukon when I ran out of money and no one would hire me till I arrived at the pizzeria. You know the rest."

"Now that you are back on your feet, you're going to quit the pizzeria, I presume!"

"I'm not going anywhere."

"Why not? You got Flavio in debt and you won't care what happens to us. That's why you couldn't be bothered to buy furniture. Well, get back to your privileged lifestyle. When I think I took you to a thrift store and advanced you money! What a joke." She stormed across the room and jerked open the door. "Goodbye, Mr. Piers Sonder Reddington!"

"Nicole, I do care. I care about Flavio, the business, and I care about you. I don't want to go back to my former life."

"Do you know what happened to the boy who cried wolf? He lied so many times that nobody believed him anymore."

Piers dragged his feet to the door. "Please, listen to me."

"I've listened. Listened plenty. I don't like being taken for a fool. But then I suppose I am a fool. I should have checked your references. All phony I suppose. See you at the pizzeria for work. You still are employed for the time being. I need time to think."

The stairs loomed at the edge of the landing, a chasm ready to swallow him up. What a mess he had created! In all that a glimmer of hope began to flicker in his heart. He was a born optimist. *I need time to think.* That meant she'd be furious with him for a while. During that interval, he needed to convince her he wanted to spend the rest of his life working for Flavio's Pizzeria.

"Nicole, please, forgive me."

She turned a stony face away from him and slammed the door shut.

***

Nicole slumped into a chair. A sharp pain clawed at her. How right she had been. He *was* a liar. The king of liars. What amazed her was that he had thrown himself wholeheartedly into the work and not only saved Flavio's Pizzeria but expanded it beyond her wildest dreams.

She had accused him of running Flavio into debt. True, the business owed more than it ever did in the past. What she hadn't credited him with was the fact that Flavio's Pizzeria stood poised to make big gains.

If he left, her heart would break into a million pieces. She was glad she didn't tell him about the son she was looking for, glad she didn't tell him that she had fallen in love.

If she had a close friend to confide in, that friend would tell her that all men are not all the same. Some are good. Some are bad. Piers didn't so much lie as omit the truth. He showed grit by sticking to his work and putting their business before his personal needs. Why the Yukon? Still the land of opportunities, she supposed. Unless he was trying to get away from his own nightmare.

More questions crowded her mind. Why did he choose to go to jail? Even minimum security jails must be awful places. Such record would follow him everywhere for the rest of his life. Though of course, with his name and family wealth, he probably didn't need to apply for a job. Unless he saw going to jail as an expiation for the accident he caused.

Compassion rose in her chest. Such a tragedy would never be forgotten. He must suffer deep down. In everyday life, at work, yet he never let it show. Only occasionally had she caught that haunted look in his eyes. He must be just as steadfast in more important matters. Like love.

The hurt came back and with it tears that stung her eyes. He had waited until after they made love to reveal the truth. That made her decision all the more difficult. She'd never have succumbed to his charm had he told her at the outset. Why was she so upset? Was it because he still belong to one of the richest families in the country? He still could at any moment go to the bank and use his trust... She slapped her head.

That's why Flavio got the loan. Piers told the bank manager who he was and secured the loan! What else did he do? She had given herself to him in the hope that it would make him discover love. No, she corrected. She hadn't thought about anything last night. Disappointment choked her. Although she never wanted to think about her foster mother, she admitted there might have been some truth in the woman's warnings. A rebellious adolescent, Nicole had known better. And now she was paying the price for her arrogance. Had been for the last ten years.

To keep her distance was the only smart thing to do. From now on, she intended to treat him like any other employee. Until he told her he was leaving, nothing would change. She had a lot of experience with the cold shoulder. If he really meant what he said, he wouldn't go away. Then she'd be able to evaluate the situation. And if not, she had one wonderful night to remember.

***

Piers lingered in the lobby. A door slammed. He looked up. Rob appeared whistling a tune. Piers swallowed his disappointment.

"Morning, Piers. If you're waiting for Nicole, she's already left. She and Tina went jogging."

"She did? Thanks. How's the house going?"

"We've run into problems. It won't be ready for another couple of months. You can't wait to get the apartment, are you?"

Piers laughed. "Would you believe that I don't mind my basement suite? I spend so little time in it."

"You're working too hard, buddy."

There was no point in trying to catch up with the women. Half-heartedly, Piers set off on a short run. On his return, he thought about waiting for her. He'd give her a ride to work. Then decided against it. It was obvious she didn't want to see him just yet. Besides, she probably had gone straight to the pizzeria.

The demands of work kept them apart for the rest of the day. Finally, Piers caught Nicole in an unguarded moment while she sat at her desk.

"Can you forgive me?"

"Give me some space." She kept on shuffling papers and didn't look up.

"Alright. Things are running smoothly. I'll take a few days off for Thanksgiving."

Her head remained bowed down. "Do. I can take care of business."

"While I'm gone, why don't you use my car? Here are the keys." He handed her the keys. When she didn't take them, he dropped them in her lap and walked off.

He checked with Flavio, and Lynne offered to drive him to the airport in the city.

"How did you guess I want to catch a plane? I didn't say so."

She shrugged. "This is sudden. I figure that either you got your marching orders from Nicole or else you want to reconcile things back home with your father."

"Both."

"Really!"

Piers fidgeted. "I told Nicole the truth. She didn't take it well. She's upset with me for not being up front from the start."

"I can tell. It shows on your face. Let's go. You want to get your bag first?"

"Please."

Chapter Forty-Six

With his bag slung over his shoulder, Piers stared up at the ornate terra cotta facade of the 1902 building that housed the offices of the Reddington Sports empire. A glance at his thrift store jeans and jacket brought a wry smile to his lips. Doubtless, his father was sitting behind his desk somewhere on the fifth floor.

Piers was ready. With an insolent spring in his step, he shoved open the door. He avoided the reception area and made a beeline for the stairs. Forrest Reddington, CEO and fitness maniac, frowned on any employee using the elevator. "Fitness begins at home," he was fond of reciting. He extended the notion of *home* to include work.

In the executive suite's outer office, a pretty blond personal assistant beamed a five-million-dollar smile at Piers. "Good morning, sir. May I help you?"

Piers came to an abrupt halt. He had expected to encounter the formidable Maxine, the appointed guardian of the door to corporate power. The girl, he guessed, was a temp. Surely Maxine hadn't retired! He smiled back at her. She was a definite improvement over Maxine. "I'm just heading in to see the old guy."

The girl jumped to her feet in a vain attempt to block Piers from entering the door marked 'F. Reddington. Chief Executive Officer'. "Sir, you can't just walk straight in. I have to call and see if Mr. Reddington is at his desk."

"No need to. He's been there every Friday morning for the last forty years."

A light of recognition appeared in her eyes. "Aren't you the man in our commercials?"

Piers blew the astonished personal assistant a kiss and breezed through the door, giving a cursory knock on his way in. "Hi Pa!"

Forrest Reddington sat at his desk absorbed in reading a report.

The old man lifted his head. A look of surprise spread over his face. A brief emotion, one soon controlled, warmed his features. "Look at what the wind's blown in."

"I came back to see you."

"You've decided to cut your vacation short by two weeks? Ran out of money, I suppose."

Piers ignored the sarcasm. "Actually, I wasn't on holiday. I've been working."

"Working? That's a new one."

"You're right. I started out as a delivery boy for a pizza parlor in Otter Lake."

That news piqued his father's curiosity. "Where is that?"

Piers continued. "In the heart of the prairies. I then worked on developing the business. We now have three pizzerias and I'm planning more stores in small towns. It provides employment and the workers keep their jobs for life."

"Any industries?"

"Not industries, I'd say artisan workshops. A small doll and accessories factory. Then we call factories a handmade furniture and a knitting plants.

A silence stretched between them. Piers watched his father's bushy eyebrows come together over the bridge of his nose, then relax.

"You did all that in what six months? Where did you get the capital?"

"The owner and I signed a bank loan. Flavio's Pizzeria has a good reputation."

Forrest's face reddened, a sign of his mounting anger. "You had to go out West to do that when you could have done it here?"

"Father, you don't know what jail does to a man."

"And don't want to know! You refused a deal. We could have got you a plea bargain. You wouldn't have a record. You wanted to go to jail. Why?"

Piers sighed. "You can't understand how sorry, how desperate I was to have killed those innocent people. Nobody can."

Forrest's face crunched up to contain the storm. "Those good for nothing, spoiled brats friends of yours getting you drunk."

"I got drunk all by myself. I didn't need any help."

"But why not come home when you were let out?"

Piers shrugged. "You didn't visit me, you prevented Mom from visiting. I was mad at you and the last thing I wanted to do was to come back here and sweep the floors as you had said you'd make me do."

"I was mad at you. Maybe I hurt too because of the accident."

Piers shook his head with a slow movement. "I didn't think you could. Getting drunk was such a stupid mistake on my part. I wanted to go to the Yukon, somewhere in the wilderness, to forget and be forgotten."

"You always were fond of your liquor."

"I've sworn off drink. Haven't touched a drop in all that time. Don't intend to ever again."

His father's granite face softened a fraction. "Running away doesn't help to forget. I'm sorry I've been so inflexible."

"I'm sorry I didn't stop to think."

"All this time, since you had been freed and I thought you were on yet another of your time-wasting *vacations,* you were working in... a pizza joint?"

Piers detected a brusque tinge of admiration in his father's voice, something he hadn't heard since his high school team won the zone football championship. "Not only worked there but saved it from going bankrupt."

Forrest pushed back his black leather chair.

"Let's go for lunch. You can tell me about the woman."

"Woman? How did you...?"

His father laughed. "Son, when a man does a one-eighty like you appear to have done, there's a woman involved somewhere."

On their way through the outer office, Forrest waved a hand at his personal assistant, "Heidi, hold all my calls for the next two hours. My son and I are going out to lunch."

Piers paused to grin at the girl's look of amazement. "You were right. I'm the same guy as in the commercials."

Her reaction was to thrust a note pad and a pen at him. "Can I have your autograph, please?"

Piers obliged with a smile, then hurried after his father. In true Reddington style they shunned the little used elevator and headed down the stairs to the main floor.

Over fettuccini on the sheltered terrace of a nearby Italian restaurant, Piers told his father everything he had done since his accidental move to Otter Lake. Almost everything, that is. He sketched over the mess he made of his relationship with Nicole. The October wind blew dead leaves from the tree branches. A feeble sun played hide and seek with the gray clouds.

Forrest drained his water glass, wiped his mouth on the linen napkin and smiled across the table. "Because you omitted to tell this lady that you call Nicole the whole truth, she is now less than enamored with you. Am I right?"

Piers didn't return the smile. The joy he felt at having won over his father was dampened by the reality that Nicole would likely not want to see his face again. "More than that. She's really pissed by my behavior."

"She'll come round. Give her time."

"You reckon she will?"

"If she's as wonderful a person you make her out to be, she'll see the good in you. A woman with those qualities will forgive your stupidities. But not immediately."

Piers ventured a weak smile. "I hope you're right."

"When she decides to forgive you, you can give her your great-grandmother's ring. I'll make sure you get it."

"The ring? It belongs to mother."

"It's an old family tradition. The ring goes to the eldest son's bride-to-be. I bought your mother a rock for our fiftieth. Practically had to mortgage the company to get it."

"Not so fast, dad. I haven't got anywhere near proposing. I'm not even sure I'm the marrying kind."

"Nonsense! You love her. You'll work it out. Your mother and I will be counting the days to our first grandchild."

"You're jumping way ahead."

Forrest ignored his son's anguished tone. "I suppose you still blame yourself for the death of, Tracy and your baby."

"It's hard not to. And that innocent family."

"Guilt is a mighty destructive force. You have to stop beating yourself up over it."

"I've tried to do just that ever since. Not much success."

"Fate. No one can change the destiny. Life has to go on as they say."

A long shuddering sigh heaved in Piers' chest. "Thanks, Father. I try, but it isn't easy."

"From what you say, this Nicole sounds like one special lady."

Piers slouched on his chair. "She is. The only problem is she now only talks to me about pizza-related matters."

Forrest chuckled. "Then your job is to find a way to repair the damage you've caused. You like a challenge. So get to it."

Piers nodded and puzzled over how he'd go about making amends to Nicole.

"Talking about business," his father said, "where do you propose to raise the capital for your expansion?"

"I intend to research what investment companies have to offer."

Forrest nodded. Before speaking again, he glanced at a buxom brunette on the sidewalk walking her poodle. "I'll sign a couple of your shares in Reddington Sporting Goods over to you. You can invest it in your venture. When you have a solid foundation, then you can invest more. And my advice, pay off that loan and open pizzerias one at a time."

Piers' throat contracted. For the first time he became aware of the depth of his father's love. "Thanks, Father. Won't that affect the family business?"

"Of course not. T-Bo's been itching to put some of his ideas into place. I held back because I had thought you'd eventually take over, being the oldest."

"I'm sorry if I disappoint you."

"Not anymore. Pizzas are just as good as sports equipment. Build an empire like I did. I'm proud of you, my boy."

To hide his emotion, Piers raised his glass of mineral water. He knew well how much his father hated displays of sentiments. His father rarely showed any himself, except for the occasional angry outburst, and was embarrassed when anybody else did.

They toasted the future.

"Are you going to stay a couple of days? See your old friends?"

"I'll stay until the day after tomorrow. Just for the Thanksgiving weekend." He chuckled. "Mark and Clayton are my only remaining friends. Don't want to talk to anybody else."

"Good. Your mother will be instantly cured. Charlotte told you she's depressed."

"I wrote to her."

"I know. It helped. I'll take the rest of the day off. We can discuss your proposed expansion, if you think your old man still knows a thing or two about business."

For the first time in his life, his father was treating Piers as an equal. Gone were the arguments and the tension-filled standoffs. Love and respect swelled in Piers' chest. The day passed too quickly and ended with a new understanding between them. Piers knew there would be many more days like it.

Chapter Forty-Seven

Lynne stripped off her apron. "We're done for the day, unless you need help."

All the while keeping her eyes on the computer screen, Nicole shook her head. "I'll just finish collating these bids for supplies, then I'll go to Flavio Porcupine. They're short of staff today because of Thanksgiving. I hope the weather improves. I've never seen October this cold and windy."

"The forecast is optimistic. Do you want me to go to Flavio Porcupine?"

"You look after Flavio. I've nothing better to do."

"Missing Piers?"

Nicole rolled back her chair, her face calm. "Not in the least. I'm mad at him. He can stay gone wherever he is, forever."

Lynne put her hand to her mouth to hide a smile. She cleared her throat. "But you still love him."

"No, I don't..." Her lower lip twitched. "Well, I do but... I don't know. If a man can lie through his teeth for six months, what else is he capable of?"

"He had a good reason."

Nicole breathed a deep sigh. "I haven't been up front with him, mind you."

"I'm no psychologist but maybe if you told him, you could start over again and see where it leads you. If he's not been up front with you, nor you with him, that sort of cancels things out, doesn't it?"

Nicole shook her head. "I'm not in his league. As a matter of curiosity, did he say when he was coming back?"

Lynne contained a smile. "He didn't, but it won't be long now."

A wistful expression settled on Nicole's face.

"You've been moping since he left. You're putting in extra long hours. I think you've got a bad case of love sickness. And it's only been two days!"

Nicole laughed but there was no humor in it. "I confess I miss him. I want to put things straight between us. Do you think he went home to mend fences with his father?"

"He didn't say, but why else would he catch a plane? See you tomorrow."

After Lynne's departure, Nicole could no longer concentrate on the figures on the screen. She saved the data and closed the computer. Roger shouldered open the door of her office. In his hands he held a plate of fragrant biscuits.

"Lookie, your very own cheese biscuits. I thought you'd like to take some home."

"What a nice thought, Roger. Thanks."

"Flavio Porcupine just phoned. They don't need you now, they've got a casual."

"Thanks, that's fine."

She took her backpack off the peg and slipped the biscuits into her plastic lunch container. Before closing it, she saved a biscuit and shouted a goodbye to the staff. She took a bite, then stopped. Snowflake was eyeing her with a mournful expression on his jet black face.

"Okay, here's your share." He delicately took the offered morsel. She played with the dog for a while before walking home.

Thoughts tumbled around in her head. One horrible scenario that kept returning was what she'd do if Piers never came back? If he had left for good? A pinch in the spiritual region of the heart made her falter. No, she couldn't believe he wouldn't return. He had committed himself to helping Flavio, and she had to admit that whatever his shortcomings, Piers would keep his promise.

She was less certain that he would love her. No one can ever be sure of love. Love was not something that could be defined and neatly packaged.

Absentmindedly, she punched in the pass code to the door of the apartment building. On her way in she collided with the solid mass of a man's chest. "Piers! You scared me."

His arms steadied her. "I missed you."

A fierce longing coiled inside her. A whirlwind of joy swirled through her body. A smile came to her lips. Piers was back and she wanted this moment to last forever. All her carefully planned reasons to keep him away from her evaporated. Her heart sang. Her skin tingled.

"I'm glad you're back." What an effort it was not to kiss him and hold him tight. "Want coffee?"

He drew her close. "And lots of other things too."

Her head began to spin. The voice of reason clamored in her head, *Careful, careful, careful. There are unresolved issues here.*

She broke free. "I have the definitive version of the Flavio Cheese Biscuit right here in my bag."

He pulled her against his chest and laughed. "We'll taste test them first, before..." He released his hold and carried her backpack upstairs.

She unlocked the door. "I'll make a salad to go with the biscuits."

"I'll set the table."

The domesticity evoked by that simple exchange tugged at her heart. Her happiness at his return was tempered by a host of questions. Would he want to stay once the debt for the extension was repaid? That wouldn't take long. The three pizzerias were already turning a healthy profit. Of course, he had been interested by the idea of establishing a series of pizza parlors in small town across the country. She wasn't sure it would be enough to keep him here. He may decide not to go on with the project.

More than what would happen to the pizza business the question that loomed large in her mind was would he stay once she told him about Christopher?

She brought him to date on the business. "Roger has good organizational skills. His position should be full time, with a flexible schedule. And we need to find an assistant manager."

"Flavio's talking about retiring?"

She nodded. "He wants to just take on the training of the cooks and staff, and said you were to train the managers in business practices. How was your holiday?"

"No holiday, really. I went to see my folks."

"Did you patch things up with your father?"

"We spent two days doing just that. Actually, I think he's proud of me. He's freed up a couple of shares of the family business to invest in our pizza expansion venture."

Nicole's face showed her surprise and shock. "He did what?"

"He thinks the pizzeria business is great. I showed him a draft of the business plan. He approved it. Said he couldn't have done better himself."

"He's got experience with multiple stores. That he's giving you your share of the family business is incredible."

"He told me he trusts me. My stupid pride refusing to go home after my time was over because my father not only didn't visit but prevented my mother from doing so served me right in some way. If it wasn't for it, I'd never have met you. All what we've accomplished together at Flavio's proved to my father I was a capable individual, not just the pretty face of his commercials."

"You've got that same self-confidence as Howard had. In a way, it frightens me." She bit her lip. She hadn't meant to blurt out what was on her mind.

"Who's Howard?"

"Howard Whitherington. My baby's father."

Piers' jaw dropped. He looked at her in silence. Then slowly, a grin lit up his face. He leaned forward.

"You have a baby?"

"Well, yes and no. I *had* a baby. I was sixteen and stupid." With a flushed face and trembling voice, she gushed out a garbled sketch of her troubled youth, of her search for her child, of kidnaping her sister.

Piers took her by the hand and led her to the sofa. His touch was soft and tender.

"How about if you tell me the story from the beginning?"

She wiped her eyes. This was her moment of truth, her defining moment. Piers might just walk away, never to return. The thought hurt deep down in her belly. Though, unless she misinterpreted, he'd looked delighted when she'd uttered the words *my baby*.

"Paula was six and I was twelve when our parents were killed in a plane crash. I wasn't quite sixteen, no I had turned fifteen a couple of months earlier, when I met a man called Howard Whitherington. He was rich and a smooth talker. At the time, life in our foster home was tough. He convinced me he could help me become a model. I was cautious because I thought help does not come free and maybe he'd want... sex. But he didn't. Or at least he said he didn't."

"Did he help you?"

"He said he was a photographer and even had some shows. He told me I needed a portfolio to send to modeling agencies. He showed me photos of his models. They were all nice-looking girls. And the work was really professional."

"So you posed for him?"

"He bought me lots of beautiful clothes. The photos he took were good. He kept telling me..." She stopped to swallow. "that I was so beautiful, such a natural. So I didn't mind posing in a bikini."

"And?"

"He started taking me out to fancy restaurants and to the theater. I was really star struck. I was only a kid. Home life was so drab, but I didn't want my foster parents to know that he bought me all these expensive clothes. So I used to change before coming home, except for a few things which wouldn't arouse the Nolans' suspicion."

"Your foster parents, right?"

"That's right."

"Did this Howard guy not want to meet them?"

"No, and I was too ashamed to let him see the dump of a house I lived in. One day he was showing me how a portfolio is made and he said that the bikini shots were good..." She broke off to blink several times. "But if I wanted to become a model, I would also have to pose without clothes on."

"The scumbag!"

She nodded. "I don't know whether I wanted to be a fashion

model, but it seemed to be a way out of that foster home. He showed me ads where the models are less than dressed. So I agreed. Then he told me he loved me. I had been secretly in love with him for months."

"The creep was a filthy pedophile!"

She nodded. "I thought my life had changed. He was rich and wanted to marry me after I finished school. A month later, I discovered I was pregnant. I was so happy when I told him. I said we could get married right away."

"What did he do?"

"He calmly told me he was already married. I got the usual blah blah blah about his wife not understanding him but he couldn't divorce her right away because her health wasn't strong. He gave me money and a phone number saying I should get rid of the baby."

Piers raised his eyebrows. "You didn't?"

"At first I thought I should, because I didn't want a child from such a despicable man. Every time I was about to go to the clinic, I knew I couldn't kill the life that was in me. When I started to show, I had to tell my foster parents. They threw me out quicker than it takes to tell you this. Paula was just nine, and she was devastated. I promised her I'd come back for her."

"That was just the first angry reaction from the people who were supposed to be caring for you and your sister."

"They cared only for the money they got from the child welfare services. There were six other kids in that home. We never got any clothes except what the neighbors discarded and used to drop off on the porch. Food was rationed."

"What did you do?"

"I lived on the streets for three months or so. A woman befriended me and took me to a shelter for teenage mothers. They have all the girls sign up their babies for adoption. I didn't want to sign. Counseling was one-sided. After I'd felt the baby move in me, I just couldn't give him up. I worked for a couple of days as a relief in a day care center. After the baby would be born, I planned to continue working and study."

"You had a boy?"

She nodded. "Christopher."

"Where is he now?"

"That's the problem. I don't know. Just before I was discharged from the hospital, the directors of the shelter came and took him away. They said he'd get a better life with adoptive parents. I was crushed. I went back to the foster home but they wouldn't take me in. Paula was crying. They were taking their anger out on her. So I... kidnaped her."

"I'm not sure the law would call that kidnaping."

"I hid in a neighbor's garden shed. When Paula came out of the house on her way to school, I called to her and we ran away. She told me she knew I'd be waiting for her and she'd stolen two twenties out of the jar of grocery money that morning. She had also crammed a couple of sweaters and undies in her backpack. She had left her books at school. We walked all day. I didn't dare take a bus in case the alarm was given and someone would remember seeing us."

"How did you manage to survive?"

"I went to a supermarket on my own, bought some basic food like bread and cheese. We kept on walking west. Toronto is a big place when you're on foot. We finally got out of the suburbs and into the country. We took what looked like less traveled roads. The first night, we slept in a disused barn."

"You must have been scared."

"I was. I kept looking over my shoulder thinking the police were going to catch us and throw me in jail. I think Paula thought it was a great adventure. We got to a town where I saw a newspaper box. We weren't on the front page. We went into a Wal-Mart so we could clean up in the washroom. We looked at the TV sets that had the news on. There was no mention of a teenage girl abducting a child."

"How did you navigate?"

"I bought a map in the Wal-Mart store. We kept on the move for several days until the money ran out. We went through bigger towns in back lanes, scrounging food behind restaurants. Do you realize the stuff that's thrown away? Once, I was offered a job washing dishes for a whole week. The money was welcome and what's more, we pretended to leave like the other employees did but slipped back into the bathroom, then slept in the break room. The owner didn't know, of course. Then we moved on, intending to get to British Columbia."

"Why British Columbia?"

"It was as far as we could get from Toronto. Being a warm place, we wouldn't need many clothes. I'd heard some people lived on the beach. So we could do it too."

"You never made it there."

Nicole gave a dry laugh. "No, we didn't. Nowhere near."

Fondness tinged his voice. "You got to Otter Lake."

"Yes. It was summer by then. School was out, so we had less fear of being stopped. But we still traveled on secondary roads. Our sneakers, the second pair I bought with the dishwashing money, were worn through. Our clothes weren't fresh at all, even though I washed them in lakes and rivers when I could. A few times I had got a job for a day or two with farmers when they caught us lurking near the barn. We took a bus once between two towns. We look for country roads to find farms. Farmers must have thought we were kids from nearby just having fun. But I was serious asking for a job. They all had gardens that needed weeding. Then we got jobs helping to make preserves and pickles. Some people are truly nice. When we got to Otter Lake, I was looking for a thrift store when I happened to see a help wanted notice in a pizza parlor - Flavio's Pizzeria."

Piers smiled. "*Déjà-vu.*"

A genuine smile lit up Nicole's face. "The idea did cross my mind when you walked in. Flavio set us up with Susan, and we stayed with her until she got married. Then Paula and I moved here. It's closer to the pizzeria."

"I don't see how you could have been charged with kidnaping. I've a hunch that the Nolans didn't alert the authorities so they could keep on receiving the foster care payments for you. They probably told the school you had moved."

"That occurred to me. All the same I couldn't take a chance. Flavio understood and paid for Paula to attend a private school. They weren't too concerned about getting her student records as long as the fees were being paid. Besides, she was so bright she became an asset for them."

"And now she's attending university. A beautiful and sharp young lady, thanks to you."

"I finished school by night classes and distance ed., then went part time to college to take a degree in accounting and business management. The rest you know."

"Did you try to find your little boy?"

His question brought renewed tears to her eyes. The realization that he understood, that he cared, struck her.

"Two years ago, I had an awful dream that my little boy was unhappy and needed me. I feared he might be in danger. I began searching for him in earnest. I couldn't have done it before Paula was eighteen. I feared the authorities would learn about me kidnaping her, even though I'm sure Flavio would have stood for us. But I've had no real luck in tracing him so far."

Piers pulled her into his arms. "We'll find him. I know we will."

Her heart beat faster. He had said *we*. She raised her face and closed her eyes as his mouth claimed hers.

Piers pulled away. "Mark, my lawyer friend, also runs a private investigation agency back home. It's useful in his line of work. He specializes in family law. I'll call him."

Nicole gave a long sigh. "I've employed one already, but I ran out of money before he got results. Right now I'm saving. I don't have enough for another PI."

"You don't need any."

Her voice rose. "He's not going to do it for free. Forget it if you think I'll let you pay."

He took her hand. Shivers ran through her, so strong she jerked her hand away.

"My friend is a real friend and he owes me," Piers said. "Time to collect."

"I've written and phoned all adoption agencies I could find in Toronto and Ottawa. Every city in the East. Although it is improbable that it'd be an agency from out of province, I started looking at Quebec and the Maritimes. It takes time to find the addresses. Not all of them have a website, maybe some are not even legitimate. Some agencies refused to talk to me. Most say they don't have any records of a baby boy matching Christopher's description at that time."

Piers ran his fingers through his hair. "It could have been a private adoption."

"I just assumed the shelter worked through an agency, since it's a shelter recommended by the welfare services. I tried to get information from them. They weren't forthcoming. They said it's regulations. All the babies are up for adoption. Closed adoptions. Mine was no exception. Jack tried too. No luck. He tried the hospital again and managed to get the name of one of the nurses on duty the day they came to take Christopher away."

"I guess you haven't found her."

"Not yet. We've been so busy. You'll probably think I need a shrink. I'm so obsessed in finding what happened to my little boy."

"You don't need a shrink. You just need some help to find him. And that should be possible. There are many channels to explore. There are ways to get information from people."

"It takes time. All I have is the internet."

"And you've been working long hours. We'll change all that."

"You really want to help?"

"You mean a lot to me."

She looked away. *You mean a lot to me, too,* she wanted to say. His interest hadn't been merely casual. A ray of hope flickered. But the insidious voice of reason and experience whispered, *Wait and see if he really means it.*

Piers' face wore a slightly deflated expression. "I suppose you don't trust me."

"You made it difficult for me. I haven't sorted out my thoughts yet." At this moment, she wanted to forget about anything. Perhaps if she were more assertive, more worldly, she'd find a smart and ready answer. But she wasn't. The few times she had gone out with Piers, Ed and Claire, she mostly remained silent, admiring their sophisticated conversation and the assured way in which they planned to rebuild the world. At the same time, she had made a list of books to read to expand her knowledge and understanding of the world.

"I'd better leave now." Piers got up and edged toward the door. "Are you going to work tomorrow?"

"I'll relieve Lynne at the end of the afternoon."

"I'm not scheduled yet, so why don't we go to the park, run, grab a hot dog and take a little drive. I'd like to look at houses."

"Houses? Do you intend to buy one?"

"My grandmother left enough to buy a house to each of us. A house was her most important goal. She was a child in France during World War Two and her house was bombed, her parents killed. She came to Canada as a child refugee."

"So sad. I understand that. A house is a home. When you own a house, it's like putting roots."

"You're right. Now let's have a picnic tomorrow."

Nicole laughed. "Okay. I'll bring a thermos." *A house. He meant to stay, to put roots down, did he not?*

"Thanks for dinner." He bent over and kissed her softly. His fingers trailed a fiery path under her jaw, down her neck, her shoulder, her arms and caught her hand. He brought it to his lips and kissed her finger tips. Slowly, so slowly he released her and stepped back. Then he was gone.

Her tongue firmly caught between her teeth hurt. She exhaled a long sigh. No, she wasn't going to give in to her impulse to call him back and hide herself from reality in his arms.

Chapter Forty-Eight

Piers pushed open the door of his apartment and grimaced. The stuffy atmosphere assailed his nostrils. He went to the window and struggled to open it. Fresh cold air flowed into the room. A house would be a definite improvement over these living quarters. His buying a house would maybe convince Nicole that he was intent on settling in this place. A house where he could bring her as his bride.

He pulled out the small blue velvet box from his bag and contemplated the ring for an instant. Its emerald stone sparkled in the center of a crown of alternating diamonds and rubies nestled in an intricate gold filigree. It brought back images of his mother wearing it. She was always so elegant, he took it for granted. When he was a young boy, though, he was fascinated by its colors and brilliance.

When his father had announced Piers was going to need it, she had jumped out of her chair to hug him, and immediately pulled the ring from her finger.

"It's meant to be handed down to the oldest son for his bride. When your son marries, it'll go to him."

"Wait, mom. I don't know for sure that Nicole loves me or that she'll marry me if I ask. I don't really know what love is."

His mother had remained silent for a minute. "Yes, you do. True love is the essence of life. Makes it all worth living. You can't let one tragic experience destroy the rest of your life. You'll have to talk to Nicole."

"I thought many times I was in love."

"It never really was love, though. You've matured. You see life in a different way. Nicole on the other hand seems totally different. She is, isn't she? You'll marry her and have half a dozen children."

A silence fell between them. Troubled, Piers took his face in his hands. After a few moments he straightened.

"I haven't even told her I love her. But yes, you're right, what I feel for her is love, deep down love."

"But you will tell her and she'll accept."

"You don't know that. She's angry with me."

"I'd be worried if she wasn't mad at you. She cares, that's why. Besides, I know you'll pursue her until she's yours."

"But you don't know her."

"If she has managed to turn you inside out, she's the daughter-in-law I've always wanted."

They had laughed. That was the end of the discussion. His loving parents had helped him let go of the burden he had been dragging. Not forgotten, just lightened. Then amazement had filled him. He was re-affirming that what he felt for Nicole wasn't simply lust, or friendship. It was all that plus something else. That little something which made him want to shout with joy when he saw her in the morning. That little something which made him want to stay on with her in the evenings. His father called it love. His mother called it love. He had believed he knew what love was and he'd recognize it if it came. He did but didn't believe he was worthy of it.

It wasn't going to be easy to make Nicole believe he loved her and he wanted to spend the rest of his life with her. First, he had to help find her child. Anger burned in his chest against the man who had abused her trust. No wonder she was so fearful of men in general. She had trusted Jack, and he too showed a side of him that had scared her.

He reached for the phone. Mark was going to kill him for waking him in the middle of the night.

A grouchy voice answered after four rings.

"Hi buddy. It's Piers."

"Do you know what time it is here? What the hell are you doing phoning at this hour?"

"I need your help."

"Can't it wait till I'm awake?"

"You are now."

Mark muttered an expletive. "This better be good!"

"I need to find a baby that was taken and adopted against the mother's wishes nine years ago."

"Hell man! If it's waited nine years, can't it wait till morning?"

"I'll email you the details."

"How much do I get paid?"

"You owe me. Remember the Preston case?"

"And now you're collecting. Okay, okay, send the file."

"Thanks."

"Who is she?"

"Who?"

"Come on, fella, it's got to be a woman. The mother, dummy."

"You're really sharp. Yeah, the mother is a girl I know."

"Man, it must be serious. Just, don't phone again at three in the morning!" Mark hung up.

A smile on his face, Piers sat at the computer and entered all the information Nicole had given him. He'd have to ask her for more details and names in the morning.

He had no doubt Mark would be able to trace the child. Mark never gave up and had a team of dedicated PIs. Then what? The baby had been adopted by a couple who badly wanted one. They must have provided him with love and all his material needs. It was common practice to tell children when they were adopted. His parents would probably agree to let him meet his biological mother so he wouldn't grow up with a feeling of rejection.

Guilt in Nicole's subconscious could have spurred the dream. Piers didn't dismiss it. Guilt was something he knew all about. He didn't believe in extra sensory perception. Yet he believed that there could be a strong spiritual connection between two people. Enough to make one of them feel for the other one.

His thoughts became hazy. Business plans and projections were things he could handle with confidence. Analyzing the human mind was a different matter altogether. One he had no knowledge of and didn't intend to find out. Sleep finally overwhelmed the workings of his brain.

Chapter Forty-Nine

The knock on his door brought a smile to his lips. "About time!" Piers' heart did a little jump when he saw Nicole in winter running gear on the landing. Her long smooth legs in Lycra tights and supple body rocketed his blood temperature to boiling point.

"Did you want to eat breakfast before we run?" she asked.

"I'd prefer not to. What about you?"

"Same here. I've got water and a couple of sandwiches in my bag."

"Come in for a couple of minutes. I need some details on Christopher."

Piers completed his email to Mark.

"How can I thank you?" She raised herself on her tiptoes to place a light kiss on his lips.

About to pull her into his arms, Piers controlled himself as he remembered his decision to let love develop slowly.

"Let's go."

As they were leaving, the buzzer to his apartment sounded.

"Who's visiting on a Sunday morning?"

Nicole tugged his arm.

"Whoever it is, we'll meet them at the front door."

However, when they reached the top of the stairs, there was nobody at the door.

Unsettled, Nicole paused at the foot of the stairs. "Do you really think it is Jack? He didn't take no for an answer. He insists I must marry him."

Anxiety suffocated Piers. "Will you?"

"He makes me uncomfortable."

"That's not a good start for a relationship." The words sounded lame even to his ears. What does it mean *He makes me uncomfortable*? But the guy had been around for a long time, helped her too. Piers' head began to spin.

They started toward the park in silence. He worried that once more someone was trying to scare her. Most likely that weasel Jack. She didn't say she wasn't going to marry the guy. Pain roiled in his belly. She couldn't do that.

***

Breathless, Nicole slowed down. A mist blurred her vision. If she needed further proof that Piers was a typical male whose interest is only to bed a woman, she had it. She hadn't really expected him to make a declaration of undying love. Just a vigorous protest that she couldn't possibly marry Jack. Then she could have jumped in his arms to say her reply was no, nothing would make her marry Jack. Not after having made love to Piers. Not since her heart had reluctantly but strongly started beating only for him.

Back at the apartment, Nicole ran upstairs. A splash of cold water on her face helped her regain her composure while she dressed for work.

***

His car sitting in the morning sun was already an oven. The October day was unusually warm. Piers turned on the air conditioning. Numb with shock from head to toe, he stared vacantly out of the window. When Nicole joined him, he opened the door for her. In silence they drove to the pizzeria. Cheerful greetings met them when they walked through the door. Piers made an effort to appear his normal self. Nicole went straight to her office.

Only Lynne threw him a curious look. "How was your trip?"

"Very good. In fact I've news for you and Flavio if you have a minute."

"We're just waiting for the shift to arrive. Roger had a performance last night so we're covering for him this morning."

A while later, they crowded into Nicole's office. Although she smiled, a hint of sadness lingered over her features.

The new filing cabinet reduced even further the space of the small office.

Flavio settled his long legs under the desk. "We're too crowded down here. I got Aldo to renovate the upstairs and make a couple of offices and a staff room. There'll still be plenty of room to store stuff. So Piers what's your news."

Piers glanced at Nicole. "I've raised the capital."

Lynne smiled. Flavio whistled in admiration.

"Well, boy, I knew you could do it. Want to elaborate?"

"It's no secret. My father turned over a couple of my shares of the family business to me. I'll invest it in Flavio's Pizzeria expansion."

Flavio crossed his arms. "So penniless Piers has a father with a business! D'you mind enlightening me?"

"Sorry. You don't know, of course."

"I'm always the last one to know anything." He kept his tone light and mocking.

"My father is Forrest Reddington, boss of Reddington Sporting Goods." In a few words, he told Flavio about his agreement with his father.

Flavio chuckled. "This is a good one. I think we'll need more than two offices upstairs."

For the next thirty minutes they discussed office space, a board of directors and strategies.

"You're bringing in serious capital, so you have the most shares," Flavio said.

"Lynne has contributed too. The van she bought after the lease was up is an investment. Therefore she has shares, and Nicole has shares too."

For the first time, Nicole spoke up. "I don't have any money to invest. So count me out."

Piers wagged a finger. "Wrong. We are calculating the time you spent without pay, plus factoring in that you kept the pizzeria afloat during Flavio's illness and recovery."

"That's not how investments works, and you know it."

"We can make it work any way we want, can't we Flavio, Lynne?"

Flavio was clearly enjoying himself. "You're the one with the MBA. If you say so, then that's how it works."

Nicole bit her lip. "I suppose we could argue till the end of time."

"Good. It's settled."

Nicole rolled her eyes. "While we're here, I'd like to bounce an idea off you all. I already talked it over with Roger. How about opening at seven in the morning and doing a breakfast special?"

Immediately everyone spoke at once. Before leaving, Lynne pulled Piers by the sleeve and they stepped outside. Snowflake greeted them enthusiastically. "What happened between you and Nicole?" Lynne asked.

"I've got a ring in my pocket but before I could put it on her finger, she told me Jack wants to marry her. I've failed, Mrs. B. All that because I didn't tell her the truth at the start. But if I had, she'd have sent me back home. She wouldn't have believed I really wanted to make it out on my own, and in the process I've lost the only woman I've ever loved."

"When is the wedding?"

He was startled. "Wedding? What wedding?"

"Yes. If he asked her and she accepted, there has to be a wedding date."

Piers looked stunned. "She hasn't said."

"Then what are you wasting your time for?"

Crestfallen, Piers bowed his head and scratched the dog's ears.

Lynn scoffed. "You don't know women very well, do you?"

"I haven't known many, no. Casual dates don't count."

A motherly look softened Lynne's features. "Then take my advice. Talk to Nicole."

The door opened and Flavio stepped outside. "Ready Mrs. B.?"

Piers watched them go and went back inside, a half smile floating on his lips. He went straight to Nicole's office.

It was empty.

Chapter Fifty

A whirlwind of meetings and conference calls to set up the corporation, besides the regular activities of the pizzeria, occupied Piers for the next few weeks. The work robbed him of a chance to talk to Nicole other than work. Her avoidance tactics were plain.

At the bottom of the stairs, he lingered debating to go up and beg a last cup of coffee. In his suite, he made a half-hearted effort to eat a couple of cheese biscuits before dropping into bed.

The phone ringing with its savage insistence awoke him. He frowned and glanced at his watch. Who on earth was phoning at 4:00 am? He fumbled for the receiver, ready to curse whoever was calling at that ungodly hour.

"Hey, sonny boy, wake up!"

"Mark Bergson!" He sat up and rubbed his eyes. "I guess it's payback time."

The two friends shared a laugh. Mark then explained his findings while Piers took notes. Piers lay in bed afterward for over an hour unable to go to sleep. He got up. After a quick shower he climbed the stairs to the top floor.

It was still early, but Nicole wouldn't mind being woken up for his news.

The sight of her as she opened the door sent electric currents through his body. Low cut jeans and a short tee hugged her figure. Her tousled hair cascaded over her shoulders. He shook off the images that sprang to his mind.

"I heard from Mark."

Her still sleepy face brightened instantly. "Come in. I'll make coffee."

"Your baby's adoption didn't go through an agency. It was a private adoption through a lawyer."

"So that's why I got nowhere."

"Mark also found Nurse Riemer and talked to her."

Her mouth fell open. "He d...did? That fast?"

"Mark's a pro. He has a lot more than the internet at his disposal."

Excitement fairly made her dance. "Can we go and see her?"

An understanding smile came to Piers. "She's now working in Edmonton. We'll phone her first to find out when she'd be available."

"Of course. I'll cook breakfast."

Seeing her absorbed in this domestic task wrenched at Piers' heart. He could settle for it any time. But Jack had asked her. Though it burned the tip of his tongue, Piers couldn't bring himself to question her as to her reply or the wedding date. She hadn't been talking to him, but news of her child made her forget why. Unless she was trying to forget about the night of love they had shared because she had accepted Jack. Cold tentacles of despair wrapped themselves around his insides. Maybe he could talk to her while they eat. What could he say? Start with congratulations about her marrying Jack, No, she hadn't given her reply yet. Or did she? Try again. *Did you know I love you? I've a ring burning a hole in my pocket. Would you marry me? I know Jack also wants to marry you, but he's a creep. You can't possibly love him....*

"Piers."

He jumped up. A tantalizing odor wafted from the kitchen. Piers poked his head through the archway. "That smells delicious."

"Wait till you eat it. Here take the plates."

He carried the plates while she brought cups and the coffee. For a while there was only silence. A grunt of pleasure preceded Piers words. "Delicious. Compliments to the chef. What is it?"

"German pancake."

"It's light and fluffy and the apples inside make it taste rich."

"Remember your idea of a veggie pizza with honey? Lynne tried it. It's really good. We are still experimenting though. We grill tofu with the honey from Ames Lake Farm you recommended we buy at the Farmers Market."

"Great. I'll have some more pancake, if you don't mind. Thanks. Do you think—"

"Oh no! we're not going to offer pancakes!"

They laughed and talked shop. A safe subject. Incurably optimistic, Piers mentally elaborated some more strategies on how he could get her to tell him what her decision was regarding Jack. Finally, Piers pointed at the clock. "Time to call Nurse Riemer."

Piers introduced himself over the phone and reminded her she had talked to his friend Mark. The conversation was brief.

"We're in luck. She just started a three-day-off cycle and would be happy to see us later this afternoon."

"Wonderful! But are you sure you want to come with me? I can drive."

A wan smile crossed his lips. "We're flying. And I want to be with you." He dialed a number.

"It might be too late to get seats for this afternoon."

"I'm chartering a Cessna Skyhawk from Flying Otter Air."

Shock coursed through her. For once she said nothing about cost. Finally she had a lead. Piers phoned the airline then ended the call.

"All set."

"Let me dress in something a bit formal."

Piers looked down at his jeans. "I guess it'd look better if I did too. See you in fifteen minutes downstairs. I'll call Lynne and tell her we won't be in today nor tomorrow."

He didn't really feel there was anything wrong with his second-hand jeans, but staying in the apartment while she changed might have prompted him to lose his cool. He had brought a suitcase from home. In his new position as CEO of Flavio's Pizzeria Enterprises, he had to dress more appropriately.

The flight passed mostly silent. From time to time Nicole expressed her worry that Nurse Riemer wouldn't remember her or what had really happened the day they took the baby away. Piers reassured her as best as he could. They rented a car and stopped for lunch. Nicole ate only a token.

"Eat more. You need your strength."

"I'm too excited."

An indulgent smile floated on his lips. "Okay, let's go and buy her flowers."

Neck craned forward, Nicole sat stiffly wringing her hands. Piers navigated the streets and at last pulled up in front of a small white house.

"This is it."

Nicole clutched the flowers and walked up the path on legs that resembled jelly.

Jovial and round-cheeked, Bea Riemer opened the door. "Hello, you must be Nicole. Come in, come in."

Nicole handed her the bouquet.

"Thank you. That's so nice of you. I'll make some coffee or would you prefer tea?"

"Coffee's fine," Nicole said.

"Make yourself at home. I can crank up the heat if you'd like."

"No need. It's very pleasant in here as it is."

They sat facing Bea Riemer. An awkward silence reigned.

Nicole took a deep breath. "I'm sure I'm imposing on you, but I wonder if you can remember the circumstances of... when my baby was taken away. I screamed so hard and so loud that I hoped you might remember." She told briefly how and why she'd been searching for her child.

Bea Riemer nodded. "Since that private investigator phoned me, I have tried to recollect everything that had happened. We were seeing all the teenage mothers from the shelter at the hospital, but I do remember your case, because if I'm not mistaken you'd come into the hospital early because your waters broke and you had a long labor. More than that, you were the only one there who wanted to keep her baby. At first we thought you would be able to. My colleagues and I were so happy that a child could live with his mother. We'd come by all the time to give you advice."

"I remember your kindness. After I got settled in Otter Lake, I contacted the shelter but they refused to tell me anything."

"Not surprising. Money was involved."

"What do you mean?"

"When you went into labor, we had to notify the shelter. That was the rule. Your baby was barely three days old when a couple arrived. They'd flown in from Winnipeg and wanted to meet you."

"Winnipeg!" The shock of learning that the adoptive parents came from Winnipeg drained the color from Nicole's face.

Piers took her hand.

"It was against the rules, so they left. Then a man turned up asking for them. I didn't speak to him. The head nurse was quite angry. Later, in the staff room, I asked her what all the fuss was about. She said it was the lawyer who'd arranged for the adoption and probably was more concerned about his big bucks than any regulations about mothers not being allowed to meet the adoptive parents. He wanted to make sure his clients didn't bypass him."

"You mean they paid more than the hospital costs? They *bought* my baby!" Nicole slumped back in her chair.

"I'm afraid so. There are no hospital costs, not in Canada. But the shelter charges a hefty fee to the adoptive parents. Except they call it a donation."

"Does it mean that the people who pay more get a baby to adopt faster?" Piers asked.

"Not through the legal channel, but privately who knows what goes on. But this was the first time a couple had come to the hospital wanting to meet the mother. They were really nice and concerned about your future."

"When I was running away...I'd planned to go to British Columbia. Instead, I landed a good job in Otter Lake. That's why I stayed."

"You wouldn't happen to remember the name of the lawyer, do you?" Piers asked.

"No, unfortunately. The only records we keep at the hospital are the mother's and that she was sponsored by the shelter. And if they won't talk to you, I don't know how else we could find out who they were."

Nicole's voice wavered. "And there must be thousands of nine-year-old boys in the city."

"Mark is going through the list of lawyers that could deal with adoption cases. When you eliminate corporate or criminal lawyers, the list gets smaller. I'd say that only a few are unethical enough to *buy* babies for their clients."

"More coffee?"

Nicole's throat was parched with anxiety. "Please."

Bea poured, then smiled. "The adoptive father impressed me. He was such a handsome man. Probably why we, the nurses that is, remember your case. It was different."

They shared a laugh. Bea was only a handful of years older than Nicole.

"He said his name and what his job was, but I'm afraid I can't remember. Sounded a bit foreign, but he looked all Canadian to me." Bea took a drink from her cup, then added as an afterthought, "The wife was nice too. We paid less attention to her. But they were a lovely couple. I'm sure your little boy is happy."

Piers passed his hand through his hair. "That's helpful. We can start looking in Winnipeg and hope that the family didn't move somewhere else."

"Maybe your friend will find the lawyer. I presume he was from the city too. At least we know he wasn't local because he ranted about the cost of the flight. It's your best bet."

"You're right, and thank you very much for talking to us," Nicole said.

They left after promising Bea to let her know the results of their search. On the way to the hotel, Nicole's hopes, if not exactly bubbling over with joy, at least were kept alive by cautious optimism.

Chapter Fifty-One

"Do you really believe the adoptive father is as nice as Bea suggested?"

Piers gave her an amused smile. "She was a young nurse easily impressed by the man's good looks."

"She said he and his wife had wanted to meet me."

"And were concerned about your welfare."

"Then that shows he is considerate. Do you think he and his wife would let me meet Christopher?"

"If they're as nice as it appears, then yes they would."

"What if something's happened? I had the dream again last night."

Piers frowned. "I don't hold any stock in dreams. We just have to be patient and wait to see what Mark finds out."

"I'm just so excited. Thank you so much for helping me."

He reached across and squeezed her hand. "I want you to find your little boy so you can be reassured he's happy and well cared for."

Nicole lapsed into an exhausted silence. Piers concentrated on the driving. He pulled up into a restaurant parking lot.

"Let's have dinner here. It's quaint."

"Why are you doing all this for me, Piers?"

"Maybe because I'm just a nice guy."

She laughed. As she watched him order and flirt with the waitress, her heart lurched out of step. No matter how hard she tried, she'd never stop loving him. If she kept it a secret, she wouldn't be as hurt as if she confessed and he rejected her. Maybe he was right. He was just a nice guy, funny at times, tender and... she blushed inwardly... When she wondered whether his tenderness could be love, she had it wrong. He was just being nice to a fellow human being. A sigh almost choked her, but she kept her composure.

The need to tell him she wasn't going to marry Jack gnawed at her. When the time was right, she'd tell Piers. At least the air would be cleared between them and they could resume their easy-going working relationship. Especially now that she had become a shareholder and a member of the board of directors. A good rapport between the members was essential. As for the future, she'd wait and see. In the meantime, it would be best for her not to engage in anything romantic.

They stayed at a hotel near the airport. Two separate rooms.

After an uneventful flight in the late morning, Piers retrieved his car from the short-term parking and drove home. They collected their mail in the lobby. Nicole bit her lower lip. "Did you want to come up for a cup of coffee?"

"No thanks. I've got some urgent work to finish, and call Mark."

"Okay. Thanks for everything."

They parted. Halfway upstairs, Nicole turned to look back at him. He was watching her. They waved.

* **

Still chewing on Nicole's revelation that Jack wanted to marry her, Piers kept himself busy. While he was at the computer making sales projections for the future stores, Flavio cornered him.

"Why don't you take the afternoon off and go for a run in the park?"

"Too much to do. Why?"

"It be better for your health to run outside. All you do is dash from your car to the lawyer's office."

Piers laughed. "Good point, Flavio."

"Are you avoiding us?" Flavio's eyes showed his compassion.

Out of embarrassment, Piers hesitated. "Not at all."

"I have the sneaky suspicion that maybe you're running away from our Nicole." A silence fell. There was no point in denying what the shrewd old man had obviously seen. "It takes a man to see another man's trouble. What's bugging you?"

"She's had a marriage proposal."

"And it's not yours." With this matter-of-fact statement, Flavio put a floury hand on Piers' shoulder. "So what are you waiting for? Go and propose. In business it's called making a counter-offer, no?"

"I can't do that when there's another man in the picture."

"Chivalry is outmoded. Did she say she's going to marry the other guy?"

Piers sighed. "I don't think she's given her answer yet."

"Why are you sitting on your butt? *Mama mia*! That's not the Piers I know. What's happened to you?"

"I don't know. She's been avoiding me a lot."

"Are you surprised? You're acting like a goofball. You must be in love! Go throw your hat in the ring. You can't win a woman by hiding behind business."

Piers remained silent. "She's been hurt before. I didn't want to pressure her. But I guess you're right. I should speak to her."

"I'm always right."

"Funny, Lynne also gave me much the same pep talk. She told me to propose to Nicole. I'm trying to find the right moment."

"Forget about waiting for the right moment. You're in love. You must stake your claim and defend it."

Piers scratched his head. "What if she doesn't want me?"

"If I know my Nicole, she will. In any case, nothing tried, nothing gained. I want to retire with Mrs. B. soon, so you better get married to keep the business in the family, so to speak. Go now. You maybe the CEO but I'm still the boss. I'll send her home if she turns up here after whatever she's doing at Flavio Silver."

Piers held out his hand. "Thanks, boss." He left.

***

Contradictory emotions threatened to give Nicole the headache of the century. She set out to do a thorough cleaning of her apartment. There was only one thing she had to do. Make sure she tells Jack she is not accepting his proposal and to stop pestering her. Then she'd show Piers how to love. She picked up the phone and dialed Jack's number.

It was busy.

Deflated, she sat looking at the phone. When it rang she jumped up. After four rings, she picked it up but said nothing as Piers had instructed her. Silence at the other end. An unpleasant feeling slithered down her spine.

She dialed Jack's number again. It was still busy. It must mean he was on the internet. He only had a dial-up connection since it was the cheaper option. She grabbed her purse. Minutes later she strode down the street returning greetings on the way. The same creepy feeling she had experienced after the empty phone calls came back. She turned her head and thought she saw a shadow disappear in a doorway. She was becoming paranoid. Then she remember Piers' warnings. She fished her mobile from her purse and speed-dialed Piers.

"Don't move. Stay in view of people. I'll be here in seconds."

The Taurus screeched to a halt in front of her. He had meant seconds. She hurried to climb in.

"Thank you."

"Right, so what were you about to do?"

"Go to Jack and tell him to stop bothering me, that I don't want to marry him."

"I'm glad you came to your senses and call me. What you were about to do is pure folly."

Sheepish, she lowered her head. "I'm sorry. I should have known."

"Let's call the police and open a file."

"Betty's brother is a policeman. We could ask for advice."

"I think we need more than advice. Let's go home."

Piers parked and after looking around the parking lot, took Nicole's arm. In her apartment, she called her friend and explained the situation. Betty promised to tell Carl, a captain.

"Shall I make coffee?" Piers said.

She nodded. Deep in thoughts, she pondered on how to make Piers love her. Small incidents flocked to mind. Piers holding her hand, smiling with tenderness, getting himself rained on while shielding her with the umbrella. His eyes widening in awe and excitement when she told him she had a child. So many images running before her eyes like an endless video loop. Her head began to spin.

And his words. *Maybe I'm just a nice guy.* A nice guy could learn to love. After coffee and cookies, Piers left and waited outside her door until she locked it.

She sat at her laptop and emailed Jack thanking him for his friendship and stating clearly that she had no romantic feelings for him and to get the idea of marriage out of his mind. Then she sent a copy of the email to Carl and Betty who had forcefully told her not to have any personal contact with Jack. Email was much more impersonal and safer. And Jack needed to know where she stood.

Sleep didn't come to her until past midnight. After confessing to lying to her for over six months Piers probably lacked the confidence to approach her. On reflection, she shouldn't have got angry. She ought to have been more compassionate. He did prove himself in so many other ways. It was time to do some repair work.

Her buoyant mood stalled. A chill reality dawned on her. Now she knew he was wealthy, she was going to appear like she was on the make. He must have had his share of women attracted more by his portfolio than his handsome profile. A dry sob raked her chest. She had made a mess of things. And she had told him Jack wanted to marry her. Now that she admitted she didn't want to marry Jack, Piers would think she had changed her mind solely because he was a better prospect than Jack.

Tears pooled under her eyelids. The last thing she wanted to appear was a money grabber, or giving an overdose of gratitude because they were so close to finding her son. She'd better tell him that although she was not marrying Jack, she had no intention of marrying anyone.

A mountain of regrets crumbled down on her. An idyllic image of herself watching from a window as Piers played ball with their two small children who looked just like him came to her mind. To complete the picture and her happiness, Christopher was coming up the walk to pay them a visit.

She shook off the impossible daydream. None of that was in her destiny. Although perhaps, she could change the course of fate. A plan formed in her head to make him fall in love with her. She would make herself more attractive. There were a thousand unknown steps before she reached her goal. The lack of experience was a challenge. Instinct would have to be her guide. One thing was sure, he would have to make the first move. She wouldn't tell him she loved him. Not until he was madly in love with her.

Chapter Fifty-Two

Next day, still chewing on Nicole's revelation that Jack had wanted to marry her, but she hadn't accepted, Piers kept himself busy. While he was at the computer making sales projections for the future stores, Flavio cornered him.

"Any progress?"

"She said she wants to tell Jack she will not marry him."

"And?"

"She left before me this morning."

Flavio took a big breath and exhaled it slowly. "Get out now. I know she left Flavio Silver half-hour ago. She phoned to ask if she was needed here. I told her to go straight home where you are going to be waiting for her."

"Thanks, boss."

On the way to the apartment, Piers wondered how he was going to approach Nicole. Maybe he should sit on top of the stairs and wait for her. Or he could knock on her door as soon as she came home and invite her out to dinner. Flowers! Yes, that was a good idea. He checked his watch and drove to the nearest florist.

He was about to drive off when his cell rang. He grabbed up the receiver.

"Mark! What's new?"

"I found a lawyer who deals with private adoption as a sideline. You still interested?"

"Where? Any hope it could be the one we're looking for?"

"I'm not sure. There are a couple of others who may have done private adoptions too. I want to interview them. I'm catching a flight in half an hour. Do you have a bed in your cave?"

"Not yet, but there'll be one when you get here. What time does your flight get in? You need to connect with Flying Otter Air."

"Already done. The bush plane will arrive at six-thirty your time. I could check into the hotel, though it's more convenient if I crash at your place."

"I'll pick you up at the airstrip."

Excitement spurred Piers' steps. This was an ideal excuse to speak to Nicole other than business. In minutes, he was at the furniture store a block away from the thrift store.

"I'll take this brown sofa-bed you have on sale. I'll take these blankets and comforters too. And throw in a couple of good pillows."

"Anything else?"

Piers smiled. "That'll do for the moment. Can you deliver this afternoon?"

"Sorry, sir. It'll have to be tomorrow."

"I need all of them tonight. How much for the delivery?"

"We just can't do it."

"Where's the manager?"

The woman rolled her eyes. She didn't have a chance to reply. Piers was already knocking on the office door. A middle-aged woman, dressed in an elegant prune linen suit, raised her head from a thick catalogue.

Her eyes flicked up and down on him as though he was an item of furniture she was putting a price tag on.

"What can I do for you?"

"You could arrange for the delivery this afternoon of the sofa and other items I just bought. Deliver before six o'clock, preferably."

"Our truck is out and not due back before five."

Piers gave her one of his charmer smile and lowered his voice. "Your clerk was most helpful with my purchases until it came to delivery. Surely you can find something. You must have casual workers who deliver, don't you?"

"We get a transfer company, but they need advanced warning."

Her sigh told Piers she must have had this problem before. He switched his voice to his business tone. "If I were running your store instead of Flavio's Pizzeria, I'd have a list of small delivery companies lined up who'd be more than happy to help without notice."

Her eyes lit up. "You're the manager of Flavio's?"

"CEO, yes."

"That's a fantastic come back Flavio Bellini made."

"I'm glad you know him."

"We attend the Chamber of Commerce meetings together. Will you be there next month?"

"I certainly will."

"The way you've expanded the pizzeria to Silver River and Porcupine Creek is just wonderful. In the meantime, leave this small matter of delivery to me. Your sofa will be delivered in good time this afternoon."

"Thank you, Ms...?"

"Jill Yarrow. Call me Jill."

Piers shook the offered hand. "I'm Piers. Pleased to meet you, Jill. We'll do business again, I'm sure."

He left the office and nearly collided with the sales clerk. He wagged his finger at her. "Naughty, naughty listening at the door."

She laughed and turned away.

Piers sauntered out and hurried home. He knew that today, Nicole was helping out with the books in Flavio Silver and according to Flavio she had already left. It couldn't be more perfect.

A few minutes before five, Piers stood guard in the lobby, with a bouquet of twelve red roses on his arm. A cube van, with the logo *We Deliver the Moon*, backed up to the main entrance. The driver jumped out waving a sheet of paper. Another man joined him. Piers opened the door to them.

"Special delivery. You Mr. Sonder?"

"That's right."

He showed them downstairs. "Looks like we got here just in time. Where do you want the sofa? We're setting it up for you."

"Thanks." Piers put the flowers on the table. "Let me move the cot to the other side."

The men carried in his purchases and tested the bed mechanism. Piers acted as a doorman. His shoulders sagged. Five o'clock had passed. Nicole must have come back and gone up to her apartment while he was downstairs. Now he had to rush to the airstrip to fetch Mark. The flowers sat forlorn on his wobbly table, but there was no time for him to call on Nicole.

Chapter Fifty-Three

When Nicole arrived, she saw a truck and two men carrying a large sofa. She assumed it was Rob and Tina moving out. She avoided the main entrance and went through the parking lot. She heard a commotion coming from the lobby and hurried upstairs to avoid being trapped between the wall and a piece of furniture.

The first thing she did was to take a shower. Then she selected her prettiest dress. Still conservative in design with its hem just at the knees, the bronze cashmere flattered her figure and enhanced her eye color.

For a while she agonized over her hair. Up in a bun, as she did it every day, or loose on her shoulders? The thick waves spoke of sensuality. Piers once said how he liked to run his fingers through the shiny mass. It wasn't in her plan to appear to go all out to seduce him. She sorted through her collection of hair clasps and settled on an antique silver barrette she had got for a song at the thrift store. Her tresses held back, she gave herself a satisfied glance in the mirror. The ponytail was not as severe as a bun, yet less provocative than loose hair over the shoulders... and the barrette would easily come off if needed. She flushed at the thought.

Sandals with a medium heel and a matching purse completed her outfit. About to walk out she remembered makeup. He might kiss her. Well, if he didn't maybe she should kiss him. No, if she had read the signs properly, he'd be sure to kiss her. According to her plan, he had to make the first move. Waterproof mascara and a light pink lipstick would do.

Her heart beating at a ragged pace, she closed her door and descended the stairs. She knocked on Piers' door.

No reply.

Six-thirty. He ought to be home. Her arms dropped to her sides.

With a heavy tread, she went back upstairs. So much for her big seduction plan. The sight of the phone lifted her mood. Call the pizzeria to find out what had delayed him.

Five minutes later her mood plunged into an abyss of gloom. He had taken the afternoon off. Sprawled on the sofa, her thoughts drifted aimlessly. Maybe she was wrong to go after him. Yet she felt she had to tell him that... that what? Tell him that she was in love with him. No, that was too direct. Sure to send him packing. Or that she valued their friendship and it seemed to have crumbled. Yes, that was a good opener.

Mentally, she rehearsed her lines. *You know, Piers, I over-reacted when you told me about your past and your background. I don't mind your lies, really. You proved you're the best possible man. I highly value your friendship. And I'm so grateful to you for your help toward finding my son. In a matter of days you made more progress than I had over the last two years.* No scrub that.

He had become cold toward her. Or was he just keeping his distances as in respect? She wound her imaginary recording tape back to the moment when she told him Jack had asked her to marry him. What a stupid mistake she had made. She still couldn't understand why she had blurted out that fact. A dry sob caught in her throat. Piers had acted honorably. He had stepped back. Unless, of course, he did so because he didn't have romantic feelings for her. But now he knew she wasn't going to marry Jack.

Back in the horrible days when she found herself wandering the streets, alone and pregnant, she never gave up. She wasn't about quit to now. Tomorrow she'd see Piers and ask him out on a date. Tonight was a failure. She chalked it up to bad luck.

As she stood up to change, there was a knock on her door. A surge of delight overcame her at the sight of the two good-looking men on her doorstep.

Piers and a stranger.

"Nicole, you look ravishing!" Piers smiled a broad smile.

"Thanks."

"Were you going out?"

"I'd hoped to find you at home."

"Nicole, this is my friend Mark Bergson. Mark, meet Nicole."

"Very pleased to meet you, Nicole."

Mark reached behind Piers' back and handed the bouquet to her. Her eyes registered surprise.

Piers voice rose in alarm. "Hey, Mark, those flowers are mine!"

A momentary ripple of confused emotion went through her. Then she burst out laughing. Piers had bought her flowers. She recovered.

Her happiness flowed back. "Come in, both of you."

She extended her hand. "Mark. I must thank you for finding Nurse Riemer for me."

"It was my pleasure, Nicole. You're even more beautiful than Piers said."

She blushed. "You're too kind."

Piers frowned at his friend. "When you've finished flirting, I'd like to speak."

Her eyes sparkled. "Please, make yourselves at home. I'll go and put these in a vase."

"Mark's just arrived, and I'd like to take you out to a restaurant."

Her heart clicked into racing mode. He had bought her flowers. He wanted to take her out to dinner. "That'd be wonderful." Of course, Mark would be there. In a way that was good. His presence would help ease any awkwardness.

In no time they arrived at the Polar Night restaurant, which of course offered Flavio's pizzas. They opted for Italian cuisine. The excellent food was enlivened with Mark's witty anecdotes about his not-so-glamorous life as a lawyer and private investigator, his hobby or so he claimed, and courtroom anecdotes.

On arriving home, it was natural for Nicole to ask them up to her apartment for a nightcap.

Piers patted the space next to him on the sofa. "Mark didn't come here on a friendly visit to me. He's on business."

"I've come to interview some lawyers, one in particular, who may have dealt with the private adoption of your baby."

Nicole leaned forward. "Is there really a chance of finding out?"

"I'd say a good chance, but no guarantee that he'll admit to anything."

"If that's the case, we'd have to threaten him with legal action as well as against the shelter," Piers said.

"It wouldn't bring Christopher back." Her voice wavered with renewed anxiety.

"You said you wanted to keep your baby and that you didn't know what papers they made you sign, plus you were underage. That will get the sympathetic ear of a judge," Mark said.

"Especially if she is a woman," Piers said.

"I was too young and too naïve to know what was happening. All these years I lived in fear of being arrested for kidnaping my sister. During that time, I never dared begin to search for my baby, never mind consult a lawyer."

Mark shook his head. "I specialized in family law. That includes finding disappearing children and spouses. My PI agency does a lot of searching for children that one parent abducted out of malice in separation cases. They're difficult to find. It's upsetting when children are used as pawns between two feuding people. I do have a few avenues to find people though."

"I only want to make sure Christopher is happy and well cared for. I want him to know I didn't abandon him."

Piers took her hand in his. "We're close to the goal."

Mark's eyes followed the gesture. He looked at his watch. "It's past my bedtime. I should turn in. Give me your apartment key."

"I guess I better hit the sack too." Piers sighed loudly and stood up. "I'll see you tomorrow, Nicole. How about a run before we go to the pizzeria?"

"That'd be nice. But excuse me butting in. Where's Mark going to sleep?"

"I bought a sofa, a new one, and got it delivered this afternoon."

Her mouth formed an O. "I should have known!"

After the door closed behind the two men, Nicole ran a caressing finger over a velvet-soft rose. In the midst of the red roses stood a tiny pink rose bud. The poignant symbolism brought tears to her eyes. Piers was more than just "a nice guy". His touching gesture proved he was caring and sensitive. Red roses meant love in the language of flowers, and pink signified sweetness, innocence, like a baby. She wished she hadn't given him the cold shoulder or ever doubted his motives. Perhaps it wasn't too late for them. Tomorrow on their run she'd make amends. An apology was definitely needed.

In a lighter mood than she'd been in for a long time she tidied up the apartment thinking of Piers and the kiss she'd bestow on his lips the following morning.

Chapter Fifty-Four

"Excuse the impertinent question. If you just bought this sofa, where the hell did you sleep before? Or is the question superfluous?"

Piers pointed to the cot disappearing under the packages of bedding. "Not what you think. I slept on this old army cot."

Mark chuckled. "You put up with an army cot with a beautiful woman upstairs, I'm surprised!"

"Nicole isn't that sort of woman. She had a suitor. That jerk. She liked him and I hadn't told her who I was."

"A suitor! What a quaint old-fashioned term. Don't tell me you bowed to the competition!"

"I wanted her to find happiness. Since then though, I've changed my mind."

"You mean you wish her to find unhappiness?"

"No, dummy, I mean I had changed my mind about sitting on the sidelines."

"Hence the roses."

Piers shrugged. "Oh! Oops! I've got to get my laundry out of the dryer. It's not fair to the other tenants to leave it for them to take out and clean the filter.

They both went to the laundry room and made short of the work. Piers picked up the basket while Mark kept the door open. A loud crash and a scream stopped them in their tracks.

"Nicole!" Piers dropped the basket and bounded upstairs. Mark rushed behind him, cell phone in hand.

***

Betty's phone played its jingle. Her brother Carl was on the line.

"It looks like the Jack Wilshire you ask me to look up may not be who he claims to be."

"Dangerous?"

"Although it's a different name, I found a predator, maybe two unless it's the same I don't know yet, who registers for courses at a university, in accounting. He picks one or two female students, takes his time then offers marriage. One was found dead in a wedding dress in a black van. The Mounties had obtained a doorbell camera video from a witness doorbell camera."

"Jack doesn't have a vehicle. But you scare me. I'll go to see Nicole, she's just told him she wouldn't marry him."

"Stay put! I have officers picking up the individual at this very moment. We just compared the video and the Wiltshire individual. It's him alright."

Carl raised his voice. "Not on your own, you don't."

"Her phone doesn't answer. I'm going!" She grabbed her purse and ran to her car. She threw the cell on the seat, put the phone hand-free mode and peeled off along the avenue.

"I'm on duty... Oh! Crap! We've got a call." Still on the phone he hollered orders in the background. "Betty! I'll meet you there. Don't go in without me!"

"Okay, but I'm driving there now."

Mindless of the speed limit, Betty arrived at the grand old house and looked for a space and parked in front of a black van. Icy fear ran into her belly. She stuck her forehead against the driver's window to see inside. She recoiled in horror and, phone in hand yelled. "Carl, there's a wedding dress in a black van at Nicole's-"

"Stay put! We're on our way!"

***

Piers shoved the open door. It flew back hitting the wall. A shelf rattled and china tumbled down. Faster than lightning, Piers had hold of Jack Wiltshire. Mark had already sped-dialed 911. The man flew in the air, his feet toward the ceiling. He landed face down with a heavy thump. Before he could move, Piers straddled him and twisted his arms on his back, bringing the hands level with the man's shoulder. Wiltshire yelled with pain.

Mark hurried to a gasping Nicole collapsed on the sofa. Still holding his phone, he put his free arm around her shoulders and pulled her against him.

"Yes, ma'am. The intruder is now subdued by the neighbor. I can hear the sirens already. Thank you."

The communication cut off but Mark kept filming with his phone.

"My arm! You broke my arm." Jack struggled against Piers powerful hold.

"Shut up! You scum!" With one hand gripping both Jack's wrists, the other one tightened his shirt collar, lifting his head just above the rug. "Shut up or I'll break your neck."

"Piers! The cavalry has arrived. Be gentle." The irony in the recommendation drew a small, sad smile from Nicole. Her breathing slowed down.

Before any time elapsed, the red and blue lights flashed on the walls. The siren cut off. The ground floor tenants' doors were open. Rob had run upstairs. He flattened himself against the wall to let the three officers enter Nicole's apartment. Betty sidled behind. Mrs. Harlow opened her door, shaken and stuttering. Although Rob wanted to know what had happened, he helped their aging landlady down to his suite and let his wife look after her. He stayed by his opened door and greeted the other neighbor also standing by his door.

The two constables had Jack handcuffed and on his feet and being told that under section 7 of the Charter of Rights anything he said during arrest would not be admissible in court.

In Piers' arms, Nicole shuddered. Carl issued a couple of orders and kneeled in front of her.

"How badly hurt are you, Nicole?"

She shook her head. Piers was examining her legs, arms, running his hand in her back. "Nothing appears broken."

She tried to shake her head again and buried closer into his arms. "I opened the door thinking it was you and Mark coming up for the last cup of coffee."

She caught sight of Betty coming out of the kitchen with a steaming cup and a glass of water. She took Mark's place.

"Sip the water slowly while the honey tea cools. You're in shock." She turned to her brother. "What about the black van?"

Carl pressed the button on his radio. "Tom, check the black van." To Nicole, "You'll give me a statement when you feel better."

"I'm okay." She told Carl about her misunderstanding of Jack's personality and how she was putting him off after he proposed and became forceful.

Mark held up his phone. "Do you want me to send you Piers' intervention? It was quite spectacular."

"Yes, please. Does it show the broken door?"

"It does."

Carl's radio crackled. "Phony licence plates."

"Get it towed to the garage for forensic examination. Send me the particulars of those Joe Watson and Jerry Worring I uncovered yesterday, J W same initials for the three IDs." He turned to his sister. "You're a good detective, but next time you want to snoop around a man's apartment you call me first, okay? You might have been next on his list."

Betty looked the picture of sweetness. "With you looking so much the cop in civilian clothes, I couldn't have gone to the bathroom while he was making coffee and seen all those pictures of Nicole, some life size, plastered on his bedroom walls."

Mark and Piers looked at each other appalled by the revelation.

Pale and trembling Nicole straightened, a look of determination on her features. "I regret being a fool and opening the door without looking through the peephole. When I saw Jack, I suddenly became frightened. He had a look on his face, so I screamed."

A while later, Betty shooed everyone out of the apartment. "I'm staying with Nicole."

Piers tried to protest it was his job, but Betty wouldn't listen. He and Mark retreated.

***

"I didn't know that Jack guy was a sicko, but I hated the sight of him. Boy! Do I feel stupid."

Mark raised his hands in a fatalistic gesture. "You couldn't have known. Nobody did."

They made up the sofa bed and Piers switched off the light. He tried to shake the rage that still made his nerves taut by reliving the earlier moment the door opened upon Nicole looking so beautiful.

Sitting in the restaurant, watching her get admiring glances from men at other tables had put him on edge. Had he not been so sure of his long-standing friendship with Mark, he'd have punched him for flirting with her.

An irrational feeling of possession welled up from deep inside. That too must be part of love. That he wanted to spend the rest of his life with her had now become ingrained in his psyche. He had to figure out a way to show he was worthy of her.

No simple task.

Chapter Fifty-Five

In the pre-dawn, Piers slipped out of the apartment without waking Mark stretched out on the sofa-bed. He took the stairs two at a time and whistled a tune softly. Nicole opened the door before he could knock. His whole body tightened at the sight of her long legs encased in winter running pants that showed her shape rather than hide it. She smiled and pushed him with one hand on his chest while she closed the door. The imprint burned him. Breathless, he controlled the sensation.

"Good morning. Are you sure you want to go jogging this early? It's still dark."

Nicole's laughter bubbled up. "Now, now, I can well imagine what you have in mind."

"Not just in mind."

Betty joined them. "I made honey tea. You should have some before you go off running in the cold."

After a recap of the previous day's events, Betty sent them out. "I'll make breakfast for when you come back. I want to make sure Nicole's has no late ill effects. Have fun."

They let themselves out of the building into the cool of the November morning.

"I had the scare of my life, but I feel okay now. And Piers?"

"I'm so glad you came up so fast."

"You're safe now. Let's speed up. It's going to be cold today, maybe a little snow too."

"That's the prairies for you."

They reached the top of the hillock. Piers took her hand. They sat on the brown grass sprinkled with a thin blanket of hard snowy frost, and sipped from their water bottles.

Both spoke at the same time.

"I must tell you something..."

They burst out laughing.

"Ladies first."

Nicole took a deep breath. "I've been wanting to tell you that although Jack had asked me to marry him, I never wanted to... because my heart belongs to another man." She bit her bottom lip and gave Piers the look of a child seeking forgiveness for a silly mistake.

Piers' jaws clenched. Thoughts tumbled in his brain. "Who?" His tone bordered on the savage.

Their gaze locked. As have all women in the world known since creation, she recognized his love. Then she laughed.

"Who? Why, the idiot sitting on the snow beside me. No cancel that, I never meant to say it." She reddened.

Piers knocked his water bottle over in his haste to throw his arms around her and pull into a tight embrace. Not giving her time to protest, he took her lips in a fiery kiss. They rolled in wild abandon in the snow. Piers' mind swam as he savored all the sweetness of her kiss. Only with effort did he lift his head.

"I love you! Oh, Nicole, how I love you!" There he had said it, and it was right.

"I love you too, Piers. I wish I'd said it before I knew you were a rich man. I can't marry you though."

For an instant he remained numb with shock. Then the obvious dawned on him. "My sweetheart, I'm a regular working guy. You can marry me. But I haven't asked you yet."

"It must be the winter heat. I'm behaving like a lovesick adolescent." A deep blush invaded her cheeks. She sat up.

"I feel like a dumb kid lying like this in the snow, but what I feel for you is a whole lot more grown up than a teenager's love. It's a grown man's love. It's forever-after kind of love." Piers drew himself up onto one knee. "Nicole, will you marry me?"

"I was determined not to tell you how much I loved you. I was awake all night trying to convince myself I wasn't going to admit my love, that you couldn't possibly want to spend the rest of your life with me. I was going to let you fall in love with me. Then I just blurted it out. I'm babbling..."

"I fell in love with you from the start. Only, I didn't understand it. I had some issues to resolve before I could tell you. I was just a bum when I turned up on your doorstep. By hiring me, even though maybe you didn't trust me, you gave me the chance to prove myself, to become someone useful. I lived through a lot of anguish. All the while, the only thing I wanted was to love you."

A pent-up breath escaped her lungs. "I'm so confused. During the time I've been looking for my baby, I've never had a relationship with anyone. It seems that when I'm in the company of people, I clam up and can't take part in the conversation. Not the sort of wife material a CEO needs."

"Get rid of all those doubts right now. You're the most wonderful woman I've met. I love you and want to marry you. Say yes now."

Her eyes misted over. "Yes."

Piers gathered her in his arms. He sealed her reply with a long kiss. His fingers trailed a light caress from her cheek, down her neck down and under her windbreaker. A wolf whistle sounded from a passing jogger. The man's footsteps faded into the distance.

Piers and Nicole sat up. "I have something that's been burning my pocket since I went home." He pulled out the ring box. "My mother gave me this when I visited. It was my great-grandmother's, and her mother before that. It's been passed down the generations to the first son for his bride." He opened the box, took out the ring and put it on her fourth finger where it fitted as if it had been made for her.

The early morning sun caught the liquid-green emerald and scattered it in a million beads of colored light.

"It fits me and it is beyond word beautiful."

"And matches the color of your eyes."

She ran an exploratory finger over the row of diamonds and rubies circling the oval stone. "I don't have any words to express what I feel."

"No need for words." He took her lips with his.

She responded eagerly leaning hard against his chest. The swish of a runner's nylon sweats and the slap-slap of sneakers reminded them they were in a very public place.

"We should go home," Nicole whispered.

They jogged back, hand in hand, looking at each other occasionally with a promise in their eyes. As they arrived at the entrance of the building, they literally collided with Mark. After they all regained their balance, Piers shoulders sagged.

"Hey, lovebirds, you're up early! Tell me where I can go and get breakfast before I start work. I've never seen a fridge so empty, Piers. What happened to you since our college days?"

"It's a long story."

"Why don't you both come upstairs and I'll cook breakfast."

Mark's eyes shone. "Now that's my kind of woman. Would you like to spend your life cooking for me?"

Nicole waggled her fingers under his nose. Her ring sparkled in the lobby's light. "Too late, Mark. I'm spoken for."

"Son of a gun!" Mark pointed his chin in Piers' direction. "And he's the lucky guy?"

"Yes, he is."

Mark shook his head. "You don't deserve her, man."

Piers punched him on the arm and they trooped inside.

Betty eyed Mark. "Just in time, breakfast is prepared."

The men's joking continued until Nicole and Betty put a plate of bacon and fluffy omelet in front of each of them. Betty's gaze settled on Mark who told of some scrapes he had got into in the course of his job. He kept glancing at her.

"This is nice and cozy, but it's time to get back to work," Mark said.

"We'll be at the office today. Call me on my cell."

Betty turned to Mark. "I'll give you a ride wherever you need to go."

"That'd be great."

They waved goodbye.

When they were gone, Nicole turned to Piers. "Did I understood that you saved his life?"

"If not his life, at least saved him from serious injury."

"So what's the story?"

"Later. Can we talk about us instead?"

"Nope. We're supposed to be at work in half an hour."

He sighed. "Not enough time for what I had in mind." He pulled Nicole into his arms and kissed her. Heat mounted between them. Their breathing shortened. He raised his head a fraction to let her take air. "We don't have to go to the office just yet."

"Yes, we do," she replied. "We have a meeting with the staff."

After Nicole, whose voice as she recounted her ordeal, the meeting started. It was conducted in the newly renovated office with some staff member from the other two locations. Piers' cell rang. He excused himself for a moment and stepped outside to answer his phone.

"What do you mean, he's looking for her?... Can't have been trying too hard."

"He concentrated his search in Toronto," Mark replied. "Can you make it in the city this afternoon at one? There's a letter, but he didn't want to give it to me."

"If we leave now, we'll be there."

Piers put his cell back in his pocket and rejoined the group. Flavio had everyone laughing with his off-beat humor.

"Can you spare Nicole and me this afternoon?" Piers asked.

"Why, are you eloping?" Lynne's voice rippled with humor.

For a brief instant Piers and Nicole looked stunned.

Lynne laughed. "I'd have to be blind not to notice the beautiful emerald weighing down Nicole's left hand."

They all turned to stare at Nicole's ring. She lifted her hand to let them admire it.

Pandemonium broke loose. The kitchen staff abandoned their work to find out what the ruckus was about. Even a few customers came over to offer congratulations.

Finally, order was re-established.

"When is the wedding?" Lynne asked.

Nicole laughed. "We haven't had time to talk about it yet."

"Good, we can go shopping and get everything ready," Lynne said.

Nicole and Piers made their way to his car.

"You didn't tell me why we're taking the afternoon off."

"The call was from Mark. He met with Lawrence Pim, a lawyer. Apparently, he's been trying to find you. He has a letter he wants to give you. We're meeting Mark at the lawyer's office at four."

Her heart beat faster. "What do you think it's all about?"

"If Bea Riemer is right, maybe the parents want to locate you."

A stricken expression crossed her face. "I've heard stories of adoptive parents searching for the biological mother because the child has a life-threatening disease. Is that why I had the dream?"

Piers put his hand over hers. "Probably not. If it were, they would have advertised in newspapers and magazines, even on the TV nationwide."

The rest of the drive passed in silence. Finally, they pulled up at the lawyer's office.

Mark was already there and made the introductions.

Agitated, Nicole couldn't hold back any longer. "Mark said you were looking for me."

"Yes, Ms. Desmond. I never thought of searching for you in Otter Lake. I had ads in the Toronto and Ottawa newspapers, unaware you had left long ago."

"Did something happen to my... my child?"

The lawyer shook his head. "Not to the child. To the mother... his adoptive mother."

She let out the breath she had been holding. The lawyer handed her an envelope.

"I'm sorry. What happened?"

"She died of cancer. Mr. Forsyth came to me shortly after his wife's death and asked me to find you. He gave me a letter addressed to you. Then every six months for the next two years, he wrote an updated letter. This is the latest one, written only a couple of months ago."

Her fingers trembling, Nicole ripped open the letter. It was handwritten in a neat sloping script.

Dear Ms. Desmond,

My name is Jostein Forsyth. Nine years ago my wife Jill and I adopted your son Christopher. We were not allowed to meet you at the time but always hoped we would eventually connect and let Christopher get to know you when he was old enough to understand.

I am sad to tell you my dear wife Jill died two years ago. Since that time I have been searching in earnest for you in order to respect my wife final wishes. She was hoping you would want to come into our son's life.

If you read this, I beg you to contact me as soon as possible. Christopher has withdrawn into himself since his mother's death, to the point he barely speaks and never laughs.

Nicole didn't read to the end. The letter slipped from her fingers and floated to the floor. Piers bent to pick it up.

Nicole got to her feet. "I must see Christopher now."

Lawrence Pim held up his hand. "Please Ms. Desmond, allow me to call Jostein first."

She sank back in her chair. "Of course."

Piers put an arm around her shoulders. "We're going to see Christopher. Just let's wait until Lawrence phones to make sure Jostein Forsyth is at home and prepares Christopher for the meeting."

All the while she waited, her impatience threatened to boil over. Pim finished talking and replaced the phone on his desk.

"Jostein's leaving his office right now and will meet you at his house. Jostein said he'd like to speak to you first before you meet the boy. There was a teachers' in-service today, so no school. His son and his housekeeper are at the zoo going through that amazing 'Journey to Churchill' polar bear sanctuary. He's picking them up after work so you'll have time to talk to him."

It was strange to hear the lawyer talk of Jostein Forsyth's *son*, just as it had been reading *our son* in the letter. Emotions she'd never experienced before churned up inside her. Piers thanked the lawyer. He steered Nicole to the door.

Downstairs, Mark halted. "I'll leave you two. Good luck, Nicole. Piers, I have the apartment key you gave me. See you later. Betty and I are going to grab some dinner."

During the short drive to Wellington Crescent, Nicole bit her finger nails. She sat on the edge of the seat. "Do you think my dress is okay?"

"It's great and makes you look even more beautiful."

"I'm so nervous. What if Christopher doesn't like me? They did call him Christopher. Isn't that sweet of them? Are we there yet? I should have worn jeans. Everybody wears jeans-"

"Slow down, sweetheart. You look fantastic. Christopher will love you. But remember it may take some time before he does. He's been traumatized. We're just turning onto Wellington. Look out for the number."

"I can't believe that all this time he was close, and I never knew."

Piers parked across from two tall Colorado spruce that partly screened an elegant house overlooking the river. Nicole leaped out. Piers grabbed her by the arm to prevent her from dashing across the street. A Cadillac SUV sat in the driveway in front of the three-car garage. Nicole saw nothing of the stone facing and the deep red trim of the double storey house. Her eyes remained glued to the oak doorway flanked by ornamental leaded windows.

A tall, handsome man opened the door without them having to press the bell.

He came forward to greet them. "Ms. Desmond? I'm Jostein Forsyth. Please come in, I..."

The words died in his throat. "Forgive me for saying so. My son... *your* son bears a striking resemblance to you." He let out a long breath and turned to Piers. "And you must be Piers Reddington?"

The two men shook hands.

Nicole extended her hand. "Please call me Nicole. I'm so happy to meet you."

Jostein took her two hands in his and held them a moment. "This is a wonderful occasion." A shadow passed over his eyes. "I only wish Jill could be here to meet you. We spent a long time trying to locate you."

Jostein led them into an airy living room. The muted decor showed off the tasteful teak furniture. Simple but intimate. He scooped magazines and books off the coffee table and stacked them on a roll-top desk.

"Please take a seat. Would you like coffee, tea, juice?"

"Juice will do fine," Piers said.

While Jostein was in the kitchen, Piers told her to breathe deeply and relax. Nicole closed her eyes. Jostein came back with a tray of glasses and a pitcher of juice.

"My housekeeper makes it."

An awkward silence settled in the room until Nicole took the initiative.

"I've been searching for Christopher because I hadn't wanted to give him up. He was adopted. I finally accepted the fact. I never wanted to take him away from his loving adoptive parents. I just wanted to be reassured... and maybe the parents would let us get to know each other. I'm babbling..."

Jostein leaned forward. "You said you *didn't* want to give him up?"

"I wanted to keep my baby. At the time I didn't know that the papers I signed were release papers."

"Heaven and earth! Your baby was taken away from you against your wishes?"

"Yes." There was a lifetime of suffering in that simple word.

Jostein ran his hand through his hair. "The adoption lawyer, Lucas Berton, assured me the baby was free to be adopted. The legal work had been professionally taken care of. He's done several adoptions with the shelter and I had no reason to doubt this one was not above board. You, we, could sue the shelter, though it might be difficult because you did sign the release."

Nicole brought her fist to her mouth and fought off the tears that threatened to spill from her eyes. His face ravaged with suppressed grief, Jostein kneeled beside her.

Piers held her hand. "Suing is something we might consider later.

Selling babies might be a charge that would hold."

"The money I paid was supposed to be for the mother's care at the home and hospital extra costs for a private room. Then another large sum was for her to get a new start in life."

"Someone pocketed that money. We can deal with that later," Piers said. "Right now, let's face the all important meeting between mother and son."

Nicole sniffed. "I had a dream two years ago. The dream came back again and again that Christopher was unhappy, was calling to me."

A look of awe came on Jostein's face. "That's uncanny. There must be some kind of bond between you and him that I can't understand. Jill died two years ago. Since that day, Christopher has been suffering from selective mutism. His teacher understands and doesn't push him to talk in class. She walks with him at recess and asks him questions that he can answer with yes or no. The school staff has been really good, especially when some kids started bullying him last year. But he hasn't talked to me in two years." Tears welled up in the man's eyes.

Nicole sucked in a breath.

"He doesn't play," Jostein said. I can't get him to do anything at home. "He keeps his room tidy, so tidy it's unnatural for a small boy. He helps Eileen, my housekeeper, in the kitchen but remains silent. All he does is read books. I'm sure he's reading at several grades above his age level. Yet he won't talk about his books or anything. Toys sit untouched in his room."

"Your wife must have loved him very much," Nicole said. Her eyes again brimmed with tears.

"She did. I do too. He lets me hold him. I talk to him, talk about all our good times and memories, but he doesn't respond."

"Did you get professional help?" Piers asked.

"I consulted three child psychologists and one psychiatrist. They said it's a childhood anxiety disorder. They had no success. It was his third-grade teacher who suggested I find his biological mother as quickly as possible. I told her I was already searching. We had told

Christopher he was adopted."

"For him it must have been losing his mother twice," Piers said.

They nodded in silence.

"So what do we do next? Do you think he will accept me?" Nicole's voice trembled with contained anxiety.

Jostein wiped the back of his hand over his forehead. "All we can do is try. I'll explain it all to him when I go and pick him up at the zoo. He's awfully smart and mature for his age. Your feelings are important too. Do you want to be part of his life?"

"Jostein, how can I express how much over the years I've been hoping to hear those very words?"

"Then I believe it was a miracle when your lawyer friend tracked down Lawrence Pim, my lawyer."

He stood up and reached into a cabinet to pull out three thick photo albums. "While I go and fetch him, I'm sure you'd like to look at photographs of Christopher's life over the past nine years."

"Thank you. And thank you for keeping the name I gave him."

"It was on his hospital bracelet. Jill and I had gone to the hospital to meet you. We were hurt that they turned us away. We were so grateful to the young mother who was giving us her child. It was only right to respect the name she had chosen, besides we really like it. My grandfather was called Christopher. While I'm out, please make yourself at home. The kitchen is at your disposal."

"Thanks, we'll look at the albums."

For the next hour, Nicole and Piers pored over the photos. They were all labeled and neatly glued in the albums. An irrational pang of envy gnawed at her at the sight of the slender woman who was holding baby Christopher. Nicole shook off the feeling quickly. Her baby looked serenely happy. She laughed at the fun snapshots, at the beach, him on his first bike.

The sound of a door opening jerked her back to the present.

A matronly woman with sparkling blue eyes came in to say hello and disappeared into the kitchen. Moments later, Jostein led in a tall, slim boy with dark hair and green eyes.

Christopher.

Nicole stared at him until Piers touched her shoulder.

Jostein put his hand on the boy's head. Without warning a furious barking erupted in the outer hall and a bundle of white fur threw itself at Christopher. He bent down and buried his face in the furry neck of a Samoyed. "Sit, Lulu." The words were barely audible. The dog sat.

The sound of his voice coursed through Nicole. She shuddered.

"As I've explained to you at the zoo, Chris, this lady is your biological mother and she wants very much to meet you."

"Hi Christopher." The greeting sounded lame to her ears, but that was all she could get out of her constricted throat.

The serious little boy looked intently at Nicole for an interminable time. "Dad told me, you're my other mother."

Jostein's eyes filled with amazement at the sound of the boy's voice, a voice a touch raspy.

"That's right. I'm the mother who carried you in her tummy."

Another long silence. The adults held their breath.

"You can't be my mom. I already have a mom, except she's gone to heaven."

Jostein wiped back a tear. "You sort of have two mothers. Your mom Jill who raised you and loved you. Then you have your biological mother Nicole who loved you and looked for you, but didn't find you until now."

Christopher's mouth puckered. Another long silence fell.

Nicole wondered whether he'd retreated into himself after his brief outburst. Then the boy took a deep breath. "Why did you give me away?"

She could see his mind working. "I didn't give you away. You were taken away from me."

He frowned and turned to his father. "Did you steal me?"

"No. We'd applied to adopt a baby. We didn't know the people in charge of the adoption had taken you away from your biological mom."

More silence. Christopher swung back to Nicole. "Did you put my picture on social media?"

Nicole struggled to answer the legitimate questions of her child.

Distress warped her features.

Piers came to her rescue. "There was no photo of you. The people who took you away weren't really bad people, only not very nice because they didn't listen to your mother."

"I wanted to keep you."

"You were lucky when your dad and your mom adopted you because they loved you," Piers said.

Another silence stretched over the tense scene. Nicole knew the nine-year-old had to work it out for himself. If his father was right, this was the most he had spoken in the last two years.

"Do you want to be my mom?"

"Very much."

He turned to his dad, opened his mouth and closed it again. Finally he spoke. "How can she be my mom if she isn't married to you?"

"You know that sometimes moms and dads are not married."

"Yeah."

Jostein put his hand on his shoulder. "You could stay with her sometimes when I have to go away on business. We can have all the family things together."

The proposition appeared interesting to Christopher. He looked up at Piers. "Are you going to be my dad too?"

"If you'd like me to, I'd love to be your dad number two."

Christopher looked thoughtful and remained silent for a while. "Some kids in my class have two dads and two moms because the first ones got divorced."

"Then it's pretty good. They get double of everything," Piers said.

"Nope. One girl cries because she prefers to have just her real mom and dad."

"Our situation is different, Chris. Those kid's parents fought and were unhappy. So they separated," Jostein said in a gentle voice.

The little boy sighed. "Right. I don't have a mom any more because she's gone to heaven, but I get another one."

Nicole opened her arms. Her heart stopped while she waited.

Christopher glanced at his father, hesitated and took a tiny step toward her, then another. She closed her arms around him, her eyes brimming with tears. Her heart threatened to jump out of her chest. He linked his arms around her neck. Hers tightened as she kissed the top of his head. "Christopher, I waited such a long time for this."

Without warning, he burst into tears. Lulu whined and stood on her hind legs to rest her head on Nicole's lap, pushing at her young master.

Jostein turned away to blow his nose. He regained some measure of control and murmured. "This is the first time he cried since Jill's death. He didn't even cry at the funeral. I can't get over how much he's just spoken."

Nicole stroke her child's hair. Big sobs still racked his body. Finally, he pulled away and touched the front of her dress.

"Look! I've made you all wet."

Piers handed her a tissue. She took it and gently dried Christopher's face.

"It'll dry, don't worry."

Christopher laughed. A crystal clear sound that brought sunshine into the room. An expectant hush fell.

"Dad, can we go to MacDonald's?"

Jostein swallowed hard. "Of course! Go put Lulu in her kennel first."

At her name the dog bounded to the door.

Jostein let out a ragged sigh. "He steadfastly refused to go to Macdonald's since Jill's death. We used to go as a special treat. Even getting him the pup didn't bring him out of his shell the way meeting you has. I can't say how happy I'm that we finally came together."

"It brought him closure," Piers said.

Jostein nodded and grasped Nicole's hand. "I hope you'll be able to spend as much time as you can with him."

"I will." The fervor in her tone didn't even begin to match her determination.

Piers chuckled. "Then you might have to consider moving to Otter Lake."

"That is a possibility, I think. Lawrence briefly mentioned that you're in the artisan pizza business and looking to expand. I worked mostly from home." Jostein was gazing at his son through the window. "You two are married?"

Nicole showed him her left hand. "Not yet!"

"We will be tomorrow," Piers said.

"Piers tends to speak for both of us. We got engaged only this morning."

Piers grinned. "Here I go again trying to be the boss. I just can't wait."

They laughed.

Jostein extended his hands to Piers and Nicole. "Then let me congratulate you both. What a momentous day it has been for you, Nicole."

"My brain is still reeling. Finally meeting Christopher still feels like a dream."

"There's a lovely Victorian house in Otter Lake next to the house we intend to buy in the old town. Very quaint. It might need a bit of work, though," Piers said.

"You mean the one that used to be pink and white? But it isn't for sale."

"Sometimes it's enough to approach an owner and give them the idea to sell," Piers said. "I know they would welcome an offer."

"You're getting bogged down, Piers. People sell when they're ready."

Jostein chuckled while Piers took on his best salesman air.

"I know it is own by an elderly couple. I delivered pizzas there. This last winter was the first time they didn't go to Santa Fe. They find the drive is getting to them. They'd like to buy one of the bungalow that were recently renovated. Mrs. Milton said the stairs are killing her knees. The problem is that the house need quite a bit of work, not just paint on the outside, and there are no buyers who want to be saddled with the bill. "

"This sound interesting. I can afford to renovate it. "

Nicole nodded. "It'd be worth it. Those old houses were solidly built. We'll talk to the Miltons."

All talk ceased when Christopher charged back into the living room followed by Eileen, who was dabbing her eyes with her apron.

"I'm ready, dad. Let's go!"

He stood between his father and Nicole, his hands in each of theirs.

***

Piers stood a little behind, eyes brimming with unshed tears. A sort of joy grew in his heart. He had helped people to find happiness. Did it count toward expiation? A shadow passed in his eyes. There were two families who didn't know happiness, who would never know it, not in the same way. Grief and sorrow crowded him. He took a deep breath to push it at the back of his mind, never forgotten, always painful.

They walked to the car. A hand on her waist, Piers drew Nicole against him. She lifted her face to him. A glow of happiness spread over her face. "I never dreamed I could be so happy."

Also by

ROMANCES
Untamed North Country Series
- Racing North
- To Love Again
- Northern Vet
Heart of the Prairies
- The Magic of Music
- Pizza for Two
- The long Trek
HISTORICAL NOVELS
All the Silences Series
- The Tears
- The Rage
- The Hope
NON-FICTION
- WWII FRANCE: A Writer's Guide
- The Inuit Dog of the Polar North
CHILDREN
Tezzero, French edition
A Dog Named Tezzero, English edition
TRANSLATIONS

L'héritage de la guerre, translation from A Touch of Magic, June Gadsby.
OTHERS
Where the River Narrows, with Kathy Fisher-Brown

www.ingramcontent.com/pod-product-compliance
Lightning Source LLC
Chambersburg PA
CBHW072117020726
47501CB00003B/862